AVALON

Artorian's Archives Book Twelve

DENNIS VANDERKERKEN
DAKOTA KROUT

MOUNTAINDALE
PRESS

ACKNOWLEDGMENTS

From Dennis:

There are many people who have made this book possible. First is Dakota himself, for without whom this entire series would never have come about. In addition to letting me write in his universe, he has taken it upon himself to be the most glorious senior editor and keep straight all the madness for which I am responsible, with resulting hilarity therein.

An eternal thank you to my late grandfather, after whom a significant chunk of Artorian's personality is indebted. He was a man of mighty strides, and is missed dearly.

A special thank you to my parents, for being ever supportive in my odd endeavors, Mountaindale Press for being a fantastic publisher, and all the fans of Artorian's Archives, Divine Dungeon, and Completionist Chronicles who are responsible for the popularity allowing this to come to pass. May your affinity channels be strong and plentiful!

Last of all, thank you. Thank you for picking this up and giving it a read. Avalon is the continuation of a multi-book series, and I dearly hope you will enjoy them as the story keeps progressing. Artorian's Archives may start before Divine Dungeon, but don't worry! It's going all the way past the end of Completionist Chronicles! So if you liked this, keep an eye out for more things from Mountaindale Press!

Please consider giving us five stars on Amazon, Audible, and anywhere else you'd like to spread the word!

CHAPTER ONE

"Done!" Alexandria wiped her hands, having placed the last Eldritch Tome in its precise, proper spot in her *fairly* acquired library. The first of many great crowning achievements in organization! Sorting and filing had been an ordeal, but Alexandria's smile told the world that she was mighty pleased. With a nod of certainty, her mind flipped the ledger onto the next to-do list. "Anansi?"

Anansi, suave man of spidery persuasion that he was, slipped from the shadows with a flat expression. One that contradicted itself with the pleasant shine of his eyes as Anansi currently felt prouder than a peacock. Much had progressed exceedingly well for the Old Autarchy. "Miss Alexandria. A delight to be called upon. Please, how may this humble old spider be of assistance? I wish to convey that the Autarchy is delighted to receive your S.O.P.s. They are as illuminating as they are clear."

Alexandria flushed. Compliments normally flew a swallow's flight over her head, but a mention directed to the quality of her work struck home. Seeing the natural composure of Anansi, she straightened herself and copied his hands-behind-the-back pose. There was no hiding the pink in her cheeks, but speaking of impending tasks while enjoying the glow of the finished ones may have as well been flirting. "Thank you, Anansi. Also for being here. Filing has been much easier with the help of you and your friends."

Anansi pressed a gloved hand to his chest, bowing gently as a sign of appreciation. "I shall tell them so. Though we are all family, and do not regard one another in the concept of a 'friend.' In the absence of our great mother Zelia, we do not function as a hive mind, but crave the unity it provides nonetheless. We work to achieve the same task, and eagerly await the day where we may show our great mother the work we have done. The promise of her praise sustains us."

"The pilgrimage down to see her resting form was akin to a spiritual journey. The reverence around her was surreal." Alexandra gave a curt nod, then accepted a leafed bundle of vellum that Anansi extended. Opening the seal to read through the contents, she multitasked and replied at the same time. "I've heard a lot about Zelia. Grandfather holds her in great esteem when he speaks of her. I hope that we get along, when we meet."

"Miss Alexandria." Anansi hummed in an amused reply. "She will be *ecstatic* to meet you. Our mother prides herself on efficiency and short lines of communication. The clarity your methods provided to otherwise complex, involved tasks, is most prized. Should you ever feel that you are not feeling up to the task to continue, please feel no burden when considering a visit to us. Any member of the Autarchy will gladly give you direct, honest, unfiltered feedback of which documents proved useful, which could be improved, and which had wording that could be clarified."

On seeing her face contort in feelings of obvious conflict, Anansi leaned in and offered an arm. "My senses appeared to be correct in their assessment. Could I have the honor of accompanying you, Miss Alexandria? It would be my great pleasure to introduce you to like-minded friends, who think like you, and are eager to ask you many questions pertaining to your new library. A fuss is doing the rounds as to the name you think to assign. Including some betting, as has become customary."

"Do we have a new currency?" Alexandria blurted out, her mind changing tracks as she absentmindedly accepted the offered arm, following along with Anansi's calm and steady walking gait. "I thought we were still testing Mr. Occultatum's honor system?"

"That was discontinued, Miss." Anansi smiled apologetically as he walked Alexandria out of the lowest segment of the Skyspear Mountain, allowing fresh rays of direct sunlight to blanket them when openings in the structure of Mayev's Spire allowed the rays to pour through.

The soft twilight of the inner library was Alexandria's comfort zone. The brighter area caused her to wince, then squint, then blink rapidly as her eyes adapted as best she could. Unlike the majority of people around her, she was not hurtling along up the cultivation track. Much more important work needed to be done! Like filing. Organizing. Instilling some order in this ragtag band of bright-eyed souls zipping up and down the mountain at every hour of the day and night.

Alexandra paused, partially turned, and shook her tiny fist up at the mountain and culprits in question. "Some of us still need to sleep, you bunch of bent bookmarks!"

With a huff and stomp of her foot, her eyes turned to regard Anansi fully. "Apologies. You were saying?"

Anansi, most amused, nodded in understanding. "The Void Dreamer's requisition system has been shelved. Last I heard, he handed it all off to some dwarves who thought they might be able to do something with it. Efforts have instead shifted to a beast-core-based economy. The efficacy of which is… not achieving the lift-off that the Dreamer was hoping for. He expects that when scarcity of a kind is reintroduced, this may change. *If* scarcity is reintroduced. With so much of the Soul Space that needs attention, I expect we will all be responsible for our own local communities. Regardless of the Dungeon trying to push anyone and everyone towards the Mage-ranks at full force, I expect that the Void Dreamer's efforts will continue to be thwarted."

Alexandria paused to watch the sky as she chewed on that answer. When her reply was not quick, Anansi turned his head to catch the object of her gaze. He had a thousand questions he wished to ask, but he would not eke a single mandible across the line of any topic that would stop Miss Alexandra from smiling. For in the sky they saw a flustered old man attempting to teach several students who were doing their utmost to be obtuse, and give him grief.

She waved at Grimaldus and Tychus, who waved back with big grins when they saw her. The effort caused Tychus to wobble and fall melodramatically from his floating sword. He was caught by the ear as Artorian snatched him up. While Alexandra couldn't quite hear the dressing-down that Tychus received, his meek expression and genuine effort to get back on the sword told her he'd been properly chastised. Good. That big man needed every peg he could find to stand on kicked out from under his feet.

"As Tychus deserves. It's the only way that lug is going to learn." Alexandria pressed her fists into her librarian-robed hips, the light blue shimmer of which stood out powerfully in the fresh light. Breathing deep, she bothered to perform an inch of 'the cultivation thing' when Artorian peered down in their direction. She could just tell he was checking on her progress. She wasn't sure how she could tell. Either way, she was certain of it, and put in a tiny bit of effort.

Effort that swiftly turned into results as Cal fell over himself to rush toward the scene, and assist with the endeavor like a maddened blacksmith doing all possible things in his power to not let the last hot embers in the furnace go out. It was a hot day in Hel when some of the potential high-note cultivators found some drive, and he certainly wanted all the Mages his definitely-not-greedy plans could acquire!

That Artorian was now holding him by the metaphorical

ear was going partially ignored. He'd be gentle! A support pace at no more than Alexandra could handle! He knew! He didn't need a fussy grandfather leaning over his shoulder with commentary!

Alright, Artorian was being silent and the commentary imaged, but Cal could imagine it really well! A whole speech complete with anecdotes, and no less than seventeen full blown distractions!

Anansi's awareness of the matter grew when a definitely-not-rogue spike of untyped Essence condensed around Alexandria's being. He released her arm and spider-bounced a healthy distance away, then fixed his posture and shot a respectful nod towards the old man in the sky.

Artorian thought the tables should be very much turned, and pressed the hands in his oversized sleeves together. He bowed deeply in Anansi's direction in thanks for his consideration and assistance. The elder spider had been instrumental in Alexandria's continued well-being, and that feeling was conveyed in the bow that Anansi received. Act as a mere butler as he might, Anansi's achievements were not overlooked, and Artorian despised treating any close family as someone not on his level.

Anansi's clear affection for Alexandria equally did not go overlooked.

Touched by such esteemed respect, Anansi still had not figured out what to say. In the Crown Game Arena, responses had come easy! Jesting and joking with cheap shots and even cheaper, cheesy puns.

Now, after having become properly accustomed to the Administrator and his people, Anansi had begun to feel out of his depth. There was a hierarchy to power, and regardless of his significant rank, Anansi was nowhere near the top.

Sometimes a hierarchy was silent. Sometimes it was loud. With Artorian, Anansi had learned that this hidden track was as quiet as a mouse. Ever polite as the Administrator may be, the visuals from several months ago once again played behind Anansi's eyes.

A sword of moonlight that cleaved a mountain.

A continent of Essence giving birth to a glittering lake.

A whole faction of foes, brought low and shelved in orderly fashion.

All by the devices of a person who was now bowing to him. *Him*, nothing and nobody but a spider son of Zelia. That his mother would be given such respect was a pill he could swallow. That *he* was the target of such profound appreciation? That was beyond Anansi.

Keeping his composure, he replied with an identical gesture out of a sheer desire to not be rude, then turned to an Essence-glow-coated Alexandria who was slowly but surely demanding the attention of all the eyes that could fall upon her. Astrea, Grim, and Ty had ceased being little pests, paying attention entirely to one of their sisters as the trio sustained a flawless pommel stance. A forgettable detail Artorian was sure to roast them for later! They'd been able to do it all along, the little electric rats!

Of the onlookers, only Artorian and Cal got a proper look at Alexandria's inner workings. She may not have had the most functional cultivation technique, but her veil to obfuscate her methods was certainly potent! Ordinary cultivators, and even low-ranked Mages, would have had difficulty peering beyond the haze that kept Alexandria's secret project safe.

"A clock?" Artorian asked as a light-mote in Alexandria's center.

"Appears to be, yes." Cal's voice was lulling and thoughtful as he cocked his head and crossed unseen arms.

"Both of you, be quiet. I am concentrating!" Alexandria snapped at the peanut gallery. "Cal, thank you for all the Essence, but please take a seat farther out. Your presence is a big flaring light and I am being blinded. I don't even have eyes in here, and I have no additional room for you to show off that you're the big-daddy dungeon around here. Uncle Eternium's technique is difficult enough to implement! Out!"

Cal shoved his unseen hands up and backed away, all the way to the very outer edge of Alexandria's center. Artorian quickly huddled up next to him in case another verbal volley was coming and he happened to be next on the chopping block.

When Alexandria got to work on improving her cultivation technique, Tim quietly slipped in next to Cal as his own dimmed-light mote. His whispers were muted, but proud. "She finished all the pieces! I have so looked forward to this moment!"

The other two leaned his way, Artorian speaking in hushed whispers. "What is she doing? This method has none of the normally used or known Essence-form factors I've come to expect. There's no tubes, only the most basic of spin, and more free-floating components than I know to label."

Tim firmly bobbed his mote to nod. "New design, with Cal's specific Essence-provision circumstances in mind. I've named it an Armillary Tourbillon. Consider it a sphere in perpetual motion. Or the parts that will make one."

Both of Tim's friends gave him a strange look for saying that first word with the two Ls, as two Ls, but then added inflection on the second word with two Ls, and said those as a single J instead. Cal dismissed the fanciful title, making a nose-motion for a quick explanation on how the cultivation technique worked.

Creating an overlay with said explanation, Tim blocked out more of his sound to prevent it from reaching a concentrating librarian. "Without a need to refine Essence, or expel corruption, I designed this technique for Alexandria purely with her mindset as a focus. She also liked the clock story, thus the design choice. This model has fifty-seven complications, two-thousand eight-hundred and twenty-six parts, and thirty-one hands. I tout it as both the most complicated timepiece and cultivation method currently in the world! In part, this technique is meant to go hand in hand with the **Order Law**, which she has expressed firm interest in. When she feels like doing so, I will be welcoming her as a protege."

Artorian shook congratulatory mote-hands with Tim. The old man was very glad that a reclusive child of his had made good friends with an equally reclusive new brother. Easing back after, the trio settled in and silently watched as Alexandria put her cultivation method together with prim and proper precision.

To the trio, it was a spectacle of intricate, complex, infuriatingly detailed design.

A clockmaker's dance.

To Alexandria, putting her technique together was akin to reading a furniture manual.

A simple one.

CHAPTER TWO

After being thrown out of Alexandria's center anyway due to incessant whispering that ended up becoming much louder, Tim, Cal, and Artorian shared a short, boisterous laugh before all shaking hands again for a result well-earned.

Alexandria formally reaching the D-ranks had been a good team effort! As a pleasant bonus, she was now irritated at what she considered to be 'loose and vague' requirements for the C-ranks. Thus, as the head librarian did, she threw herself at the problem and had made Craig come sprinting over with a single yell of his name! A yell that made it all the way up the mountain with the Essence she'd packed in.

Cal giggled, having a quick look around her vicinity before feeling the urge to return to work. "One more person being one step closer to the Mage-ranks is a big thumbs up from me. Thumbs optional. Now where did Anansi go?"

Tim chimed in. "I had need of him elsewhere. I'm sure he'll return to the library right after he sends me the briefing on the last of the Pylons being recycled. We've about got all of them in your Soul Space now, Cal. The ones in my Soul Space aren't having much luck being mined out from permafrost rubble.

We're at the stage where, in your space, we can begin clearing out the critical backups in the Sun."

His checkered mote straightened up at a thought. "Speaking of. Artorian, those were supposed to be your Archives. You don't spend much time there do you? Also, terribly sorry for nicking Anansi from you all the time. I know the original plan was for him to be in your vicinity as a permanent fixture."

"Anansi goes where he pleases, my friend. I prefer free agents to have agency, and if he chooses to be a permanent fixture around Alexandria instead, then I certainly do not disapprove." Artorian's mote bobbed in their shared forum space. "Apologies for my lack of attention to Elysium, as I do not. The intent of the Archives was kind, but it's got all the use of a storage shed in the backyard."

He used a celestine tendril to rub at his own mote's forehead. "With methods of communication going back to the era of birds, couriers, vellum, and paper, I have felt a strong need to remain aboard Zephyr for everyone to retain easy access to my office. Even if I had been previously adamant about a spot in the Academy. I'm still trying to smooth out divisions of work and command structures, as too much work is still making it to me that shouldn't. I'm at the point where I can take several hours out of the day to take care of that old list of things I counted out on my hand. Though, I forget if it was lefty or righty."

Cal made a mental push to eke the Administrator's vision towards the three cultivators balancing on their flying swords. Tychus was being chased by Astrea who... Was she throwing snowballs at him? Why yes, yes she was. "Aren't they full-fledged adults now?"

Artorian released a tired sigh as reply to Cal. "My boy, never misconstrue a person's age with their ability to be a complete child. The correlation has no bearing. Was I not proof of concept enough? It doesn't matter what age someone is when having fun is on the table. We never truly stop being children."

Tim nodded sagely, but remained silent at first until he

recalled that snowballs should be outside of the Astrea's C-rank zero wheelhouse. "I see she acquired a new minor channel? That's a strong indicator of personal growth as far as I am concerned. Speaking of. Cal, we're still avoiding opening up everyone's affinities, yes? Even if they request it?"

Cal bobbed to affirm, but paused midway. "*Mmmno-yes?* There's an exception now. We're still holding off from unlocking anything new for anyone. That is correct. The sudden mental changes are highly undesirable. And while Artorian makes for a good case study for what happens if things go well, Zephyr makes an excellent case study for when they do not. All-affinity Essences do not suit her and she still refuses to not be a boat. She's a nice boat, but still. She was an outgoing and confident Air-cultivator that could not be stopped from moving forwards, then became a reclusive, uncertain, discomforted-to-exist boat that needs several plushies in her hold. So she can *hold* them."

Cal waited for his pun to land, but got no responses, deflating. "Difficult to pun that with the word needing to be repeated. Zephyr is with the best people possible who could help on the job, all the resources one could imagine, and *Artorian* on board as a semi-permanent fixture. I'm doing all I can to help here."

Tim needed to reach out and pause Cal. "You're doing great, bud. Tackle the madness you can handle, not the one you can't. You mentioned an exception?"

Cal took a stabilizing breath, filled with Zen-like calm while Artorian rubbed over the diamond dungeon-mote's back with a tendril of soft celestine light. "Preamble: I am still keeping close control over who can, and who cannot, cultivate. Not everyone has the go-ahead, no matter how badly I want more Mages. On that topic, some Mages I am locking out of any growth as soon as they make the jump. Anyone old-world-guild-related, as an example. I'm still expecting daggers in my back. Most Mages will have a very difficult time improving. All Mages lose the freebie Essence-gathering effect that I have going for non-Mages."

Steady now, he continued smoothly on the affinity topic. "For those who can cultivate: Yes. Anyone who reaches a 'Strong' quality affinity channel can ask to have it upgraded to 'Perfect' quality. The mental difference is… barely noticeable. Whereas the output and efficiency differences are serious. Most important is that Perfect affinities cause less 'strain' to me."

He held up a diamond tendril to block questions. "There's a lot to unpack there that I don't want to get into right now. Just remember that Perfect is better, and just like people at the B-ranks, we want more of them. I've not had a single individual even think to complain when I've approached them with: 'Hey, do you want a power up? It's a freebie.' They go rabid for them. Honestly, I'm fair! Not everything costs an arm, a leg, and all your memories!"

Artorian stopped rubbing the dungeon-mote's back and poked him in the side. "Got a rewards system for helping out up and running yet? Are tokens suddenly of any value again at all? Do I have to list off the other one-hundred and twenty-seven items on that particular list?"

Cal grumbled and inched away. "Okay, I know. Fair point. The only people actively helping out right now are either the ones who have to, the ones who can't stand being bored, or the ones who are driven to some kind of goal. Oh, eh. Speaking of that nugget. Artorian, I might have to steal you away for a *smaaahl* chat about Henry and Marie?"

"I already know." Artorian gave Cal a cheeky little smile. "Keep it off your plate. That meal is mine. I'll handle that matter this go around, and then you can neatly wrap a bow around the bundle and call it a volume. Supervisor-level individuals not doing their required job and only doing the job they want is very difficult to ignore. They haven't come to speak to me yet, but I equally doubt they've even realized more than a day has passed since the last time they thought to try. Some of us in the group have a tendency to blindly 'fall into our work.' They're in that hole now, and I expect they will come knocking any day for some silliness or another that will let me drag their noses over the grindstone."

Tim quipped. "According to chitter-chatter, they don't even know Odin is out of the picture, or that you did it."

Artorian shrugged. "Can't say I'm surprised, really. I unfortunately can't handle this problem the same way. Odin was an actual pain in the keister. He was only going to respect a display of power that he truly could not contend with. Old-world rules. Henry, I believe, just hasn't pulled his head out of the dirt long enough to realize or remember there was more to life."

The celestine mote waggled a hand. "From some faint connections I can play like a harp, he just wants to make Marie happy. Marie, on the other hand, is *really* leaning into that **Law** of hers. I theorize that **Glory** has some… tendencies? Let's call it that. To shine only in the face of strife. No conflict? No glory. She needs to defeat an obstacle, or accomplish something grand. If she wants to do it with kingdom building, that might take more time than she has remaining patience for. I'm expecting her to dip into more forceful methods if she's in a rush for ranks. I have the feeling she's on the Exemplar Track. If she's even an A-ranker?"

Cal crossed his diamond light-tendrils. "No kingdom-cleaving, then? Shame. Loved that Olympus lightshow. Spent some time with Grace rewatching the event from different angles. She ogled the moonlight effect every time. Personally, I liked the rainbow one."

Cal then returned to the topic. "Both Henry and Marie are at A-rank zero, though only because I pushed and provided all the Mana they needed. Dawn showed up to help when the compressions and contractions of the A-ranks started. A miracle for them to both avoid being bricked, since they still don't have their Auras under control. They are currently both *stuck* at A-rank zero, and likely will be for the foreseeable future."

He grumbled about the unforeseen difficulty. "I could help in the B-ranks, but conditions get tacked on in the A-ranks. I don't know if the hold up to A-rank one is their nearly nonexistent Auric control, or A-ranker circumstances, but Mana-provisions from me aren't making a dent. I'm going to keep that freebie-flow going a while longer because I want that data, but I'm already having doubts. I'm not giving infinite-Mana freebies to anyone else until I understand why it isn't working with my A-rank test cases."

Artorian mentally filed away that Henry and Marie effectively had infinite Mana reserves while this test was ongoing. He remembered the feeling very distinctly back when he had put 'The Grid' together. He had been the B-ranked test case. That kind of power went to your head, and fast. Firing that Stargazer Cannon had been such a rush! On the other hand, its use had turned his body at the time into fine particles.

The dungeon mulled something over, reclaiming Artorian's attention. "The 'zero' rank is where a lot of people are currently stuck. The C, B, and A-ranks slam into a skill ceiling after making the leap. Only the F, E, and D rankers are flying up the track. Are you sure you can't just knock this out nice and quick? I like nice and quick. My to-do list is fatter than Chandra's recipe for thrice-stuffed carp."

Tim scoffed. "Same."

Artorian firmly shook his head no. "Sorry. Not at all. Odin was a smack-it-down solution. For Henry and Marie, people who I count as friends, I intend to approach the task from their level. **Law**-Tier and all. If I come at them from the seven-twenty Tier, and we have the inevitable fight…"

Tim nodded powerfully, understanding where this was going when Artorian let the sentence hang. "Marie will never let this issue drop. Henry might. **Valor** and **Glory** are both on Tier ninety-eight. If you're wanting a more evened-out fight… then you may need to drop lower than that Tier for the math to work out, given you're at A-rank seven."

Artorian agreed. "Indeed. So when we have the inevitable fight, I believe I will have the opposite problem to Odin. If I defeat Marie with an objectively stronger method or power, then she will balk, begin claiming I cheated, or otherwise commence the same downward spiral kids do when they don't want to admit they've lost. It will only get ugly, and keep getting ugly, and down the drain it goes until it's all gone to Asgard."

Nods of understanding followed, so Artorian continued. "What I feel like I have to do for Marie is drop myself down to her Tier level. Or lower, as you said, Tim. What does the **Love**-Tier divided-by-seven math come out to, for my *oomph*-calculation to ruffle be in the area of an A-rank zero? Somewhere between Tier twelve and fourteen?"

"Ruffle?" Cal poked with a smirk. "Did you mean roughly?"

"Yes, Mr. *Porrible.*" Artorian swiped at, and missed, the diamond mote's shoulder when Cal sidestepped, getting him back with a reminder to his own famous flub instead. "It's *possible* that I did."

Tim replied with a thumbs up to Artorian's question, then motioned for him to continue.

Artorian drew breath, and soldiered on. "I will admit that, after the Odin fight, going up and down Tiers made me feel like I'd been run over by a horde of Morovian Boars. A whole month I sat at my desk; puffing, melting into a puddle, and waking up with my face pressed to the vellum. My cheek was covered in ink and letters, with a line of drool that went all the way to the floor because I was just so infernally tired. I looked like the definition of a smear."

Tim chuckled, but cleared his throat so the old man would get back on track. Artorian did so. "Right. Doing it again. The A-ranks help a lot, but there are forms of tiredness and exhaustion that truly don't care about what you're made of. Back to Henry and Marie; I intend to show up on their Tier, unarmed, with the intent to talk it out first. If that falls through, then when they start pulling out toys, I shall call for some of mine after, to make it seem that I am trying to match them. **Glory** will drive Marie to greater heights if I look like a worthy challenge, but it is just Marie that will face me if I keep a step below that activation requirement. Since it is Marie, *the friend*, that I want to help, this remains the goal."

He tapped the side of his mote's nose, then winked at Cal. "I mucked around in your Tower-**Law** attempt. Running up and down all those stairs personally, tiring as it was, provided some good insight that is now coming in handy. Thanks, Cal. Good job."

Cal smirked wide, slapping in another pun. "I **Love** it when that happens."

CHAPTER THREE

Tim approved while Artorian buckled with a groan, defeated by the cheap-shot punnage. "Sounds like you have the matter handled, or will, in due time. I'm aware your to-do list is as long as the record of your schemes. On that note. Artorian, I know you're going to try to help where you can, and this is going to be a strange request, but could you avoid traveling to my Soul Space until the Henry and Marie matter is resolved? There are some... significant problems that your re-entry would cause, and I'm not ready to handle them."

Cal queried an interested eyebrow at the checkered mote. "Is it his body and state of being?"

Tim instantly confirmed this to be true. "Very much! I'm actually not certain he can re-enter at all with the current body. A whole nested Pylon bank may just up and explode because his presence required something of them, and those same areas are the only thing giving the frozen waste that is Eternia spots of hospitable land and life at the moment. I had to play serious hopscotch with some of the wiring and connective tissue between Pylons to make his efforts worthwhile. Particularly in order to get Barry sorted. All that hotwiring and kludge came back to bite me. It was already annoying even before we became aware that the *irritant* left some 'gifts' behind."

Artorian tapped his foot. "Am I going to get the details to any of this any time soon? This has been eating at me, you know. Both the 'what am I now' question, and the 'what exactly am I supposed to be helping you out with,' Tim?"

Cal hung his mote's head and sighed. "Sorry, Artorian. We just can't tell you yet. As soon as you know, you are not going to be able to stop yourself from throwing your attention face-first into the fray, and we're just. Not. Ready. We will tell you everything when it's time, and will even hold the door open for you when you want to run and get it done. Right now…"

Tim apologized in tandem. "We don't have a door to open for you. There's only an ice wall, and Cal and I currently haven't figured out a way to the other side that doesn't require squeezing down to the size of a household sponge. Don't look too glum, we've both got our pickaxes out and prospector hats on. When one of the Incarnates comes back with something useful, we'll get right on it. For now… Any non-Incarnate or non-native should *absolutely* stay out. Ammy is a heavenly sent gift in buying us about as much new time as we keep losing, and Ricky… sorry, Occultatum, is hard at work getting new bodies to be an option when he's not with me. If you don't see much of the Incarnates, don't be surprised."

Artorian brushed a tendril over his own mote's head, just how he did when running a palm over his actual bald head. "That's the way of it then. Very well, I'll try. I have plenty to do, and after a few months of getting the lay of the land, and the hang of how I can manage my time, I've become aware that it's not going to be possible to see everyone. That's life. One will always miss out somewhere. The trick is not to *feel* like you are missing out when it happens. I might have to write a book about it. Perhaps it will help someone?"

Cal smirked. "With what time?"

Tim and Artorian both released a short laugh, both saying the exact same words, at the same time. "Ha! I know, right?"

Tim and Artorian pointed at one another in full exaggeration, big smiles on their motes.

Artorian then fell back into Administration mode. "Good times. Was there anything else we needed a quick catch-up for, or are we getting back to it?"

Cal held up a tendril. "A curiosity question. How have the people in my Soul Space been? Overall, I mean. Do we have civilizations forming, or is it every man for himself? My attention has been on major problem solving, and while I do take time out of the schedule to come enjoy bonfire-night at the capital with Dani and Grace, I haven't kept eyes elsewhere. I know your Lunella and such are doing great, but that's all."

Artorian counted and formed pinpricks of light to represent the list. "Limited success. Some communities are building up well, while others give me a headache. We do have some lone wolves, but overall people are *trying*."

He illuminated a larger blip above the smaller ones. "As a general overview; after being decanted, people have banded together in groups of their liking, most commonly on racial or familiarity lines. Most have found a nice spot on your planet to settle."

Artorian moved to a smaller dot. "We've skipped the early phases of civilization growth since knowledge of 'the old way it was done' was a baseline, and people are trying to go from there. Nobody is trying to 'reinvent the fire' or some such."

The Administrator made new dots below that topic for each new detail. "We have a few stranger outliers, such as the New Fringe being the only location to have Wisp support. The Dwarves are still in the middle of their grand construction projects, but from a glance in their direction, anyone and their blind grandmother can tell that they're going to outshine anything else we might be accomplishing when it's done. Nidavellir will more than likely be taking over the 'capitol' spot when it's all shiny and finished. The boys are going hard on their 'Art Deco' and 'Radiator Buildings' and 'Massive Suspension Bridges.' The last note I saw on my desk was something about a collaborative dam project with the Beavers. There was some joke about naming it 'Hoover,' but it escaped me as to why that was funny."

He began a second list. "Smaller in scope, we have factions based on preference and ability. As example: Emilia Nerys got wind of other people with her inclinations existing. Tim, I believe the moniker 'Vampires' has come up a few times, and they existed in your Soul Space as well. I believe I was in part responsible for their genesis via the Suncurse thing?"

Tim nodded, so Artorian continued. "Emilia is one of the Mages who has gathered disparate individuals and made clans out of them, in between her lessons plans. Kellen Shadowbeard —one of the Dwarves in the big raid, I believe—is at the fore-front of her current main clan prospects. Many of the non-native Eternia goers who were of that persuasion have done the same, though there is still some difficulty with adapting to the lack of a gamified existence."

He paused to turn towards Tim for this. "They keep shouting out terms that do nothing, and become both fearful and depressive when everything that seemingly made them special is now moot, or nonfunctional. I'm… handling it, but not well. I'm aware that on the Moon, there are both clans and septs, but Caltopia has not reached sept levels yet. We're dealing with allegiances, spots where Supervisors have set up shop, places of power, possibly some fiefdoms in the making, plenty of tribes, and then whatever Henry and Marie think they're doing. I have not touched that pile yet."

Artorian made a face when shifting to the topic, like he'd expected more, or better. "The only reports from that region consist of 'things are going poorly, m'lord.' So I haven't gone. With all the experience they supposedly have, I expect some kind of stable kingdom to be up and running before I knock on their front gate. I've had them on the schedule a few times, but each time I've checked, the courier who came to relay the state-of-the-state news suddenly looked very tired, and quietly shook his head no. Best to wait. I need something to work with, not more problems on my desk that weren't already going to end up on the pile."

Tim grumbled. "Could I have a minor example on the gamified existence problem?"

Artorian did so. "Let's take Kellen. He was dubbed a 'Dark Paladin' by the Exodus crowd, and had learned the Essence-variant abilities from Emilia involving giving and taking health in the form of energy. Heavy emphasis on blood-themed abilities; including draining either blood or energy, to gain might or replenish himself. Also jumping high into the air in order to come down very hard onto a foe? The Exodus crowd was calling that a 'Dragoon' ability. Abyss if I know what they meant by it, but that same crowd is also firmly stuck in the mindset that titles come with abilities that they are... well, *en-titled* to."

He folded his mote's tendrils together like hands. "They're so used to living with their game abilities and character sheets that not having those anymore has introduced a barrier which prevents them from learning the Essence-variants of those *same* abilities. I thought experiences in Eternia would make Essence methods more readily available, but even with my own limited testing, that has not been at all the case."

Artorian tried to show an example, but failed in the Forum space. "I can either do it because my Mana moved to accomplish the idea, Invoking and the like, or not at all. I can't replicate zip without my Mana doing all the hard lifting now. I'm back to using the expensive invocations without the Pylons alternatives that I, too, had begun leaning on. I think I've only still got a hold of Artifacting because I began using it right away after I got out. That and the Seed Core damage that physically got better."

Artorian held up a celestine tendril from the reactions he received. "Don't give me such a hard look, I'm recovering in all the other aspects as well. Seeing Zephyr slowly do better is helping heaps. I can tap into the Orbital Rail Palm from Eternia, but it feels like it was learned by someone else and I'm performing a poor man's copy. I'm not sure what changed there. I *should* be able to just throw those out like they're second nature. I cannot."

Tim held his face with his entire hand. "That would be the lack of Pylons. I was hoping that wasn't going to come up again, but I see now that the transition sickness is more of a disease, and persists powerfully. *Great.* I'll add the problem to my to-do list. I take it the reason had more to do with 'we use Essence here' rather than 'we're using complex pre-designed Pylons that let people do fancy things easily'? Or does it feel like the lack of Pylons in Cal is kneecapping you?"

Artorian waffled, no longer certain. "I didn't notice the Pylons no longer doing heavy lifting on account of them being gone. I know we used to seamlessly transition the skills from Eternia to Cal and back? I clearly remember knowing what it was like to have Supreme Weapon Mastery. That's more of a faded dream now. Is this something you want me to hand off to you and take off my plate? This is far away from my area of expertise. So is anything with the Exodus people. I can handle reintegration by introducing them to individuals that can slowly teach them cultivator building blocks again, but I am at a loss for what to do about the game-world-dependency."

Tim affirmed that question, taking the burden. "Yes. Please do. I would prefer to handle issues like that since it directly pertains to the very same gamified world that we are going to put back up in my Soul Space. This is not an insignificant problem and needs a dedicated Gnome team. Thanks for asking."

Artorian replied with a curt nod. "Consider it done. I shall have a courier provide you all my documents on the topic."

Cal gave them all a comical salute. "Good information all around. Let's get back to it?"

After agreement, the motes all popped out of the Forum space and returned to their own mountain of work.

CHAPTER FOUR

Artorian opened his eyes in the middle of the blooming blue sky. His white and gray robes fluttered wildly, as he'd dressed for the colder weather high above the ground. Senses returning, he felt that he was still standing on the hilt of his floating sword. Though, Polly of **Pride** could likely be referred to as a full and proper *flying* sword. Given the name options available, Artorian went with what he currently felt fitting. "Excalibur, I'm back."

He then looked down at the broken blade. "Doing alright down there?"

The androgynous ex-parrot in sword-form scoffed at the insinuation. "Excuse you. Who do you think I am? I wasn't going to let you *fall*. Yes, I'm very well."

The prideful blade bristled and gained a sharp glow when Polly's thoughts turned to its charges. "I've been instructing the other blades while your people made a mockery of not being able to balance right. So I sent them off on a tiny obstacle course, and now, as is appropriate, they are hanging on for dear life. Their showing of pride was incongruent with the amount they could reasonably hold on to. They're definitely learning to hold on properly now! Pride is to be measured and tested. One needs a precise amount of it! Too much, or too little, are no good! The excess will be shaved away, and insufficiency shall be mended by practice and steadily grown confidence! Maybe a nudge or two."

Artorian nodded. "As you say. Excalibur, are we floating here for oversight, or just because you were determined for me to stay put while I was off in mental conversation land?"

Polly stuck its metaphorical chest out. "The latter! Honestly, I can't even see them anymore. The route I sent their swords on was meant to bang them up and be meticulously unfriendly."

The sword relaxed at the pleasant thoughts; the pertinent question asked as the hilt stopped attempting to vibrate into another layer of existence, Polly's sharp glow fading. "Where would you like to go?"

Artorian motioned at a distant cloud bank, where Zephyr had nested herself cozily in the whitest of fluff. "The office, please. I have some documents I need to prepare for handoff to Tim, and I need to check and reorganize my to-do list. I have one major item that needs attending, but the rest escapes me, and I did have a pile sitting on my desk that I needed to peruse. Best to make a fresh list, get nice and on-top of what I need to accomplish, and see what my difficulties will be. I expect some direct conflict and strife in my future; I need to plan around that. Gotta make plans for the plans, and plans for those plans!"

Excalibur chuckled as it flew towards the cloud bank with the Administrator flawlessly balanced on the hilt, and the chunk of blade available. "I've noticed you do that perhaps a bit too much? Is there really such a need to front-load all your work?"

Artorian was firm in his answer. He had become steadily more fond of this method as life progressed. "The more effort you put in beforehand, the less one must do during, or after. Frontloading is partially how I managed to make such significant gains in the early cultivation track. Had it not been for the large number of clerics being readily available during my earliest days, I would not have thrown myself so callously into clearing and connecting Meridians. However, because they were there, and I could account for it, I was able to push harder and faster in order to accomplish the goal. It was hard to say no to putting an entire medical wing to work. I gave them such forehead creases!"

"You are a living headache to all the prideful, Administrator." Sharing in laughter, Polly deposited him on Zephyr's deck before popping into the form of a rainbow parrot and finding a nice perch to claim. "I'll be here if you need me. Unless the other blades swing by, then I need to check how green in the gills your little monsters are! I want them chartreuse! Or another lap for them!"

Amused by Polly's continued bristling before the bird did some preening, Artorian wandered across the deck, patting a new looking handrail that hadn't been here last time.

"Welcome back, Administrator." Zephyr chimed from one of the many ports in the wall that she had developed purely for convenient conversation. "Fond of the improvements?"

Artorian paused, and tried to find all that she had changed. "Perhaps if I could suss them all out, Zephy? I haven't gone for a stroll without coming back to something or other being different. Is it the sails? No. Perhaps this railing? You're giving me a craving for enthusiastic walks through the woods."

"The railing is one, yes. Perhaps I should have waited for you to go inside." Closing that porthole to open another as Artorian had advanced, Zephyr kept speaking. "I have moved the internal design around. That hallway that used to run straight through the middle? I've moved it against the starboard wall instead. I've also widened that hall, and coated as much of the starboard wall in windows as I could without sacrificing integrity. Too many people were going back and forth and bumping into one another, and the rooms you and Decorum occupy were swiftly becoming too small for all the documents that needed to be held. Please do something about the records room? This is the third time I've had to steal space from elsewhere to enlarge it."

Artorian acquiesced to the request. "Please add it as a leaflet to the pile on my desk so I can make it a procedure and get someone on it."

"On it!" Zephyr sounded chipper before opening the new, larger mahogany door for him. "Please tell me if I did the office right this time. The assigned Wisps do their best, but their suggestions are so... drab. No flavor! All utility. I expected the Gnomes to be stuck up, but every one of those I've met, I've liked. Wasn't it supposed to be reversed, or do we only get the interesting cases?"

Artorian quietly looked at the porthole, his hands behind his back. Zephyr took a few seconds too long before picking up that his silence was directed at her so she could stop, and he could begin doing all the things being asked of him. "Right! Sorry, the other affinities are still... I'll be quiet now."

"You're fine, dear. Practice makes for the best confidence booster. Eventually, this hesitation you are feeling will be a fleeting reminiscence. A memory. You will stride through the clouds with all the confidence that little High Elves look up to." Artorian chuckled, patted the hull, and looked about as Zephyr thinned the ceiling of his office to a veil of crystalline matter. Moissanite? Was that a *moissanite* panel? The skylight properly allowed Artorian to see without needing to adjust his vision, or make his own light, and the fiery side-effects made him believe that Polly had had a wing in the material's selection.

Pacing around the room, Artorian slowly took the revamp in. One slow breath at a time. One smell. One touch. The mahogany desk preference had bled over heavily into other aspects of the room. In her attempts to improve the place, Zephyr seems to have adopted 'more means better' as a design ideal.

Paneled flooring? Zebrawood. Extra dark, with ridiculous graining. He might as well be walking on animal stripes.

Furniture? Mahogany. Vibrant light browns, unnatural smoothness to the touch, and a finish coating each surface that no amount of rubbing diminished. Very good protection against repetitive wrist motions when he needed to sign document after document.

Walls? Healthy, bright, white Calacatta-patterned quartz.

The brightness of the walls freshened up the room, and made it feel larger in volume.

Chair? Possibly his favorite addition! One of Deverash's snugly-fits-anything triple-padded Iridium doohickies. In a pinch, that chair also doubled as an emergency leg-maintenance station. Well... A pinch wasn't applicable. Every visit from his Gnomish friend came with a mandatory checkup. Mr. Deverash didn't leave Mr. Administrator to his work unless a pass on the ol' knees occurred. Not like monthly checkups on prosthetics were a bad thing! Rather a checkup than discovering another fracture too late.

If he had to one-legged hop across an entire town one more time, swinging the broken-off leg above his head, he might actually throw the Striker next time. He had no idea what Lunella was thinking with her no-fly rule, but it was her rule to make. Likely his own fault for telling the Solar Gate story.

Pressing his rump down into the seat, a sound of relaxation left him as he sank back into its cushions, which adapted and moved to fit him before pushing from the floor and bringing his arms up to ergonomic desk-level. He took a steadying breath; his hands hovered over quills, vials of readied spare ink, and work, work, work. "Sometimes I wonder what I liked about being a scribe so much..."

Then he picked up a new quill and smiled at the design of it, as he read the attached note explaining the rune engraved in the nib. "Then, of course, I find an Iridium-tipped quill that never runs out of electric-cobalt ink so long as there's a source around for it to draw from, and I get giddy."

A detail from the corner of his eye stole his attention.

"Before I begin..." Placing the quill back in its specialized holder, he laced his hands and exhaled firmly as he turned his gaze towards the seemingly vacant wall. The only one devoid of book-cases, sporting a brand new door to an adjoined room. He'd only had the main entryway before? This second door was new, and likely led to that enlarged records room. "Would you three terribly clever youngsters mind telling me why you're skulking? Or were the three of you intent on standing there all prim and silent until I had need of you?"

A male humanized Arachnid, female Dark Elf, and green-colored fire Wisp all became visible at his mention. The Arachnid man had skin whiter than the pale moon, and donned a dark butler attire similar to Anansi's. The Dark Elf was his opposite; dark in skin, wearing a bright, but simple robe. While the Wisp...

Alright, Artorian needed to pause and turn his full attention to the glowing green orb. There was a lot going on here and a sideways glance wasn't doing the Wisp justice.

Artorian chimed in again, voice focused on the Wisp as he balanced curiosity and care. "My apologies, lad. My eyes see many things, and currently I would love some elucidation. Could you tell me why I am deducing: 'screaming rock,' 'Gnome,' and 'Wisp' all at the same time from you?"

C'towl out of the bag, the green Wisp hovered to be directly in front of the Administrator's desk. "My name is Luopa. I am..."

Uncertain of how to proceed without making it compli-cated, the Wisp dropped the other half of his guise that the Administrator could clearly already see through. While the green ball of light remained, a disconnected body formed beneath it, in the rough shape and posture of a Gnome. Luopa even had the clothing to match! That his frame inside of the clothing appeared to be made of... Wisp energy? Wenergy? Wispergy? Wuju? Best stick with Wuju. Based on how the hands had been copied to be Gnomelike, raised Artorian's interest.

Especially with the Rune-carved rock floating in the center of Luopa's light-ball head.

Luopa, liberated from the guise, introduced himself and his protective compatriots properly. "I am a Gnisp. The not-so-secret love-child between a Gnome and a Wisp, which is also the reason I am being attended by such security. Please meet Merciful Chaos, on my left, and Painful Serenity, on my right."

Artorian nodded at them as they were introduced, shelved the naming convention for later, then tapped his fingers together. "Could I ask about the rock?"

The Gnisp cleared his throat, hovered up to be on Artorian's desk, and dropped his efforts to maintain his look to answer the question, returning to being a... stone? With a *thunk*, the carved rock fell exactly like a rock should. The unmoving chunk of stone now nested in a pile of papers, everyone's attention drawn to the surprisingly mundane spectacle that couldn't help but feel intriguing. Artorian expected more to happen, but no. They were engaged in the profound and newly minted sport of rock-watching. *Thrilling.*

When Artorian looked back up, both the Dark Elf and Arachnid assistant approached his desk. They both made some symbolic movement that Artorian decoded as a gesture of obeisance before adopting matching poses, their hands clasped together in front of them. When they seemed to wait for him to designate one of them to explain, Artorian motioned at the lady. One day he would get people to treat him like any other grandfather, but the current topic was too important, and the comment too minor.

The Dark Elven lady bowed respectfully, then provided clarity. "Administrator. Thank you for allowing me to speak. My actual name is Silentra, and my other half is an Arachne that has agreed to go by the name of Uvo. By the grace of a... very complicated peace agreement between the Gnome and Wisp factions, Luopa is the cornerstone of their not-so-temporary ceasefire. Our presence is a security measure against those who wish to see that bond undone, and we have been assigned to be Mr. Luopa's body-guards. In our efforts to perform this function, we have had to be... violent. This behavior has given us embarrassing nicknames, and Mr. Luopa secretly finds great enjoyment in introducing us with those titles. Even if they make us quietly cringe."

Artorian rubbed at the tip of his nose, laced and unlaced his fingers, then gave her an intent-filled look to continue. Silentra did so. "Mr. Luopa is currently the only Gnisp in existence, and as much as we would like to safeguard him under far more persnickety circumstances, his base form is as you see before you."

"I see the rock." Artorian drummed his fingers on the mahogany desk, his mind churning to rapidly connect strings together. "I still don't *understand* the rock. Or why it was important you sneakily waited all invisible against my office wall. I do take appointments."

Silentra slid her hands together, apologizing with a light bow.

The Administrator wanted a change of pace, and motioned for the Arachne to approach.

When Uvo stepped forwards, Silentra stepped back. Uvo spoke with a mixture of calm tones and easy exhales, like a diplomat doing his utmost to offend nobody. "Mr. Luopa's origin is a *screaming* rock. One of the initial creations of Master Cal's dungeon. A Wisp and Gnome who cared nothing for the brewing faction strife would meet at this rock, and it is reported that, due to a strange influence of 'pink colored Mana,' something came of their affection for one another."

Artorian instantly held his face.

That couldn't have been anything but him.

Now he was partially responsible, and the pieces were starting to fit. He didn't remember when this might have happened, but it sounded so quintessentially him, that he was just going to accept that it may as well have been. "My boy, may I infer that your sneakiness is due to not wanting anyone to know that the Gnisp is here? It is abundantly clear that he needs to be kept safe. I heard 'Wisp and Gnome peace agreement,' and with that alone you would have gotten all of my help to keep it that way."

The Arachne bowed lightly with a subtle nod, then reached over to tap the rock. Luopa hovered to become an orb of green light, before re-adopting the full 'dapper energy Gnome with a light ball for a head' look and speaking. "I apologize for the less than subtle introduction, Administrator. There is, however, another reason why I had to try to come here and ask for sanctuary."

Artorian nodded, already determined that he was going to adopt this one. "Please, do go on."

"It has to do with being a screaming rock, sir." Luopa watched carefully as the Administrator's eyebrow rose. "We all scream for a reason, and I was screaming because, from where I sat as a rock, I had a direct view of the workrooms where people would take documents and adjust them to make them fit a filing system, before making copies. The spelling and grammar errors they made were driving me up the wall, and all I could do was scream at their choice of comma placements and incorrect filings. When I suddenly gained the ability to do more, I was hoisted on my own petard by flying in at full pace and 'fixing' each document that I could. I was caught and started an entire political drama."

Artorian tilted his head. "I'm not seeing a downside here, save for the part where screaming rocks do that for a reason. It means I need to send a note to Cal. In fact, let me draft that while you explain to me why that tidbit had anything to do with you being, specifically, here."

Luopa cleared his throat again, hands of energy fidgeting. "Those... documents I went wild on? They came from the Zephyr."

Artorian felt like he'd been turned to cold stone, his movements frozen before ever so slowly thawing out as the implications percolated. If Alexandria ever got wind that documents originating from either his or Decorum's office were not being properly filed, she would be picking up the entirety of Skyspear and beating him with it.

His voice was ice. "Mr. Luopa?"

"Yes, sir?" The Gnisp continued to wring his hands together, apprehensive.

"Please tell me…" Artorian laced his fingers, leaning forwards. *Everything.*

CHAPTER FIVE

A powerful handshake many hours later, after a hefty discussion, and Luopa the Gnisp was officially in charge of the records room located between his and Decorum's office, where Mr. Luopa would perform mighty line and copy editing passes over all the material before it was ready for out-processing.

Intake was easy! His desk got piled up by a mixture of documents, and items with tags on them. Sending documents out with all the bits and bobs in the right place so the next step didn't fudge the filing system? Well, that was sorted now as well, complete with a hefty letter for Alexandria forewarning her of the change, and likelihood of errors in the files coming her way.

When the Gnisp and his guards were out of his office and creating a kerfuffle next door, Artorian tuned out the noise. Luopa was clearly rearranging the entire room already. With full screaming-rock fervor.

"Zephyr, dear. You could have warned me?" He offhandedly murmured while using both hands to claw down his beard. He wanted to keep out of politics as much as possible.

"Nah." Zephyr smirked like a crass High Elf enjoying a tropical hammock, swirling a fancy drink. "I said I liked

Gnomes, and that was all the hint I felt you needed. As if you weren't going to notice they were there."

Exhaling through his nose, he supposed he couldn't fault her for poked fun. "Very well. Any more surprises, or can I get started?"

"No more surprises that I'm keeping from you, no." Zephyr adjusted her sails with such obvious, eye-brow bouncing, oozing cheek in her tone that Artorian leaned on his elbow to hold his face.

"Which one?" He held his beard with obviously controlled emotion.

"The axe." Steadying her sails back out, Zephyr corrected her words with a far less teenager-styled attitude, starting to feel that her desire to poke fun was once again flooding over the boundaries of accepted levels.

"Thank you." Artorian released his beard and appreciated the quick cut to seriousness, leaning back before inspecting his desk as Zephyr went quiet. He drummed his digits on the mahogany, then figured it was the double bit throwing axe. He reached out with a motion of the wrist, brought the item to him with telekinesis, and read the tag after turning it upside down so the text was legible. "Spotter Axe-a-lot."

A few more finger-drum motions on the table, and he wasn't any the wiser as to what that might mean. "Suppose there's nothing else to it except to pour some energy in and—*whoooops!*"

A spark of pink energy flared from his fingertips as he once again lost some control over his Mana. Artorian stabilized his output, but the damage was done.

The flare arced from his cobalt ink and onto the axe, connecting both together like they were drawn by gravity. Smashing together in a frazzled mess of electric fireworks, a cobalt-blue, coursing with electricity Axolotl wiggled his little tiny legs in midair before normal gravity took the reins again.

Artorian reached out, then caught the Axolotl, who clung to his hand and fingers for dear life. His feelers and eyes frantically looked about before settling on an equally puzzled old man.

The blue creature's paw rose, one digit extending as miniscule static ringlets of electricity rolled off his skin. The Axolotl spoke dreamily, his voice similar to his Dwarven friends. "Could Ah offer ye a spot of tea?"

Artorian blinked, chose not to question anything, and fell into stride. "I'm quite set on beverages at the moment. Who might you be?"

Looking himself over after learning there was no imminent threat to limb and life, the Axolotl replied. "Ah... was? A Dwarven Spotter. Spotter being mah profession. Ah was making a pun a second ago? 'Don't sit there, you'll rune that experiment,' is what Ah said. Then pop! M'here! My name... My fellows used to call me Axe-a-lot. I'm a pun-thusiast and tea aficionado."

"I will admit that is a little difficult to say in casual conversation, Mr. Axe-a-lot. Though it does explain the form." Artorian mused, starting to become amused.

"Blue, then. Call me Blue. Blue Lightning was the first thought, given my... Yes." Wriggling for comfort, the Dwarven-spotter-turned-Axolotl oohed at the bits of cobalt flashing over his fins. "Don't suppose yah know a way for me to return to a form Ah'm a wee touch more used tah?"

"Why, it so happens to be the case that I do! Would you mind sitting around while I call someone?" Artorian smiled, putting the tiny critter down.

"Lady luck be shinin' on me today!" The Axolotl sat down as requested, watching the old man click a device latched to his chest pocket before not being able to help himself and laying the puns on thick. "I'm ec-static you're here. Hopefully you won't charge for that service."

"Operations Team?" Artorian requested, his messenger orb ringing a bell elsewhere on Caltopia.

A click was heard from the device, followed by a Gnomish voice. "This is Operations. How may we help, Administrator?"

"Good afternoon, Operations. I have a Dwarf in my office that is trapped in the form of an Axolotl. He needs transport to Nidavellir, and a Wisp assigned to him for humanization training. Could you please direct one to my office? This is sadly not something I could leave to the filing system. I do apologize for using up a messenger charge, I know we're running out."

Operations crackled through the connection. "The beast cores will be acquired, Administrator. Please do not be concerned with the charges. When you need us, we will be here. A liaison has been sent out to the Wisp Courts, I expect one will arrive within the hour. Anything else, Administrator?"

Artorian considered it. "Please send a note to Deverash that I've once again had an instance of losing Mana-control. I'm unsure if the legs are responsible, but this didn't happen before I had them, and would like it added to the next scheduled checkup."

"Understood, Administrator. Your requests have been logged and are processing. Operations out." The orb crackled once more, then went still as the light on the dials dimmed.

"Administrator, then?" The Axolotl felt very nice, very nice indeed to have been unpacked by someone who could solve his problem in a hurry. "Thank ye! Ah be shocked, but thankful ye could help! If you couldn't, it really wouldn't be your volt."

Artorian, for a moment, wondered if he couldn't get that Wisp here faster. He did not want a miniature Cal sitting on his desk like a talkative ornament. No, one moment, hold the Axolotl up. Did he not know someone else who also shared this proclivity, aside from Cal? "Blue, when you are all settled with your form, there is a person named Wo'ah the Wise who I would like you to meet. He shares your... sense of humor? You may find yourself a new friend, though I will forewarn you that he is a Lunar Elf. Also Anansi, should you run into him. He's all about cheese."

The Axolotl looked like tiny gears were turning in his head. "Wo'ah the Empyreal?"

Artorian's brows shot up. "You know each other?"

"I know *of* him." Blue waffled a fin, his information not

exactly fresh. "I hope he has space in his schedule to planet, I bet we'll be laughing like lunatics."

Artorian wondered if he'd made a terrible mistake. "I may regret this."

"I hope you do." The silver Wisp that hovered into his office sneered, nose shooting to the air, the door opening for him. Invictus, who was still sore from their last encounter, stopped before the desk. With a heavy breath and obvious exhale that painted entire pictures of just how much he did not want to be here, Invictus formed his humanized being, then stood firm. "Invictus of the Winter Court, reporting for assistance to the Administrator. Regarding... *that*, I assume."

"Can Ah punch 'im?" The Axolotl ground his knuckles together with full brazen forwardness when the Wisp addressed him with such callousness. "Just a wee bit?"

"Blue, my friend, your Dwarf is showing." Artorian rebuked him by placing two fingers on his head. Though only with the faintest of intent as the Axolotl puffed up and stood on his hind legs, front paws crossed before a bulked out chest. "Please accompany Invictus to Nidavellir."

Blue grunted like a displeased Dwarf, but all that came out was an adorable, drawn out squeak. Artorian looked away so he wouldn't make a noise in response, covering his move before turning his attention to Invictus when he was good. "Invictus. I am aware our history is rocky. Do you have... issues with this arrangement?"

Invictus kneaded both his eyebrows with deep pressure. "*Sir*, it is my intent—please do recognize that I said the word intent —to be cordial, useful, and work in accordance with the rules. As much as that is possible. That said, what you did to me, and what your friend followed up with, has haunted me, and will continue to haunt me, for every remaining second of what will be a considerably long life. Deeds and stories already had the propensity to follow a Wisp around. The tale of 'Invictus the Cube' is currently a new staple in the entirety of Wisp society. I will *never* escape it, and my only saving grace is that it replaced the story of 'Invictus the Frazzled.' Which came from my telling you of certain inner societal workings."

Artorian pursed his lips, hushed, and then laced his fingers together. "I see."

"Good day, sir." Invictus curtly bowed far too swift, and far too crass, before extending a hand to the table so Blue could climb onto the offered glove. "Mr. Dwarf, if you would please accompany me? I wish to have you where you need to be as swiftly as possible."

Still glaring, Blue waddled onto the offered hand, then kept glaring every moment after as Invictus removed himself from the room and premises.

With his office once again vacant, Artorian wondered if there was a way to turn that sour mood upside down. He'd shot himself in the foot with Invictus, and a way out of that mire looked neither easy, nor convenient. He had to shelve the thought, then considered the workload piled on his desk. "That will need attending another day. For now, perhaps I need a secretary? I cannot have my desk be this much of an unorganized mess anytime another matter is brought in. It's too much."

"Is this a bad time for me to add my note to the pile?" Zephyr formed a pneumatic tube from the wall, giving her an easy opportunity to cut the tension.

Artorian looked at the mess, then extended a hand upwards and made a grabby motion. "Might as well be now. Give it to me, please."

A leaflet formed from the ceiling, detaching to flutter and fall like a leaf before being caught between the old man's extended fingers. Giving it a glance, Luopa's addition to the records room had already been noted. "I see we're ahead of the curve. Dear, is this a space problem or a resources problem? Last I recall, you began as a much larger ship. Are you trying to maintain certain dimensions, thus the efficiency request? Or is it something else?"

Zephyr stabilized her new tube system, then lectured energetically. "The first one. I am trying to keep a certain line and figure. I've had to cannibalize many places internally, and currently am still in the process of doing so. The main areas in my hold come down to a complicated portal room, two large offices, a records room, and a connective hallway. I want to put a place to sleep or cook back where I had them, but that space is thoroughly taken and I can't conveniently squeeze them in elsewhere. The records room is currently taking half of all available space, and I don't see why copies need to be kept there in the first place. I don't have the room to keep expanding it."

Artorian considered that, and felt agreement. "I also don't know why we are keeping copies of documents there. We have an entire mountain, complete with a library, and more space than we know what to do with available at the Skyspear. Let me amend this note of yours and forge a fully-fledged work order. Luopa's room would function better as a dedicated editing and out-processing area. In that same vein, I would very much like an in-processing area, with a secretary. I can't have pile after pile of random problems dropped on my desk. Some of these are bound to be more important than others and this just doesn't work."

"It was fine before?" Zephyr had difficulty spotting a difference, seeing the just as messy desk that happened to have more piles.

"It was!" Artorian broadly motioned across the warehouse that was his desk, then clarified before leaning back in the chair. "Before, the intake volume was minor to small. Now I come back here and there's more pile than desk! In the beginning, I could neatly section incoming work away to a corner of the desk, now I barely have room to place the quill. Let me work on this and get the records room sorted."

"Would Yvessa be a good choice? Sorry, Titania?" Zephyr adjusted her shutters, trying to be helpful and increasing the light intake.

"I'm afraid not, dear." Artorian intoned while picking up a different cobalt quill and flurrying it between his fingers.

"Yvessa is my caretaker. She will look after me, but probably not the work I do. She will gladly make that clear the moment it is asked of her, and tell me to find someone else so she can focus on me. Surely you know her by now."

"I have learned to strategically widen the hallway at times, Administrator." Zephyr practiced as she joked, some warping heard outside the main door. "Some people are given more space so the environment is not in their way. Even if they float above the heads of others."

"Is that why the hallways change when I'm in them?" Yvessa zipped onto the scene and chimed in, her tone sharper than ordinary as her green light filled the office. Though Artorian picked up a hint of playfulness. "Here I thought someone believed I was fat."

Zephyr instantly panicked when the caretaker Wisp appeared in the open doorway, having been too distracted with moving furniture around. "*Nononono!*"

"I'm joking, Zephy." Yvessa's light calmed as she whispered to the wall with a much larger smile, before her perspective snapped towards the old man, her tone serious. "Just like Artorian was *joking* when he said I would not be the secretary. I am never going to forget your weasel-y little antics in the Old Fringe, you sly codger! What we had going during bonfire-night worked exceptionally well, and we will be returning to that model. Plus, I do *not* want to be anywhere near the middle of Wisp society as Titania. A nice and cozy spot on the best boat in the entire sky as Yvessa? Yes, I'll be there, thank you."

"Awwww." Zephyr drifted a donut in the cloudscape as she flushed pink and gushed. "You sweetie. I guess there will be two fire Wisps on board then!"

Right before the spoon appeared, Artorian knew that Zephyr did not know that this detail had not been the best to introduce right now. Because Yvessa doubled in size, and bristled. The old man's caretaker released the very expected, and slightly angry: "Artoriaaaaaaaaan!"

CHAPTER SIX

After Titania's steam was sufficiently discharged, she let Artorian sit back down after having chased him about his own office. She surged to speak with Luopa, then returned with redoubled vigor, stating that part of her caretaker role involved the type and amount of work that made it to him. "This task is mine, and this is final. The only person I would ever consider handing the role off to is Zelia."

Artorian put his hands up to surrender, Luopa screamed his way back to work, and Zephyr discovered it was difficult to hide when being the object that people were meant to hide in. Titania quietly summoned a small host of other Wisps to organize his desk, her temperament shrewd. The veteran caretaker efficiently picked out improvements to the workspace, so it would allow for her proper involvement.

When Titania spoke, she addressed Zephyr. "Dear. Please make a floor below this one. Connect a new hallway to the portal room, place it beneath the current one, and place my secretarial office right below Sunny's. I want a direct staircase connecting the two offices. Make my hallway the intake hallway, and the original hallway the exit hallway. Connect both at the end with a staircase so people don't run into one another. I want one-way traffic only. They pass my office on the way in, they pass this office on the way out."

Grinding sounds below them were indicative of Zephyr getting started with remodeling, while Titania made a loud noise of approval. "Good."

She then moved certain documents closer to Artorian's hands. "These first, please. They're important and need priority processing."

Artorian picked them up, and gave them a look. "Oh. Yes, indeed. This is exactly what I was talking about earlier with some documents being more important!"

Swiftly nabbing a quill, he pulled close fresh sheets of thin vellum and got right to work on approving Father Richard, Decorum, and Mahogany's Supervisor statuses! "Promotions!"

Artorian added a footnote that Zelia really should get bumped to Administrator as well, then slid the vellum to his 'outbox.' A prized space that was now visible after Titania had cleared up the debris field. The Administrator then nodded at the general situation as this was much better already. He then waited to see if more priority documents would appear under his nose, but those promotions appeared to have been it so far. Reaching out to the still-being-organized heap, he nabbed the top sheets and got to work.

"An approval request to implement sugar glider racing in the Nidavellir skyways, and gyrosphere racing in the Nidavellir underground. Project name: Need for Speed. I remember seeing that development start on the moon's workshops. The S.G.R. project, I believe?" That was easy enough to approve. Artorian only felt surprised that this had made it to his desk at all. Had his Dwarves wanted it, they'd have just done so? Checking the details, his copper fell and he went 'ah.'

The idea did not originate from his Dwarves, and had been given the runaround. "Let's see, these were submitted by... Nixie? The one with the tubes and the glowy lights? Nice to confirm he's actually around."

Tapping the end of his quill to his mouth, he then shrugged and dropped the matter. He knew nothing about Dwarven politics or what might be going on over there, and if all that was required for some good entertainment to be added to Nidavellir was a tiny signature? Fine by him.

His friends were going to need it after their work-frenzy faded. "Giant Sugar Gliders? Checkmark of approval. We already have Blanket, so the more the merrier. Decals and lights on the Gliders and Gyros? Sure, why not. Checkmark."

Artorian then scratched behind his ear. "Bugatti Sugar Glider variants. What… What does that mean?"

He read on a few more lines, his confusion packing on. "Approval requests for improved hydraulic assisted joints, approval requests to name some of the Gliders: 'Storm Rider,' 'Audible,' and 'Stardust.' Strange…"

Another few lines down, and he was reading some serious nonsense on turning Sugar Glider coats 'hot-rod red.' "I have the powerful feeling that some of this should not be my choice. This ought to be up to the individual Sugar Glider. Not *me*. Does the rest of this document get into ever more esoteric details?"

Taking more pages from the top of the organized piles and shuffling them so they were in numerical order, he went over the racing approval documents again, and came to the decision that very little of this should be something he decided. Overall allowance to hold races? Sure, that he could understand. If they could name a glider something, or muck with fur color? That should be up to the glider.

It was the 'assisted joints' request that gave him pause. "That sounds like *internal* tampering. I'm not supportive of changes to a glider that the being itself did not approve of. Unless it's about matters involving emergency healing. I don't want any kind of situation where I might walk into a charnel house because some doofus is doing business 'by the part.' That would make me *very angry*."

Mind set on how he wanted to approach this, he redid the

entire vellum of answers and replies with significant emphasis on agency, Sugar Glider choice in all matters, and that he would look very, very unfavorably on this all getting out of hand. Artorian strictly demanded overt public rules on every part of the operation, full transparency, and a whole host of other ethical additions that had him by the beard.

Nixie likely hadn't meant or intended his requests to garner the kind of awful side-effects currently running through the old man's mind, but Artorian's quill was a furious set of scribbles in order to account for them anyway. The Gyroscopes received much more leeway due to being non-sentient machines, but Sugar Gliders were living, breathing beasties. Overhauling a Gyro? No problem. Want to change so much as a hair on a Glider's nose?

Artorian fumed. "Not without their direct approval, you didn't!"

Hours had passed by the time Artorian was done. His stack of vellum was three times as thick as the request had been, with his mustache visibly bristled before he leaned into his chair and began smoothing it out, swimming in righteous indignation the whole time. "These boys have no sense of foresight. I changed my mind. This coming across my desk was *excellent.*"

Titania agreed with a hum, a small cauldron of soup placed on the corner of the desk. "Drink something. I'll get these to Luopa, and please ignore the noise downstairs. I have about twelve other Wisps setting up my office."

Artorian hadn't previously noticed the noise below that his ears now picked up, having been too absorbed into turning a simple request into an ethical book. He'd kept much of the ruling vague so the Dwarves—or more likely the Gnomes, based on some of the strangely technical details—could make their own. Still, he'd been abundantly clear on the direction those rules ought to take. Artorian picked up the cauldron and drained it, placing it back empty. "Thank you, Yvessa. My work up until this point has seemed so simple in comparison, and I was not expecting something like this."

Titania bobbed her green orb in understanding. "It may be exactly the case that the document needing such a ruling is why you received it?"

Artorian drummed his digits. "I... If that is the case, then I'm going to approach all the rest of my work with far higher scrutiny. I doubt all of them will be like this, but now I know to be on the lookout. I may not have the free time to write all the books I want to, or research my Flash Runes, but if I think I need to spend several hours beating the ethics into an answer, then by Cal, I will!"

Titania remained supportive, taking the cauldron and replacing it with an oversized mug of hot leaf juice. "You'll find the time eventually, and honestly, why don't you just outsource some of those research projects to some Wisp or Gnome teams? You saw the workshop on the moon. They're even expanding because it's no longer important to defend the surface with all the demons booked."

She sprinkled in additional details of comfort. "The Goats, Gators, Geese, and the like, have also been moved Caltopia-side. Complete removal of natural threats opened up the S.A.S. and the septs to contributing to more projects. They're, of course, still going to play their crown games, but if I'm the first you've heard it from, they're not particularly happy about no longer having an important purpose. They want one. Halcyon keeps them all together, but that doesn't change how most of the inhabitants on the moon feel."

Artorian pulled a piece of vellum in front of him while nodding. "I'll address that now. On a tangential thought, I don't suppose you remember what my old left-hand and right-hand lists were?"

Titania rattled it off as if Halcyon had told her five minutes ago. "Your right-handed list included: Tribulation seven. Diplomacy and Accords. Skyspear. Decanting adults, and decanting children. You finished all of those. Your left-handed list included mending your Soul pillow, teaching cultivation, letting visitors come to you, scribing, and administrative work. Unlisted tasks include Flash Runes, Henry and Marie, secretly sneaking help into Tatum's projects, and weaseling out information on what's going on with your body from Tim. I suggest you outsource most of them."

"I'm reminded of Invictus." Artorian tapped his quill, then offhandedly voiced his concerns as he listened to his caretaker recount his to-do list. "Or should I really just leave that be?"

"You definitely should leave that be, Sunny." Titania stopped in place, her glow altering to a comforting hue. "Invictus might be unhappy with you, however, Ammy has already picked up that task and you'll be getting in front of her feet if you begin to meddle. Might as well leave it alone until it explodes, and he creates something of it. In which case it's his own fault for acting out."

The Administrator put his hands up as he let go of the issue, then reached over towards the pile and picked up the next problem. "So it is, then. Thank you. On my old list, even pillow mending is an activity I will need to schedule in time for. This pile isn't going to diminish by itself."

"It might." Titania plumply puffed herself into a pillow shape, correcting him as she picked up an entire pile of papers and carted them off to her own office downstairs. "None of these are worth your time. They're either busywork or extraordinarily plain requests. Some shouldn't have even been requested. There's also an adequate stack of complaints I'm still compiling, but those go to Decorum. He has specifically requested work where he can go see a problem firsthand and give an on-the-spot verdict. For the truly problematic ones, those will make it to you just like the racing approval did. I know how to filter them."

"Oh." Artorian hummed, seeing some room open up in his work life. "Might not need a strict schedule after all then. I take it this means that all the matters on my desk will include the truly strange ones?"

"You're holding one, Sunny." Titania released her pillow shape, returning to glowing orb form before vanishing below the floor to cart off documents. He heard her speak to some of her helpers shortly after, and saw them zip up and come pick up piece after piece from a specifically segregated work pile.

Out of sheer curiosity, he plucked a scroll from the pile no longer meant for him, and read the text off. "Missive from a Mage: What do you want to do when you have no needs? What do you need to do when you have no wants?"

He blinked at it, then put the scroll back. "I see. Questions I would love to answer, except that they would steal whole days of my time from the actual work I need to get through. That's unfortunate. I would have enjoyed delving into this topic."

Attention turning to the paper previously in his hand, he gave the contents a read. His eyebrows quickly went up as he uncovered the very problematic information kept within. His finger began to trace the sentences, speaking them out loud from the middle of the report. "Why do you keep showing up in my dreams? Says the assassin woman to a person she should never have met, but had in prior iterations as someone else."

Artorian squeezed his chin, eyes glued to the text as he skimmed down. "A Dwarven father was seen tightly hugging an Elf, profusely apologizing as if to a young son. While the Elf, both older than the Dwarf, and a lady, cried heavy tears on endless questions as to why 'he' had to go through life alone. Both the Dwarven man and Elven lady were speaking of humans that they were in different lives, yet clearly remembered these lives well enough both to speak on the topic; including finding one another, regardless of their new lives never having intersected before. At the point of first meeting, both appeared to remember the full breadth of their prior lives at the same time. The 'son' did eventually forgive the 'father,' resulting in a strange merger of houses where that duo is now living two lives at once, while the rest of their families are awkwardly coping with the news."

Artorian scratched his head at that one. "*Uh-oh.* I thought only Tussle and his missus had the full breadth of their other lives recounted to them. Was it everyone? Or was it everyone in a more muted capacity, and now the other lives are bleeding over? I don't recall what Genevieve said. Something about the effect being based on her skill? I was hoping there would be a stronger buffer between iteration-based memories, but if they were carved onto the soul…"

Quickly pulling a fresh vellum from the pile, he addressed this one to the Wisps, with a copy for Tatum. If they were going to have to deal with people not knowing who they were, combined with a mess of mixed memories, that could go poorly. Best to have a counseling location set up when more cracks like those spread through the foundation.

Artorian paused, letting his mind spin some wheels. "Crackers and toast… That's… That's *everyone*."

Titania nudged him in the shoulder after returning for another pile, seeing him stare a thousand leagues ahead. "Everyone what, Sunny?"

Artorian put his quill back and all his papers down, hands pressed flat to the desk. "Save for the Supervisors, and a few key individuals, the grand majority of Cal's Soul Space occupants have lived multiple lives. Each fully separate and disparate. This document just brought to light that the barriers between those memories are coming apart. Some people might be able to handle this, but not many. I'm going to warn everyone, and send a separate missive to Lunella so she can make preparations for a place where people with this issue can seek shelter and sanctuary. This is not a small cookie, and will not be easy to chew. We're going to be wrestling with this for a while, and if not addressed properly, could turn into an avalanche that buries all our efforts."

Titania then added an unfortunate nugget to this unpleasant information. "Most all the Beasts too. Plus anyone that was ever a Pylon. Plus everyone in Eternia. Iteration changes happened there as well, and I've seen the lists where souls needed to be recycled and used again in a new form. They're… they're very extensive, Sunny. Only the people kept in Memory cores—until Cal was forced to decant everyone—had shielding."

A helpful detail came to her mind. "I actually talked to Genevieve about this not too long ago? According to Genevieve, we only just recently got everyone back into their original body. As original as we could make it, anyway. Very few showed any signs of form-rejection, but you're likely onto something here. Dwarves thinking they are Elves, and Elves thinking they are Dwarves, is not going to be a pretty sight. Especially not when they're *all correct*, but they can't figure out which is right."

Yvessa then turned apologetic. "You don't have the time to handle this personally."

Artorian squeezed the bridge of his nose, then snatched his cobalt-crackling quill back up and pulled close a whole stack of blank vellum like it could save the world. He was going to need it. His mind churned with solutions, his eyes burning bright pink as the crackling cobalt on the quill began to seep and mix with Artorian's **Love** and passion for people. "They will *all* need a home. I have solutions. I need more vellum!"

Titania saw him pour his heart into his work, quickly lost to the world as the Administrator put effort into his namesake. His hand was a blur, the vellum filling with glowing text as Essence and Mana poured into the pages and words. The very air around him felt his concern, whistled for its counterparts, then surged into him as Artorian wrote down anything and everything he could think of to tackle this dilemma. Being unable to do it himself, he would need to be both crisp and informative. The instructions were to be clean, simple, and most importantly of all: **Loving**. Filled with consideration for the fellow mind and soul. Regardless of its many possible mixtures, and many possible forms. To see past the flesh, and into the spirit of things.

Artorian never noticed that the clouds around Zephyr swirled away into her hold, brightening the room further as a growing zone of Mana around the old man responded to his raw will. The energy, not even his, saw his conviction to do good, and chose its path as Zephyr kept herself steady on the sudden stormy current. Visible waves of Mana brushed against her hull until Artorian, eyes closed but still aglow with purpose, raised his crackling quill to the air.

Sound stopped, motion ceased, and Mana paused in place.

His other hand, without thought, moved a fresh vellum into place, then struck it with the fall of gravity. The impact of quill tip to paper sent out a whistled shockwave that flattened all waves with the mere power of a single water drop, turning the raging skysea that had begun to roil into a flat, calm, endless lake.

Artorian's mind was consumed with thoughts of others. His heart went to them. His hand followed. Pink ink glowed to life on Mana-infused pages. The sky around Zephyr copied his words onto the flat lake, making them free for all to read, should one so much as look up.

Yvessa couldn't help but feel pride, and whispered her response, even if her emotions gave it more supportive weight than her whispers betrayed. "Then more vellum you will have."

CHAPTER SEVEN

Artorian woke in the dead of night, inhaling sharply as he blinked the sleep away.

Had he fallen asleep? He couldn't recall doing so.

There was paperwork before him, a fried quill still in his hand. The work stacked on a dark desk, illuminated only by the moissanite panel above. Mountains of vellum now lived on his shelves. He'd gotten through one of Halcyon's requests, and after placing the bundle in his outbox, he had sat back for a moment of comfort. That comfort must have come with severe snoring, because he found himself covered in a new blanket.

Words of wisdom came to mind.

"If you don't schedule maintenance on your system, then your system will schedule it for you." Wiping his eyes with the back of his hand, Artorian sat up more, the chair accommodating his movements. "That's what I get for trying to stay up and power through the work."

Folding the blanket and laying it over his chair, the silence struck him. No editor working next door. No Wisps kerfuffling a floor below. No party on the deck. No mid-ship grinding of Zephyr moving yet another beam.

He peeked through a porthole. Zephyr was holding steady in a cloudbank, a canvas of stars filling a dark sky above the pasty white puffs. A glance through solid matter over the shoulder revealed that Decorum was present on the ship, also asleep in his office. Artorian grinned. His brother snoozed in an equally comfortable chair. He'd done away with the prior monstrosity, it seemed. A shame, that old chair had some good weight to it.

One of Decorum's ears twitched when Artorian looked too long, Gomez sitting up with the telltale nerves-on-edge expression that revealed he knew he was being watched. Artorian chuckled, stopping that particular method of sight.

He ambled his way to the other office.

Gomez had his nose out of the door before Artorian got there, the old man whispering while his knuckles ticked against the doorframe. "My boy. I believe we may have woken during everyone's naptime."

Gomez nodded, his eyes catlike before shifting to their humanoid counterparts. He whispered back all conspiratorial, like it was a game. "This happens from time to time when Cal needs to repair something major, or change something without notice. We might be first up. Should you see déjà vu cats, that's normal."

Artorian had thought this unscheduled doze had been an off the cuff nap, not actual, serious, unscheduled maintenance. He whispered while holding his beard, at a loss since he wasn't keen on being the reason more people woke up. "I see. What should we do?"

Gomez's stomach rumbled in reply, the stately man looking away with a flush. Artorian stifled his snickering, his brother managing to growl out a response. "I'm always hungry when I first wake up. I also want to fight something. The old Liger instincts at play. No amount of being a statesmanship-loving humanoid can repress or replace those urges."

"I'm up for a hunt." Artorian grinned back, his teeth showing. "I always have more rust to wipe off my fighting skills, and we *did* need to go on that run together. Plus, I have hundreds of years of your memories of being a Liger, but no actual use. Know anywhere we could go tussle with anything that won't cause other problems?"

Gomez shot him back a feral smile. "The Mononoke Rainforest."

After sneaking off Zephyr's deck, Artorian and Gomez silently made themselves scarce. Decorum knew a few hunting spots, all of those places the kind of knowledge that came with an equally silent tap to the side of the nose, and an overt wink that fooled nobody.

Artorian gave Gomez his replacement storage ring that he'd gotten from Minya, since he wasn't going to be at risk of bursting out from nice clothing with a transformation. He was still barred from transformations after all, and he wasn't particularly attached to the object. It held Ammy's Spirit-quality glass table and accompanying chairs, but little else. Perhaps his stately brother knew of a good spot for them.

Gomez, on the other hand, treasured the gift.

After Decorum stretched out in his full Liger form, paws and claws kneading the dirt to get a feel for the freedom of it all, Artorian carefully paneled himself in with his Presence. The flip in perspective from a human being encased, to the creature doing the encasing, came at the exact point when enough of the Liger-form was complete. When he could blink as the Light-Liger, he was the Light-Liger.

First order of business, turning down the brightness!

Decorum chuffed in amusement. The entire forest had likely seen them. Speaking as a beast came with more gruffness, but Gomez managed it. "So much for our element of surprise. On the *bright* side, the boars will come find us instead. They're very territorial."

"Don't you start with the puns, too! I've had enough of random new people who all ascribe to the madness of Cal."

Artorian huffed, his voice normal even when the Liger's mouth moved, as it was still his original body speaking. "First Anansi and Wo'ah, then a Dwarven Spotter? I'm lucky that Luopa gives me peace."

Artorian stretched out in his Liger form, feeling his new back pop, stretch, and feel sooo incredibly good from that cat-specific stretch. He then copied Decorum and kneaded the ground, tearing up some roots and grass beneath him as the light from his panels dimmed to a matte gray finish. "*Mmm, there we go.*"

Hcweeeeei!

The boar that exploded from the brush had the time to stampede towards Artorian before cat-like reflexes kicked in and a flashing Liger claw crushed the attacker while simultaneously ripping the entire boar's tusked head off. It wasn't clean as the claws dug deep, the panicked swipe felling a tree along with the boar. The charging giant hog exploded in hot... unpleasantness, all over him. Draping him in... dead boar remains.

The cry from the now-dead C-ranking beastie had alerted at least fifty more feral hogs to his exact position, amusing Decorum greatly. Artorian invested his Starlight effect into his Liger shape, and cleaned himself right up, the unwelcome gore sloughing off him and leaving him pristine. "Ew."

"That's a neat effect." Decorum chuffed, reducing his size to that of the average Puma before lounging in some branches that were barely able to support his density and mass. "The constellation pattern on you, I mean. The cleaning effect I knew about."

Artorian curled awkwardly to try and get a good look at himself as the sound of a growing stampede grew closer. Remembering he could make a mirror instead, he boxed himself in with four of them. "The boars can wait a minute. What pattern?"

Decorum said nothing, believing the mirror would do a better job of answering his brother's question. In front of Artorian, a blocky Liger made of mixed celestial paints, dots of lights, and lines connecting them swirled in the slow, steady movements of thick liquids. Grinding his claw against wood confirmed that the effect was merely visual, and he wasn't a paintbrush.

Artorian could have easily been convinced otherwise given the view. "Delightful. I don't think it did this previously? I also had less problems standing last time. I remember being able to run. I feel very wobbly?"

"Talk later, fight now." Decorum growled as he dropped from the tree. The rainforest kapok unable to do more than barely hold him, as the wood croaked and groaned to re-settle when Decorum's pressure left.

Absorbing his mirrors, Artorian came snout-to-snout with more than a mere fifty feral hogs that had previously piled in on the dark side of the mirrors. None of them cared in the least about the size difference. He also suddenly doubted they were feral. Most of these boars were dumb and C-ranked, but it wasn't possible for the few B-ranked ones thinking they were clever at the back of the pack to actually hide.

He remembered something Halcyon mentioned about Beasts normally not challenging creatures stronger than them. Or that there was some difficulty? That problem had either been resolved, or perhaps only applied to A-ranking Beasts and up? Because this horde definitely did not care and did not have a restraint problem.

When the unique-patterned invader that looked like a piece of the night sky had fallen into their territory became visible, all the Mononoke Tribe Hogs released that awful sound and went for the throat. Tumbling and crashing over one another to get gnashers and tusks into the enemy.

Artorian, after becoming buried under a pile of hogs, needed a few more seconds to come to terms with the pile not having done to him anything save make for a very awkward huddle. Attacks from Strong-Cored Beasts... well. It was cute? Interesting was perhaps a better word. He was, after all, in something else's territory. What a C-ranked entity thought it was going to do against an A-ranked Aura...?

A bite to the back of his neck that felt like a chastising nip dragged him from the squealing hive as Decorum 'saved' him from the predicament. Running off with Artorian's Liger form like it was a kit that hadn't realized it was in trouble.

The kit being six to seven times the Puma's size.

Decorum deposited Liger-torian on a stone ridge, then bapped him hard in the face with a paw. Several times. The more experienced Liger chastised him further. "Brother, what are you doing? I'm lucky you kept a mere single rank in your form and I could move you, but come on. I even warned you!"

"I..." Artorian said half-heartedly, not exactly sure. "I think I was for some reason expecting to have all of a Liger's inclinations? I *whapped* the first boar as a reaction, but then the rest were suddenly there, and I froze up. I had no thoughts. No clue what to do. They just piled on me and I sat there with question marks above my head."

Decorum grumbled, looking at the rainforest below and the swath of hogs all beelining for them. They likely had an extra few minutes due to the elevation, but normally Artorian was more on the ball than this. Decorum exhaled from his nose, and laid on his stomach with crossed front paws. This was his brother. His brother was not one to 'Dale it' without choosing to.

Fun hunt or not, his brother needed to find his feet first. "You expect that you know what it is to be something, from memories alone? You must feel the wind against your fur. The flavor of meat in your jaws. The sensations of claws rending your enemies. Merely knowing is not enough. Having the memories is not enough. Those are *my* experiences you have. A veil, or lens, separates you from them, even if you believe you have experienced my early years firsthand. My memories are in your possession, but they are not part of your *Pattern*, brother. The acts are not engraved on your soul."

He grinned wide, incisors showing. "Knowing what to do

does not mean being able to react without thought, and doing them. That is the realm of the practiced, and ingrained. Until you practice, and engrave the pattern into the canvas of your memories, your own memories, thus making them part of your soul, you will not feel like a natural Liger. How could you? Did being a dragon come naturally? Did you know how to play with your bonescripting purely because you had it?"

Artorian grumbled in retort, as his brother was driving the point home rather hard. The response came with a growl from the throat, his Aura picking up the slack for the gruffness his own body could not create. "Alright, alright. I just go and stumble around in that pile of hogs, then? They have no chance. There's no real threat here."

Decorum grinned wider. "That there is no threat is not the point, brother. They are the chaff. The practice. The strong ones come later, but how do you expect to hunt them when you have forgotten how to walk? How to prowl? How to stalk? Come! Watch me! I shall teach you."

With a gust of sharpest wind, Decorum zipped away like the slice of a blade. A blade that formed claws, and turned the front wave of boars into a plate of charcuterie.

When Decorum came to a dramatic halt in the middle of them, he drew a massive breath, and roared at the lot. Challenging the boars to their territory. A challenge they couldn't ignore, if only because Decorum was completely repressing his rank, and not letting them cower due to his sheer presence alone. That, and this was possibly not the first time he had come and rained on their truffle-snuffling parade.

Something Artorian should also do! If it didn't seem to be the case that… he was also not emitting the pressure of his rank? "That's odd, I didn't direct my Aura to do that, and it seems to be doing it already. Mimicking Decorum, are we? Convenience!"

Shaking himself out as he got to his feet, Artorian compressed his own form to not be so ridiculously oversized. He got down to about twice Decorum's volume before the dimensions threatened to take space away from where he was keeping his actual body, but that was a grand improvement from the six to seven times volume that it had been. His acuity also felt better? It wasn't exactly right, but the smaller size matched up better with Decorum's memories.

"Well, no time like the present to let off some steam!" Artorian braced himself, and jumped! A whole three inches as the ground behind him broke and gave way, smashing him face first into the rock as physics wondered what he thought he was doing. Building tension strength on loose gravel? How was that ever going to provide stable footing?

Tumbling down the hill instead, Liger-torian rolled straight into the horde of angry boars, and remembered some lessons from the noodle days. "When in doubt, flail!"

Also Fireball, but, baby steps!

Dozens of squealing hogs went flying through the air as the constellation Liger rolled, thrashed, clawed, gripped, and launched itself at nothing in particular. Focused only on making as big of a mess in his surroundings as possible, while trying to get a grip on which limb went where and what his range of motion with it was. That he turned with enough force to destroy a charging hog into a bloody mist with a **kpaf**! was just happenstance.

The Starlight effect kept him clean! Just him, though, but that was acceptable.

Decorum had intended to teach methodically, but was too busy wheezing and laughing as he watched the oversized Liger with dexterity equal to a blind cub thrash and flail about. Lessons... lessons were going to have to wait. Merely existing as a Liger was going to come first. He slapped a boar away, then needed to slap the ground to cope between bouts of laughter. "We... Okay. Brother? We are going to take a day out of every week, and practice this. We will hunt when you *can* hunt."

"I've got one!" Artorian enthusiastically replied, a hog having bitten his tail while refusing to let go as he rolled through a few trees, felling and crushing them to splinters beneath him. "Sounds good! I'm getting the hang of this!"

Artorian was most certainly not 'getting the hang of this,' as Decorum quipped. "Brother... you do not have it. It has you. By the tail. Which is the start of a new joke that I will never let die. Work on your balance! *Balance!*"

CHAPTER EIGHT

Months later, Artorian stood on a sword in the sky.

Still working on his balance.

A whole host of students in matching green robes accompanied him, including the prior three that Polly had put effort into educating. She was an excellent Parrot. Purveyor of all things **Pride**. Her efforts to teach the floating swords to stay airborne helped tremendously, while providing the students a measure of confidence.

"Very good!" Artorian applauded, then called out to the whole class, his eyes gliding from one student to the other as they balanced on the part of their floating swords that they liked the best. Some were pommel-people. Others liked the long stance, with one foot directly on the blade. "Exem, watch the arms, my boy."

"Yes, teacher!" Exem flailed regardless; first backwards, then forwards, before finding some comfort in the art of intimidating a scarecrow with how his arms twisted like antennae. The child peeped out false bravado. "I'm alright, teacher!"

Artorian gave it a second to make sure the boy was balancing on his sword properly, then nodded and smoothly hovered in a loose circle around them all. "Very well then. Now! While some of the other classes are still working on getting airborne, you've all graduated from novices to beginners. This means you are privy to the same lessons that the class before you received. This is mostly down to keeping your ears open, so pay attention and you'll graduate from beginner to apprentice very quickly. Remember that this ranking is about competence in the Academy introductory course, not overall power. A lower-ranked cultivator who is an apprentice still has something to teach you! Anyone that actually makes it to student rank will get to join the Academy proper, and be given introductions by Ali and Razor."

He motioned at the two specific individuals, who were here to take Artorian's class for the sake of having taken it.

Artorian drew a breath, opening his lecture to an attentive class. "Let's begin! Basic cultivation in Cal's Soul Space is a trifle compared to the real deal outside, that you will one day face. This event is inevitable, so it is important to have an exceptional grasp of the basics, should you not be in a position to conveniently meet one of the requirements to re-gather your power."

He stuck a firm digit into the air. "Remember! Regardless of how far you advance in Cal, this is the practice round! The harder you work now, the better your real results later! Some of your efforts will transfer, but some will not. Any of you that breach the Mage-ranks, as example, will be happy to hear that the same Tier will be attained a second time with considerable ease, when you breach that threshold on the outside again."

Coming to a standstill in a position where the sun was in his face, rather than at his back so his students needed to squint, Artorian folded his arms behind his lumbar. "You've all done well attending both the basic and supplementary lessons, but I'm here for the problematic stuff that occurs out of the ordinary. Your teachers will have their own methods, and as some of you have swiftly learned..."

Artorian shot a meaningful glance to Ian and Exem, who

had failed entirely to thrive under Craig or Emilia due to their own reclusive natures. Astrea was a good substitute instructor, but even she was here for lessons. The bards were doing better, but not by much.

Artorian picked up his dropped thread. "That not all methods are helpful to everyone. Nor do all methods work for everyone. Some of you like to 'Dale it.' Some of you like to ponder. We've got some free thinkers in the group! A person or two with their head in the clouds. Plus at least one scholar that needs every last detail hammered into stone so it can be read and re-read a thousand times before any of the information sticks."

Giggling did the rounds, accompanying some hushed whispers about Amber being dragged face-deep in mud while people pried a basket of cookies out of her hands. That had certainly stuck!

Artorian chuckled, also fondly remembering Amber getting her comeuppance when faced with the cookie-envious wrath of slighted children. Her own fault for thinking she was going to get away with it. She'd made it a full week before being hunted down by the ravenous horde became too much, and the last cookie left her possession, before they'd left her in the mud. Amazing how well they listened to schemes when united under the same banner. He, unlike Amber, would surely get away with it. Surely.

He recaptured attention, motioning at the Ziggurat brats. "Astrea, Grim, Ty. You're all near the C-ranks to my eyes. I noticed the number fluctuated earlier as well. You explosively pumped up to C-rank four, then dropped down to nothing again. Has this become a common occurrence?"

Astrea stuck her hand in the air, looking sheepish.

When motioned at, she answered. "We're all stuck at C-rank zero and we're not sure why. Then again, we've also, erm... been lacking in the 'asking for help' department. Most everyone has been having too much fun going around and blasting critters that roam about—especially around the Skyspear—with the limited one or two techniques they kind of know. The Essence replenishment happening by itself and in vast quantities is great! Actually improving... We might have been a little lazy."

A glance at Grim and Ty confirmed much the same story.

Grimaldus did appear to have a nugget of insight as he raised a hand. "There was a point where I felt like 'extra help' went away, and something changed. Like the mechanism responsible for keeping me stable at C-rank two poofed, and I crashed right back down to zero. My advancements didn't change, but my rank did. I lost none of my progress in Aura work, but for whoever does the accounting now, that doesn't seem to be worth the tally. C-rank zero for me, like everyone else. We've seen some people jump from C-rank zero to B-rank zero, but I could swear they were done with all their infusions and building, and the like."

"Pylon problem. Cal's on it. Grim, so long as you're making infusion progress, you should be just fine." Artorian exhaled, then turned to the host of other students. "Does anyone have any questions before I break this lecture open?"

A few hands shot to the sky.

Artorian motioned at Alexandria, who had an entire notepad nested in the crook of her arm. "I am having difficulty *entering* the C-ranks. What is wrong?"

Direct and to the point as always.

Artorian considered her request, studied her current progress for a moment, then held his beard before the standard pensive stroking began. "Alexandria, dear, since I know you will ask me in depth anyway, I will give you the answer to both the old circumstance, and the current one. I feel you will find better use by having the comparison."

She nodded fervently, eyes eager for knowledge.

Artorian got lost on a short segue before correcting himself. "Regarding our old world, should anyone want more knowledge on that topic, Alexandria was there. So feel free to ask her for records or clarifications. She can always steer you to a better source, though it will likely be the bards."

The bardic students in attendance all clicked their tongues and shot crossbow fingers at everyone.

He cleared his throat, and tried again. "In our old world, there was a barrier to entry where the C-ranks were concerned. I myself encountered this problem. For convenience, I will be using the old Guild rank measurement system, since that's spreading around anyway. It's not as correct as I would like it to be, but it will do until I sit down with Discord and the gang and cobble together a more detailed one."

He wove some Mana together, doing his best to create a list-like format. It... didn't go so well. Without Pylons, clean lines and arrow-points didn't look pretty. He dismissed the mess and went right back to making a bunch of multicolored orbs.

The orbs never failed!

He began at the green orb all the way on the left. "First up. G-rank. Also called Moss rank. In general, these aren't cultivators. Think of G-rank as anything that qualifies as a noun, that happens to have a teensy bit of Essence. Any person, place, or thing with at minimum a tiny bit of Essence in it is G-rank. Any noun *without* Essence in it is either mundane, or nothing but corruption. For the most part, we're talking about plant life when the G-ranks come up in conversation, starting at non-organic matter like rocks and ash for the lower G's. Mid-G begins with small plants such as moss and mushrooms, while the upper ranks form most of the other flora in the world."

Artorian moved to the yellow orb. "The F-ranks are where beings become sentient and sapient, able to gather their own food and make short-term plans. As a side note, we can once again just say 'nouns' here. More than just people, places and things can have this happen as well. You've all seen the talking brooms, and Cal's mountain of puns. I suppose he had to keep them all somewhere... We're equally in no shortage of talking rocks. On that topic, I do not yet have permission for a field trip to the

Silverwood. The Wisps are having a debate on safety regulations, as they don't trust some of you dastardly youngsters not to touch one of the dungeon Cores and start an avalanche of problems."

The Administrator glared severely in the direction of all the younger bardic students, like Megheara, Meave, Moza, Ash, and their ilk. Their quick-flashed innocent smiles weren't fooling anyone, except perhaps Ali and Razor, who had the same Abyss-eating grins on their faces.

"Behave!" Artorian fussed, getting back to the ranks. "The mid-F ranks are what most humans reach before adulthood, without cultivating. Once cultivation becomes a focus, this is known as the fishy or 'failure' rank for people who can't crack into the next one. I'm not fond of the title, but Alexandria is tearing that paper up."

Alexandria's eyes snapped up for a moment, her command clear. "More!"

Artorian chuffed. Tapping the yellow orb, a few smaller cubes escaped it, rotating around the orb like small square moons. "Confusion often happens here, because we can be talking about both cultivators and non-cultivators when referring to F-ranks. When it comes to cultivators, this is the bit where you clean up your body, and prepare your Meridians. You can distinguish between the two when you figure out how to look at someone else's center. A clean center is a cultivator, a... muddled one with corruption swirling, that's a non-cultivator."

Rolling his shoulders to get the thought out of his head, the old man cracked on. "People generally have one or two Meridians open before the D-ranks, as most of the effort here is stuffed into getting your Core cultivation technique up and running. Attain a 'good enough' Core in the F-ranks, and you're D-rank. Congratulations. F-rank is all about Essence storage and getting the engine going."

He then considered some problematic looks directed at Jiivra, and thought it best to address that detail. Even if she was just here to listen in for a few minutes. "This is also why E-rank is such an odd duck."

"Quack." Jiivra mimicked said duck. A massive grin formed on her face only after she made the students' composure break with shrieking laughter. "I can't stay, but do tell them the story. Echo was always a weird one."

"That it was." Artorian plucked one of the cubes out of the air to squeeze it like a stress ball before letting it go. Then he agreed, moving on to the orange orb once enough of the students had gotten themselves together. "E-rank is known as the Echo rank, and in old world terms is used to prepare a body for intense cultivation. Which is a fancy way of saying that someone else is undergoing all the effort to place a copy of their own technique into you. The cultivation technique must be suitable for the person, needs to be of a complexity they can handle, and has to be a shape they can understand. It's not simple. Much like trying to turn another person's spiral into a fractal, this process is highly intensive, prone to severe downsides, and has a rather high chance of sudden, instant death. I've echoed a few times myself, and the first time just about killed me off."

He made an apologetic gesture to Jiivra. "Worth it, dear. I assure you I have no regrets. You being with us makes my world feel all the more whole."

She flushed bright pink, her face squeezing to stay serious before hovering over and crushing him with a hug. "Hush, you. No more story. I'm heading out before what I die of is embarrassment."

Returning the affection, Artorian waved as he watched her go, then spoke without turning back to the students. "If you're not a Mage, put doing this for someone out of mind. In general, I would avoid this altogether. The only time I've done this was to save a life on the brink of failure, such as Jii's. Or with a literal year of constant, sustained effort, as with Yuki. Consider someone with an Echo rank to be a survivor or victim more than some lucky punk. They need hugs, not judgment."

Some flushed cheeks and meek mumbles did the rounds, but Artorian got his point across and moved on to the next orb. This one was going to take the most effort, since he needed to unpack it twice. He was interrupted by a raised hand from Ian, who he motioned to while the boy was making Infernal flowers grow on his hand. "Does this mean we should give Yuki hugs?"

"Yes! Plenty!" Artorian smiled extra wide. "She could surely use them to thaw."

Those who were in the know broke down laughing, but Ian was clearly dead-set on the hugs-solution. He was making a determined face. Artorian was not going to stop him!

CHAPTER NINE

"Let's move on to the D-ranks then." Artorian laid his finger on the red orb. Plenty of cubes poured out of this one before keeping a stable orbit. "The D-ranks are where most people get stuck. Or at least the time they will remember the most, given it has the heaviest *physical* struggles. Most first-time failures happen at this stage. Trackable, demonstrable, and utterly necessary, these hard-coated points of progress that must be met tend to stick with people. You'll technically spend more time in the C-ranks overall, but Aura building is what most people call esoteric nonsense, before kicking a rock and slumping away all grumpy. It did not escape my notice that the majority of people are internal cultivators."

Artorian released the orb, and began tapping individual cubes to make them glow. "This is the rank where a cultivator starts to become actually dangerous, and that's what's sold to all the newbloods to put the shine in their eyes. A single D-ranked individual can usually fight off ten F-ranked beings without issue. Since at this stage people are still very much mortal, with mortal problems, this is very enticing. Who hasn't thought of walking into their workplace and throwing all of their managers out an open window? I know I have. Remember, kids! Thinking is not illegal! Actually throwing them out the window… probably is. That reminds me of this one time, when…"

"*Eh-hem.*" A look from the head librarian made him skip some of the storytelling.

Artorian pressed his hands down his robes and kept lecturing like he hadn't just gotten terribly distracted. "Old world-wise, D-rankers were characterized by a 'fractal' in their Chi spiral. As many of you know, that is… no longer quite the case. Fractals and geometric cultivation techniques are still fine, but we encourage the adoption of any Core technique that your mind is able to handle and keep spinning. Alexandria had a list, I hear."

The head librarian waved said list above her head, handing out copies.

Artorian enlarged his red cubes, each representing a detail of a cultivator's growth. "In the D-ranks, old world rules had very little wiggle room. Current knowledge instead says almost any of the steps are interchangeable, but it is more convenient to do some before others. Overall, the main issue people had in the old world came down to time, willpower, and resources. There's plenty of Essence in Cal, but out in the real, you had to put significant, life-changing effort into going somewhere that had any. Not to mention Essence that matched your Affinity types. *Exactly*, mind you. Locations that match your Affinity types exactly. If you have Air, Wind, and Fire, your cultivation spot better have all three, or you'll be drinking in corruption like you're on a Dwarven bender. Better if the weak to strong variables match as well, but at that point you have wiggle room."

He motioned at Maeve when her hand went up, one of the sharp-tongued bardic students now fully on the cultivator path. She steadied her voice to not harm it, or anyone around her with what the infernal additions tended to do when she spoke. "Is this why fighting in dungeons was so common? I remember spending years traveling through the mountains with you, but aside from some significant improvements to our Core techniques, Meridians, and general physical condition, we didn't power-up all that much. Essence was hard to get."

"Correct!" Artorian clapped his hands together, easing back before smoothing out a flutter in his robes as the wind whisked by. "Gathering Essence is done best in an Essence-rich environment. The frozen north did not help, and it was solely due to your affinities that we got the Essence from the environment that we did. Mind you that it took... What? Seven years? Eight? For your whole class to ease into the D-ranks. Cultivators who went for the dungeons cut that time into considerably smaller chunks. This is also why the entire endeavor created an industry, and why people kept attempting to monopolize those situations."

Appeased by the answer, Maeve dropped her hand.

Tapping another cube, Artorian continued. "It is entirely possible to focus on your Aura while in the D-ranks, but it is more difficult without all your Meridians clean, open, and well-connected. It is also more difficult without a good Core technique, a healthy Essence pool, and favorable circumstances. Having an Essence-infused brain certainly helps, but that's not a step to take without preparation, and someone next to you. Let's never forget that improvements for a cultivator come with very real and lethal side-effects if something goes wrong in the middle of a process, or you find yourself short on Essence when you really need not to be."

Artorian tapped the side of his nose. "Aura requires more mental work than physical work, which is why it tends to be moved to the C-ranks. If you got your body-building all worked out in the D-ranks, then it's considered good progress! Infusion stage? Incredible. Rebuilding stage? Majestic. If your form is cleaned, infused, *and* rebuilt with Essence? Go hit a bell, because you beat the bell curve, you madlad internal cultivator you."

He then motioned at the inevitable, impending question from Alexandria. "Yes, dear. I'm getting to it. The bodies, right?"

Alexandria's hand dropped before her mouth ever needed to open, so her old man explained while he got a few confused looks. "In Cal, the bodies you are using are very complicated, very powerful copies of what you should have. Squeezed down to be on par with what you can handle. With these bodies, you are skipping almost all the physical steps we've just described."

Artorian made a tower of cubes so he could point at each ridiculous convenience, one at a time. "You will never need to clean your body of impurities. There is no need to clean Meridian paths. All your Meridians begin completely opened, infused, and built. Essence cycling happens without you needing to do anything. Your Affinities are side-stepped because Cal provides unaligned Essence anyone can use, in quantities that are frankly unbelievable to old world cultivators. Nobody will ever need to piggyback from a Gathering Webway into a cultivation technique since the supply is always abundant. So not only is it easy to make a Core technique, but people can quickly make a *good* one."

He nodded at Alexandria. "Some of us are skipping whole volumes of natural progression and arriving straight at some outright remarkable end results."

She shot him a smile back, one that proudly showed all her teeth before she made a swirly motion at her notes. He should be talking!

"Refining Essence and corruption rebuking is thus a thing of the past. Meaning that 'capacity' suddenly gets the gold medal, and even capacity feels like a hunk of metal gilded for show because of how quickly replenishment works." Artorian continued, his circular hover re-adopted in lieu of pacing. "Thus I expect that all the aspects people normally familiarize themselves with to receive a 'but this is already done' retort, in questioned or confused tones. This is why I mentioned it best to familiarize yourself with the steps."

He then turned to Alexandria fully. "You are not doing anything wrong, dear. D-rank nine to zenith has hidden conditions for breaking into the C-ranks, and they're not very intuitive. I do not expect you to simply cross them off from a checklist. Attaining D-rank nine is easy. All you need is to achieve a well enough built body, with a center and Core cultivation technique that can handle a large enough amount of Essence to make the breach."

The silence of his students told him they were all being very attentive. So he enlarged the orange orb, and washed waves of watery Mana over the shell again, and again, and again. "The hold-up to the C-ranks is that the limitation-barrier of your own being needs to be eroded, like waves over a rock, by the constant push and pull of your Essence against what you feel to be your walls. Eventually, like a breached dam during a storm, those barriers will give way, and you will find that your actual maximum to hold Essence was far greater than what you thought it was."

The puzzled look on Alexandria's face made him clarify, motioning at Grim, Astrea, and Tychus. "Your brothers and sisters are good examples. They constantly flex their techniques, expend their reserves, and let them fill back up. This in and out method is one of the ways to erode the barriers. The other is to meditate, and mentally push your supply against the esoteric walls from your center, to chip them away from inside-out. Most everyone likes to do outside-in as a method, that being throwing out a bunch of flashy techniques to enjoy watching their enemies turn into frizzled confetti."

Her hand went up, so he took the request. Alexandra needed a beat to find her words, her frown deep. "I am having… difficulty with the concept of these 'walls,' Grandfather."

Artorian attacked his beard with grooming hands to think. "*Hmm.* So, normally one begins to play around with Essence either in their center, or at their fingertips. Please do not confuse this for the difference between internal and external cultivators. Some people first encounter Essence internally, as I did. Or externally, as most others. The entire endeavor of controlling Essence is contained within your center, where you keep your cultivation technique. This space can be considered to have 'walls.'"

He checked whether to see if she got it, but that did not appear to be the case. More words it was! "From one's center, people normally branch out to form their Meridian paths. This teaches them 'hey, I've got a lot more space in here than I thought'! Then, when a cultivator starts cleaning their body up, they realize that they can begin storing Essence in their cells. That storage suddenly becomes much better when they later replace their cells with the Essence variant."

Another check, and Alexandria still hadn't made the leap. Even more words, then! "The walls change from one's center, to part of the body, to the entirety of the body, to the entirety of the body completely stuffed full of Essence like it just suffered through an entire holiday dedicated to eating. Unfortunately, satiation to the limit—by itself—is not enough to break that limit. Normally when one does break it, they become aware that their Aura is much more than it appears to be, because all that energy still has to go somewhere, while remaining a part of you."

He added a spicing of personal experience. "I had a lot of difficulty with this because I had access to the tools afforded by an Aura before reaching this point, and the change from D-rank to C-rank was underwhelming, to say the least. I got some benefit out of it, but nothing like what I was told. You become better at holding Essence, mostly because there's storage space in between what accounts for 'your body' and 'your Aura,' but for the most part, something else is now holding the slack. You may have also heard of a 'death plane' before? That would be the same connective space, and if you feel it run dry, you're dying as a cultivator. Approaching your death plane is a cold, stomach-sucking feeling with unpleasant tingles. Like ice running through your veins. Being near it will debilitate you, being in it…"

He'd hammed that up a bit much, but better to give the worst-case warning. He himself had, after all, pulled through after getting dangerously close to his death plane while dealing with Blighty. Being in it meant you were dying, but bottoming it out was a final fate. Seeing some of the students who were present from back then sternly nod in both warning and agreement, they filled in the wayward questions at the back of the class.

The old man then squeezed his beard, thinking of relatable information for the younger crowd. "Jiivra's jump into the C-ranks makes for a better example. The speed by which she was able to control her Essence had easily jumped tenfold. By her own words, Essence had felt 'immediate,' like it was 'just there.' Her capacity to store Essence went up so significantly that she felt like a person two, if not three, times her current size. If referring to Essence storage by structures, then her 'house' became a 'castle.'"

Another check, and still nothing. Maybe if he sprinkled in some knowledge on old world limitations? "I suppose it also helps that pearlescence of Core techniques is a thing of the past. Or, at the minimum, it doesn't trigger in Cal. No more feeling like your refinement process takes up physical space in your center before the B-ranks. No more losing it all if you need to start over. Breaking through the wall used to be very costly, mixed in with needing to pay the pearlescence transformation tax. Jiivra only dropped back down to D-rank three! Me? F-*two*! From a very healthy D-rank zenith. I couldn't even stand back up! I had horses eating hay off my bald head!"

That got some smiles and giggles, which was a clean break from the heavier topic earlier. "When I hit C-rank, my influx and Essence-draw improved, but my storage... barely dented. If at all. I didn't feel like I had any sort of castle, and if anything, it just felt like I'd lost a house and was now standing on a lake. Like my house had been in a basin and was now flooded over. No going back. Abyss, storing Essence became *more* difficult. I had to refine Essence *extra* just so it would pour back into my Aura."

Artorian compressed the breakdown of his experience. "In

my case, as an external cultivator, no additional space, no additional control, and Essence didn't move any faster than it had. My Core 'improved.' Faster draw. Better refining. While I drew in Essence at greater speed, now it needed a greater level of refinement before it could be stored. When I moved some high-celestially tainted Essence into my Aura, that seemed to work fine. The intermediate variant was the problem. Partially refined Essence, or refined but not refined well enough, didn't budge. C-ranking changed the 'filter' which my Essence moved through in order to ease from my body, to my Aura, or back."

Check number four, and Alexandria's face was a contorted mess. Maybe he was going the wrong direction? Last try! "Perhaps 'wall' is where I'm losing you. There is… a space between one's center and one's body. A differentiator between the physical and… the Wuju, as I call it. In the records, you may have found I kept a hexagonal beehive webway, or a gathering webway, in that location. If you pour Essence into that area, and flood it, then you will find a 'between' space. The feeling you get from doing that is similar to the feeling of C-ranking. It's… not always pleasant. Please don't mix up your center's 'between' with 'The Between,' because that's a real place, and is part of the Mage lecture."

For a moment, his mind blanked, and he forgot the right words. Artorian snapped his fingers to recover the term. "The… Essence-drawing circuit? Ah! Affinity channels, that was the proper name. Those are kept in that space, though they are not initially accessible. I expect Mana is needed to open that second door, as I don't recall ever managing to access it without Mana previously having altered that space. Or having Mana myself to accomplish the feat. Please do recall that we're still under the no-affinity-opening mandate. I can see some of you thinking."

He then frowned. "Where was I going with this? Right! Alexandria, for you, this 'between' space is where Meridians connect to your center. That bit you should have access to, no Mana required. That's all Essence. You'll recognize your Meridians as holes in your center, that you can push Essence through. Do not be surprised if you can't see or notice them at first, just throw some Essence around in there and you'll see where the paint doesn't stick. For what loops to where, please consult the wall scroll on the library's first floor."

He'd gotten off topic again, but saw that the head librarian had enough pieces to put what was bothering her together. Alexandria's eyes lit up with a hum. "It's not that there is a 'wall,' but a lack of 'connection.' I theorize that pushing Essence back and forth doesn't 'erode' a barrier, so much as it 'connects' the disparate 'Wuju space' between one's physical body, and non-physical Aura. A bridge for the between."

Artorian was going to ask if she grasped the material with that statement, but her preemptive response was to pull a functional, physical Nixie tube out of her bag and make it flicker to life with a pleasant orange hue.

Her old man reared back to laugh! What a pleasant jest! "Understood!"

CHAPTER TEN

With Alexandria on the right track and furiously taking notes to rectify what she'd misunderstood, Artorian focused his attention on other students. "I recall there being more hands earlier?"

Several of the bardic students had minor questions like: How do I not blow my environment up by speaking again? Which was part of why they were up in the sky to begin with. And questions about basic functions of infernal Essence, ending with reminders on skills and tricks to control their power and output. Which mostly came down to them having better control of themselves. Much of the advice was 'find a safe place, let out as much as you can, then you know your maximum and you can reel back in safely.'

The non-bards received opposite advice, frequently along the lines of starting slow and letting the skills develop rather than cranking the power out. As the non-infernal students were not at risk of devastating their environment by sneezing, they required a more inside-out approach to growth.

Artorian achieved his true goal when the two groups got into an argument over if he'd given the first group the method that the second group was supposed to use instead. Many didn't believe his words and thought that the infernal users should be practicing the inside-out method. Giving the old man plenty of big grins, and time to sally away to check in with other students when said argument got heated.

A bit of rivalry was healthy, and so were opposing viewpoints to test.

When he got to Astrea, Grim, and Ty, they appeared to have several problems ready for him. Artorian shoved his hands into his pockets, and began with a distraught exhale. He could see the schemes falling out from their Cheshire expressions. "Please tell me these are serious questions, and not the ones where I'm being walked off a hill to end up in a cold river?"

The smirks faded, replaced by scowls. Grim was the first to recover, chuckling. "Were we that obvious about it?"

Their Grandfather rubbed his forehead. "My boy, must I really answer?"

Grimaldus snapped his fingers and clicked his tongue. "Don't suppose there was ever a clean answer on if I could summon my old familiar back? I know Sarcopenia was a demon, but she was… different? Perhaps not the Soni, Caro, or Ludere kind of different, but different still."

"I'm afraid that we just booked them all with one-way tickets to library-ville. Cal would not be happy. I would not be happy." Artorian intoned his reply apologetically while folding his hands over one another like books being closed and shelved. "What did she do that was different?"

Grim felt dejected, but answered his grandfather. "She was polite. She could see snippets of the future, now and again. She was fond of riddles. She…"

Artorian hovered close enough to hold his grandson's shoulder when it was clear the boy was having difficulty beyond just recounting a memory. "My boy? I don't think this is about the familiar. Do you want to tell me?"

Grim grit his teeth, face buckling into a constipated frown. "I do, but when I try to think about that time, my mind becomes awash with distractions. There is pain, and loss, and I can't go back to those thoughts without becoming sick. I wish I could show you."

Artorian cocked his head, as that was not outside the realm of possibility. "That is an option, my boy. Wood Elven tricks have that in the Arsenal. Would you like me to see what's bothering you?"

Grim paused, untensed his shoulders and face, then began to nod before squeezing his own hand over Artorian's. "I think that would help. Yes. How does it work?"

Artorian beamed. "Close your eyes, don't smash my face in with yours when we touch foreheads, and think of the snippets you want to come to the forefront. When you're done, and want it to be over, just pull away. That's all. I'll see what you see."

Doing so, Grimaldus went through the motions, forehead pressed to Artorian's as his grandfather did all of the heavy lifting with techniques. His **Love** Mana worked particularly effective magic here, with so many sympathies aligning.

The flashes of Grim's memories were crude at first. Artorian saw an image of his grandson receiving titles. Grim, the Eversmile; Moth of Ghreziz; Vizier of the Mistress; Summoner of Sarcopenia, the livid sphinx.

Then a swirl of smog and fire turned the scene, and Grim had managed to focus on his familiar. The lion-bodied beast hung seamlessly and without effort from some railing. Sarcopenia's smoky wings flapped with thick feathers, as her ashen leopard fur outlined the incredible humanness of her feminine face. She growled and rolled her 'r's on purpose, but mimicked human speech well enough. "An intruder approaches, master."

A nice visual! Artorian now had a firm grasp on what the familiar looked like, but once again the scene turned. Time had passed, circumstances different. Sarcopenia's voice suddenly lacked any forced accents, and she spoke with perfect clarity when it was not required for the ruse. Now, her voice was breathy and mellow. "Death comes in the form of a burning sun. Seat yourself, master, for all demons shall die this day."

A flash of light cracked the memory, and Artorian experienced what Grim had meant with his mind turning to other thoughts. They swirled several times to moments in time that held no cohesion, and he could not deduce the events before Grim grabbed hold of something... acidic? His mind did not want to hold onto the memory. Not in the slightest!

Still, Grim held to it, as he needed it to be seen.

When the scene settled, Artorian could see a younger version of his grandson pacing around a room. The room itself was hazy as all Abyss, but memories were never without flaw. The focus was on his summoned familiar.

Sarcopenia had been calm. Too calm. Her usual destructive tendencies were replaced with peaceful lounging. It had been the first sign that something else was wrong. Grim, and thus Artorian who was listening in, heard the devastation, explosions, and sounds of battle occurring outside. Demons playing with a church thing, no doubt.

Sarcopenia merely smiled at her summoner. She never smiled at him, nor was she thankful, or anything other than a selfish half-cat. So it came as a surprise when she spoke with gratitude. "I have enjoyed... not being in the Abyss. I doubt we will see each other again. Thank you, Grimaldus of the Fringe, for these painless years."

With that, a cylindrical hole twisted into her chest, and she closed her eyes before dissolving, falling apart into a heap of soot and ash. Grim lamented over the loss, but he felt the grip on his soul loosen shortly after, the clawed hold tearing free as the bonds that clamped him were released, and whisked away. He was Moth of Ghreziz no more.

It was silent then, and the silence was deafening.

Artorian felt the connection break when his grandson pulled away, firmly holding his head with both hands. Grimaldus was a bundle of unpleasant groans, and yet Artorian could not help but notice that the balance retained on the floating sword was flawless.

Someone had been practicing!

Astrea and Ty caught Grim, acting the part of a soothing-whispers squad while their grandfather mulled over the information. He stood on Excalibur quietly, and thought.

"Grimaldus?" Artorian's Mana nudged along with his words, prompting Grim to hover back, after spending a few minutes repeating to the other two that he was in fact, *fine*. "Are you certain that Sarcopenia originated from the Abyss? I know that memory fragment said so, but... there's a significant plot hole in the story. I can't reconcile the cause of death with the behavior shown. Obviously, that wound did her in. Though her manner of being doesn't fit. Tell me about her?"

His son frowned, scratching the side of his head. "Sarcopenia was a known schemer. I have also known her to be surprisingly honest with me. I always took it as a perk of being her summoner. What is the hiccup, Grandfather?"

Artorian offered a weak smile. "Infernal creatures can't future-sight, my boy. Infernal is all about perfection of the 'now.' A focus on the improvement of a singular aspect. Events that have yet come to pass? That's a trick from the Celestials."

He considered the words of his feathered friend. "If I understood Adam correctly, it's all about how Celestial Essence is intertwined with a predetermined set of actions and events which are meant to occur. He can future-sight all the time, yet it also happens to not be correct all the time, because people exist who change the narrative and expected flow of those events. What it comes down to is that this effect is tied specifically to that Essence type. Infernals can't do it. In fact, they can't do it so intensely that when you look at them with an effect similar to future-sight, you can't see them at all. No impending actions. No information on expectations. Nothing."

Artorian momentarily grumbled, shaking a fist at the sky. "I could have really used my prediction lines in those fights!"

Moving his hands back behind his back, he huffed. "I think I've managed it once or twice with other means, but when I try to remember how, my memories also go hazy. I think it can be done, but Abyss with me to remember how. Maybe it happened in Eternia? I'll need to ask Tim."

"Regardless!" He kicked himself out of the hole and shot his finger up. "Sarcopenia can't be a demon, nor from the Abyss, if she had so much as an inkling of that ability. I know I give lectures on all the Essence types being able to do all the things, but I will admit I have run into exceptions. *That* being one of them. Let me put this matter to swift rest, and consult an expert."

Grimaldus nodded, and hovered away to let the now-glowing grandfather work. A humming light and choir's call from the sky above them later, and down feathers rained upon them as Adam descended in that arms-wide pose of his that he'd come to like so much. Artorian secretly knew it helped with descending without being tackled out of his down-feathers effect. Like Hans, Rose, and Dale had done. With Rose currently in the lead by three whole tackles, if his secret ledgers were correct. *Ehehehehe!*

"Wipe that smug smile off your face, Artorian." Adam chuckled as his descent brought him to eye level with the old man, foregoing his normal overly polite speech while retaining the cadence. "I know what you're thinking and I don't appreciate it… Also, none of them are here. Right? You're not hiding Rose under your robe to release her like a wild C'towl seeing a mouse to pounce? I do not like my wings being wrangled like a rogue rooster."

"Y'know, I haven't seen any C'towl lately. I should amend that!" Artorian grinned back, perhaps not talking about the animal at all to unsettle his Celestial friend. "So many fluffy mice abound! Floofs galore! Though I would consider a 'Floof' to be a calling, rather than some species designator. All Floofs can be chickens, but not all chickens can be Floofs. One must have a paladin's pluck for that kind of cluck!"

"I should know better than to call fowl around you." Adam shook his head, but there was a big smile on his face. His tone expected a clever ruse. "You called, Administrator?"

"Not in that capacity!" The old man pressed an offended hand to his sternum, swiftly amending. "It's about my boy's familiar. Can I Wood Elf bonk you the memories? They don't add up and I think she was one of yours. Secretly."

That detail caused Adam's brow to quirk, his face inches from Artorian's shortly after. Artorian took that as an open invitation, and smiled wide. Then, he slammed his forehead into Adam's. "Dwarven hello!"

The Celestial got thunked right out of his precious down-feathers effect, held his forehead, and was forced to hover back up into position as his effect chased him with growing concern. Half of the students weren't sure what to think, but the other half burst out in laughter as they understood the complex sequence of past events and references that made that entire interaction hilarious.

Adam replied only when he was done groaning, fingers rubbing the headache away. "*Ha. ha.* Very funny. No, I didn't see that coming, before you ask. No, Sarcopenia is definitely not a demon. Heavily affected by the Abyss at the time of memory, but still a no."

Fixing himself, his attire, and his looks to be once again in line with acceptable angelic standards, Adam appeared to take the head-butt in the spirit of which it was given. "I'll get you back for that one day, Sunny. You just wait."

Artorian grinned like a fool. "Now we're getting somewhere! Alright then! So, Sarcopenia?"

"Is a Sphinx." Adam rubbed his forehead again. "Which, by itself, tells me everything I need to know about the situation. Including why your adopted son would have nary a clue as to her actual origins. She's not Celestial, either."

Artorian's mirth stopped cold, his expression dropping to contemplative confusion. "Wait, what?"

Grimaldus hovered into the conversational sphere, his arms crossed. "I would like to know everything, please. This has caused me much heartache."

The Celestial turned to him.

"Your loss of a stable position and place in life is what causes you such heartache, son of the Old Fringe." Adam hung a wide wing around Grim, amending some additional clarity while the feathered limb draped like a politician's cape from the cultivator's shoulders. "You're a person who finds comfort in being part of a deep, intricate system, when your place in it is both secure and impactful. Not an out of the ordinary trait, but exceptionally strong within you. Which is why you took the blow of loss so intensely in the memory I was provided."

Adam then nudged the old man. "Sunny. Improve society some. Your boy needs a far more intricate structure than what anything around here has, and he needs a task that is as complex as it can get. I mean that in a social sphere, not a shove-him-in-with-Deverash sphere."

Artorian nodded short and curt in understanding. He made a hand motion that caused a Wisp to appear next to him, and he whispered the details of Adam's request before turning back to the situation before the Wisp outright vanished.

Grim's face was a picture begging for answers, his arms swinging in clear impatience. Adam considered the clouds a moment, then turned to the man. "Sphinxes come from a layer that is... I don't want to say 'unique' to them, but they do stick to it almost exclusively. They are known for being sly, in love with tricksters, and long to spend time with anyone who loves a good riddle. If you meet a Sphinx, then how they feel about you, and treat you, for the rest of their entire existence, depends on how you answer them on the first meeting."

"*Huh.*" Grimaldus pressed his hands to his hips, copying a trait from his grandfather. "Well that explains much. Also why she opened with a riddle when she first showed up. I thought I'd done something wrong, I'd never seen such a bored demon. She rattled it off with her face melting into the ground and her body puddling as if she were a liquid. I mean, she was as solid as a cat could be, but I was *convinced.*"

Adam chuckled. "What was the riddle?"

Grim threw his hands up. "I still don't understand it! All she asked me was: 'How much wood could a Woodchuck chuck if a Woodchuck could chuck wood?' I was baffled."

Artorian giggled. "Now I need to hear what you said!"

Grim shrugged. "Well, she looked like a cat who'd just spent the last day and a half gorging on fowl, so I said: 'Depends on if you ate it before it could try.' Her head came right up like that is not what she expected to hear, she turned her face to look at me, then smiled with nothing but teeth. Sarcopenia stuck with me ever since, and blended into Ziggurat's society like water filling a glass."

"Sounds like a Sphinx alright." Adam stole his wing back from Grim's shoulders. "They're morphous all-affinity creatures that roam looking for entertainment, and mostly stick to a layer filled with moss, plants, mushrooms, and fungus that acts as different flavors of catnip."

Grim mulled that over, his arms crossing while he chewed on his tongue. "Sooo... I summon?"

Artorian wasn't certain, and transferred his question to Adam with a look. "What does deterministic future say about this cat?"

Adam wasn't certain either, so he focused to have a look at the possible future. He had to pause a few seconds in, because he broke down laughing. "Oh... Oh, that's so stupid. Yes, I am a-okay with Sarcopenia. Oh, oh, that was golden. *Ha-haaa.*"

Being the entity of good that he was, Adam swiftly pointed at Grimaldus with the smile still on his face, relaying a cryptic message. "*You...* are going to be okay."

The celestial pulled in his wings for an amused flap, then grinned at Artorian as Grim sped off to a patch of open space to get started. "Sunny, remember how I said a moment ago that I was going to get you back for the Dwarven hello? I'm going to enjoy this. You? Not so much."

Artorian's face grew concerned. "What did you do?"

Adam failed to hide his giggles, his hand pressing to his own chest in a mocking copy of what Artorian had done before. "Me? Oh, I've done nothing! Grim is the one doing the summoning."

Concerned eyes flicked from Adam, to Grim, back to

Adam, before Artorian murmured a comment. "Summoning can't happen in Cal anyway. He blocked it."

"Actually!" Adam clapped his hands together, causing a luminous pop before his voice schmoozed in. "*Tim* blocked the summoning effect. In Eternia. Cal was doing it with Pylons."

"You wouldn't... happen to be referring to the same Pylons we no longer have?" Artorian's nose tingled unpleasantly, the sensation increasing with ever-growing concern. Concern that peaked when Adam made a face and giggled like a forest witch.

Artorian turned on his sword and sped to his grandson. "Grim, wait!"

It was too late.

CHAPTER ELEVEN

Sarcopenia popped into existence like a stressed and confused cat that had just landed on all fours in the most marginal puddle of water, offended as could be that her paws had been stained by such a grave, wet insult.

Grimaldus cheered in great success, and Artorian stopped short to bury his face into his hand. This was going to end poorly.

A statement that became true when Cal showed up in the body of the scholar D. Kota, looking equally as offended as the cat, with an equal spoonful of confusion to match it. Cal's tone was as demanding as it was inquisitive. "Who? *Just.*"

Cal then saw Adam shrieking with laughter, a host of confused students, Astrea and Tychus hiding in embarrassment, Artorian standing there with his face in his hand, and Grimaldus prancing around a summoned creature that shouldn't be there. While said summoned creature made a 'what the Abyss' face.

"I see." Cal tapped his fingers together, and clarified to himself; not actually understanding what he saw, but acting regardless. He first motioned to Grimaldus. "You! Big no-no!

Reflect on your actions. In fact, some bookish studies would do you well."

With a snap of the fingers, Grimaldus turned into a fancy black and green book, then flew straight into Cal's extended hand. "You are now Grimaldus *the Grimoire*. You wanna toy around with summoning? Fine! You're going to learn more about summoning than you ever wanted to know."

Artorian slowly turned to Adam. He made a silent hand motion to convey the question. 'Is this your get-back-at-me moment?'

To which Adam grinned wide, and spoke. "Have fun dealing with that! Especially after I just told you about the social activity he needs. I mean, he's going to have plenty, in his own way. Good luck!"

Artorian was going to begin a long litany of complaints, but Adam flew off and left them all behind. He'd helped!

Cal cleared his throat while a mere two feet away from Artorian, the book tucked under his arm while a confused Sarcopenia padded on solidifying chunks of air while she looked around at this mystical wonderland. Being in a Soul Space, by itself, was throwing her for a loop. Everything else involved added to the question marks populating her eyes.

"Administrator?" Cal pointedly looked in his direction, the words flat in tone.

"Yes, boss?" Artorian gave the dungeon his full attention, his face finally pulling up from his hand.

"I'm going to take this book to the library. It will be filed. The summon is coming with me, and being put to work as front-door guardian to the section I'm placing him in." A meaningful look from Cal told Artorian that was neither a request, nor an opening for debate. That was a statement of fact and he was going to need to live with it.

Artorian sighed, and dropped his hand towards the group of students. "Alexandria is right there and will be able to give you the optimal placement… I'll… I'll come visit later to talk to him. Or when life permits."

Cal smiled coldly. "He's going to have plenty of people to talk to! I'm shoving him in the demon section. That'll teach him. That'll teach him sooooo many things."

Artorian made the wanting to speak but not being able to speak mouth and hand motions, but Cal was already gone. He'd nabbed Alexandria and left, leaving Artorian to hover dejectedly back to Astrea and Tychus. "Well. That happened."

Tychus nodded with strength. "Was going to happen eventually."

Astrea joined him, copying Tychus's pose of certainty. "We're walking examples of trouble. You should see us with Craig and Frank. Also, Scilla is a hoot. Interesting perspectives from that one, and acts more like you than you'd want to know."

Artorian reached out a hand to the horizon, then dropped it. He didn't know what to say. "Now what do I do?"

Tychus had a thought. "I have more C-rank questions. Astrea and I are, in fact, stuck. Grim as well, but Grim is going to have other problems for a while. I think he will enjoy wrestling with the demon books."

Artorian could not pretend that wasn't an interesting view-point. "You... You do?"

Tychus nodded like it was the most obvious thing in the world. "Well, yes? Fancy Feathers had the right of it. Grimmy is best in big groups of people where he can be all political. He says he doesn't like it, but he's good at it, and we see him smiling when he can sneak it in. *Eversmile* was an earned title. Leftovers from the Ziggurat days where it was all survival all the time and our hearts were pounding to get by. Those days have passed, but the experiences never leave you. I, too, admit I miss some of it. Not the Abyss that it was, nor the horrors, but the... sensation? I'm not sure how to say it. We experienced a kind of stress that became normal, and not having that stress is strange. I crave it sometimes?"

Astrea shrugged to agree when Artorian looked at her, the

old man holding his beard afterwards. Their grandfather exhaled, and relented. "I see."

Artorian thought on Tychus's words a moment, then straightened up. "What would you like to do about it?"

Astrea shot her hand up. "C-rank chats! You were about to get to it when explaining to Alexandria, but you stopped at the D-ranks."

"You wish me to pick up where I left off, and continue?" Artorian brushed his beard curiously, the beaming faces all the answers he needed. "Very well. Let's head to the colored orbs still hanging with the rest of the students."

Returning to become a cohesive group once more, Artorian resumed teaching. He reached out to conglomerate the red D-rank cubes back around their orb, as the students had been playing around with them. He then tapped the violet one to make cubes eject from the C-ranked orb. Artorian spoke as if there had never been a break in the lesson. "Those in the C-ranks usually have opened all of their Meridians. Those who have not tend to finish doing so at this rank. A C-ranked cultivator can usually fight off ten D-ranked or one-hundred F-ranked beings without being overwhelmed."

He paused to check expressions, and found most of the students were nodding. When Artorian's eyes fell on Tychus and Astrea, they were making 'get to it' hand motions. Better to address that detail. "I saw that. What topic needs focus?"

The duo shared a look, and Tychus spoke when Astrea motioned at him with her chin. "We were actually curious as to why so many other people seem to have problems in the C-ranks, in the hope it would help us with our bottleneck. As we don't know what our bottleneck actually is. We thought we were doing everything right, but we're making no progress."

Artorian tapped his fingers on his own chin, brushing them through the beard after. "Well, I could just tell you, but if you want to puzzle it out yourself... then I will explain it thusly: when you hit the C-ranks, a problem happens."

Needing a visual component for this, Artorian plucked one

of the violet cubes from their orbit. "In the old world, the problem was a person's attention span. Instead of just having one thing to work on, gathering Essence and applying it to oneself for continued betterment in the physical sense, you now have two foci. Only one of which can be done at a time."

Several more cubes flocked to his open palm, and he made one glow. "You can focus on infusing your body with Essence, to make it better at everything a body does. That 'cell replacement' I was speaking of earlier. Normally that happens at this rank."

Some nodding followed from the clarification.

"Or." A different cube gained a glow. "You can infuse and build your Aura, to make it better at things an Aura does. Such as defending yourself when someone chucks a fireball at your face."

Dismissing both cubes back to the orb, he moved his hands behind his back. "It is very difficult to do option one and option two at the same time. Because you have to focus on one, and that's where your limited time and Essence resources go. This is also where your aptitude comes in, as you will most certainly be better at one over the other, and the one you are not versed in will seem impossible in comparison."

Exem's hand shot up, and Artorian gave him the floor. "Is this the bit about the difference between an 'Internal' cultivator and an 'External' cultivator?"

"Yes!" Artorian swirled a few cubes around his hand, feeling pride. "Very good! Body cultivators *think* differently than Aura cultivators. One is hard facts, powerful grounding, steady brick by brick measurements. The other is more ethereal, flexible, less concerned with worldly matters and more fluent in the methods of malleability. It's like working with a cloud, rather than a brick. Brianna and her Elves use a similar concept called 'Persona' and 'Anima.' For more on that, library, first floor, the Algorithm section, book seven in the series, first chapter."

Exem flushed red, so their instructor kept speaking to distract everyone. "Since people can easily spend two centuries of life in the C-ranks, it may look from an outside perspective that 'there is plenty of time and plenty of resources.' Especially here in Cal."

Artorian shook his head. "The main problem back out in the real world was that in order to gain Essence quickly, that meant fighting, risking life and limb, and in general putting yourself in some pretty unpleasant situations. You're not thinking about the years needed to build an Aura, you're thinking about your injuries from yesterday. Your tasks today. Worries that will come tomorrow. Then, by that time, you're distracted with friends you really can't put off again. Needs of the organization you might be with. Other circumstances that eat holes in your time. Time that, to improve in the C-ranks, needs *devoted* attention."

Artorian momentarily pointed to the next orb over, the blue one. "To get into the B-ranks, you need to finish both the internal and external cultivator track. Please mind, that is merely the barrier to *entry*. It normally does not mean even seeing the door, much less getting it open or moving through. You can't just shoot off like a firework when you're all done with the last patch of Aura! You need to fully replenish all your Essence, know where you're going, and have a smattering of other details squared away."

That comment silenced some of the background kerfuffle and whispers, with Tychus looking like he was trying to figure out where he'd gone wrong. The expression on his face spoke volumes that he felt so stuck, that he wasn't making any progress understanding, either. Either Ty didn't have enough pieces for a solution, or Artorian hadn't been giving him what was needed. There was no point in wanting the man to do it himself if he didn't have the requisite components to do so. That was unfair.

Personal attention was going to be the solution here, with the answers provided.

Artorian's hand resumed drawing attention to the violet cubes. "Remember that not everything that weighs you down is yours to carry. Cultivation, like many other tasks in life, comprises an arduous journey. Don't do it alone. Definitely don't be afraid to ask for help when you're stuck. Very few people are scholars, and fewer still have an understanding on the actual way of things."

Pausing to let that sink in, Artorian recalled all the cubes, and dismissed all the orbs. He made some motions for people to mingle, and that he needed a minute.

After the chatting picked back up, he motioned at Tychus. "My boy, your focus has been on what you knew. You know how to improve your body. Infusing is all done. Replacing cells, when you have already replaced them once, doesn't actually do anything. I can see that's what you tried to do. You're stuck because your body came pre-finished, and those are the steps you know how to do, but going through them got you nowhere. Aura is your next step, and that requires sitting, meditating, dropping yourself into your center, and working on that thin feeling you sense glued to your skin. Cal did nothing to help you with that aspect."

Tychus ran his nails over his scalp. "I don't really know where to start. Or what it looks like. I'm a 'bricks' person."

To give an example; Artorian made his own Aura, currently kept skin-tight like a thin mesh, glow slightly. Not too much, because then he would blind people. Extending an arm, he motioned at it. "This shiny bit is my finished Aura. In my case, my three Auras have merged—as I am a Mage, and that happens to the inner, body, and outer layers in the Mage-ranks —to become a full-formed Presence. This is what you're looking for while you are in your center, and reaching outwards. You may encounter your inner or body Aura, before you find this outer Aura, but the story is the same. You need to patch it up, make it better, and spend a few years on it. Locate. Infuse. Rebuild. If you want a full lesson on Aura, you're in luck! Do come prepared to take notes, because I will be both long-winded and detailed."

Tychus formed a complicated face, then scratched his head

wildly. It told both Artorian and Astrea that, help as the old man might want, it was time for a break before more words happened. Tychus was not Alexandria, and the same method would not work.

Artorian then wondered if there wasn't an alternative to sensing an Aura.

Tychus wasn't a classroom learner, and Artorian did not want to use live combat practice as the solution. Not unless there were no other options.

"Let's pick this back up in a bit?" He then pointed at the ground and picked up his voice so all the students could hear. "I suggest we call this lesson here for anyone who has had their questions answered. We've been busy, a lot happened, and your minds need to ruminate on the information provided. A few of you also look primed to play around in your centers, and I do not suggest doing that while balancing on a sword hilt in the middle of the sky. Down you all go! Go play!"

Artorian watched most of them go, including Astrea and her brother, who were taking a break for the sake of a break.

When he looked back up, he smiled wide. "I was hoping you'd stay."

Kinnan, Jillian, Pollard, and several other bardic students had remained, along with some other welcomed faces. They hovered closer on their swords, but were clearly still experiencing the wonder and awe of it all. Jillian opened with a greeting. "Hello again! We didn't want to interrupt the lessons with the people who seemed to actually know what they were doing, or needed. We're still just little D-rank babies."

"You got out of the F-ranks and that is a great accomplishment." Artorian laid his arms across their shoulders to squeeze and shake them. "I remember you three always struggling, and you made it! The only direction to go is up. Perhaps not on the swords, though. This is about the stable zone for floating. Now, you have questions?"

"Commentary." Kinnan smirked as she leaned into the shoulder grip, her voice sounding older since the last time Artorian had heard it. A slight touch more hoarse. As if she spent much of her time chasing Pollard and Jillian. "How do you always get the kids to listen to you?"

Artorian smiled with a chuckle and shrug, then provided her with his small nugget of wisdom. "Written on the wall of virtues, in a section oft forgotten, philosophers of old scribed the sentence: Do not train a child to learn by force or harshness, but direct them to it by what amuses their minds, so that you may be better able to discover with accuracy the peculiar bent of the genius of each."

CHAPTER TWELVE

Pollard, the oldest of the three, was the grump today. "That's good, poetic, and well, but I don't know how to convince them to care about other people. Our brats are all wrapped up in themselves."

He shot several of his old students, most who were now better at both music and cultivation than him, jealous sideways glances. "I call it the diva complex."

Artorian looked over at the bardic bunch, those with ombre-colored hair not denying the accusation. Those who appeared to prepare some kind of defense were mostly bristling that the accusation had been made in the first place.

The Administrator attempted to diffuse the situation. "Performance arts are demanding. Standing in front of a crowd requires stones, and a not-so-subtle amount of self-confidence."

He winked at a few who cracked smiles at his 'understanding.' Then addressed those with thicker heads. "I cannot teach anybody anything. I can only make them think. To think otherwise is a delusion that infringes on the assumption that another being can absorb the knowledge you have, as you have it. Doesn't quite work that way, so I'm always glad to have attentive students who come with questions. Lecturing to a hall might as well be attempting to make the entire student body sleep. Granted, that is also something I want, but generally not at the same time."

He then flashed a crude smile after those who were more stubborn also broke their stern facial facades and cracked. "As to caring about things. Fairly easy. Suffering and joint misfortune! There's a reason that people who have never had anything bad happen to them are frequently the worst of the bunch. One needs to encounter hardship to build empathy. Otherwise how are they to understand what is difficult for another? People are mercurial! Not merely inclined to unpredictable change in mood or mind, but mercurial as an adaptive mechanism. Trap people together in a room and they'll leave either as fast friends and newfound family, or sworn enemies. The mind swirls with an ever-present need; curious of the new, hungry to sate desires, and unfathomably powerful at finding ways to escape unpleasantry."

Kinnan squinted at him. "That sounds like a hidden lecture."

Artorian held his hand up to his eye, then squeezed his fingers together until only a smidge of space remained between them. "I've got a whole flock of angry squirrels on my shoulder when it comes to merchants and most nobles. They're all the same, and tend to share in certain traits that have me by the beard."

The old man separated himself from that topic, then nudged his nose over to the bardic students. "When the student is ready, the teacher will appear. When the student is truly ready… the teacher will *disappear*."

That shut them all up, and made Meg shoot her arm into the sky. Artorian locked eyes with her, and that was enough for her to start talking. "Are you on your Oak's fumes again? What was that supposed to mean? I would like *more* instruction when I'm good to go!"

Artorian shook his head. "There comes a point in the accumulation of knowledge where any good teacher sees that what the student needs is not more words filtering into one ear and out the other. It is, rather, to get out from under their feet, and let them put into practice what they think they know. Failure and the drive to continue will teach them more than most of my words ever could. Sure, I could tell you every detail on how it feels to mold an Aura and what the differences between upholding different Essence combinations are. Yet, is that the same as experiencing it yourself, and knowing what it truly *feels* like?"

Meg paused, chewed on that, then frowned, and disagreed. "No. Tell me anyway!"

Artorian released a singular 'Ha!', then shook his head. "Meg, it's like your voice shredding the environment to particles when you spoke with an Infernal-Essence-laced sound. Or perhaps as it was with that mentioned vibration weapon of yours that I have so far not been able to do much with. What good is power that you're not accustomed to? Skills you aren't adapted for? People need to practice. Achieve a bit of balance."

The old man made a hexagonal red shape appear above his hand for just a moment, the spinning object filled with a chaotic variety of essences. "If you knew everything there was to know about the color red, everything possible, yet you'd never seen it before, wouldn't you still learn something new by seeing it for the first time?"

Maeve smirked at the comments about adaptation and practice. "Like smashing into the ground over and over because the body you're in doesn't work as you expect? Mr. Noodle-flag?"

She'd been attempting to get in a jab, but Artorian nodded sagely, and the effort to insult passed over him like mere water. "Correct. Your weapon training is the mirrored image of that notion. Swing, my girl. Swing until your arm falls off. Then do it again the next day and swing some more!"

Maeve felt nonplussed about the retort, not a fan of overzealous, endless hard work. That wasn't going to make her sing better. She chose to remain quiet about her lack of dagger proficiency. "If you can't make it rhyme, then don't give it the time."

Pollard rounded on her. "Maeve, it took you hard effort and years of practice to sing as well as you do. Ease up on your diva trait. You just don't want to do hard work *again*. Do what Sunny says."

"Fine." She huffed, looking away with crossed arms.

Artorian shook his head. There was little to do about certain personalities, so he checked the remaining crowd, landing eyes on Ash. Meg's friend. He followed Ash's gaze downwards, seeing some crop circles in the fields below. "What's on your mind, Ash?"

She looked up, surprised to be addressed, then right back down to the indented design in the grass. "I can't help but wonder what makes those."

They all looked down, and Kinnan said what came to mind. "Animals completely rocked out of their minds from the same Oaken blend that Meg was talking about earlier. It's almost as bad as cats when the sun is down, zipping all over the place like wild mouths looking for something to bite."

Some chuckling did the rounds, after which Artorian hovered next to Jillian, who had looked both bothered and distracted. A small nudge with the elbow broke Jillian from that mire. "You alright, old boy?"

Jillian took a moment, his eyes regaining focus before his mouth caught up with his mind. "Yes? I think so. Sorry, Sunny. I was distracted by some thoughts when you were talking about Mages earlier. I've been picking up bits and pieces everywhere, and I could not stop thinking about how we're 'something else' when we're Mages? Yet, I feel like we're already 'something else' when we willingly replace our bodies with... what do I even call this? Bits of energy? My meat is important to me, it's part of what makes me myself."

Artorian waited patiently for the older bard to finish,

tugging Jillian away from the rest with a slight hover. "What about it, my friend?"

Jillian brushed a hand across his black stubble that was turning gray, then scratched his cheek with a nervous tick. "Am I going to be different? When I do the internal cultivation changes, I mean. It's not going to be me anymore. Is it? It scares me. Sure, the bigger, better, stronger, is a nice sell. That's not what's bothering me. Am I going to be different?"

Artorian unpacked that one slowly. Very slowly. "Are you… against change? Change was always a constant, even before cultivation. Every meal, every year of age, every new memory, was a bit of something that changed you over time. Are you the same you from when you were a baby? A child? A youngin'? Do those changes feel so frightening, from where you are now? Or is it the changes you can't see yet, those lying ahead?"

Jillian shook his finger at the last bit of what Artorian said. "That. That second bit. I admit, I feel a little silly when thinking of how different I am now than when I was a child. I was a dumb youngster, and I cringe at some of my past actions that I now regret. Still. I feel like that's inevitable for anyone? I worry for my humanity."

"It is indeed." Artorian firmly rubbed Jillian's back. "Now you are the same, yet someone else. Do you feel like you lost anything you did not wish to lose? Please exclude external changes, my boy. We're all fraught with a handful of relationships that went sour. The bit about you. Just you."

Jillian did not have convenient answers for the man prone to falling out of the skies. "I don't know, old man. People a lot smarter than me need to wrestle with that one. I just know it bothers me, and I think I just wanted to tell someone."

Artorian felt a Nixie tube light over his head. "I recall my friend Tatum mentioning that he wanted to delve into this very topic with someone. Though, it was about if people were still themselves when they were Mages. Something about… psychological changes?"

"Yes. That!" Jillian perked up. "I want to talk about that. He was already getting started? Do you think he'd have time for me?"

"I can certainly send him a missive on your behalf, Jillian. I don't know when he'll get it, but I can certainly put it in the pipeline." Artorian confirmed this while thinking of Dev's attempts to explain Dwarven pneumatic message tubes, clearing Jillian's heavy expression up to one with some hope. "Can I include anything to him about what kind of topics or concerns you have? The more I can write to him, the better it will be when you both have a moment."

Jillian's lack of dark attitude brought the words to the fore with increased ease. "Well. As a bard, I have a lot of stories about how power corrupts, how people in power change, and how different people process a sudden spike in their personal might. Whether it be physical, societal, implied, soft power, or hard power, the change in ability causes people to act differently. Well, most of the time. I know you're still an ancient weirdo who falls from the sky. One day we're going to update that song, just you wait."

"I look forward to it! Do your worst!" Artorian joked with a grin and a heavy pat on the back, spurring Jillian on, very much on purpose to give the man some momentum. "I still don't have anything to write down."

Jillian exhaled through his pursed lips, taking that challenge. "I hear Mages take a **Law**, and that this **Law** changes a person's priorities. I'd like more on that. When I undergo this change, is anyone going to understand how I feel? If this is traumatic to me, can I talk to anyone? This is going to bother the Abyss out of me."

With the old bard finding his stride, Artorian kept his mouth shut so the ball would keep rolling. Anxiety was best kept off the chest, and Jillian appeared to have plenty to shed. "Is there any type of therapy, or someone to discuss the concept of no longer being truly human? I would need someone to relate to and understand why I am what I am, and if, after replacing every piece of my body, am I still me? I know the boat metaphor was brought up before, but I think this would plague me. Otherwise I wouldn't think like this. Am I too old and stuck in my ways?"

The old man considered, and rather than taking mental notes, spent the effort to teleport a notepad to himself and physically write down Jillian's concerns. Seeing actual results make it onto paper would likely help the man who needed a more hands-on set of solutions.

Jillian clearly liked this, and kept talking. "I have this heavy thought that instead of searching for healthy outlets, I would delve into past obsessions. I mean, my body isn't even human anymore, I hear, so what stops me from drinking Dwarven brandy over and over, or falling into one of Oak's dens for months on end, or throwing myself into a fight just to get some sort of kick to feel human again? Obviously it's not a good path, but feeling pain, feeling human would, in a weird sense, connect me back to what I was?"

Artorian was about to mention that these words were dark, but the bard was here for a serious talk, and was aware. He also appeared to be able to read the worried wrinkles right from Artorian's face. "I know that's dark, but it's true. When you feel that lack of human connection and dissociate, that really affects me. So when, on a biological level, I am no longer who I was, how can I feel like me anymore? Just because the soul is the same doesn't mean the mind is comforted by the body changing so drastically."

Artorian paused him right there. That was enough.

"Jillian." Artorian spoke softly, both his hands holding the man's shoulders as he moved to be directly in front of him. "Look at me."

Jillian at first looked down, spurred on to move his head up when Artorian put light supportive squeezes into his grip. "My friend, look at me."

When their eyes met, Jillian knew that regardless of what his worries were, he had taken the right steps forward, and would never be alone. The pink energy radiating from Artorian, by itself, gave him that feeling with uncanny certainty.

Efforts made to focus on the kindness in his voice, Artorian steadied his friend. "Jillian, you are going to be alright. This was never something you *had* to do. If this causes you more stress than it is worth, you can, and may always, stop at any time. If you wish to continue regardless, you are not alone. You are one of my people, whose mind races ahead. A scholar hidden in a body that can't keep up. I *understand*. When you need people to speak to about this, even if it is merely to be an ear, merely for you to speak, and empty your lungs, I will be here. Others will be as well."

Jillian swallowed, his hands not knowing where to come to a stop as they moved with frantic effort. "I don't... I don't want to stop cultivating, Sunny. I'm just afraid of outcomes that I can't control. I know it's stupid but..."

"They are not stupid." Artorian gripped Jillian firmly, rebuking the statement outright. "If you are worried about it, then you are worried, and that by itself was, and is, always enough to voice yourself. Your worries do not need to make sense for them to burden you. They do not need to be logical. That they are there, at all, is enough. Step into my office, take a chair, and speak. Tell me what it is that you do not want to happen, and we *will* find some people to sit with you when you go through certain stages. If you feel that you should repeat yourself, then repeat yourself. To worry is very much human. To contradict oneself is human. To be hypocritical, saying one thing yet believing another, is human. We are but a bundle of flaws, doing our best to make the best of it, and get things right."

Jillian held Artorian's arms, his discomfort fading.

"Am I going to be alright?" His voice cracked, Jillian's muscles tense when he whispered.

"You are going to be alright." Artorian brimmed with confidence, firmly stating the response to pull the tension right out of his friend. "This is the same as when the conversation began. Are you *the same you* from ten years ago? Do you feel the loss? Do you feel like you are who you should be? If not, who do you want to be? Heave your efforts into being that person, and doing the things a person like that would do. You will find yourself moving towards that point, and your worries of what you could have been will fade. You will avoid taking actions that do not lead to your desired destination. I believe in you, my friend. I always have."

Artorian then clarified a misconception of Jillian's core issue. "Your capacity to feel, and experience, will not change as you think it does. Internal cultivation will increase your capacity for such notions. *Increase*, Jillian. Not decrease. You will feel more. You will hear more. Smell better... or worse, in some ways. Stay away from latrines by an extra league when you do that one. If you thought opening the Meridian was a big shift on the nose, I have baby-booty-bad news for you. For it is a very green situation that you are obligated to handle, and I completely understand if the thought of *that* kind of experience makes you flee to the hills. The upwind hills."

He released the bard's shoulders when Jillian chuckled. "New information is supposed to make you rethink your views. That is normal. It is meant to happen. Not looking at a problem again, in light of new information... That is where issues brew and fester. If you feel that you will worry about this regardless, spend time around others when going through those paces."

Artorian waved the clipboard covered in scrawl. "I will get all of this to Tatum and Decorum. Gomez may be better for your immediate needs with Tatum not being easily accessible. We will try to get a class or Forum together in the New Fringe so people can meet and gather to speak on the topic. Some kind of round table setting where everyone can share. Maybe that'll give him a use for that spirit glass."

Artorian then focused on Jillian, a scheming twinkle in his eyes as an idea of how to empower his friend and put some pep back in the step came to mind. "Are you at all interested in helping to get that movement going? I'd hate to hear that there were hundreds more with this same worry as you, and it was going unaddressed."

Something about the mantle of responsibility made Jillian feel a need to grip the flagpole, and hoist it high. "That... That would honestly give me a lot of control over what I could be doing about this as an active participant, rather than a passive observer just waiting on others. I would like that a lot, Sunny. I want to hold that flag."

"Then we will make it so!" Artorian proudly spoke as he rolled an arm about the bard's shoulders, his other hand dropping forwards like a prime directive. "Now let's get you back to your people. I suggest a big meal, heavy sleep, and a few days of downtime just doing fun things. I'll get this flag of yours for you. Or, this little one here will."

Jillian paused in the sky when the old man winked at a mustard yellow Wisp that existed in the visible spectrum just briefly enough to take the notepad from Artorian, and get it to where it needed to be. This pause forced Artorian to jerk to a sudden halt and raise an eyebrow. Jillian then fidgeted, and looked at him like the effort had meant the world while his voice wavered. "I love that you fell into our camp all those years ago, Sunny. I never would have expected this life, but I'm really, really happy that I have it, and that you are in it. Yours has been my favorite boat to get picked up by. Thanks, captain."

"Anytime, my dear bard in the snow." Artorian smiled, trying not to let his emotions bleed out as wet streaks from his eyes. "Anytime."

CHAPTER THIRTEEN

With the bards back in their huddle, Artorian took a moment to acquire some breathing space. Jillian and company were going to need a few hands of time to sort their new volition out. Which made it a great moment for Irene to hover her floating sword over to the old man. Her younger voice was a mixture of pleasantry and pride, that Morovian Revivification skill getting a workout. She looked almost twenty again! "Always the community-carver wherever you go."

He nodded while feeling solemn, still composing himself from the emotional waves. "I... Yes. I do what I can. I've the thought roiling in my head that, as heartfelt as Jillian was, that entire problem would have slipped right by me had it not just come up."

Irene looked wistful, but otherwise appeared to be waiting for him.

Righting himself, he tugged on his own sleeves to mend minor details. The tiny victory over a tiny detail did the trick for now, his head tilting towards Irene. "How can I help? You wouldn't have huddled in without some question."

"The Aura guidance you gave to your troublesome trio?

Well, duo. It's insufficient for me as well." Irene flexed her arm and muscle, right to the point as she put D-rankers to shame with the finely tuned force contained within. Like a large cat that was bristling with impatience now that she could address the irritation crawling across her skin. "I found nothing while looking out from my center, and succeeded only in permanently making my skin itch. Now I can't focus or concentrate enough to meditate. I need… something else. I know Aura is an internal affair, but is there anything that might help make me sense it from the outside? Some resistance? Something that can push back? *Anything* that won't make me feel like a fish out of water."

Artorian held his chin as all his concerns melted into the background when the heavy thinking began. "I…"

Pwaaaaamp!

A red blinking light noisily blaring from the hilt of every floating sword grabbed his, and everyone else's, attention. Artorian looked down to Polly a moment, expecting an explanation.

Excalibur figuratively jumped at the change, otherwise Artorian would bounce off the handle. "The external Cores are close to depletion. None of the birds will be able to retain their sword shape when the affixed Cores have run completely dry. We have to land."

A sharp nod from Artorian got the sword moving. He sharply whistled to inform people it was time to descend, but a pink flare from his elbow crackled before he could complete the shrill canary call. He grumbled at the outburst of energy that he once again did not intend. "I really need to figure out what's causing that."

Clearing his throat, he addressed the group after seeing the nice, clear spot on the plains below that Polly headed towards leisurely. "Landing time, everyone! About down there-ish will do. Please dismount and take a moment, and if everyone could stay off the yellow grass, that'd be great. I'm about to pull some wild ideas out of my pocket."

The gathered class reached ground with ease, the floating blades all eager to return to their animal forms. Some even shed the external Core early, the blades turning back into Starlings, Sparrows, and Tufted Titmice.

When Artorian hopped off Polly, she too, returned to being a glorious parrot. Shaking out her tail feathers, she inclined her head towards the Administrator, then bounced off with successive hops. Break time meant play time!

Artorian chuckled at seeing the birds go and become a pile of shrieks and tweets while all fighting over the same random stick one of them had found. His attention then turned to the floating saber hovering next to Irene. The weapon, much like the person who had been on the blade, waited for him. He inclined his head at the saber to copy Polly's motion, in the event that it was bird-language for a meeting, greeting, or goodbye.

Kevin Penkins, composer and grand musician, maestro of a thousand strings, and wizard in the ways of the warble during the times of the Crown Game, adopted the form of a bright yellow Oriole.

The head incline was returned, before the conductor fluttered to Irene's shoulder and addressed Artorian with a surprisingly easy human tone and voice. "I treasure the chance to actually converse, but must be swift with my needs. I volunteered for the floating sword and external Core test-bed specifically to come ask you if I could observe your work outside of scheduled time. I require a muse for my musical work, and your influence has plagued my thoughts since the games. The bards I have met are all content with carving their own path, but my dreams are still enthralled with the paint in your sky. The music demands it of me!"

Artorian found the request to be more amusing, rather than how serious Penkins intended it. He nodded and took a few steps towards the short yellow grass, serving as a clear separator to indicate the domain lines that Cal was carving into the world for reasons yet unknown. "Feel free, conductor. Please do be mindful when silence is the order of the day? I have no problem with you visiting the office, but I believe I might, should it always be noisy."

"I assure you that will not be a problem." The conductor brandished his Oriole wings, already bouncing around on Irene's shoulder, whose attention was entirely on the movements of Essence in the area. The old man was already spinning his complicated magic with the stirring swirl of a finger.

Irene studied, then frowned at the thick paste that the air was turning into.

"What am I looking at?" Her hand reached out to press into the strange, shimmery edge of a cube that began to look like a faint oil slick. "Is this still air? The sensation feels like water, but not. The ratios are becoming incomprehensible."

Artorian didn't reply right away, drawing inspiration from the conductor as he raised both his hands to the air and waved them as if he was holding a baton in both. Each swirl and sharp jab made several of the onlookers think of incantations, sans words. His antics also summoned the other half of the class that had descended beforehand, as he was being interesting. Observation was always worth it when the old teacher did something interesting.

Artorian overheard their banter when it began, including wild guesses and naming attempts for what he was doing. He was not going to stand on them making a mess of his current, improvised efforts. He'd need to name the trick or it would all go awry. A thought occurred, and he smirked while throwing his hands up, causing the one-hundred by one-hundred meter cube to flash. "Aquarium!"

Penkins the Oriole fell off Irene's shoulder, scrambling up a tweet-storm to summon his musicians from the pack still fighting over a twig. Inspiration was dawning! There would be music!

Irene chuckled at the conductor's antics, then pushed her hand through the cube's edge now that it was more than a vague barrier. "The inside is dry. Definitely a mixture of air and water. The prickly feeling on my fingers moves through with ease, but my actual hand feels slowed."

Artorian beamed, ecstatic of his success. "Very good! Indeed it is. You were always excellent with ratios."

An intrigued look from Irene made him quickly delve into a deeper explanation. "Ratios that I can't pin down anymore. It's coming apart into individual components, even if slowly. What did you actually do?"

He loved an attentive student! "I mixed up the properties of Air Essence and Water Essence. Breathing in there won't be any different than usual. However! I've altered the pool of Air Essence present in that area to provide water's resistance. Specifically against anything that *isn't* Aura. Fashion a properly developed Aura that is covering you as intended, and you will glide through this aquarium as if you were one of the fish. If not, you'll learn what it's like to be stuck in pudding. You *can* muscle your way through, however, I obviously encourage you to focus on your Aura while you do so."

He paused and considered something he'd said. "That was one 'however' too many. I should be careful about those. In short, your comment reminded me of a difficulty I had with my Dragon form, and being underwater gave me the tactile sensation I needed for my body to make sense."

He tailed on his fingers. "Resistance. Pressure. Difficulty. A noticeable substance to work against. I warn you, the pressure in there is harmless, but thick as paste. Possibly vanilla flavored?"

Irene wasted no time in stepping through the cube's outer wall. Her movements slowed to a crawl instantly, like she was trapped in jelly, or some kind of sludge. Mud, perhaps? No, pudding was exactly right. She nervously drew a heavy breath, but that came and went without any difficulty.

Irene sounded very surprised, her voice muted and dulled from speaking inside of the Aquarium. "I did not expect to get stuck right away. For your information, only the outside looks all rainbow-like. The inside is identical to being underwater. Easy, bright, translucent blues with some hints of color where the sun is passing through the exterior shell. My hair and clothes aren't floating like they do under actual water. That's a little weird. Shame I can't see the prickle-prickle on my skin."

Artorian cocked his head in confusion, but deduced that Irene must have been talking about a sensation that described how she felt her Aura. "I can do something about that. Let me think. A sprinkling of Celestial Essence, perhaps?"

Wibbly-wobbling his hands and playing havoc with the ratios before choosing to Invoke the idea, Artorian swiftly gained the alteration to his Aquarium that he'd been wanting. Now seeing the Essence coursing across her skin without needing to adapt his modes of vision, he observed her beginner's Aura spike, then ease, then spike again. Hopefully, she could see it as well. "Looks like we found your Aura!"

Artorian was very thankful that Irene confirmed his thoughts.

"I can see a spiky field of some kind coating my skin? Is *that* my Aura? It's barely covering me!" She then howled, beaming a wide grin at him. "This is so easy now!"

Her head was then stuck in that direction when she lost focus, the enthusiasm spent when hubris tackled her down into the yellow grass. "Maybe I spoke too soon. I had it for a second! Being able to both see and feel this itch is of significant help. I think everyone struggling with Aura is going to like this a lot."

Artorian was pleased as fresh biscuits in a well-arranged box that the Aquarium worked so well! Penkins and company were already making music, but even Artorian with his terrible musical talent could tell that it needed work. He reached out to run a finger down the edge of the oil-slick's surface out of curiosity, then cursed when a spark of pink energy once again fluttered free. He had to press the flat of his palm against the cube's edge to prevent it from expanding out in the direction of the students, causing the cube to instead consume all the space on Cal's cordoned off yellow grass.

The full square league.

"Abyss. Really?" Pulling his hand away, he waved off the problem when people gave him strange looks. A quick flight upwards allowed him to check the dimensions from above. "Looks like I managed to curtail the Aquarium from going wild, but now it's taking up that entire chunk of landmass. Undoing that is going to be very annoying."

Irene joked from within with a yell when he descended without entering the Aquarium, the Morovian woman entirely unharmed. "I like it! I will overcome this obstacle!"

He pensively rubbed his chin, rethinking the idea. "I could leave it?"

A shrug later, he landed and went with the route of owning his mistake. First he got word out, informing whichever invisible Wisp was keeping tabs on his location that he'd crafted people a new space to practice Aura in, should they be having difficulties that meditation simply wasn't solving. Wisps were kings of gossip, and this development was too juicy of a pastry not to make a thousand copies of.

Five minutes hadn't passed before all of Skyspear knew.

He made sure to grip Tychus and Astrea tight by the sleeves when they both came running, slapping them with a warning that was going to fall on deaf ears. "This is not a substitute for meditation!"

He was sure they both heard him, but the wide-grin expressions on their faces told Artorian volumes about how that information went in one ear and out the other. He let them go and kneaded his brows as the news spread like wildfire.

Half an hour in, and C-rankers from all over were hurrying to the... Well, it wasn't a cube anymore. Square-ish, sure, but not as tall as it was wide. Was that a rectangle? That was probably called a rectangle. A quiet wave of the hand eked the dimensions out to be a proper cube. Surely nobody would notice. "There. Cube."

An hour later, the walls of the Aquarium looked like ants having found sugar. Artorian merely sat on the sidelines, wondering what to do about this. All the while watching Tychus find the kind of success that put a significant smile on his grandson's face.

How could he take this away now? He couldn't. Not after that. A physical solution to an otherwise esoteric problem should be of some use. "Yes, I should leave it. Unless Cal had plans for the yellow grass zone over there. I think it was meant as a hedgehog playground? We'll have to start them off in the Green Hill Zone. Or make it interesting with a city escape, see them rolling around at the speed of sound. That'll make things interesting." *He-he*.

Artorian's nose then tingled, a smile curling on his lips. "Speaking of…"

When Cal popped in with a vast look of confusion pre-set on his face, he waltzed straight to a contemplative Artorian. Cal said nothing, mouth half open with his brows furrowed as his pointer finger moved from the Administrator to the oil-slicked cube, and back a few times.

When he crossed his arms and finished his mental math, the expressions cleared up. "*Huh.* Know what? Changed my mind. This is helpful. I like this. I'm moving that zone's plan over one tile. I'll combine it with the rainbow roads."

Artorian nodded with an appreciative throaty hum, his mind instantly distracted. "How'd shelving my boy go?"

Cal scratched at his cheek as he watched people enter the Aquarium, only to get stuck at its edges. He spoke to himself rather than the peanut gallery. "Alright, that's *very* amusing. Cultivators *must* have some Aura control to move around in there, or it's not going to work. Zones like that would be fantastic for one of my upcoming dungeon projects. I want twelve. Mages are going to find that place equally helpful."

Cal then focused on his Administrator, clearly appreciative of the work as he compensated Artorian by refilling his Mana supply. "Artorian, do you mind if I alter that effect so it slowly pushes them back out? Many of them are completely stuck, challenging a pudding too big for their britches."

"Be my guest, and thank you kindly for the energy. Creating

a stable space of energy is unfathomably costly." Artorian offered a confirming hand motion towards the Aquarium of modified Essence. "I'm still trying to think of what to call it other than an Aquarium. Knowing it can take up that spot is nice."

Cal chuckled, pulling up his sleeves. "That's a dungeon specialty. Trying it as a non-dungeon causes something like eight times the cost. Strangely enough, eight times the cost is coming up a lot for Tim and I lately. Many techniques people aren't suited for keep rounding out to about that modifier when performed, regardless of inclination and suitability. We're likely going to implement that for the game's cross-class abilities when we can get the ball rolling again."

The old man then studied the Aquarium further, commenting on its construction after learning that mathematical nugget. "That type of Essence is now so stable I was honestly surprised that it didn't collapse on me and return to disparate units, after my Aura 'sparked' it. Your Soul Space hasn't 'nommed' it like I thought it would either. I'm glad not to be a dungeon Core, Cal. This kind of spatial control isn't for me."

"I admit, tasty vanilla." Cal smacked his lips and joked as he touched it, the dungeon daydreaming thoughts and theories for what kind of dungeon Artorian might put together. New ideas instantly began to percolate like coffee within the great overlord. "Though, now you have me curious as to what kind you'd be."

Cal made the Aquarium's adjustments in record time, then checked to see the occupants slowly being ejected, before quality controlling the consistency of the Aquarium's Essence as the topic took a sharp left turn back into Artorian as a dungeon. "Definitely not a green earth Core. My guess would be a Celestial type mixed with a lot of water. I'm thinking of a nice round chunk of white gold mixed with teal and pink swirls as the basis. I see you wanting to avoid conflict, but that conflict then happens regardless of your attempts to help. Specifically with the water trait of being distracted by something else. I can see you making something majestic, leaving for a moment, then walking back in through the door with a box of pastries, and the entire region being on fire."

The dungeon squinted, paused, and glanced over his shoulder at the Silverwood to see how much water that theory could hold. "Abyss! *Red* basis. That does explain all the green Wisps. I was way off on the survey. I'm gonna blame Ricky."

Artorian mulled that over while Cal gave the Aquarium a once over, adding to the old man's prior deconstruction while slapping it like a sack of rice acquiring a seal of approval. "You've made an emulsion out of it, but you added a touch of **Love** somewhere, or it would have begun to come apart. It's really interesting what you made here. That's not just stable Essence, that's *stable-stable* Essence. We're going to need to call that mixture something."

"If I name it, will you tell me what you did with my boy?" Artorian inhaled with an over-the-glasses look, hooking into a topic closer to the heart. "I know he's unharmed but I'm still a worrying grandpa."

Cal was about to make a quip, then thought better of it and relented. "Yes."

CHAPTER FOURTEEN

"Looks like Shin's soup to me." Amaterasu appeared from thin air, interrupting the conversation. Around her, the black-hole effect she walked through folded inwards with solar radiance, like space collapsing in a controlled measure.

Artorian's eyes abandoned Cal, turning to his dearest and taking in her current getup. Ammy's carmine-colored attire was finely robed and powerfully elegant, with layered cloaks and several belts holding it all together. Her hair was currently being a show-stealing spectacle, being the live and moving version of the bards' popular rainbow-ombre hair.

She wrapped her arms around her boy when he stood up to greet her, Ammy squeezing Artorian in like a favored plushie. Her words, slowly spoken, were like being wrapped in winter blankets. "Hi sugar. I had a minute. Hold me and tell me what that strange look on your face is about."

"S-soup?" He lost the disparate thread of his thoughts before refocusing on current events, and why he hadn't expected to see her. "Tim commented that the Incarnates were indisposed. I thought I wasn't going to see you for a while!"

Ammy chuckled, kissed the top of his head, then rested her

cheek against him before releasing the heaviest sigh and kneading his back with her fingers. As if he really were the coziest plushie in all of existence. "I needed a moment out of Eternium. I gazeboed out. Felt you here, stepped over, noticed the soup, and had memories from my stairway journey surface. This is the second time I've seen this emulsion. First time that it has been stable, but still."

Artorian squeezed back, relaxing in the comfort of her Presence as she expanded her Aura like wings from her back to wrap him up. "I take it you don't have too long? Also, I'd love to hear it."

Ammy released him after a counter-squeeze, took his hand, and folded fingers with him, claiming them while she was here. She then pointed at the Aquarium with her free hand, and filled in. "During the time of Amaterasu, the ranker whose life I'm going through, the joke about this emulsion was that it was called 'Shin's soup.' A man named Shin put the effect together while tripping over his pot of soup, and injuring his shin. He made a field like that out of his soup on the way down, catching his fall. Nobody could let the joke go."

Artorian mouthed an 'oh,' surprised it was that simple.

She then winked, pulled a trinket out of one of her belts, and pressed it into his open hand. "First, take this. Decorum had a very lengthy letter for me, *gushing* about how you gave him your previous one. This is a better storage ring, though we got the dimensions wrong with the unique feature we were trying to implement, so it's more of a bracelet."

Ammy beamed, holding up her hand to show off a similar bracelet around her own wrist. "I made it! Okay, Incursus helped. The dungeon, I mean. This storage ring will work here, in Eternium, and every other dungeon Core you might need to visit. I made it out of Silverwood, thus the nice bark texture and dull metallic sheen."

She then gave his hand a squeeze as she moved it back down, her expression apologetic. "Second, I'm sorry, sugar, I'm already out of time. I wanted a big hug and to give you this goodie. Eternium needs me to keep the temperature in Eternia's permafrost wreckage above a crisp arctic chill. Tatum and I are chipping away at the problem, and we've long passed the point where we could do it without more help. All the Geese, and even Yasura, were given very lucrative offers in order to render aid."

Artorian froze, the thought of wearing the bracelet right away slipping from his mind. "Yasura? The Incarnate demon? But... I thought we got them all?"

"Tut tut!" Ammy kept both her arms around him. "Daemon. There's an A in there. Not that you should expect me to stand up for either variant."

She then pointed at Cal, who gave Artorian an apologetic smile when the Administrator rounded on him with a fuming expression. "Yasura was an Eldritch Tome for a short while, but needs must. If Tim needs more hands, then more hands he's going to have. Even if that means concessions to entities we would really rather not deal with. Luckily, there really is a big difference between a demon and a daemon. That A matters. After discovering the difference, I felt much less awful about offering the deal. He's bound by the same conditions Soni and company are, so no betrayal chances. Oaths are oaths. That Yasura and the Geese now get along like quacks in a pond... a little more concerning."

Ammy added some details onto the being getting Sunny's beard in a twist. "He's named Yasura the Yamata No Orochi, now. He copied Wagner, and now also has a serpent form with eight heads and eight tails."

Artorian kneaded his face, then turned and pressed into Dawn to squeeze the abyss out of her for comfort, and provide that requested bigger hug. She made a happy sound, and tried not to crush him with the return-squish, keeping his face tucked in the crook of her neck. "It'll be alright. If he acts up, he's all mine."

"I'll consider you to have 'dibs,' dear." When he was set and felt the irritation leave, he let go and released a steam-based exhale while fiddling with the bracelet he'd been given. Artorian's attention returned to the Aquarium, and the prior topic. "Well, I don't want to call this effect Shin's soup. Only actual soup is allowed to be that big of a mouthful."

Cal cackled at his Administrator's grumpy retort. "What about Airlightenment?"

Artorian hid his face in his hands in surrender. "I... Forget it. May I just please be told about my boy?"

The dungeon snickered, and took the victory. "Alright. Yes. I suppose the emulsion doesn't *need* a name. Aquarium is fine for a new landmark. Otherwise all mixtures would need them as well, and on second thought, I don't want to be in that mess."

"Boys, I have to head out." Ammy clapped her palms as she smiled cheerfully, breaking up the conversation. "I'll come visit when I can, sugar! If not, well, you know where I am."

Artorian let her go reluctantly, but he understood.

Before she stepped away with a short wave and vanished outright, she blew Sunny a kiss, the same black hole effect trailing her path as before as she poofed.

Cal watched her go, his eyes flicking to the direction of the Silverwood tree before nodding. "Progress is good. Breaks equally so. If people need to step out and breathe, then they should."

The dungeon then stated a profound discovery. "I, too, am people."

Artorian almost couldn't believe his ears! Mentally, his arms went up. He wasn't going to need to rush through his tribulations to kick his overlord's rear all the way up and back down another frosty iceberg! Progress!

Cal couldn't remain introspective for long. His response to Artorian was filled with amusement, as if sensing the old man celebrated schadenfreude. "Grim acquired an emotional support eldritch abomination. He's doing great! He's pretending to be someone named Solomon, and has two demons in his pocket already. Sarcopenia told me mid-giggle that they're each proudly holding an adorable hand-drawn sigil!"

Cal flourished his arm, enjoying the recollection. "In no time at all, Grim carved himself a spot in the new Libr-archy. Hierarch-shelvery? I'll just stick to hierarchy. Good news! Sarcopenia took to her library spot like water filling a bowl, and turned out to be an avid reader. She also chews on the ones that mouth off to her. *Hehehehe.* Back to Grim! In no time at all, he conjured this magical story of a powerful tome called the Key of Solomon. Sarcopenia said he weaved this beautiful tapestry of Demon classifications, capturing their attention hook, line, and sinker."

Cal pressed a proud hand to his own chest. "I, of course, poked my nose in. You can't get me that curious and not risk my attention! Grim, posing as Solomon, expounded with political prowess on Ars Goetia, Ars Theurgia-Goetia, Ars Paulina, Ars Almadel, and Ars Notoria. He was delving into the Greater and Lesser keys, the Clavicula Salomonis and Lemegeton, when I slipped out. Fascinating speechcraft."

Artorian blinked. "Please unpack *all* of that."

Cal looked at the horizon rather than reply. "Unfortunately, that will have to wait. Your appointments have arrived, and I, too, can't stay."

Artorian followed Cal's hand when the scholar pointed, seeing Henry and Marie flying towards them. The Administrator grit his teeth, then whistled at the part of his class not currently stuck in the Aquarium. When he had their attention, he made a finger-swirl motion in the air, telling them they were dismissed and to get a move on. The students had been somewhat expecting this, as this was not the first lesson that had been wrapped up because larger forces dropped in to take their teacher's time.

Conductor Penkins lamented the loss of his muse, but one glance at the sky-bending people approaching made him change his tune. He directed all birds to pick up their mostly expended Cores, and get out of here with the people they flew in on.

By the time Henry and Marie slammed into the green grass

next to Artorian, the class was gone, Cal nowhere to be seen, and a few hundred cultivators were stuck in the Aquarium. They were slowly being pushed free thanks to Cal, but a few were actively fighting the interference. Irene, unsurprisingly, was one of them.

The land around the duo buckled, pressured, and flattened to crushed biomass when their frankly insulting Auric control loosed and fielded without warning. They may not have been bothered by the emanations of the other, but Artorian found it an affront. He grabbed both of their fielded Auras as they shed them like puffy coats, then pinched with the mood inherently found in an ornery crab.

"Auw!" Both of them jumped and yelped in unison.

"Pull that back in!" Artorian snapped both verbally and with his fingers, his expression already in the realm of displeased. "You're going to crush anything you land on or near with your Auras shed off like that. I don't want you anywhere near C-rankers or below! Those poor cultivators will barely be able to breathe with you both walking around like that! If they can even pick themselves up from the ground."

"We have it *handled*." Marie glared at him, reaching out with her hands to physically snatch back her Aura like Artorian had not been allowed to touch it. What interested Artorian was that this worked, and the very physical action was causing Marie's Aura to react like a proper, corporeal entity to be interacted with.

Well, that was certainly new. Is that what happened when you left your Aura fielded all the time, and barely worked on it? It became a weight? He was secretly glad for Tatum's new-body projects, because these two were going to have to start over completely.

He frowned and pressed his hands to his hips as he let go of Henry's Aura, eyes darting between the two. "Celestial feces! Just what have you two been doing to your Auras? Your Mage Presence will never work properly at this rate. It's just turning into a big weight that you're slumping about with. What happened to make you both unable to address this?"

"Unlike you, we are busy!" Marie snapped her fingers back with vitriol, chiding him with an insulted tone. Her diplomacy sounded long expended.

Artorian was taken aback from the clear, direct hostility and irritation in her voice. He pressed a hand to his chest. "Me, *not* busy?"

Henry tried to deflect, his hand up. "She didn't mean it like…"

Artorian copied Henry's motion, his words matching Marie's heat. "No. She meant it how she said it. Do not defend her when the first words she speaks to me after not seeing me for so long are anything but a pleasant hello."

"Well, to be fair, you also…" Henry fidgeted and muttered, petering off.

"Henry, you and your lady both arrived with your power splayed and out. That can *kill* people. Especially A-ranker Auras. That takes precedence over the hello." Artorian turned to Marie sharply. "What's wrong? You were never such an over-drawn bow. The tension is so palpable it's almost rolling from your skin."

"Don't pretend to care *now*." She dismissed him with the back of her hand, clearly too upset to be cordial. "We have been spending years and years on our monarchies, and you can't even find the time to come visit. We had to come to *you*. We have had to come to you *twice*! That you were unconscious the first time? Fine. That you still didn't come after you woke up? Insulting! We are busy! We barely have the time to eat between court procedures; a wild, crazy influx of people looking for a home, and cultivators galore not knowing what to do with themselves. We have been nearly dethroned seven times in the last month alone, and that 'problem' you so indelicately keep poking at is the reason I do not have a dagger in my spine!"

Artorian was unsure if he should be offended or not. More was at play here than he was aware of.

Henry allowed a sheepish smile. "Crushed a hidden B-ranker who thought they were being stealthy with some drapery. Seeing him back the following day to apologize was an *event*."

Turning back to Henry, Artorian motioned loosely at the sky. "What's going on?"

"And now you *ignore* me?" Marie fumed, her anger bleeding through powerful enough for the grass under her Aura to ignite. "Forget this, I'm leaving!"

Artorian's hands motioned from Henry to a flying-away Marie in utter confusion. "Henry… What? *Huh?*"

"I'm sorry, old friend. Things aren't going well." Henry cringed, his words becoming ever more meek. "Try to come by when you can? Here, take this invitation. Give it to the steward and he can squeeze you into the schedule. Circumstances are tight right now."

Artorian accepted the fancy letter from his friend, but that was not at all the answer or response he'd been hoping for. When he looked up to ask for clarity, Henry was already chasing after Marie, leaving Artorian dumbfounded as he doused the grass to put the fire out. "Okay, *what?*"

CHAPTER FIFTEEN

Thinking to equip the Silverwood bracelet, he storage-pocketed the invitation letter. Artorian then threw his hands into the air and grasped at the people still stuck in the cube. He wasn't going to be able to babysit them to make sure Cal's insurance worked. He pulled them free with Mana so they spilled out from the outer membrane, then huffed and walked his foul mood off with some wide laps around the Aquarium. The whole Aquarium. The entire square league of it.

He stopped to stomp his foot several hours later, still frustrated while wracked with indecision and conflicting emotion. "What am I supposed to do with this? Now I don't *want* to go visit them."

A Nixie tube lit above his head. "Oh my word, this is what Aiden feels like. I get it now."

Surrendering to gravity and falling into the tall grass, he laid on his back and made grass indentations by moving his arms and legs. Closing his eyes, he took the time to breathe, lay there, and soak up some evening sun.

When a shadow fell over his face, he opened his swirling blue eyes to see Yvessa standing there with a hand on her hip.

Her voice was more one of concern than chiding caretaker. "You all right? You weren't at the office."

"Been better." Artorian exhaled, his eyes betraying the equally strong swirling thoughts still churning away. "I can tackle philosophy all day long, wrestle with papers, and fix problems like I'm eating cookies. Dealing with people who are making choices through emotion, rather than letting their emotion be the guide-point for their rational actions... not so much. It's not a problem in and of itself, but boy am I bad at it when that emotion is lashing-out anger and directed at anything it can get a hold of. I know Marie wasn't mad at me, but whatever is making her be that way isn't going to conveniently go away."

"Ah." Yvessa released her hip, grasping the conversation. "Was wondering what you were all sullen about. You didn't come to Zephyr, so I figured Zephyr ought to come to you."

She motioned overhead, guiding Artorian to look at the clouds and spot the skyship. "I've given the task you were putting together for Tatum purely to Decorum instead. He actually has the time, and some experience on the topic. Tot doesn't, and I've got a note from Cal to try to avoid nudging the Incarnates."

Artorian began his morning stretches from the old times, merely to have something to do while listening. "For the best, I suppose. Do you mind if I take a few tasks while on the grass? I'm feeling all off from that surprise interaction. I didn't even get an answer out of them."

Yvessa smiled. "Of course we can. Most of it is minor."

Artorian extended a hand, expecting a paper or some rolled up vellum. Instead he received a fully prepared, itemized folder. He read the content briefings off with a mumble. "Neurotic Clan Necrohamsters are having a tiff with Godhand Clan Glitterflits."

He flipped a page, then a few more. "Sand skiff requests for the desert. Economics are important and Cal is already bored of any system where money purely flows to the top... I thought

Tatum had… Right. Not here to keep testing his ideas. That Beast Core economy might be something?"

He flipped another few pages. "Silverwood Tree Ice Canopy plans. Non-Pylon Senate functions don't function… Yvessa, I thought you said this was minor? All of these are extended projects."

His caretaker flopped into the grass next to him, making her own grass indentations. "All the small and easy projects, you've managed to delegate away. Which I'm happy about. That was the plan, and now all you have left are the involved projects. I was making a joke about it being minor. The best thing to do now would honestly be to skip town and stick your nose into The Camel-lot. See what Henry and Marie are actually struggling with."

Artorian had to push up from the greenery. "The what?"

"Not what." Yvessa reached down and tapped a spot at the top of the page where the document noted a location. "Where. The Camel-lot is a lot of land where they keep the camels. That same lot is where those two are building up, and all the old world ideas are gathering. That sounds as messy on the surface level as it is in practice."

Artorian winced, and adopted the pose that told Yvessa she could continue. She rattled off the groups as a list. "There's a Guild faction, Church faction, Necromancer faction, Valkyrie faction in place of Amazons, and an Olympian faction in place of Northmen or Asgardians."

The old man squinted at the text for a moment. "Asgar… didn't this used to be spelled as guard? With a U in it? It no longer has the U. Did it ever have the U or is Preceptor Mandela rising from the grave to laugh at me?"

Yvessa leaned to look, but shook her head. "Both are probably fine, just gloss over it and move on."

Artorian shrugged, did what his caretaker told him, and moved on. "All the old stuff is here. Except for a merchant faction? That spot was absorbed by a combination of Foxes and the S.A.S., wasn't it? There's an asterisk here with the name 'Tyler' attached, but the snippet isn't rosy."

She clarified why there were no old world merchants for a moment. "Dale ended up asking for someone named Tyler, but explaining to him that non-cultivators couldn't be brought back like cultivators could be? That was difficult. Not having Tot to explain 'inviolable' information is rough. I got as far as having him accept Tyler wasn't going to magically join us like the Wood Elves and Gnomes managed to. He met Frank and we had to… curtail some hopes. They still get along swimmingly, as good news. I heard them laughing as they caught up. Frank was trying to console Dale as the stories of his death were neither pleasant nor exaggerated."

"Sorry to hear. Good that he met Frank." Artorian laced his fingers and nodded, deciding that there was no way he was tackling all of those factions at once, and that the other project list would still need disseminating. "Any information about this camel place? Given this sounds like a bad joke by Cal waiting to happen, this better be an abyss-good location."

Yvessa was happy to not be pressed about inviolable information and how Essence connecting to information made it somehow retainable. How it all worked was completely beyond her. Some people could come back, but not everyone, and not infinitely. Tatum had an entire wall covered with nothing but angry red text and multicolored strings per what worked and what didn't. Most of it didn't.

Taking a page out of Genevieve's playbook, Yvessa turned chipper. "The Camel-lot area is situated at the merger of a bunch of rivers, in a wide estuary. So it became a very popular and easy place for roamers to end up at. Or did you not look at Cal's new world map?"

Artorian's voice pitched. "We had a *world map*?"

"Yes?" Yvessa grinned wide with significant amusement. "I've had the world map up in my office for a month. We keep updating it. Did you not come down to see?"

"No…" Artorian deflated like a balloon, mentally adding

the need to see this map to his to-do list. "I'll... I'll take a stroll around Zephyr when we're back up there. I stopped paying attention to all the changes because they kept happening."

Going back to the list, he glossed over it again, but he wasn't reading the material. His eyes slid over the letters, and he put it right back down. "You're right. I just need to go myself. Please give the skiff issue to Dev, economics to Decorum, the canopy to Chandra, and the Senate functions... Honestly, I didn't realize those were supposed to work without Pylons. The Essence variant is not easy to do. Give it to Mahogany; that's a problem for his neck of the woods."

His caretaker motioned at a spot in empty space each time he said something. A smaller Wisp became visible there for a short moment before zipping away to relay the order. A whole invisible array of Wisps served as her perpetual retinue.

She encouraged Artorian to continue when the delegation slowed. "More?"

"Well." Artorian clicked his tongue. "I'm not sure what Necrohamsters means. So I don't know if I want to give it to Richard, or just go myself."

The Administrator mulled it over, choosing to delegate after all. "Give it to Richard for now. Also, dear, I didn't hear you mention any Elves in your list, of any variety. No Spotter faction either?"

"That topic will make much more sense when you see the map." Yvessa motioned helpfully towards Zephyr. "All the Elves, of every faction, live at the base of the Silverwood tree. Not directly on it or next to it, but as close as they can get without causing friction with the Wisps. The Spotters have joined the Gnomes inside of the moon, and us Wisps are sort of all over the place. We have some rest stops in the New Fringe, however, the majority live in and on the Silverwood."

While she was at it, Yvessa listed the remaining landmarks off on her fingers. "Olympus Lake holds everyone who became a weapon. Excalibur considers the basin a new home, and I have the feeling that Yuki will like it a lot when she wakes up. El

Dorado is a city situated on a natural gold vein where Olympians who wanted to turn over a new leaf went, for anyone too far away to find the camel estuary. Think a bunch of people like Tyrian and Pim?"

Artorian motioned that he was following and let her continue. "Aiden is doing well with Atlantis, which is where you last saw it. Then there's the moon, but the surface is still being vacated. Halcyon is deliberating a place on Caltopia to resettle, and seems to be going for a bunch of loosely connected islands on the equator. I hear it's so the various animal races can run around freely, or swim, while keeping plenty warm."

She took a breath, and soldiered on. "Dwarves of every variety are still having a frenzy over at Nidavellir. A few have mellowed out and started actually living life on the outskirts, such as the marines. Dale and company still have their family farm, tucked away in the middle of nowhere. Basically impossible to find even if it's right next to the desert. Then you've got Avalanche-ville, with your people. Skyspear with the old Portal guild, new vampire clans, the old academy, and a new library faction. Lastly, Anansi and the Arachnid Autarchy set up shop underneath the mountain, and have the run of most underground tunnels that have been mapped. There's a few other places, but those are the major ones right now."

"Wait. Stop. Back up. Why is the New Fringe called Avalanche-ville?" Artorian wildly shook his arms, begging for a pause with a burning need to know. "That's almost as bad as the Camel-lot. Also, very difficult to say!"

"Do you have something better it could be called?" The caretaker received a freshly unfurled vellum from one of her attendants, quill at the ready. Her request joined an obvious raised brow.

"Camelot for one. One word. Easy. Straight." Artorian waggled his finger while making a cutting motion with the edge of his other hand. "As to Avalanche-ville... I must be sending too many problems their way. Aval... something."

Silenced by swirling thoughts, the old man suddenly could

not help but think of Bob. The best goblin. He mouthed some old words, thinking out loud. "Projects that dragged on…"

"Avalon." Artorian rose to his full height. Declaring the statement with a sudden, sturdy, and confident voice. "No more New Fringe. Change the name to Avalon. Bob would have liked that."

Artorian felt determined, but it wasn't his lot to name. "Run it by Lunella, see what she thinks. That will make it easier than needing to refer to Fringes all the time. I should honestly do the same for the Skyspear, but please send that renaming request up to Amber, Emilia, and whoever else lives up there. Have them form and convene a council."

Yvessa saluted. "I shall make it so."

CHAPTER SIXTEEN

The click of a disappointed tongue stole Artorian's attention.

"No luck, this time." Brianna smiled as her Presence entered the scene, her eyes looking up at Zephyr as the airship bobbed through the pasty clouds. "I was so looking forward to walking in on the best parts of the conversation. No subtle offers for me to stab anyone this time? Though, I may have good knowledge on how to assemble quality councils."

Artorian looked up and behind him, then flashed a wide grin at the assassin Queen's extended hand. He gripped the offered palm, and hoisted himself up as he shared gossip. "Portal Mage Amber is behaving very well! No stabbings to plan, I'm afraid. As for council skills, should one of your adjutants have time to speak to my caretaker, that would be very helpful."

"I shall have someone sent." Brianna chuckled, the back of her hand wiping some grass from his outfit, as he looked like a farmhand who'd crawled through an entire hay bale while fleeing from a bite-y weasel. "The only time being afraid is applicable, Administrator, would be when I *am* planning a stabbing."

Artorian posed to make the cleaning efforts convenient. The old man intoned his quip playfully. "Isn't that all the time?"

A most innocent expression formed on her face that unsettled Artorian more than a month of paperwork could. Her voice was cheerful as she plucked blades of grass off him. "Of course!"

Her pleasant expression faded when she looked the Administrator up and down, her gaze inspecting him for a detail other than the cleaning effort. "Abyss. Does it affect you as well? Celestial feces, I was hoping you would be the exception so I could wiggle some kind of workaround into place."

Artorian didn't follow her change of topic. "*What* affects me, dear? There's been a whole slew of confusions with the Pylons out of commission. No Senate. No Forum. Eternia abilities being difficult to recall or implement. Such and so on."

"You are A-rank zero to my eyes, Artorian." Brianna flicked his shoulder as she answered demurely. Holding her chin, Brianna made bitter bunny noises before her eyes slashed a path towards the supposedly empty space behind her. Artorian had spotted the host of retainers hiding unseen in her wake, but considered it polite not to bring that detail up. "It was my hope you would be exempt, and still read as A-rank seven. With every Mage reading as the bottom of their B-rank or A-rank, accurate measurements have been... problematic."

Artorian cocked his head to the side, really not following. "I grasp why that might be a problem for the people attempting to break into the next rank, but not why measuring would be. We haven't truly been using the zero to zenith rankings for anything more than chevrons to wear on a sleeve. Progress is tracked differently for our current purposes, and people are likely to slam face-first into the C-ranks before truly encountering problems."

Brianna's gaze was narrow, until she grasped that Artorian wasn't talking about the same topic she had in mind. "I see where we have diverged in thought. I was not referring to the growth of the Essence-babies, Administrator. They will grow, of that I have no doubt. In truth, I am baffled instead by those that choose to eschew the ways of cultivation, but as it is very clear that the greater-hearted among us support this measure, I thus do as well."

Her stance straightened, hands easing behind the small of her back before a small, sly smile crossed her face. "My concern has to do with keeping problems in check. I was not joking when I said that I have plans to *stab*. The fallen Olympians are behaving for the most part, but many are bitter. They truly believed they were in the right, and joining Marie's little hodge-podge has only given them room to work those irritations out. Some among them require a hushed whisper to the ear, and a sharp reminder buried in their kidney. Many are not graceful losers, newfound arachnophobia or not. A whole pile of them vie for her throne."

Brianna waved that portion of the pie chart off. "Those do not concern me. The ones that act against Cal's interests by attempting to exploit loopholes? Life is to be made unpleasant for them. A few deaths can do so much good."

Artorian frowned, then rubbed the growing crease. "They'll just come back. Please elucidate on what this is meant to accomplish? I also have the nose-itch that I should delve into Camelot soon. Paperwork piles endlessly on the desk, but after what happened a few hours ago, I feel the burning need to sniff around personally. I have a mighty difficult time believing that after... what? Fifty? More? Iterations of Henry and Marie practicing kingdom management, that they would not be excellent at the skill. That I keep hearing of rampant problems was... honestly not the expectation. I'm very confused. They even came from a royal lineage!"

Brianna laid a hand on his upper bicep when the old man began to pace in circles, throwing his arms up while getting ever louder about the matter. The quiet motion made him realize he'd been going off on a bender, and stopped him cold when she spoke. "Had the conditions of the old world remained, they would have done very well. That carpet was pulled from under their feet, and now every journey is akin to scaling a new mountain."

Her words were even, measured, and full of understanding. "Administrator. Ruling, and sovereignty, is not a smooth, predictable, or easy path to tread. I can tell you from experience that it is never the problems you expect to kneecap you that do. Small, little things come from below, and mire you. Preventing you from moving when you should. Moving *as* you should."

She released him, but kept her gaze firm. "Politics are a game with arcane rules all to themselves, and that duo has not managed a realm where those rules have not been fluid. Each new attempt, they tried something different to cut off a problem in the prior attempt. Each attempt was thus rife with new problems, and no amount of repetition of a task will let you expect the unexpected. Attempting to govern when your people are not in unison is a misery that I cannot abide. The Camel-lot may as well be a zoo. One where the pens are open, and the keepers find more safety within the cages of their own making."

Artorian nodded pensively, before Brianna continued. "An 'educated' Olympian who returns after a short death remembers the pain for long enough to reconsider acting out against Cal's rules again. Henry and Marie's, they may flaunt. That is their problem to sort. My allegiances, on the other hand, are very clear. I may be the pinnacle of the Dark and Moon Elves, and likely will be until the last of my days, but even I have learned that my personal path of tyranny was lacking. It is therefore good that I have places, and people, to look for when seeking guidance."

Her voice dipped, whispering supportively. "You do not understand the grandiose boon it is to have you as an Administrator, Artorian."

He frowned once more at that. "My apologies, my dear. Now you've lost me on an entirely separate topic. I merely do the little I can, from my little office, with all my papers. That I can sneak off to teach classes, and have found the time to patch up my Soul Item to completion, has been my highlight. I'm not certain how I could be a boon to a ruler that has already far exceeded anyone else's skillset in the ruling topic. I think Halcyon and Zelia may be close to your prowess? I'm a walking fumble."

Brianna covered her mouth daintily as she giggled, her expression fond and amused. "You are such a grandfather at heart, Artorian. Now I understand why Polly makes such a fuss about sticking to you. Your **Pride** needs bolstering. I shall keep my opinion short, as compliments fluster you easily when they are true, and you cannot convince yourself to accept them."

That made the old grump huff, but he took an attentive stance to listen as Yvessa popped into her orb form. She hovered to stabilize, then wandered away to coordinate Wisp work.

Artorian lightened his own mood with a joke. "Might know a thing or two about being kneecapped."

A guffaw from Brianna was the prize for his effort. The loud, boisterous belly laugh was unexpected from her, but a smile was a smile. "Cheap distractions will not work on me, Administrator. My view is easy to understand: no matter the prowess of my society, the control I had over it, or the exactness of its functions, my Monarchy of the Mist was lacking. The goals pursued were not those that saw to the betterment of anything but my own desires. The goals you pursue may as well be the pursuit of that lofty philosophical ideal called 'The Good.' I admit I felt little draw to an ethical standpoint not solidly entrenched in scales of gray, but I equally cannot deny that what forms in the wake of your passing are events I would have craved to see unfurl after decades of work. Flowers and health bloom where you tread."

Artorian crossed his arms, cheeks slightly flushed. Those were high compliments. "Yes, well, thank you."

"Let me explain why I consider you a boon, Administrator." Brianna squeezed him fondly, capitalizing on his flustered mood. "I began my rulership with the question: how do you pick the best of the best? Because clearly, to float on the very top, that is what one must have."

She tapped the side of her nose. "It is in asking this very question that I went wrong."

Artorian recovered from his fluster, attention pulled towards the philosophical opening. He did not know this side of Brianna, but the scholar in him wanted to. Without interfering, he observed as she drew a graph in the air in front of them, using a very familiar Mana trick. Her lines, unlike his, were sharp as a tack.

He commented on her graph's listed values. "Performance versus trust?"

"*Mhm.*" Brianna continued her work as the chart became ever more crisp, motioning at the sections to come. "There's a saying among the mortal warrior clans of old. 'I may trust you with my life, but do I trust you with my money and my wife?' Clever, no?"

Artorian chuffed and crossed his arms, but provided no comment. Brianna took the silence as leeway to draw her graph. Starting with drawing a square in the bottom left corner, closest to the minimal values, and a second one in the top right of the graph, with the maximum values. "Nobody wants a person who has low performance and low trust. Everyone wants a high and high."

Artorian nodded; that was common sense.

She then drew a circle high on the performance metric, but abysmally low in the trust metric. The very top left of the graph. "This type of person. The high performer of low trust? This person will get everything you need them to get done. However, they are a toxic leader, a toxic ally, and a toxic team member. This is the kind of person who will do anything, and strive through anything, to achieve their goal. People like this are obsessed with hitting the pinnacle of the given dominance hierarchy they are in. As such, they are often difficult to negotiate or speak with, nail focused on their tasks and goals, and incredibly hard-headed. They're outstanding at what they do, but abysmal at anything that doesn't contribute to their pinnacle, and frequently have views that aren't healthy for common social interaction."

"My apologies, Brianna." Artorian scratched his chin, hesitantly interjecting. "You just described the stereotype of most old world Elves."

"I did." She nodded casually, not at all bothered by the observation. "Specifically, I have described old world Dark Elves. Including my own views up to the point when I was… forcibly taught to see the error of my ways, in Niflheim."

Artorian grumbled in discomfort, but Brianna moved the focus back to the graph. Specifically, moving all the way to the right on the trust scale. "I would rather have a medium performance person of high trust, or even a low performance person of high trust, than more of the prior category. I tried that. It went to the Abyss. I learned that the only direction it can go with any organization that values and empowers these people is to the Abyss. Making it equally as annoying that these are *exactly the kind of people* who end up in those positions to begin with."

She held her own hands, gracing him with a weak smile. "The realization comes only after you've fallen down the hole. We have a million methods to measure performance, but almost no methods to measure trust. Which is bad for the long game, because it destroys the organization."

Artorian was beginning to comprehend her direction, though she erased the Mana graph too soon for his liking. "With the long game being what's important. I see."

Brianna pressed her digit to his robed chest. "Continue to be you, as you have proven to be of high trust, and place the wellbeing of your people above any other goal you might set. Attempting to do otherwise in the pursuit of a goal would only steer you astray."

She pulled her finger away, having driven home her point. "Henry and Marie keep attempting to appease their **Laws**, their governments, and their idealized pursuits of being 'good' monarchs. Being too hasty, I would say their core problem stems from relying on high performance people, rather than high trust people, but that is not where I see the issue being. They're barely relying on other people at all, and are becoming the very type of person I've just said would wreck the 'age of empires' wonder."

Artorian perked up, his eyebrows high. "Could I have your full opinion?"

Brianna was glad to, and delivered it like midday gossip served over spiced tea. "They have forgotten entirely—as those bloated wrecks that can't competently be called an Aura clearly show—that growth comes from within. They, *as people*, need a break, and need help. That the people around them are too disparate to fit into an unorganized culture, much less function, is not even secondary to them. It's barely tertiary. Abyss, Artorian, it might not even crack their top ten list."

Her voice turned a notch up on the judgmental scale. "They are trying—far too hard—to stabilize a society they don't even have a proper grip on. Only after internal struggles have ceased will external efforts have merit. My belief is that they should step back and focus on themselves, but I have already told them such, and they would not listen. One cannot build clever workarounds on a foundation that is crumbling."

She smirked, sensing an opportunity. "Much like that city in Muspelheim you destroyed by moving the equivalent of a toothpick."

"Ha!" Artorian shook his head, mightily amused at the reference. This friendly banter was doing wonders for his mood. A detail of Brianna's effort that didn't escape him. "Fell right down in a heap!"

Brianna wrapped up her opinion with cold hard truth. "They are devolving into the ways of the iron gauntlet, and that style of management only has one outcome. Rebellion."

CHAPTER SEVENTEEN

Artorian considered Brianna's opinion with the weight that it was due when the joke elapsed. "I'll keep the advice in mind, Brianna."

She looked at him with the expectation of receiving his own opinion, but he didn't want to talk further about Henry and Marie. A swift segue would surely save him. "Personally, I still rebuke the idea of rulership. Administration is a toe over the line, but a toe I can manage. I'm quite happy being a little old codger, sticking his nose in to make trouble or break trouble. As to clever workarounds, that only made me think of personal projects that I don't know where to place. I did like your growth from within mention, dear. Good stuff, that."

He then shot her a squinted look. "A bit on the nose with the compliment reference."

The Dark Elf grinned. "I am fully in the know about the prank pulled on you when the 'Tsun' Pylons were still functional."

"Bri!" Artorian loudly fussed, both hands shooting across one another before he devolved in a set of mumbled grumbling that wasn't particularly serious. She was just pushing buttons.

Realizing those actions were on purpose, his mind moved the topic over to make room. With fresh space to think in, a Nixie tube lit up. He'd found the correct question, and it was what Brianna was doing here in the first place.

The Supervisor before him instead looked both curious and hesitant when she detected the shift in his demeanor. No amount of subtle change was going to make it past the trained assassin, as her words gained an edge of opportunism. "Would these personal projects be anything I could assist with, by chance?"

The old man shrugged lightly. "Only if you want to hear me babble about my Flashrunes idea that so far has gone nowhere at great speed. Could I ask why you came to find me?"

"We used to cover entire buildings in complex and intricate Runes that made people forget we were there." Brianna slid in with a not-insignificant amount of mischief in her tone. "Gave Dale the run around a few times as well. We kept a running tally of how often we befuddled him. I came out like a bandit with my bets."

Avoiding his question further, Brianna attempted a sly side-step. "I understand the Spotters or Gnomes may be what you're looking for in terms of hard mathematics, but if you seek Runeworks that are more flexibly explained, the Dark Elves are no strangers to their secrets."

Artorian flattened his face in the Tibbins expression, making Brianna break from her fancy pose. She'd skipped out on his question and they both knew it. A short sigh later, and she gave in to his curiosity. "Happenstance, this time. I was on a walk with my retainers and judges, to get fresh air away from the Wisps near the Silverwood. They delight in dreaming up new rules for those who wish to visit, and I was getting irritated by their games. Then I heard our Administrator plunked down a land effect, and that was my excuse to proverbially get out of the house."

She shrugged when the look didn't let up. "No more, no less. There is surprisingly little for me and mine to do at the moment, save for scaring full-grown Mages as if they were mere children afraid of the rattling beneath their beds."

The grins on the faces of every hidden judge and retainer behind Brianna told Artorian this was anything but a disliked pastime. They delighted in being the scary thing hidden away in the dark, now that they had reclaimed that spot from the booked, spined, and shelved demons.

Artorian let it slide, and supposed that he could use the help. Convenient that Brianna had offered, he supposed, as he was stuck either way. No time to do it himself, combined with the small matter of lacking the expertise to properly commence, didn't bode well. "I see. Well, why not?"

Turning only his shoulders, he addressed his caretaker. "Yvessa, I mean, Titania. Since this is actual, official work, would you happen to know where my notes on Flashrunes fled off to? Brianna is going to need a copy."

The change of name made his caretaker pause the conversation with her attendant Wisps, and snap straight into secretary mode. "Of course, Administrator. I will fetch them and get them into Brianna's hands. Until then, may I suggest a short explanation?"

"Good thought." Artorian considered that, nodded, and let her get back to her own coordination work as Titania huddled up her congregation of newlights and left. The Wisps held clean rank and file positions as they beelined for Zephyr.

Turning his shoulders back to face Brianna, he tasted the ideas in his mouth and spoke when he had enough of an order together. "Flashrunes are this idea I had for getting around a problem I foresaw, when we need to step back into mortal bodies. Because we—or at minimum, I—do not have a grasp on how long we inhabit those before we become Mages again, I conjured a contingency. Sadly, I don't know how to put Flashrunes together. Perhaps verbalizing my thoughts will clear the air."

Brianna made a generous 'go ahead' hand motion.

"Flashrunes, as an ability, are meant to be a new method of

achieving an existing effect, that circumvents a well-known difficulty. I'm going to meander for a bit to establish concepts, and then it'll all suddenly make a lot of sense." Artorian formed sigils in the open space next to him, drawing as if on a chalkboard with his finger. He spoke out loud, half for his own clarity to make sure he had his foundations correct. "Mages use Mana, and craft their full techniques within their own forms, otherwise currently known as our bodies. We can change our bodies, but interestingly, how that affects our ability to use the effects we know changes surprisingly little."

He drew a quick draconic stick figure. "This is a symptom which I believe to be a side-effect of us actually having Spirit bodies. I'm convinced that dragon-forming in a non-Cal body would render me completely incapable of using my normal Mage skills. Having no legs in my current form was enough to throw the entire effort off, and that tipped me off to not trust the convenience. Having a fully different shape I feel would crash the whole party entirely."

"I will require more, Administrator." Brianna was doing her best to understand where he was going, and openly made a hand-motion for her retainers to come out of hiding, listen in, and take mental notes. They did so without a word, taking in Artorian's idea while looking very blasé about the endeavor. Lack of enthusiasm prevented none of them from doing exactly as they were ordered.

"The core of the matter remains that we form these patterns to create specific effects, and the most stable types of these effects we have come to call Runes." Artorian surmised while tapping his lip, swiftly adding a qualifier. "I know Cal has 'Spells' and 'Spellforms,' but those are not suitable for Mageminds. I straight up failed to duplicate one when attempting. So, 'Runes' is about what I feel an A-ranker mind can keep a good enough hold of, in order for quality casting to occur."

That detail got the attention of some of the Moon Elves who had written this interaction off as a lost cause before it had begun, regardless of obeying Brianna. Spells could not be properly cast by Mages without assistance? How intriguing. The old man had garnered their interest now. This conversation was leaning towards efficiency, and the Dark Elven people loved their efficiency.

Not particularly displeased by having everyone's attention, Artorian happily soldiered on in full academia mode.

"External cultivator that I am, my main drawback is that my repertoire of actual Runes and down-to-earth unit-combination Essence patterns is embarrassingly limited. Due to my penchant for invoking effects, my skill set has leaned the entire other direction. Unfortunately, invoking is both costly, and about as inefficient as you can get trying to accomplish your intended desire."

He drew some firework effects on the board as some of the Dark Elves cringed when Moon Elves informed them of the inefficiency being referenced. "The Essence will get it done, but it will cost both your legs and possibly half an arm."

Artorian paced during his sermon, wanting to be very clear when he made his points. "Runes are the king of cost-effective casting, while being of a complexity that is still manageable. Spells clearly being superior in output notwithstanding, if I *can't* cast it, it's *no good*. Runes I have successfully cast with and without Pylon help, and that's where my ideas began to find fertile ground to grow. As those old Pylons we had for the same Rune, but of different quality levels, strongly comes to mind."

His chalkboard writings were now filled with pictures and diagrams. "If all that is needed for an effect to occur…"

Some extra notes were swiftly added to the improvised chalkboard as he slapped in an example cost-benefit formula. "…is the correct Rune getting the correct amount of power. Then… Why would I need an inscription? Or an enchantment? Or an array? I don't need the fireball pattern on a stick, forever embossed to be fueled and used as needed. No complicated engraving or expensive equipment. I only need the pattern for a moment. Only long enough for the circuit to complete."

Artorian then finally explained the name. "I need the Rune

'in a flash.' Just me, moving my Presence to form the pattern. Add the juice. Pop goes the effect. Back in goes my Aura. Done!"

Brianna prodded at a detail in his tactile and mossy-feeling air-board scribbles. "How is this different from an incantation? You have described an incantation. Taking all the power of an enchantment and expending the pattern in a single burst."

"That's just it!" Artorian gladly waggled his finger to the air like an over-enthused professor. He gleefully kept lecturing. "There are no *Runes* being used in that fashion! Enchantments are temporary Essence patterns, yes, but those effects have never been at Rune-quality. By which I do not mean the difference between 'Runes' commonly known as 'permanent effects' and 'Enhancements' as 'temporary effects.' Rather that there is a clear *quality* difference between both instances of an otherwise similar pattern. A Rune is better than an Enchantment, both in output, and effect to cost ratio."

Artorian added a detail that he thought this class might find useful. "This is also why Mages have such a hard time struggling with technique efficiency, because they are using the patterns they know, and those patterns are *not* the Rune-variants. Thus the leaking, Mana-loss, and patchwork problems."

Brianna squeezed the bridge of her nose, her tone questioning. "Mages would also not need this Flashrune idea to perform any of their abilities?"

Artorian handily agreed. "Correct! This idea was not for Mages. Did I mention it was for when we have the mortal forms? Consider this. We have the redo, the one we must go through in order to get out of Cal, due to our current Tower-binding being through Cal as a proxy. We get to the C-ranks, and then..."

He made fanciful hand motions at the sky, and posed as if in a silly performance.

The motions were a jest, and got the retainers to chuckle.

Brianna's mind kept focused on the actual issue, and when her thoughts clicked in the pieces, her eyes shot wide. "My beloved shadowed blades, we will be *stuck* as C-rankers until the exact moment we can leave Cal!"

That ended the judges' chuckles, causing questioning looks to be respectfully levered at the assassin Queen.

Artorian smiled wide, then took on a more solemn look before nodding with repetition. "You got it!"

CHAPTER EIGHTEEN

While Brianna had grasped the issue, Artorian saw the confusion grow in her retinue. He explained the problem to them when they started less than subtly flicking their eyes toward him. They didn't outright *ask*, but Artorian wasn't going to make it difficult for them. His rolling lecture on Flashrunes was already complicated enough.

This was a freebie, and he took it slow. "If we reconnect as a Mage to the Tower in Cal, we'll merely reconnect to *Cal*, and the whole affair of building your cultivation back up from scratch, in a body that's actually yours, is moot. We'd have to do the whole mortality and cultivation redo a third time, since achieving Magehood in Cal returns us to our current predicament, except in our own Mage-bodies rather than a Cal-made one, which is *not* the fix we are looking for."

He held up some digits to help keep track, still speaking slowly. "A direct Tower connection to our **Laws** means that we are completely cut off in Cal's Soul Space. Like we were during our initial entry. A connection with Cal as a proxy means cultivating in here is possible, but likely means that being outside of Cal comes with restrictions and strings that nobody is going to like. Ascending to Magehood means we have to be C-rank. The conditions we want to reconnect to the Tower require us to be out of Cal. Those same conditions lead to us having to make the gamble of being in Cal, as a C-ranker, until exit time. Which… nobody knows when that might be."

Discomfort ran through the crowd of Dark Elves, several hanging their heads in deep contemplation, while others looked on with worry.

Artorian continued the topic in stride. "Begin the mortal life too early, and Mages stuck in C-ranker bodies will get antsy. You have to live out that time the old fashioned way. I'm also told there's no more convenient seed Core body-hopping, and the like. Meaning anyone stronger than you has a lot of say over you, should they choose to press it. As you will be stuck using Essence—locked out of Mana, and your **Law**, *and the rest*—until Ascension."

That seemed to drive his point home, but he lost no stride while lecturing. "That's a recipe for disaster and strife, and we already know how that song and dance ends. Begin the mortal life too late, and you won't be able to leave right away once the way out appears, unless you're fine with Ascending while forever looking fourteen, or something equally young, as nobody is exempt from the problem that your Mage body follows the Essence paths you've built as a C-ranker."

That turned some of the Dark Elven expressions bleak.

"Sure, you *can*, but…" He shrugged lightly. "Given that Ascension is likely to happen the moment you're out of Cal, it's all about risk assessment, and good old gambling. We currently have the luxury of very malleable bodies and forms. I expect all those shortcuts and easy solutions are going to vanish into thin air when we're back out in the old world. Most certainly including our bountiful Essence access. So, it's best to consider the risk and aim for the desired outcome in the first arrow volley."

Many judges behind Brianna devolved into hushed whispers, most of them not accepting the concept of spending a few hundred years looking like a child. They could freely change their appearance in Cal. Out in the real world? They remembered their appearance to be rather permanent. An Incarnation event used to be necessary for any kind of visual update, and unlike in Cal, you only got the one.

Seeing that he'd engaged the minds of his audience, Artorian clarified the original question that he was trying to tackle. "So, how do we retain the ability, efficiency, and power that we have gotten very used to as Mages, in bodies that can't hope to sustain those kinds of stressors?"

He let the premise hang, speaking again when the hushing whispers were traded out for attentive, and hopeful stares. "My idea was to create the Mage-quality effects we are accustomed to, outside of the body instead of inside the body, because there is simply no way a C-ranking body and some quality Meridian paths are going to hold up to the Mana madness I tend to sling around without second thought."

He actually got chuckles and wry grins out of some of the judges! Progress! "Needing to puzzle out exact Essence-units to patterns is also not my forte. Lucky for me, 'good' Runes have that ratio pre-prepared. Again, not as well or as complete as Spells do, but still. That the method is Aura-based happens to be a convenient benefit. Personally, I think it's about time external cultivators got more toys and tools."

A few of the Dark Elves actually nodded. Dark Elves had a higher ratio of external to internal cultivators? *Interesting.*

Artorian exhaled heavily, and leveled some personal complaints while he was on the topic. Not at all to distract from the glances he was stealing to gauge the judges' reactions, of course. "Internally-formed Mage patterns will not be attainable when we're meandering about in the C-ranker forms. My invocations would be a death trap without Cal being *very* generous with the Essence, and I don't want to get more used to slinging those around on every occasion, in the likely event that the real world is not remotely so kind with the energy supply. I know I've repeated that point, but I must. We've all gotten very used to our non-aligned Essence, and long past are the days where specific ratios and scarcity were a prime focus for where to cultivate. Days that we must expect to return. My invoking, therefore, requires replacement."

The same Dark Elves who had nodded now did so again with vast head motions. They had clearly tried invoking, and the insane cost it had siphoned from them was not something any were keen to repeat. Spending entire *ranks* worth of Mana? For *one* effect?

Abyss to the *no*.

Artorian wrung his hands together, continuing his lecture while suppressing his facial twitches at seeing not one, but two of the Dark Elves have very dramatic reactions at recalling an attempt to invoke. "Going up the ranks the first time had major setbacks for me, because this was my go-to method. I doubt I'll have that avenue available next time. There won't be a society to sit on the corner of, to recover for a few years."

He frowned at a sudden realization. "I also need a bit more than some sunlight now."

Artorian ruminated on that thought for a moment, wondering how he was going to actually cultivate outside now that he needed all six affinity types.

Noting the metaphorical thundercloud hanging over the old man's head, Brianna interjected to give his mind something else to chew on. He did have a whole host of judges waiting on him. "In that ease-of-transition vein of thought, when it comes to retaining power, or otherwise having methods of easier external access: enchantment items are difficult to manufacture when a dungeon doesn't do it. Rune-variants even more so, and Cal simply doesn't have the time or inclination to equip people with Runic armaments for no reason. He doesn't even have a token or reward system up and running yet. So any power we wish to keep needs a *skill* solution, not an *item* solution."

Brianna tapped her lips, seeing Artorian pull himself out of the mental mire and reach for her rope. "So you thought of Flashrunes. A mixture of an incantation application, combined with the activation of a high-quality Rune. Instead of the not-as-functional patterns most cultivators have a hold of, which you are referring to as 'enchantment-quality.' Your bottleneck sounds like it is Runelore. Knowing what the patterns you want to form actually are. 'Feeling' the correct form is not the same as 'knowing' it. This will require practice, study, and toil. *Disciplined* toil. Months to years of it. A negligible cost for a Mage's time, but a major one when other obligations are piled before you on a desk."

Artorian could not disagree. "So it is… and I've neither the time to study Runes, complicated three-dimensional messes that they are, nor practice the limited forms I do know. I'm not even sure the concept can be more than a theory? C-rankers using their Auras to make Runes? That's not entry-level material. That's high-difficulty Auric control, and the batch of people we have with an Aura as malleable as mine is tiny, unless my charts have holes in them."

A few of the Dark Elves mutedly hid their facial expressions at the mention.

Artorian chose not to dig deeper for the moment. "Using the flash feature in order to make the Rune-pattern duration as short as possible seemed more a necessity than some amusing naming convention."

Brianna was thoroughly in the boat now, reiterating the point back to him. "I understand. As Mages, we have a pleasant and convenient innate sense of pattern making. There's a muscle-memory to the process, like flexing an arm. We don't really think about it without directly focusing on that aspect of the process. If I want a Mana blade, then I have one, because the feeling of how to form that pattern is ingrained. I never even think of what shape that Rune is supposed to be. My knowledge, will, and Mana manipulation all share the same level of mastery."

She formed a Mana dagger above her hand to prove the point, not even giving the method thought. The gleaming weapon was simply there. "Performing that same process *exter-*

nally requires both extreme Auric skill, and a not-insignificant working knowledge on the specific Rune you are forming. Given that the goal is Runes, you must also get the pattern correct enough for what you have formed to qualify as such, or it is likely to blow up… well, you. Especially if you're using your own Aura as the medium. You have seen what happens to items that have casting flaws?"

"Plenty!" Artorian laughed with a far too chipper response, his hands making upwards motions to mimic an explosion. "Goes up like a tinderbox! Big kaboom!"

Artorian's caretaker glowed a suspicious green when she arrived with a copy of the Flashrune notes for Brianna, her voice sharp. "Is that, by chance, why you haven't handed this over to Dev? I was dead set in my expectation that you were going to hand Flashrunes off to Dev."

"They explode on their own enough as is." Artorian crossed his arms all glum, then grumbled as a not-so-pleasant confirmation. "I secretly snuck Dev a copy of my notes ages ago, while it was still just myself and Decorum on Zephyr, but the basic note I got back is that for such a high-risk project, he'd need to dedicate an amount of time he currently didn't have."

Feeling like a weary Administrator, he rubbed at his eyebrows. "The Gnomes are all working on Cal's projects, and since those are about fixing the Soul Space, their importance ranks higher. That same reason is also why I have not felt inclined to sneak my way into the moon."

Yvessa's glow dimmed, the Wisp bobbing in understanding as she got the notes into Brianna's possession.

"I could, sure!" Artorian shrugged, his voice having fallen. "Don't feel like it."

The old man waggled his pointer finger up at the orbital body. "Access to Operations by itself already feels like I am pulling resources away from tasks I would otherwise rather not interrupt. Do I understand why some Beast Cores are exceedingly rare, and other times seemingly plentiful? Not in the slightest. I can do my part of the help, but shuffling tasks around for the best match is not the same as making sure the ground you're standing on is real."

He raised his hands to drop them. "We're not even tackling the new Pylon plans yet, and from the chatter I'm aware of, the blueprints are nothing but trouble. Anything so big a problem that makes Wisps and Gnomes work together *without* complaints is not a lake I want to dip my toes into. There's sharks in there."

He then made an open-palm motion towards Brianna, pulling up his own mood and shifting to the positive by complimenting someone else. "Bri-Bri spoke with great wisdom when she was tackling the 'fix it from within' topic. Everyone who is in the Supervisor class has a particular skill set that is best used when playing to their strengths. I am great at social issues, but a Sugar-Glider-racer wreck when it comes to economics, or mechanics, or really anything that does not boil down to dealing with people or esoteric energy."

Brianna raised an eyebrow, her smile kept polite.

"If what you're looking at doesn't make sense to anybody else?" Artorian adopted a comical pose, twisting a twirl like a performer trying to make an entrance on a new stage. "Then I'm probably your guy!"

CHAPTER NINETEEN

Artorian pressed a hand to his own chest when the joke didn't land, his mind wandering to Camelot. "I couldn't tell you how to run a good government. I'm clueless. I can, on the other hand, roll up some of my papers and whack some ill-intended fools until they grasp that the intent behind their actions is as valuable as the end result it procures. I can also weave a mean basket!"

Brianna chuckled with deep understanding, her coy expression back in full force from the old man using one of her friends-only nicknames. Her retinue, on the other hand, looked horrified at both the colloquialism and behavior this old man was enacting in front of their ruler, their eyes darting back and forth between their Queen, and potential new stabbing victim.

They were stabbing him now, yes?

The man just twirled!

Brianna declined their desires, as she'd rather enjoyed the warm familiarity. "That, unfortunately, a government does not make. Luckily, Administrator, you have many in your circle who are proficient in such things. This is not a weight you must carry, nor carry out. Zelia is a walking masterclass in rulership,

DENNIS VANDERKERKEN & DAKOTA KROUT

but I am biased as my own views are in line with her methods. Halcyon perhaps, would be the best overall choice if you ever truly needed to press your nose against the shopping window of the topic. What I have read of her work as Daimyo was... *enlightening.* I find I excel more when I can keep to my profession, rather than the rigors of rule. Of course, *you* really could do wonders, had you the interest."

The old man kicked at some grass without much drive. "*Bhah.* I would merely be another tyrant. Brianna, I appreciate your sentiment, I do, but I believe my methods would be too close to yours. I, too, would consolidate to an extreme, before I ameliorate living standards and pull people into councils and groups to get laws drafted. The requirements for me even starting such a venture are historically painted in blood, and I doubt I have the heart to commence walking the path. If I cannot begin with a unified land, then I don't believe I'll ever begin at all."

With her hands already hidden behind the small of her back, Artorian did not see the hand-signal she shot to her judges. Without stirring one iota, they all mentally tallied that the Administrator's latest words were something their Queen wanted them to keep in mind.

Brianna herself retained an innocent expression, shuffling the attention by pulling the topic back to its prior standpoint. "I shall bother you no further on it today. Was there more to Flashrunes? Or was what you have explained the entirety of the concept, notes notwithstanding?"

"That was about it." Artorian stretched and affirmed breathily, straightening up.

"Unless you want to hear me ramble about the theoretical Incarnate or Heavenly versions I conjured up." Artorian exhaled, about out of steam. "Getting the basic form of Flashrunes off the ground would already be considered a great success. I know incantations function as a proof of concept, but it's simply not the same when we're using Rune-quality patterns as a baseline."

Brianna blinked. "Please, Administrator. Ramble."

"Very well." Artorian hummed, not seeing why putting the last few cards on the table could hurt at this point. "So, the best patterns are the **Laws** in the Tower. They are the direct concept of an idea, and that concept has a shape, or pattern, or most ideal way it can be. This 'most ideal way it can be' can be expressed in many ways, but the more correct and closer one is to the complete pattern, the better."

He erased his existing Mana chalkboard, and drew a pyramid. "Thus, while we have a Tower version of a pattern, we can trickle that down to Spells, then Runes, then Enchantments, or however we are forming the quality hierarchy now. A Spell is the closest design that has been reached to copy and match these concepts to date. With Spellforms being multiple of these Spells bundled together in an Array, to accomplish an effect that a mere single spell couldn't. Usually due to complexity."

He stabbed his finger near the top of the pyramid. "When it comes to patterns I can and cannot work with, Spellforms are unquestionably out. Spells, Incarnates can do without strain, while I got a terrible headache, and flummoxed the result. The good, high-efficiency Runes are on-mark for A-rankers, while the normal, low-to-mid efficiency Runes are better suited to B-rankers."

There was a pause for commentary.

"Nothing between Spells and the Tower per quality thresholds?" Brianna asked curiously.

"Oh, most probably!" Artorian moved his digit to the spot in question, making space for the vacant entry. "Spells are merely the closest matches we've found, but there could be Soulforms, or Living Patterns, or Living Spells, or more vivacious ones like Wisp-patterns that have their own eccentricities. I'm pulling examples out of my sleeve here, and I'm making them up, but the possibility remains thoroughly open. Here, let me show you something incredible."

The Dark Elves in the loose huddle tensed.

Where the Administrator had felt like a small blip to their

senses before, the pull of Mana he enacted should not have caused all available energy in the entire region to flock towards him. Like a pet bounding and bumbling through the halls at top speed to tackle their most favorite-est person.

The Presence of the Administrator changed.

To the Dark Elves, who had their own idea of a measuring stick, Artorian tended to feel like a lazy fortress plunked on a hill. All his ranks but one invested in his Aura was noticeable, even if they couldn't get a correct measure. Auric signature was an easy method of pinpointing people and going 'that one is over there,' but there was also the measurement of how well one blended together with the landscape.

A skill heavily prized in their culture.

In general, Artorian didn't leverage the weight that could accompany his Presence, and thus he felt functionally identical to wherever he might be. Like a structure that ambled, but one not exerting a zone of control. One did not have to field their Aura, taking it off like a coat, to apply pressure to their general surroundings. There was more than one way to lay gravity on people and force them to a knee, after all.

This was not what Artorian was doing. To the Elves present, his Auric feeling altered from one comfortably indifferent from the landscape, to one of a looming mountain hoisting a great weight. A part of the world had just stood up.

They now all felt very, *very small*.

Artorian turned his palm up, gathering focus.

To the Elves, the feeling of the world standing up collapsed and condensed into a small ball. This inadvertently forced everyone except for Brianna to jump back dozens of feet with a spider-sense panic response as a miniature **Sun** flared to life above his hand, filling the region with crisp daylight, and the sound of a heavy *wub* that shuddered through the ground.

The Administrator casually commented on the orb as he adjusted the brightness. There would be no eye-stabbing today! "Amaterasu, for example, has the actual Tower-quality pattern of a **Sun**, which is where I drew the term from. I myself couldn't deduce all the details while being the post-bird for it, but its existence means it deserves a spot in the list. I had proof of concept, after all."

The Moon Elven judges jumped in front of their Dark Elven brethren, defensive techniques hastily deployed. Their eyes were wide with the realization that their combined efforts would not be able to stop an assault from that cosmic *thing* hovering above the old man's palm. The feeling it exuded to their senses made their skin crawl, their warning mechanisms scream, and caused the distinct sensation of impending death to loom over them. While incomplete, woefully lacking, and not remotely true to what it could actually be, a Tower pattern existed before them.

The **Sun Law**.

Awe and fear alike rattled the Elves to their centers.

Closing his hand, the **Sun** was snuffed out in Artorian's palm like an evening candle, all the Mana it contained pouring back out into the world in the form of a stiff, hot, desert wind. More than an edified showcase, he could not sustain. The strain was no joke, and he didn't want to do that again anytime soon.

"Very educational." Brianna nodded, keeping her reaction indifferent to the display as her clothes fluttered, her proximity to Artorian unchanged. She deeply enjoyed the incredulous looks on the faces of her judges, who had suddenly learned an important lesson. A lesson that may or may not have been Brianna's goal.

Artorian felt a need to wrap up. "I know it may be a fruitless effort, given internal pattern making, but Flashrunes could easily have an Incarnate equivalent. Call the thought Flash Spells if you'd like? It's just meant to be another method of accomplishing an effect we already know about. This could be scaled up or down, but if you go down, then I do expect people are going to hold up the Incantations pitchfork, and point at it with a frown on their face."

Brianna mused with a smile, listening to her judges recover from a display that had not been meant to show off, but had left an impact regardless. "They *do* sound very similar, aside from the tiny details that Flash Enchantments would not require you to use gestures or words if you avoided the incantation route, and are still rooted in the requirement that one is using their Aura as a medium to create the representation of the pattern. Where Incantations are a rooted, very Persona-minded solution to a sudden-cast method. 'Flash' is an equal, but looser variant that I find very fitting as an Anima-minded solution."

She paced, more to tell her judges that it was fine not to play statue and shake themselves out. "The first requires detail, meticulously repeated. The second requires esoteric control, stringently held. I honestly believe you could go down all the way to Inscription-quality, with how we are assigning them, and see results."

Brianna paused to watch the caretaker Wisp furiously take notes.

"Of course…" Her face broke open into a big grin. With uncharacteristic drama, and vigorous flair, her hands copied Artorian's earlier explosion motion. "There is always the danger of the kaboom."

Artorian lost all seriousness, and broke down laughing.

Brianna grinned proudly, and swung her arm around his shoulders to drag him along on her walk while he was still wiping the tears from his eyes. Her judges looked on, bewildered. None of them dared say a word, and trundled along behind the duo. The old man had earned their respect, and they now knew better than to wonder what their Queen was up to. Brianna was Queen for a reason, and being friends with a walking fortress that kept its head in the clouds was not a feat they could accomplish.

Not one that could make suns at a whim, with the help of the land and surrounding Mana itself. They had never, *never*, seen Mana act that way towards anyone! For most of them, making Mana do what they wanted was a struggle. Like it had a mood, preferences, and apparently, a loyalty. Which was how they chose to interpret what they'd just seen and felt, because neither Essence nor Mana acted like that for any of them.

"Enough serious topics!" Brianna marched as she declared. "Come, spend some time with a friend, and join me on my enthusiastic walk through the woods away from work. I have thoughts about these Flashrunes. You are in luck, Administrator! For the Dark Elves are not only knowledgeable in the secrets of Runes, but we are Abyss-fine Aura controllers. We will develop these Flashrunes of yours, and perhaps Eternium can find a quicker way to teach them to you?"

"I'd like that, Bri-Bri." Artorian was feeling in too good a mood to fight the widely smiling Elf. "A walk it is, then! I believe I'll poke my nose into Camelot afterwards. I'm now curious if there are actual camels?"

Brianna giggled, sharing the nickname moment as she inserted her own brand of humor. "Sunny, when you inevitably poke your large, curious nose in, even if you do not see them, they are always in *spitting distance*."

CHAPTER TWENTY

The detour with Brianna took a few days over what had been expected. Enthusiastic walks through the woods had adventurous consequences, ending up in Brianna's home territory near the Silverwood. The path leading up to Brianna's home region was shrouded in mist, but Artorian had expected that. Unlike the Beasts they'd kept running into and had needed to spank out of the way, teaching more than a few of them that the Beasts were in Dark Elven territory, and not the other way around.

No animals were harmed in the clarification of these rules.

What Artorian had not expected on arrival was the atmosphere present in Brianna's corner of society. Nested in fields of Hyacinth, with symbols of forgiveness and devotion littering the space when the winding path through the woods cleared, the entryway was laden with the weight of respect one tended to sense in a graveyard. As they tread, the symbolism of the entrance gave way to a haunting festival. Strewn around the eight octagonal pagodas that made up the center of the hidden village serving as a welcome wagon, carnations and epitaphs were stuffed into every vacant spot where one could be made to fit. Only the walkways were kept clear, not a roof safe nor spared from Hyacinth decorations.

Artorian looked up, noting that this village was overshadowed by a monstrous stone stairway, leading up to an equally massive mausoleum that saw scores of Dark Elven traffic enter and exit between the brutalism-designed pillars and architecture.

The old man kept his thoughts to himself. They had clearly not built that landmark, but the sight kept coming second to the picture of serenity that stuck to his senses. Here was a place where life slowed down, was considered in full, and given the respect it deserved so one could hold their especially long funerals.

Cal, Artorian decided, had been very much right. People needed breaks, and he too, was people. "I think... I'll do as is silently suggested, and take it slow for a short while longer."

Brianna hooked an arm around his, her expression equal measures sad, and glad that the Administrator understood what they were about here. "Your insight has wisdom all on its own, Sunny. Come, let me teach you of the Dark and Moon Elves, and our ways."

Before tackling Camelot, Bri-Bri had ended up with a whole slew of interesting and fun little ideas to take a troubled mind off its worries. He'd gotten a tour, tried the local delicacies, gotten to nap in several high quality beds, attended a few groups all focused on their own thing, sat in on a Mana class or two, and generally played tourist. He'd been well received, but was uncertain if this was due to all the hushed whispers preceding him, or Brianna never being too far behind.

All in all, a well-organized, functional, getting-things-done society. Roads made of baked bricks were a good sign! He'd thought to sneak that detail to Lunella, if the Spring Court Wisps hadn't already unleashed their boredom upon the topic.

Palaces, pagodas, and citadels were common fare for structure choices. Though none of the zones were free from Hyacinth. Brianna had clearly opted for taking all the space she'd been allotted, and making a display of it. Traditional Dark Elven architecture, he was told, involved wooden structures and steep roofs. Both large and small buildings ought to have an odd number of compartments, with sets of beams and rafters to provide support. The depth of the interior of a house should be determined by the number of columns in each compartment, which was a nifty detail, even if Artorian's attention stuck with the choice of steep roof design. Curved at four ends, roof edges decorated with high relief motifs, the gables coated in art.

Elven interactions were friendly, but Artorian was completely thrown by the lack of family units as he'd come to expect them. There was also a rather notable lack of children, or anyone not Mage-ranked. Dark Elves kept together based on mutual interests, as far as he could deduce. Chosen family, rather than one knit by blood. Local environments were easily separated by those topics of interest, as the cultivation-focused ones were barren homes, while the Elves that had gotten stuck or couldn't cultivate had shifted their attention to crafts, arts, and other material to keep busy.

Those locations were anything but barren.

The furniture shop was exceptionally busy, noisy, and full of life. Filled with people all arguing with one another on the wood they could provide, how much, how soon, and what furniture they wanted from it. Including why they should get to have their furniture made before someone else. The whole social rumble was completely up Artorian's alley, and he was sorely tempted to wiggle his way in and argue for a cup, just to be involved in the liveliness.

That half the populace seemed to be using him for stealth practice was equally very amusing. A glance in their direction, and a set of curses followed by a Dark Elf stomping away was really putting a smile on his face. Nobody 'winning' made them try all the harder.

Today's start of the day had begun with a large outdoor breakfast; smoked meat and vegetables shoved into a hot, crunchy bread bun. After sucking his fingers clean from having perhaps one too many with extra spicy sauce, he'd gone off on one of his soapbox thoughts; involving a group of Elves being far too attentive on his commentary that some cloth awnings would go very well with how they'd designed their buildings, and Brianna arriving with a huge grin on her face.

She was flanked by a whole host of judges very politely holding bolts of cloth.

Artorian had the terrible feeling that he knew exactly where today was heading.

Brianna beamed, having totally not leaned into Rosewood's bag of tricks to use the old man as a mannequin. Her rolling commentary two hours later, really drove that home. "Exquisite! You prove to look exceptional in both Dark and Moon Elven attire. Though I admit, 'dapper rogue' did not suit you. A variety of greens? Much better. The lime stands out, and I expect it will match well with the surprise."

Artorian tugged on the sleeves of the 'Ao Dai' design, as it was called. His first fitting had been a simple white robe, as he'd seen Silentra wear. One of the Gnisp's hidden arms. That robe had turned out to be an 'interim' piece, until more suitable attire was chosen. That it doubled for measuring and fitting was this society's way of designing. "You mentioned this was for Moon Elves? I honestly can't say I understand the difference between 'Dark' and 'Moon' too well anymore, Bri. Apologies."

Brianna motioned at a Rune engraved next to the window, which glowed a moment before the entire wall slid away, parting like a screen door to let in some more light and providing a breathtaking view of the Silverwood Tree in all its sunrise glory.

The light streaming in through the window had been filtered, allowing only simple, mundane colors. The direct light that passed through the tree's canopy, on the other hand, revealed the ultraviolet patterns that shone yellow on Artorian's Ao Dai.

A myriad of blazing suns.

"*Ooooh*! It shimmers!" He gasped, hands shooting to the little designs to rub over them. There was no distinct feeling, but the visuals were certainly appealing. "How nice!"

Brianna agreed, already rifling through other bundles of cloth that more judges had come in to hold up. All of them acted exceptionally polite both in behavior and speech. She then paused, and stood next to one with a quirky brow. Artorian, noting the sudden expression, spot-checked the room but didn't find anything out of place. Just a line of Dark Elves that all... "Oh! They're all B-ranked! Is that it?"

A cackle from Brianna, who also donned a brand new blue and orange Ao Dai that hugged her form, confirmed that he was correct. "It certainly is now. Previously, Administrator, the Moon Elven few were a hand-picked selection that were meant to denote the best of the best. Since life in Cal, our culture has... mellowed."

"Gomei?" Brianna's soft words were followed by the hint of air displacement. A moment later, the familiar face of Dale's grumpy old Moon Elven instructor stood next to her. To Artorian's interest, Gomei was also dressed in an Ao Dai, though with a far more militant, exacting edge than his own.

"My Queen?" The general bowed with respectful demeanor, his question combined with his greeting.

Brianna nodded in approval, causing Gomei to stand at ease as she motioned towards him, while her eyes turned to Artorian. "My general is one of the most potent, powerful, and pristinely skilled masters of Presence."

Gomei stood a little straighter at that assessment.

"It was he who came to me with the idea to open the honor up to all those who climbed to the A-ranks. Such a feat, after all, is no minor trifle." Her hands eased over one another. "The mere act of gathering power in order to climb the B-ranks is insufficient for an Elf. We are all required to take the more difficult route, part of the virtue of what makes us distinct as 'Elves' in the first place."

Artorian leaned on his hip to think. "You mean, such as the difficulties in the A-ranks?"

"Not quite." She observed the ceiling, organizing her thoughts. "The burden of proof that we must show our **Laws**, that of understanding, is more exacting. My own **Law**, as example, barely paid me a hint of attention until I wrote an entire treatise on the topic. That got me from B-rank zero to B-rank one."

She emphasized the number. "One rank, Sunny. That's all three years of wracking my head in the finest royal glasshouses got me. Not counting the additional seven years it took me to gather enough Mana to allow the leap."

Artorian made an uncertain face at that detail. "Glasshouses?"

Brianna backpedaled. "Academies. High Elves make the majority... *made* the majority of their structures out of special glass. From the smallest domus to the grandest palace. They all look like conservatories. Gardens under glimmering glass, of which they were the prized showpieces. The purpose of the structure took a backseat to visual appeal."

Gomei made a similar surprised face. He'd never heard Brianna speak of her progress before, much less admit that there had ever been difficulties at all. His eyes then narrowed, as that by itself was incredibly suspicious behavior. When Brianna turned to look at him, however, he was back in his prior pose.

Stiff as a statue.

Artorian worked his fingers through his freshly braided beard, except that this time it was in the Elven style. Exactly how they got all that hair so finely together, bound in refined artwork was beyond him. He also thought they'd cheated and brought in experts. "So your society of Elves has 'Dark' as the B-rankers, and 'Moon' as the A-rankers. I honestly thought there was some kind of species difference, but I suppose I was wrong. My apologies again, and thank you for the show and tell."

He then resumed being enthralled with his ultraviolet patterns. He would ask why she'd actually called for Gomei afterwards, the clothing question was gnawing at him. "Bri, out of curiosity, these do not appear to be Wisp-made? Did your society really do all this themselves?"

Gomei's pride visibly increased by a step.

"By requirement, yes. We trade with the Autarchy for their spider silk." Brianna spoke more cautiously than before. A few saintly silent steps, and she was next to the Administrator to adjust one of his sleeves. Her voice dropped to even more of a whisper. That it could be heard easily if anyone wanted to was not an important detail. By the very act of her whispering, all those around her did their best to pay attention elsewhere. "Wisps do not help, much less show themselves, to people they neither trust, nor like. Only in your 'Avalon,' was it?"

A shocked look from Artorian made her reply with a wink, and a continued whispering as she cut his question off. "I heard you in the field. I prefer it over the New Fringe. I hope Lunella does as well. My people quietly helped them get settled. I promised I would, if you recall."

CHAPTER TWENTY-ONE

Panic averted, Artorian nodded and leaned in for Brianna to whisper her secret message. "Unlike other societies, the Dark Elven Tomb of Kha-Din, hidden under the forests of green, is fully self-sufficient. In Olympus, Odin's old playpen, he failed to get even the most basic of crafts together. It will *not* do for power to be more prominent than culture. Even if I must flex my power to ensure that remains the case."

Artorian pressed a digit to his lips, burdened with more questions that he was preventing from escaping. Brianna on the other hand, appeared to be able to read minds. That or his expression was an open book. "Clothing for my culture has been made less restrictive. Only my Dark Elves must be dressed as shadows. While I would prefer my entire realm in battle-ready uniform, that desire is not a detail I can create, much less enforce. We must make everything ourselves, or trade in kind. The type and quality of goods we actually like—that being Rune-inscribed everything, down to the socks—are simply not available. The energy may be aplenty, but permanently adding a Rune to an object is still an effort that can take months for a single item. Outside of Cal, that used to be years."

Pulling away to stop whispering, Brianna boldly stepped to the side of the room where a window and wall used to be, breathing in the fresh air as it breezed through a sea of leaves. "Enough of my woes, Administrator. I did indeed call Gomei for a reason, but it is exactly the reason why you think I would call for one of the most professed masters of Presence and Aura. Flashrunes require the kind of skill that only Moon Elves could possess, and I will not hide that the whole idea of quality in Runes has my attention."

Artorian sat on a small stone bench, lacing his fingers. He'd grasped where she was going with this. "Bri, it is not my place to micro-manage your choices. While Gomei and I have had our differences, the matter of Dale has been... smoothened. I appreciate the extra effort to ease the transition, but it is honestly not needed. If you want Gomei to take the project, then that is your decision. Administrator or not, I will not be the loose spoke in your wheel here."

That answered Gomei's question on why he was here, and where he stood with the old man. It also answered the source on the bizarre report on Flashrunes. It was a madman's creation! No wonder it was delegated to him. Someone else would get it wrong.

A look at Brianna, which got Gomei a wave in reply, was taken as official dismissal. He'd half expected his Queen to make him sit down and speak with the Administrator to smooth over old grievances they might have had, but the matter appeared sorted. He knew when to take the olive branch. Gomei vanished on the same gust of wind he'd arrived on, swiftly followed by the other Mages who were all there to hold fabric. They had interpreted Brianna's movement as a group dismissal.

She clearly did not mind, as it allowed her to forcibly exhale and deflate from her rigid posture. "I don't know how you do it, Sunny. To be so at ease around those that look on you with the highest of expectations. I try, but the steel slips back into my spine when I feel their eyes."

The old man got up and waddled up next to her, replying only by opening his arms wide like grandfathers did. One squeeze-hug later, and Brianna felt much better about life, the grandfather being his supportive self. "If that is a goal you wish to achieve, then I have no doubt that you will reach it, dear."

Exhaling through her nose in lieu of a laugh, she crossed her arms and turned back to the open scenery. "I know. I... Some victories come slower than others, and when the expectation of ease does not bear fruit, doubt creeps in. Doubt that is squelched by friends who remind you that you're doing just fine."

"And doing just fine, you are." Artorian agreed sagely, his eyes also turning to the massive set of stairs. "So, can I ask? Why a tomb? Is that some serious foreshadowing I need to be worried about, or memories entrenched in the past that are being resolved?"

"The past." Brianna covered her mouth with a hand, a half-giggle to her words. "You have the uncanny ability to amuse me, Sunny. Nobody makes my face ache with the peculiar pain of smiling as often as you manage it."

"I am glad for it!" The old man huffed and straightened, rattling off his tangential thoughts. "Really, though, no Wisps? I was convinced this wasn't going to be a problem."

Brianna shoved her nose towards the distance, angling off towards the Silverwood. "Wisps are divided into different factions, that part I am certain you knew. Think... about the difference between a Wood Elf and a Moon Elf. We're actually all the same as far as Elves go, but our beliefs and methods clash. We accomplish our goals differently, and accept different limitations in doing so."

She squeezed her own hands. "Tomb felt... fitting. After spending so much time in Niflheim, it has become a source of discomfort to be out in the open for too long. Life in a continent-sized maze will change one's perspective. The lack of Phogen, hive-minded fungus, and equally dastardly cheese also helps. Even if I am trying to re-implement cheese as a currency."

Artorian laughed. "Ha! Cheese."

The Queen's attention shifted to a large clearing visible in the distance, a single festive Mahogany at its center coated in hanging cloth. "We came to a very appealing agreement with Mahogany and Birch. They ring around the Silverwood on the surface, as a visible barrier."

Brianna made a broad circling motion, drawing a Mana diagram with layers that eased downwards. "Entrance to our Tomb aside, as we needed a space where others could come to trade and rest, we ring around the Silverwood beneath their roots, nested snugly in vast caverns between the passageways where the Autarchy likes to play. We are not cramped, as regardless of how that sounds, there is a premium of available space. Mahogany is happy, I'm happy, and Anansi is happy."

"Glad you found something that worked so well!" Artorian beamed, delighted at this good news as he studied the diagram. That was a lot of protection around the Silverwood, and it didn't even account for what the Wisps or Adam were doing.

"As I am equally glad that you are rarely in the habit of micro-managing, Administrator." She poked at him for fun, validating his earlier decision to trust her.

A hand then shot in front of her face at a thought, stifling her own smile. "There is, of course, the story of why we do not trade with the Wisps, save for that we do not intend to play along with their silly rules that change every week. We strongly prefer the Sodgi Caravans and their enthusiastic Foxes. Their headquarters being on a beach along the Coast of Rica also adds to their appeal. The dark may speak to me, but a strong drink on bright sands doesn't go misplaced either."

"Do tell!" Artorian released his Mana, telekinetically pulling a larger stone bench closer so they could sit and watch the flora. Thankfully, no stray pink sparks this time.

Brianna began after sitting. "When we first attempted nego-tiations, we learned several problematic things about our Wisp neighbors, and I don't mean that we didn't get the Spring Court to deal with. Trading for the major structures went easy enough. Then, they made them big and bulky, without finesse. That was the first cause for concern."

She frowned, pulling at the front of her own Ao Dai. "When we asked for clothing, they brought us rags with holes in them, loosely positioned where a head and arms needed to go, but care had clearly not been added."

She clasped her hands, her grin wide. "The Wisp who came to deliver and collect says, 'It's clothing. Deal's done.' I say that if the details of a deal don't matter, then I will happily bring it up every single time they want something."

Artorian laughed boisterously at that thought. "Wisps? Not holding to the most exact details of a contract? Them? *Haaaa hahaha.*"

Brianna held her face, her smile wide as she bobbed in the same boat. "Wisps don't do things for free for most people. You and yours receive much leeway, but you are also dealing with the Spring Court. The rest of us? Has to be with deals. Wisps don't show themselves to a whole lot of individuals, and when they do it is because they want something. Usually, something they cannot make themselves."

She smiled, but then steered the boat of their conversation in a slightly new direction. "The problem has honestly not been with the Wisps."

Artorian collected himself quickly, expression changing to a frown. "I have sincere doubts that you would be indulging them in trouble."

Brianna sat up, waving her hand in front of her face as that was not what she meant. "Trading with Wisps causes the 'craving what someone else has' problem. They can make anything, like the cheaters they are, but not make it of *quality* most of the time. Our clothing is one such example. There are maybe a handful of Wisps who can do quality, and I believe you actually know all of them already."

The Administrator took those thoughts and ground them

with a mental mortar and pestle. "Why would we need Wisps to make anything of quality? I know they worked magic in Avalon's early days, but surely we could just do that ourselves? I saw you had a whole bunch of people indulging in crafting professions."

Brianna took the moment to unpack the details. "Are you aware that our entire environment is actually made of unaligned Essence?"

A confirming nod made her continue. "Wisps have free access when it comes to making changes to Caltopia directly, via Cal's choice. The world does not block or hamper them. If they wish to turn a ton of sand into a ton of berries, they can just do that, so long as they know how to make berries, which is the big limiter."

She upturned her palm, and made a dagger appear that had a rather poor berry design for a handle, showcasing her point. She didn't properly know how to make a berry herself, and barely had the shape down. "While it would be convenient to consider a single Wisp nigh-omnipotent, they are all instead specialized in their own field. Keeping the inability to do or make certain objects and things close to the chest."

She vanished her dagger. "When it comes to structures, you want *air* Wisps. The purple ones. Preferably *not* from the Winter Court. Lapis Core dungeons, also the air ones, cannot build their own dungeons themselves, so the matching Wisps pick up all the slack. With their skills in abundant demand, it is not as easy to merely request that purple Wisps make something."

Brianna delved into Wisp lore for a moment. "Cal has first dibs on everything, and any Wisp not in the Spring or Summer faction is as reclusive as you recall them. Any Fall faction Wisp outright refuses to leave their dungeon's side unless it's a task for Cal, and any deal a Winter faction Wisp might offer you is never worth taking. The Spring Wisps work exclusively for Avalon, Cal, and their assigned cores; and the Summer ones are... almost never available. Meaning that they are extra *expen-*

sive if you get a slot. Luckily, their deals don't come with fine print, and that means a lot to me."

Artorian followed and inclined his head for part two, which the lady was gleeful to indulge on. "For anyone not a Wisp, the other reason that most people cannot simply raise the land and turn it into bars of gold, is because that particular *skill…*"

She paused and corrected herself. "Perhaps I should call it a privilege? Is barred behind being an A-ranker. The granular understanding of how to take solid energy and turn it fluid is innate to our being. B-rankers, whose Mana is all still liquid and glue in comparison, could not change a blade of grass any more than ordinarily possible. They cannot turn any material into the aspect components of its being."

Brianna took a breath. "As there is a frighteningly limited number of A-rankers who also have the knowledge one would only find in Master Transmuters, doing things the difficult way is becoming more of a norm."

Artorian pressed his hand to his Ao Dai, and thanked her with a short bow, as he doubted that information was anything but hidden knowledge, before asking a follow up query. "Does this cause problems?"

Brianna waggled her hand, delighted by the small gesture of appreciation and respect. "The problem is twofold. Other cultures of people look at successful Wisp trades and grumble. Or the Wisps themselves are denied their deals, put their foot down, and die mad about it."

"Ha." Artorian flatly released his words with more air than meaning. "Well, I suppose they can't all be like the Spring Court. I figured they would have their own problems."

"They do." Brianna's expression fell remarkably flat at the quip, matching Artorian's not-laugh. "The news doesn't travel past the edge of the forest, but with the Wisp-Gnome war over, the Wisp-Moth war is now in full swing."

"The *what?*" Artorian needed to clamp his eyes shut, and shake that sentence through his head a few times to mouth the words. "How big of a problem is this?"

"Nothing we can't handle." She laced her hands, cheerfully adding details. "In short, Moths like lamps, and Wisps are the ultimate lamps of the Moth tribes. Capture a Wisp, and that Moth tribe is now in charge of the other tribes. Thus: Wisp-Moth wars. The Wisps keep wanting to make complicated deals. The Moths keep trying to circumvent the deal to bag them. It would have all been a much bigger issue if a core component of the Moths' perspective wasn't that they need the Wisp healthy, alive, and making a lot of noise."

Brianna smiled with her teeth showing. "Wisps become brighter when they make noise, and they are well versed in the art of complaints. What a shame it is, then, that Winter Court Wisps create such satisfying blues."

Artorian held his forehead. "Out. Standing."

CHAPTER TWENTY-TWO

A week after his extended visit to Brianna's corner of the woods, which Artorian had begrudgingly spent cleaning up the last vestiges of some unavoidable paperwork, it had become time to pay the piper. Camel time.

His flight to Camelot had not been without kinks, as he'd taken the wrong left turn at a corner point called 'Albuquirky,' but in truth he blamed the most heinous, uncooperative rabbit he'd encountered when needing directions. The daft gray hare seemed convinced he'd been a doctor, and had steered him wrong twice before realizing that the rabbit was changing the direction of the signpost around. Why he oughta...

Artorian hit the ground just to grumble and move his feet.

Walking towards the nearby region at a sedate pace after landing, the wet slap of a dead fish impacting the rocky ground next to him brought his thoughts to a dead halt. Backpedaling to make sure he hadn't imagined that, Artorian swung his attention to the long-dead creature crusted in ice.

For a reason not yet known to him, its dead eyes showed only relief, like an insufferable journey was finally over. Artorian inhaled apprehensively. "Why am I getting 'happy to finally be done' vibes from a fish that's been dead a month?"

Another fish, a salmon with impact marks that were a dead giveaway for it having been used as a blunt instrument, crashed not too far from him in much the same state.

Died a month ago. Nothing but relief.

Artorian ran a hand over his bald head, looking up at the distance that these had angled from. "Camelot is in that direction. I haven't seen an outer wall yet. Also no castle? This stinks. Or is that the fish?"

He'd been informed Henry and Marie had a structure, and he should be very close at this point. So where was it? Blocking the sun with a hand, he peered to the distance, but found no kingdom's edge.

Another sound of rapid descent pulled his gaze upwards. Instead of a fish, this time the sky was raining a man. He thought that he shouldn't really call a falling object 'rain' when there was only one. Rain implied multiple…

"Gotcha!" Artorian whisked himself from his tangent to catch the cultivator before the man turned into a rain of splatters on the rocky plains. Another tangential thought that splatters on the ground also shouldn't qualify as rain. "Are you all right?"

The staggering cultivator was scrawny for a cultivator. A B-rank… zero? That wasn't right, B-rank something, sure, but not zero. Artorian slapped himself for forgetting the circumstances-du-jour.

Getting to his feet with help, the man dressed in well-organized rags brushed himself off. Getting chunks of dead fish, scales, and everything except for the smell out of his attire. Also a stain… right there…

Artorian waved a hand over the cultivator and cleaned the man without a second thought. "Better?"

Inhaling like this was the first fresh air he'd had in months, the man's facial expression melted into a blissful mixture. "My divines... Two blessings in one day. Thank you, kind sir. Thank you."

"I am..." Straightening up, the scrawny, tanned, middle-aged man with a mop of cropped hair reached out a hand accompanied by a severe smile. Both of which dropped when his brown eyes froze to the sight, his tan giving way to a pale hue, as all the blood escaped from his face.

The sound of a slow, pained, throaty inhale that made one of those higher pitched yelps was all that followed.

Artorian leaned into the joke. "That's a little difficult to say."

He inhaled to make the same throaty, elongated yelp. "A name really would be better. Or have people lost their names all of a sudden?"

"Torburn Flagstaff." The staggered man choked out, his hand shooting back up, a tremble impossible to hide living within his movements.

Artorian shook the grip, but did not let go. "Is this a good time to ask why you're about to invoke brown magic? The only person who I know has managed playing the brown note with musical means is Hans, but if others know it, I can't say my inner five year old isn't intrigued."

The hard left from expected conversation brought some life back to Torburn's face. "Oh... uh... I..."

He looked down at the handhold, and realized that he was not the one currently not letting go. "Do... Do you remember anyone by the name of Ellis? If I got the description in the story right, I think you turned him into a door?"

"I do, and I did." Artorian confirmed with a calm nod, dying to know where this was going. "Continue."

"I... was his friend. We were in the old guild together. There are a lot of people who don't know who you are, or have only been made aware of you by story, song, or tale..." Torburn stopped cold at the sudden darkness in the old man's expression. To be expected, really. Even the great Kere Nolsen had been rumored to break down when the baron of some mountain land joked that songs had been made about him. Making a fake one up on the spot had been enough to bring the Slayer of Shades to his knees! Or so the story went.

Torburn swallowed hard and quick.

"I think this 'story' is going to make people start off on the wrong foot with me." Artorian raised an eyebrow as he surmised the situation. Bothered not about the story existing, but that it was going to prevent him from indulging in a favorite pastime. Sneaking in somewhere and poking his nose in to cause a little havoc, just like Chasuble. "You may call me Sunny, Torburn. Though, this has given me concern for people's mental wealth and hel-being."

He stopped to frown, correcting himself. "Mental health and well-being."

Torburn beaded sweat, muttering. "I honestly liked the first one a bit better…"

Artorian couldn't help it. He agreed. "I think so too."

Releasing the grip made Torburn feel better, who tried to adjust his ragtag clothing to no avail or notable result. He knew he was still going to need to answer. "Thank ye for the kindness, and not turning me in a door."

Artorian nodded with a foul feeling in his stomach, but hid it well enough. "Are you well, Torburn?"

The nervous man tried to get his bearings, but rambled off his feelings. "I wasn't. Then I got out of the Camel-lot. Getting over that border, even the hard way, made my day. I was expecting a hard fall with how gravity is supposedly lethal outside the zone and all."

Artorian held a hand up. "Stop."

Torburn froze.

"Gravity is lethal outside the zone? What zone? This isn't Eternium." Artorian frowned swiftly, eyes narrowed as the gears in his head were oiling up for a spin.

Torburn sheepishly pointed over his shoulder, in the exact direction Artorian was heading. "The Camel-lot?"

Artorian closed his eyes, pruned his lips, made a few facial expressions that indicated coping. He dropped his hand before his face resumed a mask of neutrality. "For once, just once, I want there to be no problems when I arrive somewhere I was expecting them. For them to be solved before I arrive. No? Too much to ask?"

Torburn meekly shrugged. "Apologies, Sir Sunny."

"Why the politeness?" Artorian raised an eyebrow, feeling like he wanted to know at least that.

"A-ranker feels, sir." Torburn rubbed his arm arms with a mutter, his stance similar to that of an unwelcome visitor who had taken off his cap and was now awkwardly standing in the doorway to address the noble of the household.

Artorian hung his head. "That... Yes, that makes sense. I forget that telling exact ranks was always a pseudoscience to most Mages. But honestly, Torburn, you're not acting like much of a Mage. Damage from a hard impact? That should be past-tense for you."

"I've been a Mage for two fortnights, sir." The cultivator shrugged meekly and clarified, getting more confident in responses as the clock ticked. Not getting smote when the A-ranker had several opportunities and reasons to was a healthy sign. "It's the only reason I braved the border. Gettin' in was easy. Gettin' out... well. The elf had to toss me."

Artorian immediately pointed at the dead fish. "Is that what this is about?"

Torburn looked, failing to suppress a grin. "No, sir. That's the morning ritual."

Artorian felt like he was balancing an Iridium brick on his head with how poorly that detail fit in any current puzzle. "I'm... I'm going to need some stories, Torburn. Would you do that for me?"

"Yes, sir." Torburn looked over his shoulder, expression falling flat. "I'm going to have to go back... aren't I?"

Artorian upturned his hand, conjuring a full plate of steaming food into it from seemingly nowhere. Nowhere being a storage bracelet he'd gotten better at using, as the stasis feature had proven most useful for keeping fresh things fresh. He wasn't going to say anything about that part of the sleight of hand. "Why don't you start by taking this fat, steaming plate of sausages and mashed potatoes, drenched in sweet onion sauce? Sit with me, and get some of that stress to go away? *Hmm?*"

The question had been kind, full of grandfatherly support. Torburn unfortunately could recognize a fox from a thousand yards, and grasped that not taking the... plate of...

Thoughts were thrown out to drown in the river as he was on the ground with the plate in his hands moments after, hungrily stuffing his face between making inappropriate sounds, and suffering a single manly tear from enjoying the meal. He spoke with his mouth full of food. "I know Mages don't need to eat, but it's sho good. It's sho gooood."

Artorian patted Torburn's back, made a fire with the raise of a finger to the tune of one of Ember's earliest showcased tricks, and tapped the ground to mentally ask it for some comfort. A pink flare from his Aura went with it, which had Artorian pulling his palm away like it had just been zapped by a moody fence.

The rocky ground morphed, churning into a circular sitting area with room for a firepit, as earthen works rose smooth as tumbled stone for eight people to lounge on. Artorian rubbed his hand, eyes narrowed at his own misbehaving Aura. "One day... I'm going to know what's causing this. When I have time."

Torburn's mouth gaped open at the display of power. His voice a bare whisper. "We can *do* that?"

"Yes?" Artorian waggled his injured hand at the scene, both shaking it out and covering up that none of this had been intentional. "You eat. Then the story. Old man is confused. Old man wants answers. Preferably before I need to enter Camelot. The circumstances I was told do not match the circumstances that are here."

After some time lounging and enjoying the air, Artorian noted Torburn was using his clothing to clean his face off.

Deploying his Starlight Aura to make cleanliness a constant made Torburn gawk. The world of Mages was one of pure wonder. The fresh B-ranker, that may have actually been B-rank zero, and not something higher as Artorian had thought, looked ready to talk. Artorian now also felt like he had a better grasp of Brianna's concerns with rank-gauging. If even he was getting it sorely wrong...

Well-fed and free from smiting, Torburn was a wealth of information.

Artorian had to make a list to keep all the factors straight, but felt certain that keeping a summary of events was going to do him more good than listing the entire tale. In order: there *used to be* good structures in Camelot. Now, it was a tent city bordering the quality of a shanty town. If being generous, a fishing village. Due to rocks they have found that burn easily, the main lighting in Camelot was red. Someone named Elizabeth was the reason the rum was always gone. The self-appointed rulers were chickens with their heads cut off from how much they keep running around like it, and those same rulers have made it a lethal endeavor to leave their boxed-in coop.

Artorian rubbed at his eyebrows, and continued with his list. Trade was scarce, the currency changed every month, haggling and bartering led to fights, and for some reason... some unfathomable reason... the only person in Camelot interested in being a fishmonger imported his fish from Atlantis, instead of catching it in the sea that was right next door.

Because Mages needed no food to eat, or could easily learn how to draw what they need from their surrounding environment, the local bunch also had no drive to do a whole lot that didn't directly benefit them. Torburn spent an entire hour explaining to the old man that this was old guild behavior that had been ingrained. "No pay? No work!"

The contrast to Avalon and the Dark Elven Tomb of Kha-Din was painful.

All the guild Mages wanted to receive something of value

for any effort they might add to something, even if that something was of crucial importance. They had wants, but no real needs, and cultivating was difficult to the point of impossible once one hit the Mage ranks. Beforehand, it was easy! Then suddenly, 'the wall.'

Artorian was aware concepts such as 'bottlenecks' were a prominent problem, but Torburn made delicate hand motions to insist that this was a different hurdle altogether. That an unseen force was stopping them from further growth, rather than their own efforts being a steep climb.

Artorian tried to sum up the Mage situation in Camelot, the situation such a far cry from Brianna's clean operations that it was difficult not to draw constant comparisons. "A group of people that all want things, but are not willing to do anything to attain those things without being provided something for it. With the rulers not managing to fill the niche."

Torburn nodded with a tired sadness, his voice labored. "When I was still a C-ranker, I was invested in where the food came from. Where I can get clothes. Basic needs and necessities. A roof over my head. Another person to huddle next to for some conversation. Then Magehood attacked. The conversion process was swift, smooth, and easy. Then afterwards... All I still needed was the huddle, and could no longer find it. I drifted out of my prior groups rather quickly. It's not that I disliked them or they disliked me? There was a disconnect that... I honestly don't know how to describe it. I just wasn't part of the group anymore."

Artorian grumbled, pushed himself up, and pressed his hands to his hips as night was beginning to give way to the next day. The red glow over the next hill was rather obvious now, the reddish hue had grown in intensity all night. "Looks like I have a lot of work to do. You said the fish-fight is a morning ritual? So, every morning?"

Torburn nodded, his face grim at needing to return. Artorian just chuckled. "So, where are you off to? Hoping for anything in particular?"

The cultivator's mind chugged to a halt at the question. The old man had never really said he'd be dragging him back. "I... I was hoping for some unity in the community. Not some squishity in the vicinity."

That didn't rhyme very well, but Artorian let it slide. He understood what Torburn meant.

"Are you willing to do work for it?" Artorian leaned as he spoke, far too flat to be natural. "Or is the tit-for-tat bird trade a necessity?"

Torburn felt cold sweat. "Sir... we have danced around this topic for an entire day and night. People from the old guild want something for their trouble. We are, on the other hand, very used to threats in order to make us get up and go. I may not be gaining anything new, but walking away with what I have is a mighty motivator. If it means I live another day, I will go delve into the dungeon. It used to be much safer than telling a superior officer anything akin to the word 'no.'"

"I was honestly taking that tidbit for granted, Torburn." Artorian chuckled and quipped. "The question is sincere. Because if you're fine with putting in some effort, then I am fine pointing you to a community where people are working together to make something for everyone. As to threats... I was going for the 'what's in it for you' angle. How did you like the sausages?"

Torburn had completely forgotten that those had to come from somewhere. His stomach growling for another helping. "They... they can pay in sausages?"

"Avalon." Artorian pointed the way. "Leave your pride at the door. Ask how you can help. You will be... very surprised as to the amount of people that will want to sit next to you at the fire, interested in your opinion of the latest sausages. Pleasant travels, Mr. Flagstaff."

Torburn looked in the suggested direction, and when he turned for more questions, the old man was gone. Torburn steeled his face, said the magic words, and went. "Gift horse. Mouth. Don't do it."

CHAPTER TWENTY-THREE

Artorian arrived at the border of the Camel-lot, and instinctively knew when he'd crossed it, regardless of there being no wall or otherwise visual indication. Marie's Aura was... everywhere. Thinned and widespread, but pervasive, and occupying the space like it was owned territory.

Turning to eke a toe over the line back out, Artorian found weight and pressure began to accumulate. As if to drop on him like a crushing boulder, ominously hovering just out of sight. "That's a very 'rocks fall' method of escape prevention, Marie."

Making one's Aura the unseen wall was one way to prevent people from exiting, he supposed. Though, making it act like this? That had to be an expensive Mana investiture. Waving a hand up and down, Artorian could feel that Marie's field was blocking Mana transfer. Any technique expenditure or loose Mana in the air within her bubble, she was slowly taking. Essence appeared to be getting through her barrier and into the region, but Mages not Marie were getting the short end of the stick.

He *could* expand his own Aura and challenge the sovereign space that Marie was claiming, but that would inform her of his presence, which… he wanted to keep quiet for now. It was a surprise that she wasn't rushing over, but he'd take the boon.

Artorian pondered the problems about stopping Mana flow in an area. "Explains more of Torburn's cultivation problems, if he's on Cal's allowed-list. Which, now that I think of it, was fairly certain to be a no-go to all old guild people? Maybe he's amending the exceptions list? Or perhaps Torburn was too close to Magehood."

He scratched his beard and chin, thinking of grabbing Marie's Aura, and joinking it. No, that was no different from his flaring his own Aura out, and he'd already decided against that idea. Better to go meandering for a while and see what else he could suss out. He guessed Henry's was holding down the other half of the zone. Speaking of, where were these camels? He still hadn't seen one!

"Torburn wasn't a humanized one, right?" Surely he'd have caught that. Artorian shook that off. "No, no. He said he was old world. That means base-model human. No bells. No whistles."

He settled on stowing the back of his hand rather than letting it strike. If he could pinch and twist Marie's Aura anytime, then he wanted a better reason. "Yes. It is not at all the case that I want to snoop around. Clearly."

He said the words, but failed to convince himself. "Ah, who am I kidding? Let's go see what kind of trouble I can cause before I have to perform my janitorial duties. Speaking of… I should likely find a nice **Law** to drop down to *now*, rather than later."

Folding his arms, he closed his eyes, and entered Cal's Tower simulacrum.

Dropping down was always easy. However, since he had zero strong sympathetic connections to anything in the Tier twelve to fourteen range, it meant dropping down the hard way. That *oomph* math formula was going to be very unhappy, but he could keep some **Love**-quality Mana in the back pocket as a just in case. Not much, though.

He mentally skipped down the stairs in Cal's simulacrum. The place was still a mess of tangled wires, but Cal had clearly put some elbow grease in after the last snide comment. Some of the cables had management to them now, bound together in neat rows.

He paused on floor forty-two out of curiosity, as he could have sworn he got nudged by a node holding the concept of a **Towel**. Nudged was a nice way of saying it had twisted up and snapped at him, missing the intended target.

"Cheeky!" Artorian smiled wide, as this was someone's ancient, incredible joke. Tier forty-two had the normal six nodes, all of them represented as basic, glowy orbs. The contents of which were:

Knowledge

Questions

Answers

Towel

Probability

Improbability

"Alright, that's very, very amusing." Artorian chuckled, dropping down to floor forty-one, which landed him on the **Law** of **Hitchhiking**. "Probably a coincidence…"

He continued traversing downwards, planning to stop at Tier fifteen. Passing floor thirty changed that plan, as he was touched by **Acceleration**, and suddenly moved considerably faster. He overshot his planned stop by three whole floors as he didn't have anything to stand on, skidding to a stop near the Tier twelve node of **Sleep**, while barely holding to the edge of the floor it resided on. "Ope! Gotcha!"

Pulling himself up onto the Tier twelve floor and rolling away from the edge, he sat up before looking around. "Alrighty! Floor twelve. What have we got?"

Around him, seemingly asleep aside from the node of **Sleep**—which was having a giggle fit, if the flickering light was anything to measure by—hovered five other glowing sconces.

"Why are they sconces?" Normally it was floaty orbs, with

other orbs in their orbit. Artorian cast some suspicious side-eye at the **Sleep** node, but asked nothing further as he scanned the space to discern its occupants.

Sleep

Empyreal

Knock

Sonder

Zeal

Kenopsia

The point of interest for Artorian was the third one. The rest he recognized easily, even if he had not expected many of those other familiar **Laws** to sit on this Tier. "Knock... knock. It doesn't *sound* familiar, but it *looks* familiar."

A yawn broke from the **Sleep** node. A sandy, spotted Cheshire C'towl sporting a cheshire grin faded into existence atop the sconce's light. The voice leaned feminine, with the natural purr of a half-asleep feline. "*Mmmm.* It's the color, pillow-boy. The color."

Artorian blinked at a node not his own talking to him so... so... *casually.* He immediately had a thousand questions. "How...?"

"*Shhh.*" The Cheshire moved a claw in front of its mouth, hushing him. "No wake-y wake-y. Ellis Henaren, Deputy of the Adventurer's Guild. Misty opaque energy. Used to be on the eighth Tier."

"Thank you?" Artorian shielded his mouth with his hand, hushing back. His initial question deftly answered as he instantly remembered Ellis. He'd *just* had a conversation about the man with Torburn. **Knock** had been Ellis's law? The man who he'd turned into a door? That... That was hilarious!

The... striped? Cheshire C'towl had just changed designs, or had done so when Artorian hadn't looked at the node. The difference was dreamlike, and... that part, at least, made sense. The shifting C'towl then grinned at him with lidded eyes. "Always wanted to meet you."

DENNIS VANDERKERKEN & DAKOTA KROUT

Artorian pressed his fingers to his sternum as he spoke at normal volume. "Am I a topic of gossip up in Heavenly land?"

The C'towl rolled onto its back, its reply hushed. "*Shhh*. No wake-y wake-y. No. I'm no demon, but I did call dibs on you, back when we were only looking at Merli of Morovia. That talent for **Sleep** didn't pass me by."

The oversized winged cat winked at him with another grin. "If not for… the circumstances, you would have ended up with me. Forgive this old feline for having a soft spot for a kitten. Did you never notice how easily the talents and skills for **Sleep** came to you, compared to the rest? You may have strong opinions on the topic of talent, but I knew. I always knew. It is no mystery why you gravitate to protecting hopes and *dreams*. You are gifted on this road, naturally inclined to nap along the path. That **Love** requested you… well. She's **Love**. Who was I to deny my kitten? I bumped my head on your butt, and pushed you from the nest."

The C'towl purred extra loud, its grin coiling to form a smile. "No regrets, my kitten. Only pride."

Artorian felt dazed. "Is that why the sleep Aura was the only one I was useful with? Fate? I don't like that…"

"No, kitten." The C'towl reached a paw out to very gently bap the top of a bald head. "Inclinations. Paths you would have taken regardless. No fate. Never fate. Not for you. Your very prancing defies it, and I delight at the cups you push from the table. Your choice in self-development. Your methods to madness. Your soft paws and the way they brush against the Essence. They would have led to superior skills in the arts of **Sleep**. Even as the next **Love**, this was not suddenly going to become false, kitten."

That set Artorian at ease.

The Cheshire, now starry-pelted C'towl, raised its paw away and pulled it back, loafing above its sconce. "Whisper, kitten. **Sleep** knows you have questions. You get two. Then you must go, or the ruckus from below will start to irritate me."

"Ruckus?" Artorian snapped up, too late to realize that had

taken one of his two allowed slots. He slapped his mouth over his hand, but it was too late. Him and his big mouth! He obviously wanted to ask more, but when a Heavenly ranked being set you a limitation, you didn't question that limitation.

Sleep snickered without making much sound, but the head bobbing and facial motions made the intent clear. "It is too early for the answer, kitten. You can do little to nothing for it. **Sleep** will tell you regardless. I do not agree with your close-ones, who would keep things from you for your health. You are a kitten gifted at noticing. Do not give in to slumber, but listen to **Sleep**."

The C'towl winked, voice dropping further and making Artorian's ears strain. "The Tower. I know you have the memories of Shaka. He came to tell us that **Sun**'s prodigy would give them to you. What you were not told is a complication we, as Heavenlies, contend with daily. That complication is that there are more concepts, meanings, and purposes crammed into the first five floors of the Tower than there are nodes in all the rest of it."

The Cheshire C'towl trailed off to let Artorian grasp the magnitude of that math, before giving him the second half of the formula. **"Each node can hold secondary, tertiary, quaternary, and many more meanings than merely the one at the forefront. Now, my clever kitten. Why would this be noisy?"**

Artorian's mind reeled. "More concepts live in the first five floors, than all the rest combined. But… that…"

He held his mouth and chin, bewildered. "That's so… That's terrible Tower design!"

Sleep exhaled a laugh that was one long, elongated high-pitched noise. A laugh without a laugh, but with the full facial gratuity of one. "Oh, kitten… if the others heard you. You would have packed on so much ire from speaking those little words."

Artorian turned as pale as Torburn.

Sleep soundlessly slammed its paw down, slapping the ground with that laugh-ridden expression plastered on the cat's face. The beast was heaving, and somehow managed to stay abyss near silent the entire way through. When the Heavenly did speak, the whisper was once again there. "*Oh*, oh kitten. I miss not having you under my wing. I never even had you as an Ascended, and I miss it still. Worry not your pale cheeks, few like to roam this equally pale imitation of the Tower. I am here because it is silent. Or was…"

The C'towl then looked at the floor, the sneer one of irritation. "Since it became possible to peek, watch, listen—and if the circumstances are correct, meddle—we have been biding, and much more attentive to those who would reach to us, and those we could reach to. All those other concepts in the lower nodes see this as a golden chance to stop being a secondary meaning, and push the rest around. They will also get a chance before the higher nodes do, with how the energy density issue works out."

Artorian bit his lip as his color came back. He had an easy seven questions, and only one left to spend. "I… I see."

The C'towl returned to a lounging position. Its face mushed to both front paws as the **Law** attentively looked at him. The swish of the tail showed clear curiosity. **Sleep** wanted to know what the question was going to be!

Fiddling with the sleeves of his Brianna-gifted outfit, identical even here where he wasn't present physically, he frowned, trying to mull it over. "I'm… I'm not sure what to ask. There's so many. I want to follow up. Or jump to philosophical problems about Essence that I haven't understood yet. Or hear more about why so many meanings are crammed into the first five floors…"

"That last one." **Sleep** stretched broadly while purring back, its expression… dangerous. "Is because the Tiers of the Tower relate to energetic density. A requirement to make refining Quintessence work properly. Or work more easily. In the days where souls pursued their hearts desire, with the intent of striving for the greatest meaning, there was no problem."

An unhealthy amount of attention was suddenly spent on

Sleep's claws, the deadly stabbers slowly extending like sharp bones from a mound of sand. "We would hear their pleas, their hearts, their drives, and we would pull them up the rest of the way when they looked at us like we were all that mattered in all the world. What is Essence *cost* when faced with a kitten who wants nothing more than to spend their life delving into what you stand for? To **Love** spending their eons and eternities in the one topic that makes them smile with glee like no other? This is the way."

The claws shimmered, and Artorian gulped, staying as quiet and unmoving as he could. "When the focus shifted to choosing **Laws** because of their power, rather than what they were meant for... the decline commenced. Lower, and lower, the quality of cultivators became. Until the fourth and fifth Tier was as high as they could go by themselves. So long did this last that **Laws** had to descend and cram into the lowest floors for attention. For survival."

Artorian held his own hands, tactically remaining silent as his eyes flicked from the dreamlike claws to the face of the speaker. There was more than one way to drag a soul into eternal slumber, and those looked like they'd definitely do the job.

With a *snikt*, the C'towl stowed its claws. Yawning hard, the oversized cat bristled and stretched itself out. "Think of your question, kitten. Think of it loud, when next you **Sleep**. I am out of energy, and my flare of anger has spent much of the energy I would have wished to retain. No more time for talks. Up you go, kitten."

The C'towl winked, before winking out of existence. "The concept you're looking for is on... floor fourteen. **Valor** and **Glory** send their grumbly regards."

CHAPTER TWENTY-FOUR

Artorian was given very little choice in the matter. With a push to his butt, he found himself on floor thirteen as if he'd been dropped in by the scruff of the neck. One blink was all he had to be aware of the transition. Pre-blink? Floor twelve. Post-blink? Floor thirteen.

He exhaled deep, hands pressing to his knees. "Celestial feces. Talking to a Heavenly-ranked being is stressful. I'm not dumb enough to test a C'towl, much less a bigshot. I didn't know if I was going to get cup-slapped from a table, or…"

He shook his head to clear the thoughts, inhaling hard and changing tracks. Artorian shelved the question allotment until later, and took in his new environment now.

Surrounding him as normal orbs of energy, Tier thirteen held:

Hunger
Bone
Violence
Sand
Annoyance
Greed

"*Huh.*" Artorian mused, looking back and forth between the lot of them. "Well, I definitely don't want to stay here longer than I have to. This reeks of a rough time. This floor is too spooky for me."

Climbing up one floor like it was a knotted rope to be braved, Artorian got to his feet on Tier fourteen and right away knew something was wrong. Only *one* node was bright to him. The other five were surely there, but... they felt like knights having taken a knee, yielding the floor. When he understood what the concept of the active node was, he spoke. "Well, I can't say I'm surprised."

On floor fourteen, the nodes were:

Redemption
Compassion
Devotion
Retribution
Empathy
Sympathy

A line of concepts indicative of a flourishing, Silver Era of kings and castles. Likely the very era that had been responsible for the game of the same name, which he enjoyed so much.

Walking up to the only glowing orb, he sighed, and shoved his hands into his pockets. A glance was spared at **Compassion**, the yielding orb feeling like it laid a hand on his shoulder before Artorian spoke to the bright node. There for him, both as a sword and as a concept. "Hello, **Redemption**."

"Greetings, Artorian." The orb of light rumbled with the voice of a heavily armored grand paladin; one of honor, ethics, and fierce purpose. The exertion alone was filled with enough strength to drag Artorian away from the speaker without him lifting either of his metal feet. The floor scraped beneath his tink-tink's with a screech.

His own expression remained flat-faced as the node boomed out laughter. Tibbins would surely feel a tingle in his metaphorical tail from this one, because Artorian didn't have a better expression to respond to such an event. Two Heavenlies in one day? What was the world coming to?

"I… was told to come with the regards of **Valor** and **Glory**?" He pulled his hands from his pockets, daring to venture. Artorian's follow up sentence cut down to the thought of one as the booming laughter stopped like a sword in danger of unsheathing.

"*Yes.*" The orb's words sent a tremor through the walls as it decreed; far more measured, and far less amused. "They have strayed. Strayed without meaning to, but strayed nonetheless. I was requested. I shall answer."

Artorian swallowed. "This part, I *am* surprised about."

"Ask your question." The orb brightened, responding in the tone of another decree, rather than a conversational manner. "I know of you, **Love**'s chosen one. **Redemption** shall not deny you. I have much to accomplish with *you*, as well."

"Well, that's ominous." Artorian tried to lighten the mood, his hands deciding they'd rather be in the pockets after all.

"No. Artorian." The orb trembled the floor as it remeasured its words. "There are no inauspicious events on the horizon. It is merely the truth. For your coming task, **Retribution** shall be your shield. **Compassion** shall be your sword. Then, when all is said, and all is done, I shall turn my attention onto you. When that time comes, we will relieve you of burdens that you should not be carrying, yet choose to regardless. I will not accept the mantra that 'someone else would have gotten it wrong.' I will *only* accept my namesake."

Artorian swallowed again, cherry picking his words with an individual that made Artorian think of a spearpoint. An honorable one that did not mean him harm, but a spearpoint nonetheless. "I… How can I help?"

"My energy is limited, Artorian. Choose the implements of **Redemption**." The orb, immediately after the declaration, lost half its brightness and luster all in one go.

The old man frowned, looking at his own hands. The answer that sprung to mind was likely not something the Heavenly was going to like. However, it was his answer. "I… I apologize, Heavenly of **Redemption.** I already have all I need. With you, I have the fairness that I lacked. The means to the path I wish to walk. The method in which I seek to tackle one burdened with **Glory**."

"To meet one's friends fairly, when they are foes, is the hallmark of a pure soul." The orb shuddered the floor once again as the Heavenly took apart Artorian's meaning. "If powerful footing is what you wish from me, Artorian, then footing is what you shall have. May you meet your friends on the field, and may they be aware of your sincerity for their plight. Know, before I fall to silence, that you would have made an *excellent* paladin of **Redemption**. You walk the path. **Love** is well off to have you, and when you rise to that station, know that I shall be delighted to follow in your wake. Call on me when you need me, walker on the road of the righteous soul. May you deliver us to the place we need to be most."

Artorian chuckled, his cheeks flushed pink. "That is… That sounds like very high praise. Thank you."

He looked around for a moment, a question striking. "No **Apathy**?"

An armored finger of light formed to point upwards, a less intense version of **Redemption's** voice speaking. That energy he'd mentioned was running out. "Tier fifteen."

Artorian realized he should not be asking questions if they had no weight. **Redemption** would answer him. But clearly that was done at the cost of the amount of strength left available. "No more questions, dear Heavenly. *Rest.* I shall go do what I must."

The bright node chuckled like a bet had been lost. "I owe **Sleep** a coin."

Artorian felt incredible elation at being at the forefront of seeing Heavenlies pull the same kind of betting pranks that he and his friends did, with Cal at the helm. He grinned wide. "Better make it a pillow!"

More chuckling followed, but Artorian felt jerked awake.

He opened his eyes in the same spot of land in the Camellot, having freshly crossed the border. He clicked his tongue. "Still no camels!"

Flexing his hands, he gave himself a once-over now that a Fourteenth-Tier **Law** sat snug and comfortable in **Love**'s seat. Artorian suddenly had doubts that other **Laws** would be as okay with this particular jumping around he did. He had accomplished it, so clearly it was possible. Perhaps not with the same kind of leeway, on the other hand.

Artorian tugged at details of his Ao Dai, even if nothing was out of place. He had meddling to do, and friends to… interrogate? That really wasn't a kind word. Also not normally a word that lived in his lexicon? What was it doing at the forefront of his thoughts? Artorian looked around suspiciously. "Interference? Who would dare? I shall show them the meaning of the back of my hand!"

Nothing visually changed, but the thought in his mind fled like a bandit who'd been noticed by the local authorities. "*Hmm. That was strange.*"

Making sure that his Aura was a veritable fortress to keep external influences out, he kept the six invested ranks steady, then cycled through some defensive concepts to have them at the ready. Powered by a Tier fourteen **Law** or not, best to be prepared, and have ready-fire-responses waiting in the pocket. He was expecting a fight, after all. It would not do to get blindsided by a **Glory** fireball. If Marie even had that in the repertoire. "No reason not to have a just-in-case."

Artorian then did some quick math. "Fourteen times… six? Yes, six ranks in my Aura. Means an *Oomph* of… sixty plus twenty four. So an *Oomph* of eighty-four. **Revelry, Valor, Glory,** and **Berserkr** are all ninety-eight *Oomph* at a single rank. Twelve points makes a big difference…"

He suddenly realized that he only knew four out of the six **Laws** on that floor. "I'm curious about what the last two on that Tier are… Anywho, so I'm a bit below both Henry and Marie, and they're both at… Let's say A-rank one for safety, because I don't actually know how to calculate A-rank zero. I should… definitely do that when I find them."

He shelved that onto the to-do list, and continued. "So if they want to put up a fight, and have no tricks or Mage-quality gear, they will need to stuff all their might either into their body, or into their Aura. Body for me is out; I have to face them with Aura regardless of what they choose. How am I gonna do that… if they suddenly prove to have gotten good at Aura?"

A glance at the field he was in made him doubt that either Henry or Marie were going to opt for the Aura route, if they were fielding it in order to make zone borders. "My bet will have to be that they choose the body option. I think they're only pulling the sovereign space trick off because they're part of Cal's A-rank infinite-Mana test. That also means I shouldn't use any techniques that expend Mana from me. If my formula changes to five times fourteen, I just lose."

With only one rank invested in his body, that meant the *Oomph* score of his physical being was a measly fourteen. Alright, that was a *lot* in normal cultivator measurements, and he was doing it in the A-ranks. So a B-rank zenith was still not going to do much, but he wasn't dealing with B-rankers as the goal. "I'd like more to work with… I've been doing this all with raw scores, but I'd like to add tips, tricks, and tools into the arsenal to make that eighty-four score more flexible."

He thought of the floor he'd just visited, and had an epiphany. "They… come when called, don't they?"

Extending his hand, he spoke the word, curious if it would work. "**Compassion**."

A pull on his Mana later, and the Albion Principe hovered before him. The blade had teleported over with the musical tones of a zither, but remained cautiously out of his extended grip. Like it knew better, and Artorian needed to catch up.

The old man snapped his hand back when he remembered the emotional cascade that came along with physically touching a weapon of this type and caliber. "Whoops! That slipped my mind. Thank you, **Compassion**. How… am I supposed to give you a good swing without **Sorrow** as a balancer?"

Another pull on his Mana, and the black katana popped into being like an indignant child, furious that it had been picked second. The blade fumed out small black clouds above the hilt, but Artorian was completely distracted by the fact that both swords were floating on their own accord. That, or that **Sorrow** was completely covered in Wisp-centric markings, floral winter lei, and… Was that a script of some kind in mid-progress of being added to the blade?

"Ho'oilo No Ka 'Oi?" Artorian levered a heavy gaze onto the katana. "I see *someone* found a nice Winter Courtyard to call home?"

Sorrow hovered back, suspiciously silent, and protective of its winter-flower lei.

A massive Nixie tube flared to life above Artorian's head as he watched the two weapons float. "Dev… you always did want me to play with Telekinesis. Today might be the day. **Compassion**, you mind?"

The musical sword twirled in place, a melody springing forth as the Principe moved through the air like a leaf on the wind, ready to stab an unsuspecting airship captain. Or perhaps that was **Sorrow**'s job? Probably **Sorrow**. That serenity-inducing spike of a katana needed to be cleaned often, and knew how to rush through a wash.

Focusing on Telekinesis, the Mage ability manifesting within, Artorian felt those same invisible arms form out of his back. They felt like his own. Like he'd used them for a hundred years. If he focused just right, he could see them as a ghostly apparition, where otherwise they were entirely unnoticeable. When fully forming the second arm, he felt some strain in his center when the effect completed. Not much, and not harmful strain, but definitely enough to notice it being there.

Telekinesis wasn't an ability he was going to call compli-cated, but the exact know-how needed a lot of doing. It was one of those riding-a-racer skills. Getting to the point where you could do it was the hard part, and once you could, you never forgot.

Compassion whirled through the air, playing a wonderful melody as Artorian practiced. The proof of concept was easy! In reality, the detailed control became more difficult when the blade moved more than ten feet from him. This was a good skill, but the ability was going to need practice. Using more of that time he didn't really have.

He let go as the zither's song finished, **Compassion** clearly glad to do some singing. He released Telekinesis internally, then tried it with his Aura instead. The difference was ridiculous. The sensation was roughly the same, but with his Aura forming the arms instead, the difference was notable. The range, reach, and flexibility especially! He could easily extend both blades a hundred feet from him, with no noticeable downside. Swirling and twirling like one of Dawn's dances.

"Well, I know what version I'll be using!" He felt mighty pleased, making both swords dance to those delightful memories. Artorian then had a terrible, devious idea, as two blades were not causing any strain. "I wonder... *How many* swords can I do this with?"

CHAPTER TWENTY-FIVE

Artorian knew he'd arrived in the right place when the sound of a fish fight reached his ears. Sidestepping the remains of a trout coming down from the sky also did the trick. The continued lack of camels, at this point, went ignored. He did need to slow and steel himself when the morning ritual brawl opened with some old world guildie bellowing a taunt. "Whale, whale, whale, what have we here?"

Artorian stopped cold, pinching the bridge of his nose.

He did not enter the haystack of poorly assorted wood covered in scavenged leafy greenery, the latter of which some people had clearly taken a bite out of. Nor did he further approach the palisade of such poor construction that pre-Bob age goblins would consider it an affront to structural design. In order to make the palisade, people had used brute strength to shove any item remotely straight down into the ground.

The only useful function of which was to add some shade.

It certainly wasn't going to keep anyone out.

Tuning his ears to break through the sounds of what was definitely a fight, one he felt very uncomfortable joining, Artorian closed his eyes for a moment and did some spying. It was

AVALON

obvious nobody had noticed him, as no nearby Mages had suffered from that memorable sharp-inhale sound Torburn had made stick in his thoughts.

"They are fresh!" The fishmonger posed like a gladiator and howled, loudly defending his wares. "Ma feesh smells like daisies!" *Whack*!

"Your fish smells like disease!" *Pif*! An Olympian shook his fish-bearing-fist and shouted, clearly in disagreement about both the aromatic scent, and quality, of said fishy goods. "They stink!"

Artorian gingerly took some extra steps closer, peeking between the unsubtly replanted trees. His focus fell on the undoubtedly big Olympian man, double checking that he was sneaking about unseen, before crossing the outer palisade and entering the inner one. Artorian wanted to bet whole bags of silver that this particular Mage was tied to a **Law** that increased his sensory perception well above the norm.

Artorian knew to trust that nose-tingling feeling.

The Olympian's tiny mustache bristled like a porcupine, which accompanied an increase in tempo to the fight, before Artorian felt like meandering onwards, shuffling towards what accounted for a big enough hole in the inner palisade to mistake for an entrance. The main gate, sans gate, led to what he was generously coining a fishing village. Alright, maybe just a hamlet. Or whatever one called mostly straight sticks pretending to play at being tents.

He muttered under his breath.

"What a disgrace. I was expecting majestic construction and a full on city for one of Henry and Marie's projects." Artorian shook his head, eyes turning to a half-collapsed pile of wood. "Can't even rightly say tents."

He paused before daring to breach the larger-than-the-rest palisade opening, his current spot doing a decent job of keeping him out of sight. Spying continued.

"Well, *my* fish is fresh and bl—" *Whack*! An old church affiliate staggered, sputtering after taking a barracuda to the teeth by the old world guildie in strong disagreement. "Blessed!"

"Lies! That fish was imported and smells like your cheese-feet forgot how to play with water!" The guildie had put both his arms into the swing, sending the torn half of the fish sailing into the sky. "Wash! You dirt-robed longnose!" *Splaf*.

The church affiliate was not taking that like a beached whale, mouth full of krill or not. "Stop giving me reef! You only make me feel carpy! I am a most holy—" *Splump*.

"No puns!" Several people roared their displeasure in unison, before the sound of wet fish slapped repeatedly on what sounded like the same target, that church-affiliated voice going rather quiet before the rest of the rowdy bundle continued the morning ritual.

"Victory goes to the one who can seas it from the jaws of defeat!" A different church-affiliate stood to take the hill, defending his old world compatriot before becoming the target of the no-pun rule, getting piled on by more pallid pisces.

"I've got the striped bass!" A third church-affiliate acted like he'd captured the flag before clearly attempting to escape the premises, her fishy prize proving too slippery to be retained as the dry impact of a tackle crashed that person to the ground.

No wonder there was no more grass left in the region.

It had been wrestled down to the bedrock.

A guildie picked up the striped bass like a slimy ball worth ten points and ran off with it. "Don't let them have anything with stripes! I am sick of them always getting anything with stripes!"

The ground-flattened church affiliate spat out mud, performing the violent action of taking the legs out from under the guildie. "All striped fish belong to the church! They are our ranks!"

There was some further shouting on how vertical stripes were slimming, and horizontal ones were bad, which caused an entirely different uproar.

Artorian could not find it within himself to listen further, so he simply stopped listening in.

He pressed his forehead to the palisade wall with a hand covering his eyes. He no longer wanted to go in there. Which was a thought immediately followed by another Olympian entering the fray, loud enough for him to not need to place any effort into spying. "Zero Wing has arrived! How are you gentlemen this morning? All your bass are belong to us!"

A frozen swordfish piercing a hole through the wood right next to where Artorian was standing cut that statement short, the sound of a group mobbing onto a single individual becoming very easy to discern as the wet slapping sounds muffled cries of pain and requests for forgiveness.

"Someone set us up the bream." A guildie beat it towards shore, the rumbling following in hot pursuit like a dust cloud made from angry shouts and swinging fish.

Artorian was busy thunking his forehead to the palisade, trying to beat the situation out of his head. Rapidly transitioning through every stage of grief, he leaned his forehead to the wood and waited for a sensical moment to give him an opening.

"*Ha-ha!*" The fishmonger celebrated. "Another successful morning!"

Artorian poked his head around the wall, hopeful. This place… this place was not one to *understand* and take apart like a puzzle box. Camelot was a location he was going to *experience*. Unfortunately, unlike at Brianna's where he could play tourist, here he was going to have to put in the work.

So, how best to ingrain himself in the local pleasantries?

He was going to have to make puns, wasn't he?

The *inhumanity*. Clearly puns were meant for dungeons, because they had no place outside of them! Brushing his Ao Dai and closing his eyes for the duration of a breath, he plastered a fake, jovial expression on his face, and strode forth onto a floor of unconscious bodies.

"Carp-e diem, fishmonger!" He spoke with a mixture of

trepidation and forced smiles. "Most fish puns are flops, and clearly all that glitters is not goldfish, but you seem to have quite the magic carp-et ride working for you here!"

The large, rotund—sporting a mustache so long it was braided—fishmonger flashed the old man a vast smile, his pudgy hands clasping together. "Sometimes they fail, sometimes they're Goldeen!"

Artorian's facade broke immediately.

His hands pressed to his knees as he bent over, his mask of false enthusiasm a crumbled mess as pain crossed his features. "Nope. No. Never mind. I can't do it. It hurts too much. I refuse to pun. To the Abyss with all of them."

"Oh, you're one of *those*, are you?" The fishmonger pushed his bulbous nose high in the air, the sizzling snideness filling his demeanor like a bucket of ice pouring into a fire. "I won't be peddling my wares to you. If you can't pay, then you can't stay!"

"Pay in what, exactly?" Artorian tapped the only sensical angle of the topic back onto the table as he straightened up, trying to find a piece of ground to stand on that wasn't a person. Not much luck, there, as the morning ritual was a popular ritual. "Does gold have value again all of a sudden?"

"What? No!" The fishmonger snapped up straight, offended. "The pun-ishments! My amusements! I get people their lunch, they pay me with entertainment, and I am treated to a good slap fight!"

Artorian held up a finger, needing to ask the question. "Olympian?"

Aghast at the accusation, the fishmonger spat on the ground and took a step away. "Excuse you. I am from Atlantis!"

That detail made Artorian's nose itch. What detail was he not seeing? No high-pitched inhale? The Atlantis comment? So either the fishmonger wasn't one of Torburn's ilk, or… No. One moment. How was a fishmonger *importing* fish? Without goods to trade or a boat to sally out with? One would need significant assistance to get that done. Outside help. Influence.

Artorian straightened to match the merchant's stature, his

expression sour and stern as he slapped his cards on the table and made his guess. "Aiden?"

The fishmonger's bright smile dropped. Along with that awful forced accent. Aiden, pretending to be the fishmonger, threw his trout down to the ground with a splat. In his normal voice, the complaints began. "Administrator! Not even a hand's worth of time of you being on the scene, and you step your foot into my fun?"

Artorian took the moment to scan the area, confirming all nearby ears were either out cold or out of sight. Satisfied, he then turned to Aiden and shot both his arms into the air. "What is going on? Did you do this?"

Aiden grinned, some of that wolfishness slipping through his features. Artorian thought to look, seeing the familiar Wolfman hiding underneath. Aiden's form was a very well-managed guise! "Well, I'm not responsible, but I'm not helping, either."

The feral grin widened, and some helpless giggling hiccupped out of the large man. "I arrived... *hi-hi*. I arrived because I couldn't do what you asked. I couldn't wait for the next round of Eternia. I came to confront them on their hubris! On Henry's constant dismissive attitude."

Aiden motioned a broad hand towards his surroundings. "Then I found this, and I couldn't help myself. All that big talk, all those 'iterations' of management, and this is what I find? I started to giggle. I started and I didn't stop. It's so bad here that I began to feel bad for the imprisoned locals who couldn't leave, formulating a plan to smuggle in some food."

Artorian squeezed his brows. "Plus destabilizing the local regions in doing so, and smearing the smuggled cake in layers of puns for a cherry on top?"

The man's grin turned excessive. "Puns are a small price to pay for my indulgence in Henry's failure. I no longer want to confront him because it might end this 'indulgence in his failures,' but with you here... the party must be coming to an end? Shame. I amassed such a hoard of them."

Artorian could hear the hidden question.

He resigned himself to it. "Aiden?"

"*Yeeees?*" The big man leaned toward him, his voice dragged out, with that toothy smile still on full display.

"If I let you get it out of your system." Artorian dropped a hand towards the man. "Will you tell me everything?"

"Carp-e diem, indeed, Administrator! I shall take that offer." The fishmonger bounced on his toes. "New, hungry mouths arrive all the time here in camel catastrophe, and I ask them: what gill are you a part of?"

Artorian held his temples, mumbling with monotone dread. "This is going to go downhill fast, isn't it?"

"Downstream, even!" Aiden laughed. "Fish puns are such a delight, no? I cod think of a few more activities for my customers to fill my days. They could attack with porpoise for my delight, and sea how many pollock they could whale against the others. Hopefully they could salmon the courage to keep fighting despite the waves of puns that I demand in payment. They might pull a mussel, but that is the cost of business. The deal is simple! One may claim any fish from my table, but it will cost them a pun, and a pun makes them the target of all others."

Artorian was already regretting everything and now held his face with both his hands.

Aiden swam on. "At first, they thought my price was small. That these puns are brilliant! So they put their heart and sole into their fighting. For newcomers, I'd recommend frozen halibut, as it's a reel great weapon. Or even a pike, if I'm feeling pointy. But after a while they start to flounder, these veterans of the morning ritual. They might distract their opponent with a red herring, to escape my presence and my cost."

He delighted in the awful language twisting. "Sometimes I throw them a bone, letting them leave early, and say: let's finnish this. It used to get an ex-stream reaction."

Aiden's voice and face fell, losing his own enthusiasm with the puns. "Then it all began to get very, very sad."

He turned, walked behind a table under a tented tarp

retaining barely half a halibut, and sat on a stool. "I expected Henry and Marie to swoop in through the region when they got wind of my whimsical Wellerman whaling! While I made a dastardly escape through the sea, breached Marie's pressure wall, and went home. I have the luxury of escape, after all."

Aiden pulled another stool from beneath the table, and offered it. When Artorian moved to approach, he recognized the table as a broken off piece of ship hull. Seating himself, he first exhaled hard and rubbed at his ears. As if to assure them the prior assault was over.

The fishmonger worked out his words, hiding a not-insignificant amount of disappointment as he moved to the serious topic. "They never came. I've seen them leave the zone a few times, but never for very long. It's usually long enough for a few people to flee, but it's such a rare occurrence that people don't hold out hope. My joke with the fish? That became something for these discarded people to look forward to. For many, it's food for the day. This zone is full of lost souls looking for a home, only to find rubble and a complete inability to leave. It's been months, Administrator. Many miserable months."

Aiden's irritation bled through, his knuckles turning white as he squeezed his own grip. "Not a peep from either of the mice. Not here, where people need it, but plenty in the center, with the frequent light shows."

"Why are there light shows?" Artorian looked to the distance as he didn't spot any, trying to scrape together all the sanity he could find. Red rocks giving off light? Yes. A show? No.

"Henry and Marie fighting." Aiden raised a hand to drop it dejectedly, rattling off his facts. "They did their best to cover their struggles up, or otherwise hide how poorly the region is doing, but every A-ranker in the zone is violently vying for those royal positions until their Mana runs dry. Or possibly to get that duo to drop their Presence effects, because that's what's making the attacker's Mana run dry. The self-appointed rulers both keep their Auras fielded indiscriminately. Too dispersed for the crushing effect to happen all the time, but more than good enough to be… unpleasant."

Aiden wrung his own hands, leaning forward on his makeshift table. It creaked under his elbows. "So far, they've both hung onto their king-of-the-hill positions, but enough new A-rankers from the old days keep joining the zone in search of respite that there's always another fight that breaks out. The B-rankers and below have learned they can't compete, and thus stay far away from the fray, which is why there's so many of them here with the rest of the grunts."

Artorian ran his hand over his head. "Why… Why would they do any of that? This is needless oppression and punishment. This is Henry and Marie we're talking about! They do this monarch stuff like it's their calling. There's no way it all went this wrong without there being more to it. There has to be a good reason."

His thoughts were distracted by the arm of one of the bodies littering the ground going up. A new, younger, female voice chimed in. Her method of speech was decidedly that of a Wood Elf. "I've got an answer."

CHAPTER TWENTY-SIX

The young Mage of **Moss** pushed herself up and out from the heap, her words cutting into the conversation. "When I met them, through their sham of a court appointment no less, I didn't even get a say."

The Mage wobbled to her feet. "They saw me, up from those fancy thrones, and *informed me* of what I was going to be doing. There was a way they wanted to do things, and that's the way it was going to be."

Her look was understandably foul. "So as far as I'm concerned, the rulers' reason for doing any of this is the same reason why the entire zone is a prison. The rich want a society based on punishment, because a society based on care would render them obsolete."

She scoffed. "Those two can't handle the idea that anything could possibly work without them, and if you're not with them, you're against them. So enjoy the gravity, it'll be a constant reminder until you bend the knee. Unless you want to brave the nine out of ten chances of being crushed to paste when leaving."

"I'm sensing some deeper ani-**Moss**-ity here." Aiden shook his hands to not crush his own knuckles. Then he growled out with a grin, aware of exactly what he'd done as Artorian closed his eyes and bent forwards, stifling a mostly muffled groan of pain.

"Please." Artorian inhaled as he pressed his forehead to the table. "No more puns."

The disguised Wolfman then backpedaled while the **Moss** Mage fiercely nodded. "There is a reason, Administrator, but I'm the wrong person to claw on the label of 'good.' When it comes to assigning blame... Let's take Henry. It's not that Henry is less to blame than Marie for the situation, it's that he's neither seeing the problem, nor fighting against the concept of 'ruling' that both he and Marie are stringently holding on to. Like an investment they've sunk too many costs into, they feel an awfully strong need to retain control and power. Even if that control and power comes at the cost of keeping their prospective citizens captive."

Artorian was glad for the shift in topic, trying to understand the mindset. "As in, they've developed tunnel vision trying to accomplish a task, and the side-effects were forced onto the back burner, where those side-effects burned to a crisp and began to smell like month old fish?"

"That's a kind interpretation of reality. I would..." Aiden bit his tongue to stifle the pun before it was said, then shoved his hands into his pockets. The wry grin still part of his face like the expression had been glued in place.

Aiden stopped giving the old man grief when Artorian looked at him with a stare that was leveled above imaginary glasses, well aware of the fine line between poking fun and being a problematic supervisor. Now that he'd had his fun, he had to turn around and be helpful.

"No more puns." Aiden bit his lip, conceding. "Aye aye, captain. Let me know what the plan is when you've got one together. Until then, Maya? Meet the Administrator. Administrator? Meet Maya the **Moss** Mage."

Artorian distracted himself by offering the **Moss** Mage a

hand, becoming entranced by the texture of the bark-like skin that... One moment. That skin wasn't bark-like. It *was* bark! His words came out as a gasp. "You're a Wood Elf?"

"I am!" Maya fulfilled the handshake, getting to her feet before adjusting a judogi that looked like it used to be Craig's. "Maya, B-ranking **Moss** Mage, Wood Elf. At your service, Starlight spirit. Though, I'll admit I'm not sure why the older generation calls you that. You give off a different feeling."

Artorian wasn't sure how to feel about that observation.

"Let's table that thought, and put a pin in your sharp commentary from earlier." Artorian mentally swiped an arm over his cognitive worktable to clear all contents, pleasing a hidden cat somewhere from all the things that hit the floor. The matter of Camelot and Aiden playing fishmonger needed to come second.

He needed to know how a Wood Elf Ascended. "I thought Wood Elves were locked to the C-ranks? Isn't the naming convention also to name oneself after the tree in question? I've never heard of a 'Maya.' Is it new?"

"I chose to go by Maya." She adopted a tree pose, stretching before resuming her more neutral footing. "My hometree is Beech. That's B-E-E-C-H."

While the spelling processed, the **Moss** Mage walked a few paces to an assemblage of sticks that was likely once a hut. Rapping her knuckles on the wood, Artorian saw that the mess of sticks was no fallen tent, but a makeshift hatch to a hole in the ground.

A hole in the ground that swung open, making way for the heads of Baobab and Olive.

Artorian shot upright. "Old friends!"

Both Wood Elves surveyed their surroundings, locked eyes on Artorian who had already thrown his arms out and adopted a horse stance for stability after shooting up from his stool, and dashed from their hidey hole to tackle him down onto the floor of groaning bodies as they both shouted in elation.

Their voices were the same from all those years ago, even if they looked different. "Sunny!"

"I've missed you two!" The old man trapped them both with an arm-about-the-neck grip before squeezing them tight to his chest. Their pounce of elation turned into a struggle to escape, but the old man wasn't about to let them. His tune changed from delighted to one handling troublemakers who had been caught stealing fresh pie red-handed. "You're also not going anywhere! I knew Aiden wouldn't have continued this all on his lonesome! He's about honor, strength, and community. You two stoked the fire, didn't you!"

Aiden looked surprised to hear that the Administrator had such a high, and admittedly correct, opinion of him. Henry and Marie may have failed this zone, but he wasn't going to just let the community here flounder and flail. His honor couldn't abide that.

"I'm immune!" Baobab bit and gnawed Artorian's shoulder like a feisty tomboy, to no avail. "Fire means nothing to meee!"

"I'm extra flammable!" Olive squirmed like a slippery rat. "It was us! Let go so we can explain properly!"

Artorian narrowed his gaze, not letting Olive's oily veneer give him any leeway as he scanned the duo over. A particular detail stood out more than any other, as regardless of them both wearing more copies of Craig's judogi, Bao's appearance being a hair-ruffled tomboy with a tooth missing in the smile, and Olive looking equally too young…

They were both B-rankers!

Artorian stood straight, and walked with both of them trapped in his arms, moving off the floor of groaning bodies to set them down on the rocks. Only then did he let go and hug them proper. "It's good to see you both again, you troublesome rascals! What's with the new bodies? What's with the rank?! I thought the Wood Elves couldn't… y'know."

Olive made some faces and stretched to pop the newly added kinks in his back. Bao, on the other hand, shot her fists to her hips and showed off her smile. "Only a problem when there's more than one mind connected to your hometree! Olive, Maya, and I got around it by accident. We were all very confused when we Ascended, to the great interest of Birch and Mahogany. They shouldn't be too far behind us now."

Olive recovered in time to comment and match poses. "We're just first, because we are awesome!"

Absconding with the knowledge like a thief in the night, Artorian's attention moved to Maya when she made a motion to speak. "I chose to, for sure. The barkskin makes me feel more unique, and I've never been without it in the first place. I was one of the old world sapling rescues. I'm actually very proud to resemble my tree as much as I do."

Artorian decided to lean into that. "Could you tell me more?"

"That's fine." Maya proudly held up part of her exposed arm to show off the resemblance. "Here is some beech knowledge for you: beech has got silvery-gray smooth bark, and beech leaves are identified by their glossy, dark green color, ovate to elliptical shape, and finely toothed margins. Young beech leaves appear lime green with fine hairs on the edges, like me! Or one of the shades that strange outfit of yours has depending on the angle that I see it from?"

Maya moved left and right, swaying her head to catch the different phases of Artorian's Ao Dai. "How is it *doing* that?"

Artorian compared Maya to the description of her tree: she had messy, shoulder length, fine, wild hair that was barely controlled by slim braids. Like a wind just blew through it and ruined all a parent's efforts of instilling order. Silvery-gray bark skin was easily overtaking the normal human skin tones that Maya's body had clearly begun with. Lastly, her dark green irises were accented by a lime and jade glow, while her stature remained child-like.

Like Bao and Olive.

Suspiciously much like Bao and Olive.

"Dark Elven weaving secrets, my dear." The grandfather's smile crept onto his own face. Rather than press his jest, he jumped to the next question. He did have things to get done today. "Is there a reason you all look so young?"

"Mortal body test from Cal." Olive turned, his own green eyes paying attention to all the bodies on the ground that were starting to stir and wake. "We were never supposed to hit Magehood, given Wood Elven lore is what it was. That we did was a surprise to everyone. We thought we could get started early with the natural-grown forms everyone is eventually going to have, so when Cal-decanting time came, we could walk out and replant. We were planning to be C-rank forever anyway."

Artorian had suspicions about this exact problem, but seeing the results firsthand did more to drive it home than one of his lectures would.

Olive motioned to himself. "Instead, we Ascended in those child forms, and I hear we're stuck this way unless we have a do-over? Mahogany was going to give us the entire explanation once we'd caused enough havoc in The Warren. That's the name of the zone next door."

Bao looked far too proud of something. "Stirring up those Necrohamsters was *such* fun. That preacher that came put a swift stop to it, and it's why we ended up here, but still!"

"Thank you for answering my questions." Artorian played cat a second time as he chose to be glad to have assigned Richard to the Hamster versus Glitterflit mess. Wiping his table clean, he turned to Aiden. "This is more trouble than I was expecting to run into."

A quick glance at Maya informed the three Wood Elves that they weren't out of the proverbial woods yet either. "We'll tackle your 'prison' comment later."

Maya shrugged. "It's not complicated. I'm young, gifted memories as a jump-start or not. I don't know the Henry and Marie that everyone else seems to know. I only know this version of them, and this version is awful. The memories I have equate the behavior of wanting to retain the kind of control they have to something rich people do. Because what do the rich care about save for control to keep their riches? This ruling type is no different."

Artorian wanted to move on, but kept himself silent and slowed his roll. Her case sounded dire, or at the minimum, burdened. Like she was glad to finally tell someone who might be able to do anything at all about the problem. The inner grandfather took the spot of the Administrator, and listened to Maya. The change in his decision was visible on his face.

The Wood Elf felt nice that the old man didn't press to delay her comment until later, her pose brimming with confidence when she was provided the floor. "We can't leave unless you're willing to brave the danger of being crushed, and those too scared to make the walk ask to be tossed. Our Mana is being stolen if we use it, and we can't replenish any while we're stuck here, so prison sounded just right."

Artorian supposed he had to bite the arrowhead and tackle it now since she was breaking the sentence down to minutiae anyway. "Then what was with the 'obsolete' portion of the comment?"

Maya's expression turned wry. "If they cared about the people here, none of this would be happening. So they don't. Meaning what they care about is something else, and if they're going to forcibly keep me trapped here when all I came to do was check on Bao and Olive, I'm going to feel a certain kind of way about that. I'm a fresh B-ranker who never expected to be one. What am I going to do against A-rankers that don't seem to run out of Mana? When I can't sit still and do nothing?"

"Be a giant pain in the keister, that's what. I see where this is going." Artorian hung his head, picking his metaphorical hat up from the coat rack to begin his actual task. "Aiden. Help. Please?"

Aiden was helping the crowd—who were collectively forming the floor as they came to—up from their morning predicament. He looked to the Administrator when he heard his name, and performed his job as a Supervisor. "There's both a lot going on, and little to do at the same time, Administrator. I'll

DENNIS VANDERKERKEN & DAKOTA KROUT

help, of course, but I do not know what kind of help you actually want. If you're here to throw fists, then my scuffle with Henry won't happen in Eternia like you suggested it to. Or is that not the capacity in which you are here?"

Aiden waggled his eyebrows. "If you're here for fun... Henry could do with some more grief."

"I'm here for work, Aiden." Artorian exhaled, his tone apologetic. "I'm sorry. This visit is to put a stamp on the document and file it to Cal as solved. You'll get your resolution, on your own terms. I know you have more to work through with him than just what happened in this corner of the world. I'll see to it that you get that chance. This time around? The back of my hand feels like it needs to administer some **Retribution** as a wakeup call. Henry may be my friend, but this is unacceptable."

Aiden chuckled. "We know the story of Cal and the iceberg. I'm glad you're seeing our perspective. Our task in the current iteration is to build society. Not... this. This deserves to be a textbook example of good intentions gone wrong."

Artorian began helping people up himself, agreeing with Aiden. "While I initially thought the problems were just two Supervisors shirking their Cal-requested duties, it now feels like a lot of people are putting sticks in Camelot's spokes because Henry and Marie have gone off the Dwarven rails."

He felt like he might have the lynchpin. "Nobody *sets up* a sovereign space Aura like this as a first measure. Needing to ramp up their counters against an ever-reactive, growing set of problems, they dug themselves into a hole as each prior solution led to a new uproar. Causing the perpetuation of the cycle. I know a downward spiral when I see one. I need to break up the pattern they've worked themselves into and give them both a good shake."

Aiden put up his hand. He liked where this was going, focusing on the earlier mention that he would not be denied his personal grudge match against Henry. "I don't think I've heard of sovereign space before when it comes to Aura."

Artorian explained. "Sovereign space is a type of Aura spreading where you 'own' all the space it occupies. Only one person can do this to an area, and only a stronger Aura can contest the claimed space."

He chuckled. "An old joke of mine is that it allows you to tax the contents, which refers to all the energy within the spread Aura. Essence, Mana, and such. The trick has many functions if you know how to use them. One of them allows you to prevent others from spreading their own Auras if you do it right, otherwise you've made a space functionally identical to the insides of a dungeon's claimed territory. It's also very convenient for knowing who or what is inside of your owned space, with a very exact measurement. I can only guess that Marie isn't here either because she hasn't looked, or because she doesn't know how, having only figured out the crushing gravity effect. How she managed to make the effect stronger at the borders... that one's new to me."

The old man shook his head. "I was wondering why their fielded Presences looked so strange, but if they tend to leave it spread out over a whole area all the time, that might explain why they felt so disconnected."

Artorian then motioned at the dazed Mages around. "Per help, gather everyone up from the region, if you can? I may be here to use the big broom, but you know that I'm unable to abandon all these people. When this is all said and done, I want them to have that respite. I appreciate that you've kept everyone fed."

Aiden confirmed the request. "Of course, Administrator. Luckily, most people who are not still fighting in the central area are already gathered here. A bonus from me serving as a food source. This task won't take me more than an evening."

The old man finally showed some relief.

"Thank you, Aiden." A rumble coursed within Artorian's body, his voice momentarily brimming with power. "Being from the old world, or of an old guild, regardless of history, does not mean they should be shafted their chance at **Redemption**."

Aiden nodded in stern approval, having some personal history with that concept. Feeling both strength and conviction ripple out from the old man, he felt his fur stand on edge. As both a Wolfman and Northerner of old who prized honor, those were qualities and conviction that he could respect. "That's the Administrator I know."

CHAPTER TWENTY-SEVEN

A guildie that Aiden helped up mumbled thanks before wiping dead fish remains from his rags, though the spoken words turned into a sharp-gasped inhale when the man saw Artorian.

"Right!" The old man snapped his fingers. "That was the response which I was supposed to expect!"

He shuffled over to the pale man, and offered a hand. "I am Artorian. Hello there! Are you old guild, by chance?"

The man turned pale, forgot how to move, and didn't stop that inhalation-shriek until Aiden prodded him in the ribs. "I... No. Yes? Alice Coinin. Of a rank that I certainly remember."

His hand shot forward like one of Dev's rusty automatons. Well, some other Gnome's automatons. Dev's wouldn't be so stiff. Alice sputtered off information in lieu of recovering and greeting the man proper. "**Grave** Mage. Eight parts infernal, four parts celestial, two parts earth. B-rank. Not evil! Definitely not evil!"

Artorian cautiously performed the handshake, then patted the man on the shoulder. "Why don't you take some deep breaths first, son? I'm gonna go with no, because the old guild having a member with both infernal and celestial channels is… very unlikely."

"Yes! I mean, no." Alice's corrections dug himself deeper into the hole he was digging. "Not of the old guild! I'm just fascinated by all their stories. I've only become a Mage recently, and the Infernal channel is not one I've had for very long. People keep telling me that, if I wasn't here in Cal, I'd be having much worse experiences."

Artorian nodded, then verbally prodded elsewhere so the man could find his bearing, his grip still holding Mr. Coinin's shoulder. "Alice the 'not evil' then, *hmm?*"

"**Grave** is not evil!" Alice hurried to put a defensive hand up, the tension in his voice suddenly melting away as Alice's gaze dulled. His thoughts only on the feeling that joined his words when he accidentally pulled on his **Law**. "It's just… that forlorn peace that you only find in the graveyard? I've always found my best moments meditating on that feeling. I have taphophilia. When I'm in the cemetery, sitting with the dead, my eyes fully drawn to the heavens while only the silent breeze acts as my companion… life makes sense. I also happen to like tombstones, and seeing people become at peace with loss. The somber calm. The melancholy peace and quiet. I have a knack for it? I can look at a person, and I can simply see…"

Alice turned to look at Artorian, and his glazed eyes that saw with his **Law** turned glossy and wet, silent tears running down his cheeks. "I can see…"

"Breathe, son. Just breathe." Artorian glowed, the general air around him adopting a pink hum as the faintly smiling old man gave the **Grave** Mage his minute. The glow blocked out what Alice had been seeing, allowing the boy to snap back. The lack of smiting and doorification also put a quick end to Alice's worries, as stories clashed with reality, and reality won out.

"I… Yes. Sorry. Thank you, I mean." The Mage then stood there stiffly, trying not to be awkward before pointing at some empty space away from people being helped up. "I'll just be over here. Off to the side."

"Don't go too far, Mr. Coinin." Artorian winked with calm instruction, thinking it better to have a group of people to ask what was going on than a few sources here purely to make more trouble. He didn't take Maya as the malicious sort, and her perspective was... unpleasantly reasonable. His tone then directed itself to both the Wood Elves and loitering crowd. "Let's help *everyone* up, and get them together. I have many questions, and too few solutions."

The Administrator did not receive verbal confirmation, but he did see the targets of his request spring to action. Action was good. The very next member of the old church he helped up gasped, priorities all over the place as he came to. "Did we get the stripes?!"

"I'm sure you did, my boy." Artorian tugged the affiliate to his feet before the smell of rotting fish registered. One foul face later, and an aggressive sweep of the hand removed all decomposition, guts, and related smells. Cleaning both the local landscape, and all the people on it as the energy wave swept out and spread. Not as far out as Artorian would have liked, as the Mana he was using to make the sweep was gobbled up by Marie's Aura before he could complete the task.

"How rude!" He snapped at the sky with a balled fist, ready to shake. "I was using that!"

A few people chuckled at his complaint, but otherwise mumbled appreciative words about the free clean up. Rather than disperse as must have been normal, the presence of the fancy-dressed old man, three Wood Elves in full attention mode, the fishmonger being genuinely helpful instead of punny, and a host of people who enjoyed swapping stories as pale as some of the fish they tended to get, people stuck around.

The gossip of respite being on the horizon was not far behind.

———

At the dawn of the next day, Artorian had serious doubts about whether the **Law** of **Redemption** had actually been meant for Henry and Marie. The gathered weary, hopeful eyes that looked at him everywhere he walked were… Alright, it was awful. Just awful. He did not like seeing B-rankers be *despondent*. He equally did not like seeing C-rankers and below scrounge for food, trying desperately to make patches of rocky ground be able to grow something.

Aiden's fish supply was a blessing.

The edible contents of his own spatial bracelet were swiftly expended, but he traded it for people's attention. And that, along with an inch of good will, was worth a lot right now.

Artorian did like that the inhale-screech-greetings came to an end. That had needed to end, and he was glad for the lack of that particular social tic. He'd spread the gossip around that he had a way out of the current predicament, and would be giving a small speech to tell everyone the details. He'd gotten a lot of stares filled with 'what is it going to cost me' questions, but the old man had shaken his head no, and moved on.

Artorian walked to where Olive and Bao were talking about an underground tunnel they'd been digging, but that the Aura's border didn't care for the concept of the ground, and that their attempt to dig their way out was a bust. "Say, Bao. I have a question."

Baobab and Olive looked up at him as he sauntered up to them. Bao crossed her arms, ready for action. "We're here to help. What can we do?"

"More of a curiosity, this one." Artorian waffled his hand. "Maya said I felt like something other than a starlight spirit? I know it was an offhand mention, but the detail is poking at my thoughts and I would rather that it didn't while I plan out how to help all these people."

Bao and Olive shared a look, with Olive picking up the branch of conversation. "No. Sunny, that was a very direct reference. When you had the old four affinities in Phantomdusk

Forest, you felt like starlight. It's how we saw you. Now you feel... different."

"Good-different?" Artorian frowned, his mumble worried. "Or bad-different?"

"You feel like a really good hug from a person that you want one from." Bao reached for the worried grandfather to hold his hand, then clarified without fuss or preamble. "There's no easy, single word for that. Good-different, as a category, but different from what we're used to, overall. In those early days in our forest, you were light that carved through blight and darkness. Now, well, you look the same way that you feel. A grandfather ready to pick up a grandchild and go on adventures with them."

Olive nodded in agreement. "With the grandchild feeling very safe."

Artorian felt comfort in that statement. "You're all being far too kind. I'm here to slap my Supervisor friends. I can't be given feedback that is so supportive."

"Yes, you can." Olive shifted his stance, not here to allow his old friend to dip into the pool of worries. "You asked what was different. We explained as best as we're able. Have this valida-tion: it's not a problem that you feel different. Or look different. I mean, look at *us!*"

Olive performed the Rosewood modeling walk, showing off himself rather than his clothing. The visual was enough to make Artorian choke on air and smile. "Alright, alright. A good hug, you say? I like that. That's pleasant."

Spirits restored well enough to address a hopeful crowd, he rubbed both of them on the top of their heads, and turned to get started. It took a minute to navigate towards the table that Aiden was standing next to, but he got on top of it either way.

"Hello, everyone." He waved broadly, greeting the crowd in a simple, calm voice. "I'm sure the gossip has gone around being the fire it tends to be, so let's not beat around the burnt down bush. I am Artorian. Cal's Administrator. The story about me turning Ellis into a door is true. I am here to reprimand the self-assigned rulers of this zone, and end this entire affair. That is an inevitability. So please breathe more comfortably, as this prison mess will all be over soon. To that end, I wanted to cover some important key points when it comes to all of you."

Artorian moved his hands behind his back. A sharp inhale, and he tackled the elephant in the room. "I'm not going to sugar coat this. Old world affiliations come with a certain... unwelcome stigma. Breaking into that big fight, on day *one*? That didn't help matters either. I know none of you meant for this. Or wanted this. That your organizations had some shifty leadership, and trickled those dark stories down to stain the members, is not something that is unknown to me. Know that I don't fault you."

Silence followed, all eyes focused and heavy on the man in green.

Many doubted the legitimacy of the man's claim to break open their undesired confinement. Many had tried. All had failed. It was easy to stand on a tall thing and swing words around. They were used to that. Nobody spoke up and interrupted because nobody wanted to. On the knife's edge of a chance that this wasn't a trick, they wanted to know the full story.

"I'm here... with an olive branch." He procured one from thin air with some sleight of hand, cracking a small smile as he looked at Olive, who waved enthusiastically at being referenced. "By which I mean a blank slate. A new chance. A new shot at life. A respite from old leanings. Old obligations. Old affiliations."

He steadied his voice. "You aren't required to take it. You aren't required to give up anything you don't want to. This is for those of you who don't want the dagger in the back for something you may never have done. Or if you have, to bury the hatchet, and forever let it lie."

Artorian brushed a hand down his beard. "I know that the Dark Elves have been lurking, interested in a peculiar few of you. I know others still, who might now have an unhealthy fear of spiders. Both of these factions are my friends."

Several Olympians turned a special shade of pale at the mention. Several others looked to share their discomfort, even if not as viscerally.

The Administrator continued. "I know that many of you ended up here to try to get away from unwanted threats like that. Some of you want… a small cave to cultivate in. A small community to build up, and call home. A small place to be left alone, and recover, and walk back to the busy places when you find your feet again. A city where you can wake up, and breathe, tasting the life it has. Ready and waiting for you to join it."

Attention and interest captured, he cast the lure. "I have that for you."

CHAPTER TWENTY-EIGHT

The old man paused when he saw unpleasant scowls on many of the old church affiliated faces. Artorian had their olive branch as well. "I'm not blind to an entire faction scowling me down, so I'll be clear. To my dear people of the faith: I'm not here to step on your beliefs. Or how you hold them. Or what you hold dear. To work in service to the heavens is commendable! For most of that work leads to helping the many who need it. Why should I get to decide what you like and dislike? Why should I get to decide what you believe, and wish to support? This is not why I am here."

The mumbling died down, expectant gazes replacing the scowls. "I'm here because I believe that you shouldn't get judged now by things that happened in the past, when you have so thoroughly, and repeatedly, been hammered for them already. I was in Chasuble shortly before moonfall. I saw the way Vicars held grip, control, and stymied direction that didn't directly serve their own agendas. This is not a boulder you should be forced to push forever up a hill, due to mere affiliation."

Artorian held up his fingers, counting down major factors. "Was losing the old world by itself not enough? Was entering

Cal and devolving into a giant murderfest not enough? Was working your frustrations out by dying, living, and dying again not enough? You have given your due penance. Was it not enough?"

A hand went up in the crowd, one of the church affiliated members. This voice stood out from the crowd. There was strength in it. Courage. A leadership quality. "Two questions."

Artorian motioned to the question, the man speaking. "I don't actually understand what you're offering me that I wouldn't have just from getting out of this zone."

"Simple, really." The old man nodded, not surprised that this came up. "I hold firm to the belief that people, Mage or otherwise, are social animals. We need each other. Even when we have times where we feel like that's not true. What I'm offering you has nothing to do with what zone you are or are not in, my friend. My offer is that, if you're willing to put all the old grievances down, leaving them behind you, and strive for a proper, better tomorrow, that I can, and will, give you that chance. A place to call home. Something to do that matters. I can't promise you the ability to cultivate, but I can tap the side of my nose, and wink at you that there might be a way."

That last detail garnered him a lot of attention. Cultivation had ground to a dead halt for most, and while the possibility of getting to leave Camelot was a stick being taken away, the possibility to keep growing was a very enticing carrot.

He broadly swept a hand over Camelot. "I want to give you everything that this place isn't. An introduction to people who would look up to you, and consider you their world from all the things you have to say, knowledge you have to offer, and perspective you can add while they build their homes. While they grow their food. While they hold your hand because you are uniquely able to give them a comfort they would find nowhere else. All by the virtue of an introduction, and a willingness to leave grievances behind. You are correct that I am not the end-all be-all, nor am offering anything you could not strive to gain by yourself. I am a foot in the door. A shortcut. A good name that will get you welcomed in a good place."

He folded his hands behind him. "I have no doubts that you would find Avalon on your own, if you so much as tried. You're all capable. You're all smart. I see only people who are incredible, and deserve recognition. I am also aware that those who deserve this recognition commonly go completely ignored. Let's also not pretend you weren't all a despondent mess not too long ago, here on a rumor."

Artorian clarified his stance. "This offer of mine doesn't care who you *used to be*. My offer is a blank slate for *who you can become*."

The affiliate appeared placated, but his gaze remained stern, a clear chip remaining on his shoulder. "I understand. Then I must apologize for my second question, because if you are who you say you are, then I do not know you to treat those who follow the same ways as I... favorably. How can I believe you?"

The old man considered this bias, and relented. He had to let it go. He couldn't offer absolution while keeping the chip on his own shoulder. That his bias was known to randomly encountered church affiliates felt like a step too far over a line that he wasn't comfortable crossing.

He knew the value of gossip all too well.

Artorian put his cards on the table, his views on the old church shed like an old, worn coat. Time to hang it up, and reference the knowledge of ancient scholar Sagan. "I'm a miser and a grump. Propositions that are unverifiable aren't worth much. Believing when there's no compelling evidence is a mistake. The idea is to hold belief until there is compelling evidence. If the universe does not comply with our predispositions, then hopefully, we have a wrenching obligation to accommodate to the way that the world really is."

The affiliate crossed his arms, hoping that classroom talk went somewhere.

"Heavenlies are real. The above exists. I must accommodate

reality, and admit I was at fault for wanting to dismiss the idea. How can I question what you serve, when I have been proven so thoroughly wrong?" Artorian looked to the church affiliate who'd asked the question. "Does this clarify my position?"

The affiliate took a moment, then nodded, appearing to bury his own hatchet as well. The chip went with it as he made a polite motion for the Administrator to continue.

Artorian gladly took that politeness. "So, it's like I said. I don't require, or ask, you to shift any of your beliefs. Or anything you might hold dear. All I'm asking is that you leave the reasons to stab the other guy in the back behind, and I'll vouch to get you into the one place you're actually, truly wanted. The one thing that no amount of cultivation will ever be able to get you. Just like that. Think of it. If you will?"

Artorian wrapped up. "I'm now going to take more questions. When questions are done, I'm going to end this charade of a kingdom. When I conclude that task, I am traveling to a nearby landmark where stone seats were raised around a fire pit. It's very recognizable, merely head for the only fire that isn't bright red. Everyone who is there when I come look, and I do mean everyone, I will assume to have accepted my offer."

Artorian had to contend with the opposition, so he tackled it. "Everyone who isn't… do as you please. I never wanted to see any of you like this in the first place. If the field comes down, and you wish to go your own way… then please do so, and be free. I will not come hunt you."

The Administrator slipped into being a grandfather for just a moment as his smile broadened and wrinkles thickened. "I will, on the other hand, try to have a spot ready for you, should you change your mind. My door is always open to those who would turn a new leaf. Perhaps a lecture on how to make friends will follow? Some of you seem lonely, and I have wisdom for that."

Artorian stepped off the table, sitting on the edge instead, awaiting questions.

An unconvinced guild member scoffed, commenting with

snark. "A lecture on friends? How would that help? Why not just stand back on that table and claim to know the purpose of life? Or someone's purpose in life, while you're at it?"

Reactions were mixed, but it would have been strange if a group of Mages, down on their luck or not, were naturally compliant to anything that came their way. Some mocking laughter from the people who hadn't taken any of it seriously supported the snark. The move could easily be taken as one meant to grasp control in a situation where they otherwise had none.

A few cold stares from others who disagreed were sent the guildie's way. Some eyes, Artorian noted, remained on him with genuine interest. That last category of people piqued Artorian's own interest. He could rebuke the man, or...

Pushing away from the table, Artorian grabbed the piece of hull by the edge and flipped it vertical, letting it serve as a makeshift chalkboard in lieu of anything better. Or chalk, he supposed. Didn't have chalk either. Artorian flashed the snarky man a 'well, you did ask' smile when the commentary died down, then pressed his finger into the wood and hand carved in some geometry. "Certainly!"

The snarky man faltered, not getting the response he'd wanted. The guildie shrunk away into the background, lost in the crowd when Artorian finished drawing four circles that all overlapped the other. Complete with a space in the middle that connected all four.

Artorian picked up a stick, and smacked it against that center spot as the people around him gave the old man some room. "This bit in the middle? One's purpose in life. *A reason for being*. Found, chosen, or otherwise. A scholar named Ikigai devised this diagram, and it was proudly displayed on a Skyspear wall. My crude copy won't do that tapestry justice."

The stick slapped to the top circle, stabbed into a part without any overlap. A teensy bit of Mana allowed for an inscription to be carved in before the sprinkle of energy was stolen away. "Major categories are fourfold. The first? My favorite! What you **Love**."

The stick slapped to the left, gathering attention. "What you are Good at."

The stick then slapped to the bottom, and right extremities of each individual circle. "What you can be Paid for, and what the World needs. These four circles are the major motivations that offer to satisfy a lack of belonging. Sources that, when pursued, can bring meaning and value to life."

The amount of interested eyes grew.

Artorian carefully stabbed the part of the diagram where only the 'what you love' and 'what you are good at' parts overlapped. "This cross section correlates to one's Passion. There's long-winded explanations on these, but I'm going to give you the quick breakdown of the full diagram, and when we reconvene at the stone seats, we can speak at length then."

Murmuring and nodding followed.

"The cross section between 'what you are good at' and 'what you can be paid for' is your Profession. The cross section between 'what you can be paid for' and 'what the world needs' is your Vocation. The cross section between 'what the world needs' and 'what you love' is your Mission."

Scribbling in the missing pieces, Artorian tackled the triple overlap zones. "Combine your Mission and your Passion? You'll have delight and fullness, but no wealth."

The stick loudly stabbed the next one. "Combine your Mission and your Profession? You'll have satisfaction but also feelings of uselessness."

Artorian stabbed the third triple overlap zone. "Combine your Profession and Vocation? You'll be comfortable, but experience feelings of emptiness."

He then stabbed the last zone. "Combine your Vocation and your Mission? You'll experience excitement and complacency, but suffer from a sense of uncertainty."

"Having all of them is, of course, best." Artorian stabbed

the exact middle, looking momentarily weary. "It is then part of life that attaining all of them is generally out of reach."

Artorian chose to halt his quick-fire lecture there. "It is the measure of an adult to balance their time, needs, and drives responsibly. Nobody can do everything, all the time."

Half of the impromptu lecture had been to stick it to the snarky man. Half to prove that he really did want to help. The latter half, it seemed, had struck home with a significant part of the crowd. Unlike the rulers, he was actually here with them, *trying*.

The same church affiliate from before approached when Artorian put down his stick, question at the ready. The man stopped before him, his face frowning while his hands opened and closed. He was visibly torn. "Why would you do any of this for us? At all?"

Artorian cocked his head to the side, the answer coming from within. He lowered his head and closed his eyes, holding his own hands as he dredged up ancient wisdom from Roberts the Ruminating. "If there is doubt, then there is no doubt."

Artorian looked up, and abandoned the idea of Mana conservation.

Valor and **Glory** had referred him to the fourteenth floor as a test. Not for dealing with their own Ascended with violence, but for showing them the way. "I could say it is because **Retribution** thinks you've paid enough. Or that **Compassion** is my sword, and this is how I chose to wield it. But… no. I want what you deserved all along. I want you, all of you, to have the opportunity as people to live a life with meaning, or at the very least the knowledge that it is open to you. You've all been bogged down by history, and I'm not about it. People should get to be people. I want you to have clean, and true…"

Artorian sucked at Runes. He was terrible at them. So, in lieu of the options and contending with the path already chosen, he took a whole rank of A-tiered Mana, and fed it into an invocation as he answered the question in its most direct, most potent, most raw form.

Breathing deep, he pressed his hands to his own knees, and spoke the **Law** into being. It was what was needed. It was what was right. "**Redemption**."

A pink flare shot out from Artorian's Aura, stealing two more ranks as rather than merely **Redemption**, the entire fourteenth floor of the Tower stood up, and formed around the old man as giants surrounding the entire village. Like armored knights, summoned from an age long beyond, they stepped from the ether and entered into being, their gauntlets pressed to pommels, their mighty astral swords stabbing the trembling ground.

In unison, the statues unfurled their wings and bellowed. "We answer the call."

CHAPTER TWENTY-NINE

From the central plains of Camelot, a man named Wilhelm must have screamed, as the exact pitch and tone brought the name to Artorian's mind shortly before the tone turned to that of Marie's! She had just gotten her fielded aura stabbed by six astral swords in a most unpleasant posterior region.

When the grand statues pulled their mountain-sized weapons from the six new gorges they'd carved, the weapons flourished above all, cutting the sky. Blade tips touched in the center of the circle, leaving just enough room for a tiny gap that allowed a godray of light to descend upon Artorian, illuminating the old man that now no longer seemed so untrustworthy. The claims of his questionable legitimacy died on dry tongues as the jaws of every church affiliate in attendance collectively hit the ground.

They recognized the feeling of a Heavenly visitor.

Even those who had never experienced the awe directly could feel the truth pressing against their skin, the power laid as hands on their shoulders. They were attuned to such experiences, receiving them more easily.

The earlier affiliate was the first to grit his teeth, speaking to the illuminated old man. "Please understand, I refuse to accept you as any kind of messenger or messiah."

Artorian sighed in relief, his age showing. "My boy, I would deeply prefer it if you did not. I do not speak for them. I merely act for them. They may have said that they answered my call, but the call was provided to me, by them, in the first place. I shall not take away from you, my boy. It is my desire to provide. And if your providence descends to aid me in this, then I can only say to have been correct, that those who serve the heavens serve those who need it most."

The Administrator suddenly looked very old, and fragile, his hand extending to the affiliate. "Would you help me with all the wayward sheep who seek only shelter? This task would be so much easier if I did not have to carry it alone."

The affiliate puffed out his chest, steeling himself as his eyes flicked to the Heavenlies above that were already partially disintegrating. The eyes of the above were on all of them. They were on him. He could feel the weight, the judgment, the expectation. He would not leave them wanting, and powerfully gripped Artorian's hand.

"I am named Caesar, and while I cannot relinquish my affiliation, I will not see it tarnished further. The taint shall be cleansed. The Church shall provide. I thank you, Administrator, for the offer. However, I seek more than **Redemption**, and I will find it by lighting the way. So may your path be luminous, Administrator, because you will not find me in the darkness, unless I am there to make it bright. I shall be the light, and carve the way."

Five more joined Caesar's immediate proximity. People of the same mind, and same inclination. Artorian felt a pull, moved to stand, and saw a golden opportunity as he laid his other hand onto that of the handshake.

Power crackled from his voice. The fragile old man was replaced by an effigy of six swords, the astral shape overlaying his being. "Then as delegator, I render unto Caesar the things that are Caesar's. **Devotion** runs through your veins.

Compassion fills your words. **Redemption** waits on the path ahead. With **Retribution** behind you, **Empathy** and **Sympathy** shall be your blades instead. Take from me these powers six, find them hosts, and build your temple with fresh bricks."

The godray shifted, moving off Artorian and onto Caesar as the old man spoke. "Show me, my new friend, this luminous new world of yours."

When the giants disintegrated fully, Caesar could swear he felt a dawning sense of approval. Both at his choice to move forward and make his own light, and from six astral hands pressing to his back, those same hands leaving the old man's shoulders for a task well done.

The field of gravity pressing them all into place lifted when the giants vanished entirely, retreating to the central plains. Many didn't hesitate. They ran for the border.

Caesar and his five closest friends did not budge, confused as to how there were actual, real, true and proper swords in their hands. Each with a different inscription carved deep into the blade, written in light. Caesar had unknowingly already chosen the heralds, as the choice was easy when those who stood by you did so in the face of grand judgment.

What they did not notice, to Artorian's vast amusement, was that a chasuble had formed around the neck of each member. The clean cloth swaying in the wind was marked with three equally luminous circles upon the ends of each. That explained much about why the old church held the clothing item in such high regard. Myth had become reality in front of his eyes.

"You give power so easily, Administrator." Caesar folded both his arms against the small of his back and whispered rather than spoke, as if he didn't believe it himself.

The old man smiled with an expression that made Caesar envision peace. "It was never mine, my friend. And even if it were, it is now in better hands. I don't *want* to judge people, or be the true arbiter of their **Redemption**. I want to be the old man you can come sit next to on the stone bench under some fat walnut tree, and pour your heart out to before you go home feeling better, to warm smiles glad to see you. This is all I want. Is it so terrible to wish for the happiness of another? It is my wish regardless, Caesar."

He reached out, and gave the affiliate a gentle push. "Now go be light. You relieved me of burdens that I should not have been carrying, yet chose to regardless. All I did was deliver them to the place they needed to be the most. "

With a glance at the horizon, Caesar turned his back to Artorian and gave the man a single, curt, understanding nod before joining the others and leaving in a hurry. His task was elsewhere, and the Administrator's was coming here. The fish-monger had hurried to the sea and vanished in its waves, while those borne of trees were nowhere to be found.

Alice too, knew to go, though the Ikigai diagram went with him.

Artorian did his best to look steady until he was out of eyesight of even Mages, but the loss of the stable platform that he'd found in **Redemption** put a serious cramp in his Mana. The Mage version of a muscle cramp going up one's entire leg.

Henry, Marie, or both, were likely on their way.

No longer having a table to lean against, Artorian held his own hands and focused inward. Being used to making the connections for quick access, his hurried approach was not without cost. Artorian went on a slip and slide in Cal's Tower, landing on Tier one after a very embarrassing set of falls that could have been avoided had he taken the proper minute. Handholds were difficult when the floor vanished from under-neath you, so he was going to have to climb up the hard way.

Standing up in the simulacrum, Artorian rubbed his butt, and looked up. "Ow."

"Ya not gonna have time, brotha. Vala' gon' be here short-ly." Shaka giggled, the node of **Fire** informing him far too cheerfully. "Ya did real good with da request, but it cost ya da victory. Ya not gonna win the fight that's comin', not like this. Four ranks worth of A-quality *Oomph* on Tier one?" *Tsk tsk tsk*.

The node drummed on his own node and joked. "You gonna be the drum that gets beat."

"Hello Shaka." Artorian cracked his back and responded casually, honestly quite glad to be speaking to the Heavenly. "That's alright, I think. If I cannot climb fast enough, well, I'm not going to regret giving **Redemption** and his floor what **Valor** and **Glory** asked for."

"True, true." The node of **Fire** hovered around him, amused for a reason Artorian couldn't discern. "I did love the show. Though they went overboard showin' off. That was almost all of dere energy! But 'ey, if that's how they wanted it. They at least gonna be happy to have made the statement!"

"I certainly hope so." The old man sighed back, looking up at the ceiling. "Apologies, Shaka. I really should go. The talk can perhaps be later?"

The node laughed. "You just wait. We'll be with you soon 'nough! It gettin' easier and easier to step out and join Calcite's playground. Not for long. Not decisively. Enough for little conversations. You right, tho. Go! **Fire** wants to see that heat in both your hearts burn. We talk soon, **Love**'s chosen. Maybe at a cute cat cafe? We talk soon."

Artorian replied with a curt nod, having been influenced by Caesar, and hurried along on his climb. That Shaka said he likely wasn't going to win… that had been a fire under his rear to make him try harder, right? He was going to interpret it as such! "I've gotta do new math anyway. Four ranks total, three in the aura, I gotta aim for a foe around ninety something… that means a **Law** around the thirties! Let's a-go!"

Like being shot upwards through a green pipeline, Artorian went up far faster than he thought he would. He definitely had help. He could feel the help. Hands on the shoulders, pushing. Hands outstretched, ready to grab and pull.

He shot past floor twenty, twenty five, then bashed his face into the ceiling of floor twenty-nine. Scrambling to get up from the floor of that Tier, the Node of **Aeris**, that being Copper, slammed into his chest like Voltekka giving him one smash of a greeting. Artorian wheezed, the air in his body having left him.

Recovering, he rubbed over the copper ball like it was his dinosaur child. "Good to see you too, **Aeris**. Thank you for having been there for my boy."

Artorian was subsequently yeeted up onto floor thirty by what felt like a giant dinosaur head. He gripped onto **Acceleration** mid-panic, and thus sustained his upwards momentum directly onto floor forty-one as if being launched out of a tube, where he gripped onto **Hitchhiking** like a climbing hold on an angled wall. That had been a strong yeet! He blinked before looking around, not having a floor to stand on before commenting. "Oh, you're *funny*! Here just in case someone hangs around, *hmmm?*"

"Don't thank me or anything." The dour node hung its metaphorical head while commenting, pulling Artorian up onto solid flooring, and speaking in an accent that Artorian had no idea what to do with. Like a depressed, homeless, automaton. "All the others tend to have a cheerful and sunny disposition. Like doors. Don't expect that from me."

"Well thank you anyway, but I think I need to be a bit lower than this for now?" Artorian deduced, seeing how high up he was. "Could you release me?"

"You should really go up. I could calculate your chances of survival if you go down." The shrugging node morosely told him. "But you wouldn't like it."

Artorian instantly pulled the Tibbins expression. This was the moment for it. "Please let me go."

"Sure. Thanks a lot for leaving me behind." The node dropped him like a hot potato. "Though I can't say I blame you. Enjoy making friends with the ground. Just don't be a whale. Or a bowl of petunias. The ground takes exception to both, particularly the petunias with it happening twice and all."

Not expecting to have been treated like a hot potato, Artorian flailed all the way back down to floor thirty-one, where he swung both arms around the node of **Celebration** and clung to it like a five legged monkey.

"Safe!" He arced a leg over the ball as he slipped and huffed, a finger shooting to the sky. A finger he quickly recouped as he needed that arm to keep holding onto the node. "Tower physics… are *far* too malleable. Whatever happened to that good set of stairs? Can we get a good set of stairs?"

"Olá! Bom dia! I can get you cachaça, Vovô. Just in time for Carnivale!" The node he clung to burst with colors, beaming pure joviality. "**Celebration**'s got that *good* stuff. Capoeira style is in season too! I can already tell I'm gonna have fun with you."

Artorian blinked. "I think I'm in the wrong place. Does Vovô mean grandfather?"

The node was far too chill and relaxed for his liking. "Haaaa! Sim, Vovô. Yes! Brasilia's gonna take good care of you. Marvin sometimes drops people in on me like this, and trust me, I know the waves, I know what to doooo. I know the motion of the ocean! Lights, music, and cheer all around. I got pinatas for days—stolen, mind you—and sunglasses that are real round."

Artorian spoke before thinking, leading to a terrible fate. "You got sunglasses? I like sunglasses."

"Bellini, we got one!" The node clicked at him, shooting proverbial crossbow fingers. "The Baja beats in your hearts, Vovô. I knew a party lived in you, old man! You made the right choice! Now let's do something about those threads while you hang with the Janeiro boys, and dance some Samba to Bellini's noise!"

"*Uh oh.*" That statement was all Artorian got out before he was awake and standing in palisade village again. He blinked with a flutter. "I have made a horrible mistake."

"You can say that again." Henry tapped his foot like a miffed rabbit, standing mere inches from him with his arms crossed, donning full and complete Cal-quality battle tyrant armor. "No really, say that again, Marie might just forgive you. Slim chance, but a chance nonetheless. She's still rolling around holding her behind, so… definitely not a *big* chance."

CHAPTER THIRTY

"Hello Henry." Artorian rubbed the sleep out of his eyes, his Mana starting to feel… problematic. He couldn't let that show, repressing the feeling of a musical beat pulsing through his Aura. Samba de Janeiro was trying really hard to take the party from the inside to the outside. He tugged the field tighter in against his skin to lessen how obvious it felt, resisting the impulses.

Marie's sovereign space was actually helping here, as Henry hadn't noticed.

What Artorian unfortunately did notice was that all the spare **Love** Mana he'd been keeping in his pocket had been spent when the fourteenth floor of the Tower had been given a door to slam through like a fat jar of fruity red liquid. He really, really did not like knowing how his Aura was doing things on its own all of a sudden.

He'd needed that **Love** Mana!

Artorian changed the subject away from his thoughts, to an action Henry hadn't taken, that he would have. "I'm surprised you didn't whop me while I had my eyes closed?"

Henry made an uncertain hand gesture to the old man's

chest. "I was confused about what I was arriving at. That the border villages were doing poorly, I sort of knew. I don't yet have the time to do anything about it, with Central being the warzone it is, but to see the place vacant with you aimlessly standing there was odd."

"That can't have been everything?" Artorian dug his heels in, knowing that Henry was making a face made of questions under that seamless helmet.

Henry moved one hand to his hip, the other rudely pointing. "Well, no. I can tell you're an A-ranker, but when I got here you were rapidly getting weaker. I'm not sure how to describe your signature... plummeting? The general density of your... feel? It went up, it went down, it went down more, then it went up some. I was too curious about what I was looking at, and then you came to. If you're here to schedule with the steward, you picked a terrible way to knock on the gates."

Artorian pointed at the insult to palisades everywhere. "Surely you don't mean *those* gates? Where is everything, Henry? Where is all the civilization? The society? The culture? There's barren bedrock in an *estuary*. I don't know how this place isn't flooded!"

Henry shifted his pointing hand to hold his helmet. "I told you that things weren't going very well."

"Yes." Artorian spun with both his arms spread wide, hiding that he was feeling irate while he motioned at the wreckage like a circus ringmaster introducing the next hilarity. "I can see that. Luckily, I'm here to fix the entire mess. Officially, as Cal's Administrator. No take-backsies."

Henry's hand fell, no helmet being able to hide that his posture could only accompany a face of surprise and elation. "That's great news! You should have opened with that!"

Henry's attempt to mimic Artorian's old joke fell on deaf ears, as the Administrator was giving him a grim look. "I don't think you're going to like it very much, Supervisor."

The armored man shrugged. "Well, if you had to stab Marie in the... y'know, never mind. Best not to mention it.

We're in her Aura so she can hear us. If... if she figured out how. I keep trying to explain it between meetings, but that isn't going very well either. Don't suppose you have time for Mage lessons? I never even figured out how to be a proper B-ranker, and as an A-ranker... I live. That's about all I've got. I live and I win fights."

Artorian raised an eyebrow. "I honestly thought you had it all under control as a C-ranker? How *did* your Aura get so... wonky? Actually, that will have to wait, and it may be moot. Are you aware of the new body project? You and Marie should give that a go, and do all of life over. Rebuild the cultivation, do the Aura properly, Ascend correctly. No rushing through stages because you *can*. None of this mishmash with trying to get a region running. Just you and Marie, living a life."

Henry released the deepest sigh Artorian had ever heard from the man. "Friend, you have *no idea* how much I would love that."

Artorian smiled like a fox. "Then perhaps... What I have come to help you with is made of good news, after all! I'll be honest, Henry, I thought I was going to need to fight you and Marie. I would prefer not to. I was expecting to, either way. You look like such a champion in that armor."

"I am a **Valorous** champion! Displaying great courage in the face of danger, especially in battle!" The armor did nothing to blunt the regent's laugh, Henry's voice cracking as the sound didn't modulate correctly from being too loud. The very air around them twisted, and Artorian chalked that up to incredibly poor Mana control. Mana that was... *pouring* out of Henry. The twisting air around the regent turned to vapor like he'd stepped into the winter cold, fresh out of a hot sauna as the fuming energy rose up from him and vanished.

With his friend standing so incredibly close, a minor shift to the eyesight allowed Artorian to see Cal's back-of-the-neck connection. Just like when he did the B-ranking Mana tests, the connection point for the A-ranking variant was the same. Henry didn't appear to notice, at complete comfort with the constant stream of overflowing power that he wasn't even aware he was spending. His body leaked Mana like a colander. Forget the sieve. The holes were massive! Marie's Aura was eating it all up, but…

A Nixie tube popped over Artorian's head. His arm waggled towards Henry as he wobbled on his metal legs and nearly fell. He stabilized before purposefully making a twisting motion that his legs certainly did not like, then fell down on purpose before failing to get up again. "Well, let's just go see Marie then and… Biscuits! Henry, this is silly, but, help, please?"

"Are you alright?" Henry rushed closer with rising surprise, noticing both the odd leg design when the fabric squeezed around the metal sticks that were not-human enough for his coin to drop, and the metallic wrenching sound that came with Artorian's stumble. "Last I heard, you lost to Odin and lost your legs. Are those the replacements? I'd forgotten entirely."

Artorian's arm slid around Henry's for support, the hamming-it-up old man clinging like a gecko.

Henry watched Artorian bristle all over, take a deep breath, and start to look better trickle by trickle. That density feeling was starting to go up again, though at a very sedate pace. The troubled regent tried lightening the mood. "I didn't know old people would still have old people's problems as Mages?"

His second joke landed about as well as his first.

"They are the replacement. There's no shame in prosthetics." Artorian gave Henry the kind of educator's over-the-spectacles-look that screamed: 'if you had ever come to lectures, you would find it very obvious that I am playing you like a fiddle.' "Did you forget I was standing when you came to visit at the Aquarium?"

"I… uh. Yes. Wait, the what-rium? You weren't anywhere near water." Henry kept Artorian close and mumbled, his head clearly not in the game. Flashing lights in the distance quickly distracted the regent, his helmet turning to what was more than likely their next destination. "Marie's fighting again. Someone must have thought that her rolling on the ground was an opportunity. That's not going to last long with the mood she's in."

"Don't worry about it, Henry. Keep me steady." The old man's own mood had lightened, but not from Henry's poor jest. Artorian was pleased as well-stirred fruit punch that his idea struck extraordinary success. Proximity to the Mana source was in fact giving him priority access to the excess Henry was bleeding off. Henry's wasted Mana normally went to Marie's Aura after it left him, but with Artorian closer, that lingering effect from Eternia where Mana just seemed to **Love** him more went to work and provided for the family.

Artorian definitely felt like a favorite child, his Mana reserves climbing back up towards the next rank. Sedately, given there was a lot of space to fill, but a gain was a gain was a gain! If he could drop down from **Celebration** before the sensations overwhelmed him, even better! Brasilia seemed like the kind of extroverted Heavenly that would drag an introvert like him all around the mountain and never listen once to even the smallest discomfort. His Bellini friend likely only made that worse. Artorian was getting a very distinctive 'two idiots, one brain cell' feel. If Brasilia began to ply roguish charm, Bellini would certainly appear from thin air with a lute, intensely strumming on the road to El Dorado.

There was partying to do! Feet to move! Shoulders to shimmy!

Artorian quickly squeezed Henry with a shuddering exhale. The **Law** of **Celebration** almost had him just then! He couldn't think about it too much. "I have been better, so it's good that you're here. Also, take this. I'm unlikely to be speaking to any stewards today and want to make the trip with you and Marie as quick, painless, and easy as possible."

Artorian retrieved the invitation Henry had given him, and returned it.

"Marie may fight you on principle." Henry pocketed the returned item in a spatial ring, an obvious smile in his tone as he spoke. "She did get stabbed, and **Glory** is a hungry beast!

DENNIS VANDERKERKEN & DAKOTA KROUT

She's going to want her piece, and just a piece of you may not be enough."

Artorian quietly noted that Henry had two spatial rings, both engraved with a bunch of shields. Keeping his grip tight on the battle tyrant gauntlet, he first made motions to get a move on, then changed his mind and dug in his heels. "Wait. Wait, wait, wait. Is *that* why the chosen always called you the *beast* Dreamer? Because **Glory** is a *beast*, and you love Marie, who is with **Glory**?"

CHAPTER THIRTY-ONE

The specific shade of pink and red that Henry turned under his helmet Artorian was going to call head-over-heels. Even with a helmet on, the old man could tell. Henry was such an open book about it that, it didn't matter if the book was hiding four-point font and trying to look away. Or whatever smallest new number Alexandria had devised for cramming more letters onto a page.

Henry choked through some of his words. "I… Well, in the early Cal days, I had a hand in Beast designs? I got my hands on a scroll from Eternium that cataloged many of the species, Beasts, and strange creatures he'd saved. The Ark, as it's called, was compiled by one of his Monkey followers named Noah. Along with a really, really smart Gorilla named Winston. Did you know that he keeps an entire collection of glasses, spectacles, and the like?"

Artorian pulled Henry's arm, making him move along and walk with him as they left the village behind. "Don't think you can distract me! Beast Dreamer details. Stroll with me. Tell!"

Henry cleared his throat, mindlessly walking along a river-bank while spilling the goods. "So I had the list, and that's how

Sleipnir came to be. I was messing about with Bandersnatches and Jabberwock, then I landed on the Nuckelavee. I didn't understand what it was, so I pulled some strings. Had one reconstituted from before it was a strange undead demon-horse thing, and when I was all proud showing him off... The Dreamer title stuck."

Henry's pauldrons slumped. "Sleipnir and I have parted ways since then. It was rough to have a chosen request to no longer be one, but I found I could take the blessing and link away, so I did. Now he's different, having ditched the cleavers, the arms, the entire human torso. He preferred the shape of a many-legged horse, running across the plains. He's happier, I hear. Trips over his own hooves sometimes."

"You realize what you just called Marie, yes?" Artorian squeezed Henry's arm with a worried change in pitch.

Sputtering, Henry tried very hard to sashay away from that insinuation. "No, no, no! Marie's great! Stringent and... very tense lately. Definitely angry a lot, and... Alright, there's very little sunshine and roses. It's been so tough and busy, and nothing goes right or works out well, and it all..."

Artorian gave his friend a considerably more supportive squeeze when the topic began to spiral. Artorian had deduced this part already. Henry was a bundle of stress. "I figured, Henry. This zone wouldn't have ended up like this without some constant back and forth where one, or both of you, felt like they needed to keep upping the ante to make progress."

Henry stopped in his tracks, helmet peering straight down at Artorian. "How... How did you even...? We didn't even explain anything yet."

The old man shrugged. "I'm Administrator for a reason, Henry, and the more you talk, the more I think that the decree I have to deliver won't be bad at all. Abyss, you and Marie might have one of those grand sighs of relief like you released earlier. Finish your story. Why is **Glory** a beast?"

Henry resumed walking. "I will have to tell you a detail about my **Law** first, or it won't make much sense."

Artorian didn't mind that one bit. "Go on then."

"**Valor** is… an odd duck." Henry felt strange about saying the words, admitting his feelings. "Think… strength of mind or spirit that enables a person to encounter danger with firmness. The **Law** is rooted in the standpoint of personal bravery. Such as the circumstance found when facing an opponent, or something that I consider to be dangerous, or to be of great danger. Something that I then stand in front of. This, I've discovered, means that in order for me to fully draw on my **Law**, use it, or grow it, *requires* me to be in that circumstance. It is a *need*. It becomes a *need*. I find myself drawn to strife, when otherwise I would have chosen diplomacy."

"Don't worry, Henry." Artorian smiled up at him, harmless and innocent. "We may have our *diplomacy* yet."

Henry, clearly oblivious to the fate of Olympus, Odin, or anything else outside of the Camel-lot, didn't catch the hidden notes. Which, of course, told Artorian volumes when Henry was quiet for a moment. The man collecting his thoughts.

"The preamble remains much the same. Which is why my standpoint is difficult, and Marie's… complicates matters." Henry continued on the **Law** topic, his stride strong. "**Glory** is… a lot of things. Instead of personal bravery, which is more of a behavior, Marie's **Law** is instead focused on high renown or honor won by notable achievements."

He immediately paused, sounding conflicted. "Figuring out what 'honor' actually is in the context required by that **Law** remains a struggle, because if it's some kind of keyword, it does not mean what we thought it meant. **Glory** can be magnificence or great beauty. Something one can take great pride or pleasure in. At the same time, it can be standing victorious on the pile of a lot, and I mean a lot, of bodies. Small piles will not do, because when that **Law** wants 'notable' achievements, it means it. Her achievement better get people talking, and if there was only one or few opponents, they better have been noteworthy."

His arm flopped to his side. "What nobody warns you about

beforehand is that there's a weight and heaviness to the concept. **Glory** looks fantastic on paper. In practice? In practice, we've got some problems. Gaining **Glory** is done via attaining praise, honor, or distinction extended by common consent. Y'know, *renown*. The ideation of vast swaths of people knowing Marie, and what she stands for. This builds her power. Having Marie's name shouted with praise across the lands, and whatnot. Worshipful praise is even better, we found. The voices of the masses, shouting, lauding her actions, proud whispers of her name ready on every set of lips."

His gauntlet waffled with a side to side motion. "Well, not this iteration, but we did find out. Anything that secures praise or renown, speaking to the events of a brilliant career, counts as something that is glorious. So that's what Marie has to do, achieve, and attain. Acquiring that praise and renown is… Well, that's the problem."

"The problem. Yes." Artorian held his forehead, having puzzled this part of the issue out. "The conditions of the zone you were placed in."

Henry was keeping silent for Artorian to explain, so the old man skipped forwards in the conversation. "Meaning that the *conditions* for those factors to exist, those that you and Marie need in order to make personal and societal progress at the same time as attaining **Law** progress, must be manufactured. Especially if they aren't naturally in place when you go to look for them. I… am seeing the larger puzzle hidden behind the small one. You already tried focusing on one over the other, and this time you attempted both."

Artorian broadly motioned at the current patch of barren land they were in. The situation of their landscape hadn't improved in the slightest. "The place was peaceful and empty when you found it, wasn't it? Its inhabitants kind? Not exactly conducive to **Glory** gain unless you're a truly stellar monarch dabbling in statesmanship. No challenges to face isn't great for **Valor** to shine either. So instead of slow and steady, you both stirred the pot."

He leveled Henry with a stern gaze. "I *believed* you both were stellar monarchs who wouldn't have a problem with this. What happened with you and Marie?"

"Can I give the 'time changes people' excuse?" Henry slumped, muttering defensively. "Marie... I love Marie. I just want to support her. Be around her. Be with her. If that requires me to play along, and then happen to find conditions where I can satisfy **Valor** as well, while getting time with her, well, that's just stellar?"

Artorian's silent, stern gaze did not let up.

Henry bit his lip, grinding out his frustrations with words. "That's also part of the problem, because this time around, you're right. We tried something different from the usual, and it has clearly not been going well. This iteration, we're seeing if we can satisfy our **Laws** by being more heavy-handed and tackling statesmanship at the same time as... well, I'm going to call it *conquest* and hope you don't take offense. While seeing if strife and *hard-won* peace leads to greater yields."

He made a sharp, irritated gesture at the horizon. "When it came to ruling, we tried to be expedient this time. Perhaps consider this a curse or downside to be an over-experienced monarch? I, at a glance, can tell where someone fits well in the larger scheme of things. Think of your basic cog in the machine reference. We tried telling the people we saw exactly where they would fit the best, because we have decades of experience understanding and finding the optimal spot for a person, from seeing what has and has not panned out. We heard the people that we might get would be aimless. So a direct, easy answer to the best spot they could fill seemed so obvious. But..."

"Nobody listened to you." Artorian patted his gauntlet. "Nobody *wanted* to listen to you."

"Right!" Henry stood firm and agreed, far too happy about the old man seeming to realize his predicament.

Artorian was trying very hard not to slap his friend until his fancy armor resembled a hang drum used by bashers for practice. "You know you could have just gone to Aiden to ask about honor, right? He is sort of an expert on the matter."

"Who?" Henry needed to double take, blurting his response out with a speed that told Artorian his friend wasn't thinking. "Oh! Right. Aiden. My friend! Yes, I suppose I could. I'll see if I can fit it into the schedule."

All Henry achieved with his outburst was to cement the idea in Artorian's head that Aiden was going to get a golden chance in the next Eternia foray to beat this man silly, and work out all his wolfish frustrations. Artorian himself flashed an innocent smile. "Good. Talk to your friends. It helps. No more conversation about comparing **Glory** to the concept of a beast. I have understood the matter. It's more of that 'manufacturing the circumstances' vibe. The motion of the ocean is easy to surf."

Artorian began doing wave motions with his arm, his method of step altering to one where he was walking to a beat. He caught himself, coughed, and clung back to Henry. "It's happening again. Henry, we need to hurry. To Marie!"

Henry deduced that Artorian was having his own problems, dropped the topic of conversation, and picked the old man up to fly him to the central zone. Now sans light show as whatever fighting was taking place had ended.

From the sky, all Artorian could see of the central plains was devastation. What had once been a perfectly good estuary was now a set of craters turned into small, muddy lakes. The sight made the back of his hand feel mighty tingly, thoughts of explosive slippers coming very easily. "I see I am going to need to do some more... *diplomacy*."

CHAPTER THIRTY-TWO

The scene Henry and Artorian arrived at was best described as a mixture of political turmoil, grandstanding, and trying too hard. The designated reception crater filled with petitioners either strangling one another, or about to strangle one another. Evidence of recent fights still littered, scarred, and marred the battlefield that was the local caldera Henry's descent aimed for.

One very trashed A-ranker appeared beaten into its very center.

Artorian was tentatively going to call that one Yamcha.

The overall landscape was a barren wreck, and not worth mentioning. The infrastructure was either blasted to barely notable chunks, or a state that may as well be non-existence. As he'd been informed, red fire burned everywhere he could see, sourced from a most interesting rock that he would need Dwarven expertise to understand.

On the caldera's tallest ridge, Marie was the center point of all the commotion.

Difficult not to be, when Marie had taken the form of a forty foot marble statue sitting on a pile of defeated Mages while holding on to a familiar-looking halberd. The flag attached to the end, showing a picture of a noodle-dragon holding on to a tree, spiked Artorian's blood pressure all by itself.

His Mana flow picked up the slack, letting him have the moment to fume and survey more of the scene, beginning with the forty foot statue as a focus as he invested considerable effort to dull the drums in his ears.

Marie's marble form was inlaid with golden lines where damage or stress fractures had accumulated. The golden material, at first glance, seemed to be a patch-job meant for healing? This trick of Marie's, Artorian wanted to know more of. He nudged Henry shortly after landing and motioned at the shiny striations on the regal statue when he got on his feet, hoping to get an answer before they got mobbed.

Henry needed the Administrator to point a second time before understanding what the old man was getting at. "Oh, the lines? Some ancient Technique, found in Phoenix Kingdom records, called Kintsugi. The art of putting broken pottery pieces back together with gold—a metaphor for embracing your flaws and imperfections. Marie took it more literally."

Artorian mumbled a sullen comment, considering the situation. "Good thing there's still room for more."

Henry didn't appear to hear him, as he just kept going. "As she increased in **Law**, her skin became more and more marble-like. She hides it with normal skin tones when visiting people. Or armor. Usually the battle tyrant armor. Currently it's back to public appeal time, since the tussle seems won. Her Mage-pile is bigger? Without bailiffs, order-keeping is difficult, so we tend to answer the ones we have answers to. I…."

His face turned foul. "Oh no, not the *rabbits* again."

Artorian peered towards the crowd, his eyebrows rising as he spotted the familiar form of Richard! Oh, good! *Backup!* "I do so enjoy being both fortuitous and lucky. Nice to see another friendly face."

Henry fished out Richard's face in the crowd, and pointed to ask if that was what the old man was talking about. Artorian nodded, then made a sideways 'let's get going' head motion as he trucked off in Richard's direction. "See to your people, Henry. Maybe quietly ask Marie how her butt is doing? She appears *suspiciously* calm and collected."

"I keep telling you, Artorian. You're going to catch hands. There's no escape." Henry nudged the man with a half-tease. "I'm certain her current seat somewhat appeases the situation."

Artorian's reaction turned into the 'I abyss-blasted knew it was going to come to this' face. Which was very similar to the Tibbins expression, except with more demure resignation and a salty sprinkling of premature pushing your sleeves up. "She can throw them, Henry, but she best be ready for more than a verbal rebuttal of rough and tumble philosophical discourse if she does."

Henry laughed under the helmet, causing another booming explosion of trembling air that made it impossible for them to go unnoticed any further. Artorian rubbed his ear closest to Henry to make a point before leveling another glare at the man. "Go see your lady. I'm going to poke my nose into whatever kerfuffle Richard is trying to sort out. I can see the Necrohamster and Glitterflit representatives going at it, but I honestly thought that was sorted? Excuse me. Administrator has to administrate."

"Don't let me stop you from taking work off my hands! I like Richard, but the rabbit problem is a microcosm of our old world, and I don't want that nostalgia trip." Henry chuckled, beelining for Marie. Arms wide, Henry could be heard dropping into politics mode and placating the crowd that swarmed him, as the mass of people stuck to him like hungry bears on honey.

Artorian vanished from the senses. Taking a page out of the Dark Elven book to insert himself into Richard's crowd without being unduly accosted, he made it within argumentation range before the effect fizzled out. The Mana he'd spent on copying the trick being siphoned away by... the **Law** he was using as a platform to stand on? He did not like that one bit! **Celebration** and sneaking were not pals, it seemed.

He could swear he heard a lute strum?

"Well, that's no good." He garnered the attention of both Richard, and the argumentative factions currently making a fuss.

"See, another agrees!" A four inch hamster in a teensy necromancer robe stomped its tiny foot. Spouting rhetoric while standing with his compatriots on an elevated rock formation that looked to have been dredged from deep below the ground. The chunk of earth was definitely a mineral of some kind, but Artorian would once again need Dwarven input for details. Some kind of 'lick to identify' ability idea came to mind, but that would have to go to Tim.

Father Richard was glad to see his scheming compatriot.

"Artorian! That was... incredibly swift? I only sent someone out a bit ago. Or was that you with the Heavenlies?" Richard smiled like a practiced schemer, putting a thumb behind his outfit to show off his new Supervisor attire, his robes splendid and new. The man had clearly taken pride in the upgrade to his threads. Richard even brushed them over when looking Artorian up and down, a flash of jealousy shooting over his features. "Must have been you, though they no longer seem to follow in your wake. I'll be asking about this at the 'big meeting' I hear Supervisors have now and again."

"Correct on all counts." Artorian gladly tackled that hungry look first. "Like it? I'm modeling for Brianna. I expect the next time there's a big round table meeting, she might bring a wardrobe."

Richard's jealousy was thrown to the wind, discarded instantly at the prospects of being able to attain his own fancy attire, and without needing to play model at that! "I cannot say I am in the least surprised about that woman desiring to spread her culture far and wide."

"Quite, though I wouldn't refer to her as Woman, unless you've got a fondness for daggers in the spleen." Artorian slid in a friendly warning since he was never truly without eyes on him. A flick of the eyes conveyed a mountain of words.

Both keeping tabs on him, and spreading her culture as incognito as possible, sounded like a very Brianna thing to do. Artorian then shot down Richard's initial assumption. "No, my friend, I'm afraid I arrived before ever being aware of any kind of missive. I'm here for the big cheese. Both big cheeses. The matter is going to get very stinky before it gets freshened up."

Richard was familiar with Brianna, but not familiar enough to get a free pass for his comment should there have been unsavory informants. The Father caught his drift on both hints, as if he'd been scheming with Artorian on cheese related topics for months, even though this was the first he'd heard of it. "Now that you mention it, *Lady* Brianna ought to be given her due respect. Thank you for the correction."

Richard's expression turned foxlike, and Artorian again felt that instant brotherly kinship.

The silent look that conveyed 'I want to be included in the festivities' was easily caught by Artorian, whose party **Law** once again attempted to break free. He repressed the sensation by shifting to a serious topic, but was starting to feel cracks form in the foundation. "I'm also glad to inform you that I've hung up my church bias coat, Richard. Some new factions have been planted, and I think rather than critique the sprouts, some nurture would do more good. I don't suppose you could go speak to Caesar and his little group after this? They were ordained with the chasuble, and want to carve their own light out from the darkness."

Artorian motioned in the direction where all those people were already gathered. "They could do with both your expertise, and your guidance on how to handle a Heavenly's personal attention."

"Tell me more when this is wrapped, Administrator." Richard physically tensed and replied tersely as he wanted to indulge, but had to contend with ongoing politics. His attention pulled back to the glares of those he was moderating. A hand motion spoke volumes that he was very much taking up that next task with Caesar, but that there was an order to things, and the Glitterflit issue was next in line. "I must attend to this matter."

"Of course, Supervisor. Congratulations, by the way." Artorian eased his hands against his lumbar, amending his stance to listen in. Though the argument had progressed from words to violence.

One of the Glitterflits, wearing her own adorable little robe to cover most of that bright golden fur, stood front and center as representative. She had gotten up on her hind legs, turned into a five foot nothing human girl in healer's attire, and was promptly pulling up her sleeves with the kind of fervor that any bar-brawler recognized as the precursor to the first bottle being broken.

Amusingly, the person retained the ears! Currently, those ears were very bristled, straight, and positively shaking with agitation. Emotion-based ears? How interesting!

Artorian currently could not tell if this was a humanization performed incompletely, or a transfiguration gone awry. Either way, the Necrohamster had snuck some comments in that he hadn't caught while distracted with Richard, which had completely ticked off the Glitterflit. Oh, right, Glitterflit! Incomplete humanization category it was.

His eyes lingered on Marie's marble form.

Transfigurations gone awry were far more complicated. Luckily, most Mages appeared to eschew being made of a material other than what their original form had been. So he didn't have to really concern himself with more instances like Ziggurat's self-proclaimed 'golden queen' that he'd dragged to the proverbial shadow realm. Okay, it was the Glitterfold, and he'd fed Meatball to space-arachnids, but shadow realm sounded like a nicer thing to say. That shaper **Law** had been such ick. Or was it shaping?

Why was he even thinking about this?

Glitterflits sort of did share a name with The Glitterfold. He should visit? Perhaps it was because it had been awhile since he'd seen a Mage be something other than a copy of their old selves. Marie knew that upholding the marble form made her weaker, right? The properties and strengths of marble were far below what basic Mage-flesh could handle. Slapping properties on your own form was a double-edged sword as a Mage. Having spent time as an opalite statue, of this he was certain.

He mumbled to himself. "A shame it's not available in the C-ranks where that would be incredibly useful. I'm certain it's feasible."

Dismissing that tangent, he didn't really want to deal with more people pulling a Dawn and turning into focusing crystal. Dodge-the-prismatic-laser was a game best played sparingly. He immediately added dodge-the-laser as an option for upcoming events when he observed the forty foot statue of Marie longer. Since that was Marie *showing off.*

A bit more fire under the keister might just be the ticket!

His attention turned to Richard's plight when the volume got out of hand.

"You have crossed the Godhands!" The Glitterflit girl stamped her foot, the tension in those ears bordering the electric as the golden fur sparked. The hamsters' latest round of abrasive commentary poised to cause more fighting. "Face our bunny-wrath!"

Artorian wondered if it shouldn't be Godpaws, since the clan was of Basher origin, but if they wanted to go with hands, then hands it was. Plenty of hands would be thrown today regardless, according to Henry, so it may as well start here.

Everyone paused when the Necrohamster slapped the Glitterflit with a carefully removed glove, throwing it down to the rocky ground in ancient challenge, before shoving its nose to the air. "Mr. Whiskers, master of the thousand dooting skeletons, rejects your wrath!"

Banter ended, as that loud *pop* drew eyes and silenced tongues.

"Summoning is on the banlist. Doot this!" In a flurry of glittery, golden motion, the Glitterflit engaged super-speed and activated the Nyoooooms of Immolation. Her hand caught on electric flames, the golden glimmer of her palm a blur of motion as she slapped the Necrohamster back with so much force that it turned the four inch tall creature into a bright straight-shot projectile, converting the static enemy into a moving object with a burning flash.

A *kpow*! thwomped along with the impact, the line of flame fizzling out when the fire ran out of fuel and physics straightened its lapels. Excess force exerted smashed conical waves of raw kinetic energy around everyone present, but with everyone present being B-ranked or up, that was no different than there being a stiff breeze.

Artorian delightedly gasped out an 'oooooh'! His head turned to follow the hamster turned projectile, observing as the beastie added a crater to the landscape in the distance. That move had been very similar to the rail palm! An Earth and Celestial variant adapted for Basher use? Lightning struck his brain as he thought of Cal's armored Basher boss. "Oh, I know! A Raile-Palm!"

The rest of the Necrohamsters looked very nervous, in full contrast to the good cheer of the two older men that were both grinning. This problem was solving itself.

"You have injured a Glitterflit. You have injured a healer!" The Glitterflit shoved her fist to the sky. She loudly proclaimed her judgment, her hand still smoking with sparking gold energy. "Therefore, you have drawn... aggro!"

CHAPTER THIRTY-THREE

The hamsters fled. Not from the wave of upset Glitterflits that easily caught up in streaks of gold and used them to practice futbol, but from the nearby boulders that came alive. Unfurling to become Raile-sized Bashers. These balls of brick then began to spin in place before launching themselves at those who held the aggro.

The healers had not come undefended, their tanks at the ready!

Richard and Artorian watched the noisy dust cloud go, not particularly fussed about the problem resolving by itself. The Father had an entire line of jokes ready, but kept them in his pocket when noticing the Administrator steal furtive glances at Marie. The man was clearly bothered by something, and the insinuation that he was here to 'take care of it' with a cheese reference was unpacked.

The Father leaned his entire torso towards Artorian without turning to face him. The motion was obvious enough that Artorian asked the leading question. "Do you want to help me?"

"Yes." Richard nodded easily, his earlier quiet request to be included properly verbalized. "Do you want me to follow your directions? Or give ideas?"

Artorian felt hope blossom in his chest. "That is my new favorite answer."

"Thank you. I was blessed with some time with the Saintess, and our chat dragged on longer than expected. I treasure the experience. Never have I met such a friendly Incarnate." Richard beamed, his smile cheeky as his nose nudged to the statue. "I have my own history with Henry, Marie, and Brianna. The first two I've always wanted to give a piece of my mind. They didn't deserve my ire in the Mountaindale days. Now, on the other holy Icon, I feel like chasing them with a smoking censer and spiked thurible while I read off litanies of betterment. I'm not blind. The road to the Abyss is paved with good intentions, and what a road they have made."

Artorian's mind encountered a slowly spinning rainbow error. "I'm sorry, Richard, I know that was very supportive, and yes please, but aren't those the same object? I am not versed in church lore to that degree."

Richard succeeded in his secret ruse, now that Artorian's mind had snapped away from whatever he'd been worried about. "They are. As nouns, the difference between a censer and a thurible is that a censer is an ornamental container for burning incense, especially during religious ceremonies. While a thurible is a type of censer."

Artorian did not have the opportunity to comment, as Marie got up and made a powerful declaration. "I have come to a deliberation!"

The Mages beneath her groaned, but barely twitched when the pressure let up.

"Ah! That must be for me." Richard perked up, his hands rubbing together before he gave the Administrator a polite nod, and hopped up to one of the taller rocks.

"First." Marie spoke, her hand making an upward motion. A slab of rock rose from the ground, engravings breaking through from within to write the words. Artorian read it like one of Tim's game prompts.

Peppers are the spicy of fire.

Mint is the spicy of ice.

Carbonation is the spicy of air.

Vinegar is the spicy of water.

Ginger is the spicy of earth.

"Second." Marie spoke again, still acting like she was making earth-shattering decisions. Artorian was still confused as to what the first question might have been, and hoped that the second slab rising from the ground held the answer. Instead, this new slab was about a whole different topic.

Power comes not to those who need it, but those who seek it.

Knowledge comes not to those who think they want it, but to those that quest for it.

What you seek is what you will gain, regardless of the activity.

If you seek a reason for anger in the most mundane of activity, then you shall find one.

If you seek wisdom in a grain of sand, then you shall find that too.

Content in her deliberation, Marie then surveyed her surroundings, as if she hadn't been aware of them prior to this moment. She instantly spotted Artorian, and her stony expression soured. "Well, look what the C'towl dragged in. Here to apologize? It better be a good one. Now that my region is finally secured and free of usurpers, I can actually get started with building. Abyss knows the place needs it. I have everything under complete control."

Artorian scratched the front of his chin. "That... Hold that thought, Marie. I've got an official notice for you first, but perhaps this is not where you'd like to hear it. Could we—"

"No." Marie cut him off without preamble or hesitation.

Artorian blinked, a hand moving to his sternum. He turned to Richard when the man got down from his rock and meandered next to him, a raised eyebrow silently asking the 'what can I do' question.

Artorian took him up on it, providing directions. "I see how this is going to go. Richard, could you please gather and abscond with the local non-cheeses to a safer location?"

Richard winked, and clapped his hands together in a motion that Artorian recognized as an old, secret hand signal. "I do want to speak to this Caesar. Please excuse my method of expediting your request."

Artorian nodded. Richard took the moment to show off, and elucidate on why he hadn't been too impressed with Artorian having the attention of a few Heavenlies. One appeared to be hanging off his shoulder, because Richard spoke with depth, and that obvious feeling of power from the beyond. "**Sonder.**"

"What is the feeling of **Sonder**?" Artorian wondered, before it hit him like a house that had pulled up from its foundations to stand on chicken legs, and tackle him like a discount Baba Yaga hut.

"Sonder." Richard clasped his own hands and spoke without invoking the **Law** again as its effect was already ongoing. "Is the profound, individual realization that each person you meet is living their own life, that each person has their own world. Filled with their own personal worries, pains, pleasures, ambitions, and routines. The sensation is that they live lives the same as yourself, in a sense, but also as intricate and as different as could be imagined."

The feeling flooded Artorian's senses, rushing through him, over him, and past him. Like fear, except warm, welcoming, and eye-opening for the duration that it lasted. This also blinded him to the world around him long enough that, when **Sonder** expired, only he, Marie, and a very confused Henry remained at the edge of the caldera. Even Yamcha was missing.

The Administrator inhaled deep, and exhaled hard.

Relief came with it, both from getting to feel that someone else was out here working for some greater good, and that he could now properly tick off Marie. Henry might take it well. Marie… "I best get to it then. Marie? Get off your high horse. You and Henry are hereby removed from your responsibilities as Supervisors. The ones that you've been shirking. You're dismissed as the assigned rulers of this region, and your task to build up is no longer on your docket. You're both taking a mandatory vacation. No more work time."

"No." Marie crossed her arms and replied with such flatness that Artorian wondered if he'd relayed the verdict just now, or if he'd imagined it.

"It… really wasn't a request, Marie." Artorian shifted to speak with his hands more, attempting to clarify.

"No." Marie's form pulsed with power, the statement rebuked. Marie was barely paying him any attention as she shook off the last of **Sonder**'s influences. "There. It's off of me. *Ew.*"

Henry rushed over while Artorian tried his best to get on the same page. "Did—Marie, did you not hear me, or do you just not care?"

"Go away, old man." She glared down at him like a mere nuisance begging for her attention, commenting sharply. "The only thing you're welcome to tell me is your deep and extended apology for *stabbing* me. Anything else that comes out of your mouth has no value until that. I don't believe the insult of words that came out of you, and I'm doing you the distinct kindness of ignoring them."

Henry pressed a hand to Artorian's shoulder. "Sunny. Was that the news? That really isn't feasible."

Artorian looked between them as abject confusion dawned on his face. "What? I—No? Are both of you alright? This wasn't a question. Pack in your Auras. You're not playing monarch here. At all."

Marie's fists cracked when she squeezed them, the stone of her knuckles not filling with Kintsugi metal. The rage on her face was easy to discern, stony features or not. "I said *no*, Artorian."

The old man squeezed the bridge of his nose, and backpedaled. "Why is it a no, Marie? When I was talking to Henry on the way over, this didn't simply sound feasible—and

I'm going to want an elaboration on that in a bit, Henry—it sounded like a desired outcome."

"No apology, then?" Marie fumed. "Fine. Why should I expect anything from you, after all?"

This underserved hostility was far too much for Artorian, who was now getting upset in turn. This was not Marie. This was not like Marie. Not at all. He turned to the armored gauntlet holding his shoulder. "Henry. I am not just confused, but confused enough to understand that more is going on than I have information to. I delivered the verdict, how is that not the end of it?"

Marie sniped sharp commentary. "How did some nobody we selected at Dale's council get more important than us? Why don't you riddle me that? *Headmaster*. We were dumped on a region of land, given yet another task to build up yet another realm, and right when we have taken care of the very last usurper Mages that flew in here to claim they would be ruling and not us, you come in and tell us this garbage?"

Artorian's comment was cut short as Marie thundered, accusatorily pointing at him from above. The Mana in the region swirled, storming from her anger and dissatisfaction. "You don't apologize for stabbing my Aura, you don't come check on us to help, you don't… You just don't!"

"There is no possible way for me to be everywhere at once, and attend to everything, Marie." Artorian moved his arms back to his lumbar, speaking with a leveled, cold tone. "You were experienced at this, I didn't expect to have to check, much less do any hand holding on the very topic you're supposed to have expertise in, and certainly not *this*. I'm about at the point where I stop caring how it came to this, and at the point where I'm about to serve your own medicine back to you. You need a fresh start. Y—"

"You do not get to decide how I live my life, old man!" Marie caused an earthquake by stomping her boot, voice booming. "You do not get to boss me around. Cal does not get to boss me around. Cal wanted us to exist in his world and do what we do, and that's exactly what I'm going to do. So you clear out, because currently you are no different from any other annoyance coming in here, demanding this and that about what we ought to do. My answer is no. Get out. You'll see us again when the Camel-lot has grown to edge the borders of your... What is it? Avalon? We're the ones who will take over. *You* take a break. *We* will rule this realm as we're supposed to, and *we* will make sure it runs right."

Artorian was, for a moment, at a loss for words. When he found them, the anger joined in full force. "Does my being the Administrator mean nothing to you? Does being a Supervisor suddenly hold no merit? You've certainly managed to make it seem like you haven't cared, but that's not what has me by the beard."

He brushed off Henry's arm, upset. "This is the iteration where our people live. Our first, proper one. You don't get to play kings and castles with this. You don't want to respect the titles? Fine. Then there's no titles at play here. No kings, no queens. Just common folk with disagreements. If I need to be just another guy to drive some sense into you, then just another guy I will be."

"Still failing to see the correct perspective as always, Artorian." Marie sneered at him and cut in. Her grip on the halberd became more than posture support. "You could never understand the outlook of a regent. What needs to be done so the most basic of groundwork can come to pass. I am someone who is meant to rule. Someone who has ruled, and keeps ruling, like it's my abyss-blasted profession. You can't come into my hard-won territory and tell me to leave. You can't tell me to do anything at this point. I am queen, and you are some lucky punk who was chosen to attend to menial administrative tasks. You have one chance to leave, or I will hold you in contempt. Henry? Prepare to throw him out."

Artorian frowned. "You don't want this, Marie. Neither you nor **Glory** wants me as an *opponent*."

Her response was to pull another slab of earth from the

ground, the engraving making her position on the conversation clear. "Clear off, *mutt*."

Artorian read the slab, his stomach turning from the subtext.

Our foe is vast.
Our land is so small.
Where will we find space,
To bury them all?

CHAPTER THIRTY-FOUR

The old man locked his gaze with the upset statue when Marie called him a mutt. The choice of insult was telling, as Artorian grasped one of the needles in the haystack that had Marie so on edge. She considered him a wolf of doubtful pedigree. Unfit to tell her what to do. A person incompetent to his station. Somewhere along the line, he had lost Marie's respect.

Henry grumbled at Artorian. "Sunny, this was a really bad way to do this. Walking in and dropping declarations makes you no different than the last twenty people who pulled that same stunt."

Artorian squeezed his eyes shut, his hands forming fists, opening wide, and forming fists again. "Henry, I take it you're going to side with Marie? No matter what?"

"No matter what, old friend." Henry slid into a combat stance and nodded apologetically, a longsword appearing on his hip in a swirl of energy. "I'm sorry, but I'm with Marie. Things will get better."

"I really wish I had more explanation here, old friend." Artorian sighed, turning as if to leave. "There's a story here. A cause for Marie's anger, and your blind loyalty. One that isn't what's getting shouted my way. Like a sickness, I remind myself that what I am experiencing are the symptoms. Not the cause."

Henry had no answer for Artorian's thoughts, a hand pressing to the old man's back in the hopes this would not come to blows after all. "Perhaps one day, we can tackle that. Are you heading out?"

Artorian didn't budge an inch, his face looking to the clear sky. He breathed in, and knocked on **Celebration**'s door. "No, Henry. It's time for *diplomacy*. I just stepped over the line where the reasons for why things got this way are secondary, and that the outcomes now stand on the forefront. You are enabling a person whose priorities now include actual conquest of regions in the world that include people whom I love. I'm no stranger to tyrants, Henry. I am one. So you best pull out that sword, because I'm not sure if you remember what I told Brianna."

"If I must." Henry's expression turned unpleasant, repeating the phrase as understanding dawned, and his non-supporting hand moved to the hilt of the longsword. "You said, *if I must.*"

"And I must, Henry." Facing the sky, he accepted a mental connection from Brasilia, and his friend Bellini. Nodes living on the same level. Artorian spoke with an air of relief, as he was releasing stress that he hadn't realized he'd been holding tight. Fighting your friends was a demanding task. "Marie? I apologize. I didn't know they would stab you. I hope you'll forgive me for the error. Yet, Marie?"

He turned just enough to face her. "They didn't stab you hard enough."

"Henry!" Marie exploded, her massive halberd aimed at the now very unwelcome interloper. "Throw him out!"

Time slowed.

Brasilia's unseen arm moved around Artorian's neck from his left, while Bellini copied the motion from his right. Two rogues here with an offer of incredible mischief. Brasilia voiced his opinion, at least understanding why Artorian had been repressing his **Law**'s concept.

The Heavenly mentally spoke in his head with one of the smoothest Forum-type connections Artorian had felt. <Vovô. You and me? We come to an understanding. Bellini and me, at first? Very confused. Now? Now we understand. We make a party deal? We have been listening in. She calls you a mutt? You show her what a mutt can do, Baja. Bellini and me? We're mutts too. So we're gonna make an exception for you.>

Bellini's voice was incredibly similar to Brasilia's, joining the conversation. <Those two? They need to relaaaax, Vovô. Work out all that stress. Let go of the livewire. The fight is here, so we will both help you out, if you do it with Capoeira and cheer. All that anger? Give it to the breeze. We'll make some music, help you eat this cheese.>

Bellini gave him a good squeeze. <Normally, we'd make you dance to our music, but Brasilia is reasonable. Seems that we should incentivize the wallflower. I got your threads ready, Baja. You party with us? We'll party with you. These two need to be shown what us mutts can do.>

Artorian considered the request for a beat.

A sharp nod followed, the active rebuking of **Celebration**'s influences turned on its head. This was not the best **Law** to face this problem with, but this was what he had. Maybe Brasilia and Bellini had a point. Rolling his shoulders as time resumed to flow normally, he suddenly *knew* Capoeira, knowledge of the martial art flowing into his mind like water pouring into a decanter.

Henry's draw and flash of steel struck vacant space, slicing through empty air as in a motion never seen before, Artorian dropped to the ground and spun. His legs swirling in a wide arc before his hands pushed him up from the rock after the initial swing of the blade passed.

When Artorian snapped up to his feet, a dull beat began to thud and resonate from the center of his chest. He dodged the next three swings that descended at lightning speed before toeing exactly out of the way of the fourth, slapping his hands together and creating an expanding glitter-cloud.

Henry, not taking chances, backed away from the expanding glitter with a swift set of shuffled hops. His armor enhanced his movements rather than deterring the effort as slits of light flared to life on the seamlessly sealed faceplate. Improvements to the battle tyrant set, taken from ideas of Dawn's old armor. Within moments, Henry was not impaired by the visual block caused by the glitter, though he also did not see any hints of danger accompanying the effect. Had it been a ruse? A smokescreen?

A smokescreen clicked into Henry's mind as answer when Artorian, dressed in a new, ridiculous outfit, held a pose while bopping his head towards his left shoulder, hearing some beat that Henry wasn't privy to. The regent sputtered at the sight. "What is *that* supposed to be?"

"An elite outfit!" Artorian posed, his beard full of glitter. Sporting a floral pattern aloha shirt, shades that fit him exactly, and bright yellow shorts covered in green palm trees. His metallic legs were on full, easy display, those animal claws gripping the ground with enough force to crack bedrock. "I present to you, Artorian! Crouching Liger, Hidden Dragon. I am the Baja-mutt!"

Artorian then moved his head and hips in circular concert while the regents stared in disbelief and wonder. The staring stopped when they could both begin to hear the music that Artorian bobbed his shoulders to in the next set of movements.

Henry waited to launch his next attack when Artorian abruptly stopped, the music skidding to a halt as his dance movements smoothed to a more snake-like slide. The sensation of sand accompanied his motions, as the music changed from clicking maracas to the strums of an Oud Instrument. One operated by a very devious Djinn.

Artorian, feeling the intended groove, improvised some lyrics as he felt the very distinct notes of more observers paying attention to him. Time for a show! Artorian broke into a song that mostly matched the magic carpet ride he was being taken along on.

Clap clap.

Scholar D, a legend is he, mighty A-kota!
Writes like ten regular men, verbose is he.
Clap clap.
He's gone and done it again.
Clap clap.
He's written a whole other tale.
Clap clap.
Something, Anything, Everything, so hale!

The old man awkwardly stopped as he lost the thread after his last line, whistling the tune of the first line again while finger twirling. Henry even commented instead of attacking. "It was good, up until the last line, where the cadence fell off a cliff."

Artorian shrugged, snapping his fingers as the music cut, the old instruments returning with far greater intensity. "That's what I get for improvising. I'm getting some strange looks, but I can hear the sky shrieking with laughter and applauding me for more. So I know the next what-for!"

Henry looked to Marie, who sternly stabbed her halberd back in the old man's direction.

"Bellini!" Artorian danced, his arms spread wide as he readied and flared his Aura, the colors covering his skin turning into spectacular displays of parrot feathers as he drew on the knowledge of Capoeira that sloshed in like a river. "*Samba!*"

Whistles, trumpets, and drums instantly followed.

Henry roared back, a lion-shaped emanation of Mana coating his helmet as parts of his armor discolored, gaining heavy tints of orange and violet. His left armored gauntlet was overlaid with a lion's claw, right hand gripping to the longsword as he called out his own current style, falling prey to a bit of show and dance as **Valor** started to kick in. "Imperial Lion!"

Henry's being flared with upwards force, his density intensifying as his sabatons sunk several inches into the ground when the increase in energetic mass took hold. Another roar broke from him and caused the air to twist. He didn't know the vaunted Gar Style from the old Lion Kingdom, but his personal growth and needs had led him to a fighting method that certainly proved effective.

Artorian recognized the flecks of intent pouring off Henry with the stance he adopted, his eyes eating up any and all hints that could provide insight to how Henry fought.

Imperial Lion was a tremendously powerful and effective fighting style if standing, or operating on the ground. The clawed left hand betrayed volumes of history with fights focused on grappling. Artorian could visualize clawing motions that could tear out or crush the throat of a man in seconds. He would have to avoid being grabbed above all. An open-claw and one-sword kind of style for mixed ranges, though this left Henry vuln—

Henry's rings activated when the Mana poured in, sealing away Artorian's ideas of weak spots and vulnerabilities as hundreds of shields formed as phantoms around him before materializing into the real thing. A warcry rumbled from each manifestation, the obviously imported Eternia items gleefully eating up their due of energy. Each of the ornate, detailed shields was inscribed with an inscription or lower-class Rune that was sure to cause headache.

Artorian spotted heaters, wankels, bucklers, coffins, kites, war-doors, and tower shields. A whole mixture of fun that hovered around Henry in stable orbits, the spinning defenses surrounding him as an adaptive, protective wall of *block*.

Artorian chalked Henry's kit up to include warcries, Beast skill copies, one-handed weapon mastery. A physical combat boy. The Mana was focused on Henry's body, with little regard for Aura. Though the infinite energy exploit was on clear display, since Henry didn't even notice the disconnect. His Aura swam back to him and globbed on like an oil spill, causing more of that orange discoloration on his armor.

Honestly, an Aura that bad should have killed the man. Henry had luckily not been dumb enough to disconnect it from himself completely, but every time Artorian saw it, something inside of him cringed. Just… how did one have an Aura *that bad*, and still…? Never mind. Later!

Artorian would have preferred to stick to his strengths, but he was definitely going to need to use his own Aura to contend with Henry's physical form. The math was ever so slightly not in his favor, but given the clear complications living on Marie's face, it appeared his prior calculations had been spot on!

Marie responded by shoving her gauntlet into the air, and making it clear that venue was more of a choice, rather than happenstance. She couldn't bring the full force of her **Law** to bear, since Artorian didn't qualify for its full use. He was weaker than her, unarmed, and fit none of the bills or tick-boxes that provided her **Law** an effective foothold. He was an opponent, yes, but in his current state, he was little more than a walking mockery that she had beef with.

Marie wasn't going to let tiny details like that stop her. "**Glory**!"

Bombastic drums drowned out Artorian's music.

"Imperia!" Marie released her power. She declared the battlefield regardless of its limited efficacy, reshaping the entire caldera with a single word into the centerpiece of a coliseum that she pulled right out of the ground. Shaped, chiseled, detailed, and all. Her memories made manifest, fueled by a disgusting amount of invoked Mana. Complete with a statue of her at the north part of the oval, with Henry's matching form at the south.

Trumpets roared as mystical illusions filled the structure with bannermen, knights, and spectators. They pulled free instruments and weapons, displaying both before breaking into a musical effort fit only for a military parade. The waves of which coated Henry and Marie in a sonic shell, defending them from incoming harm.

Artorian had sussed this detail out correctly as well, it seemed. With Henry shielding, and Marie buffing, this meant that their opponents were forced to power up or otherwise bring more of their capacities to bear. To face a more powerful opponent was good for **Glory**. To make them notable before being crushed was best.

With the entire structure forming around Artorian and Henry, it was difficult not to be awed. Then again, calling on your **Law** was supposed to result in bombastic effects like this. Anything less would not be worth the cost. Cost that Marie didn't even feel as she poured energy into the connection and let the effects rip.

The landscape rumbled, rocked, broke, and gave way to structure after structure rising from the ground. Artorian recognized many buildings from the Phoenix Kingdom capital. Including a certain courthouse that he'd once run out of at full speed after ticking off every single occupant except for the Great Phoenix themselves.

Marie then appeared in front of her statue, taking a seat in a throne that evolved out of a newly formed plinth. "I, Queen of the Phoenix, scion of **Glory**, decree the beginning of the new Lionix Empire! Let Lion and Phoenix live as one, let judgment fall, my will be done!"

CHAPTER THIRTY-FIVE

Brasilia whistled, Artorian able to sense arms mentally being crossed. <Oke, *now* I'm upset. She calls you a mutt? I can work with that. She steps on our *Carnivale*?>

Brasilia clicked his tongue in quick repetition, intensely disappointed. <*No, no, no.* This is unacceptable. Drowning out Bellini's music with that... *pwaaamping*? That tempo is as bad as their Mana control! At least you sounded like you took drum lessons once, even if you are not inclined. No. Vovô? Change of party plan. You *survive*. Bellini is gonna be here for you, Brasilia needs to go upstairs.>

Making some snapping actions in a Z-patterned motion, Brasilia left the building and left Artorian alone with Bellini, who was feeling equally as upset, the mental image being one where his head was kept slanted and eyes open wide as he took in the insult caused by Marie's trumpets. <Vovô?>

<Yes, Bellini?> Artorian turned to ask, watching his situation turn ever more grim as the math was thrown out of the window, the numbers now so far out of his favor that 'survive' might be exactly right. The math was only good for 'no special

DENNIS VANDERKERKEN & DAKOTA KROUT

tricks' being accounted for, but neither Henry or Marie were giving him that advantage.

Both were spending an egregious amount of Mana, and both were in highly advanced armor. Marie was doing something to the environment by having dictated the field, and was heavily boosting the both of them. With that sonic shield being the most obvious, and trumpeting certainly doing something else. Her Aura fully claimed the area as sovereign space, liberally trying to draw Mana out of him. Not to any success, but it was trying.

Artorian had the distinct sensation that while the bannermen might be for show, those mystical illusion knights were definitely not. Her halberd being coated in that same sonic layer was also a dead giveaway that she would absolutely take a free swipe at him if he got too close.

Henry was fully pumping his output, had enhanced armaments up and running with those Lion-overlays of his that did abyss-knew what, and was using Runed gear to fuel a constant spiral ring of shields that each had their own little gimmick. The longsword looked like the least of his problems, and Artorian had no doubts that it was another imported Eternia goodie that also did Cal-knew-what.

Both of them were displaying the full force of Tier ninety-eight **Laws**. Marie was invoking hers and was able to not give two sticks about the cost, and Henry didn't look to be too far behind since Artorian had certainly ticked some boxes in the **Valor** activation spreadsheet. All Henry had to do was face dangers to the goal, and while Artorian wasn't much of a threat yet, Artorian hadn't come here to get beaten into the ground without putting up a fight.

He just needed… to be very careful about the fine line between **Valor** and **Glory**. **Valor,** he could likely tussle with, but if he triggered **Glory's** requirements, then this became a two-on-one that he did not want to bet on.

"I think Shaka called it." Artorian metaphorically threw his hat on the ground. The old man murmured to himself, jumping on the tip-toes of his metal claws as he surveyed his diminishing odds swirling down the drain. He was sitting on a Tier thirty-one **Law**, and the amount of units invested between the body and his Aura didn't hold a candle to his opponents, who seemed to have maxed numbers in both. Whatever those numbers might be. So much for trying to figure out A-rank zero. He couldn't even get a correct measurement.

At A-rank one, you could likely put half a rank into Aura, and half a rank into your body, and reach a nice equilibrium. A-rank zero? The mystery continued.

"Well, this is scuffed." He tried to exert Bellini's Samba only for it to get *pwaaaped* down by Marie's trumpets. "Nice gear, Henry!"

"Thanks!" The armored man clearly felt good about the prospective outcome. "All these weapons are straight out of good old Tim-booki-tooki!"

He held up the longsword, gleeful to show it off. "This is Rend of the World. It doesn't cut, it rends! Also surprisingly effective against split ends."

"Way to make me feel better, buddy." Artorian dropped his gaze, mumbling demurely.

"Sorry, Sunny." Henry shrugged and apologized, sounding truly genuine. "Now that it's come to this, I'm going to have to beat you down until Marie is satisfied. Throwing you out changed into making an example out of you when Marie pulled in a setting. I'll be at this until I win! Unless you pull out something really interesting and get Marie involved. Don't worry, though! I don't enjoy any of this, and I'll be sure to help find you a good spot in our new kingdom. You're still my friend, regardless of our current disagreements. I'm not going to hold back! I know you."

"The happenstance of the situation does not change the pattern of the outcome, Henry." Artorian grit his teeth. "I think we would have ended up here regardless, if this is how you and Marie kept doing things. To rule by strength is a fleeting endeavor."

Henry was curious, flourishing his sword behind the defensive cocoon of his shields. "Oh yeah? Why is that?"

"People won't necessarily remember what you said! But they will always remember how you made them feel." Artorian adopted a lecturing stance. "The effect you have on others is the most valuable currency there is, and the amount of animosity Marie scraped together, from the people I've met here alone, would have guaranteed your downfall. Even if I'm not the one to bring you both down today... The grave is dug, buddy, and you dug it."

"Then they should have come and scheduled a meeting or shown up for the public—" Henry began to speak, but was cut off.

"'What cannot be said will be wept,' said scholar Sappho of the ancients." Artorian interrupted with a finger waggle. "Those who I met wouldn't have gone to you for anything, and it doesn't change how they felt. 'Right is right even if no one is doing it; wrong is wrong even if everyone is doing it,' said scholar Augustine of the ancients."

Henry adopted an attacking pose, tired of being backhanded by morality lessons. He launched himself at Artorian with a concordant boom of displaced air. "I'm not here to be lectured. Fight!"

Artorian dipped past the oncoming shield bashes, slid under a kite shield with some homing capacity, Capoeira leg-spun between Henry's legs, and jump-spun over the shields that followed in his wake. A buckler still caught him in the side of the head, the inscription on it activating. The buckler repulsed him with force directly into the path of a war-door, which slammed him into the coliseum wall with a pressurized cold snap and crack of ice.

Artorian pulled himself from the rubble, stumbling out before the wall mended. The arena floor absorbed the broken chunks, leaving behind only a pristine fighting area, ready for more splendor. He rubbed at his chest, not feeling any signs of frost damage on his aloha shirt. "Ow."

Artorian then rubbed the back of his neck, and popped his back as Henry needed to pause and laugh. This was barely a fight, and Artorian took the moment to mumble to himself. "*How* am I gonna do this? I had a trap card of swords up my sleeve, but even with mass TK to refine their movements, that's not gonna accomplish much. Polly would have a field day, but lacks the Tier to lay down some law without me having the Mana to help. The concept weapons... might give me an opening. Really, it's the *venue* causing me problems. *Hmmmm.* And that sonic shell..."

An image flashed through his head, thoughts of the Aquarium swimming by. How poor was Henry's Aura control again? Would that work? It *was* a block of **Love**-quality goodness. Something to keep in the pocket, for sure.

He momentarily wondered what his own Aura would look like in there, then turned tail and ran the perimeter when Henry went after him, lion roar and sword-tip first.

Henry was not amused as Artorian pulled some Glitterflit maneuvers and used Rail Palms from his feet, of all places, to steal moments of acceleration. Keeping him out of shield-intersect range as Artorian used the self-repairing function of the coliseum to his benefit and put proper oomph into his escape bounces.

Henry chased the floppy beard, yelling with irritation. "Why are you running! Stop running!"

"Crackers and toast!" Artorian ran faster, playing a trap card and immediately flipping it to face-up position. He whistled loud, like an admiral had just stepped onto a ship's deck, the shrill canary-call cutting through the trumpets. "Admiral on deck!"

A quick dodge and duck got him below the swing of an oversized halberd when he provoked Marie's attack of opportunity, the fleeing rabbit complaining to feel better. "Ineffective or not, I need help. I need flying swords. A lot of flying swords. Wings made of swords! The Baja-mutt will soar!"

He shook his fist at Marie on the pass by her plinth. "I know you're using your Aura to keep me pinned down, lady! Don't think I didn't notice that!"

"Get 'im, Henry." Marie smirked in satisfaction, her eyes following the chase as Artorian ran away from her plinth. "I expected more."

Marie quietly twirled her halberd as she watched her Lion chase the Hare, reviewing all fifty motions of the Mauling Phoenix, and picking out which she wanted to employ. Artorian knew at least up to... the twelfth motion? There was a betraying twist inherent in one of his side-steps with the way his body turned to dodge. The dancing-dodges... those were new. She'd never seen that before, but without the music around Artorian, his ability to perform those arts was diminished.

Her bannermen may be mere illusions, but with enough Mana, even those could be corporeal. She was keeping her war drums in reserve for now, along with most of her arsenal. Artorian, annoying runt that he may be, became exceptional when cornered or in a bind. He had a reputation for doing a lot, with little, and Marie was too upset at not having been given help when she'd needed it to let him off lightly.

The addition of a darkened sky and impending rain was interesting, if only because she was trying to keep the skies clear. How was there rain when—

Her grip on the throne squeezed reflexively when she picked out a hail of swords coming down. That was no water! Those were weapons! Hundreds of them! "Henry, above you! He was stalling!"

Henry glanced up in time to see the impending shower of stabby death, a motion pulling all his shields together moments before hundreds of flying swords plinked, tinked, and stabbed into his defenses. Defenses that activated in massive groups. Gouts of flame, torrents of ice, bursts of steam, cracks of force, and whips of acid all belched forth from the inscriptions of his shields. Sending the majority of the sword hail back out into the sky.

"Nice trick!" Henry howled at the effectiveness of his

protections, a smile in his voice now that Artorian's plan had been revealed. "Shame that they—*Wow!*"

Henry shut up and put up, parrying a fencing blade with his longsword as it deftly and with incredible accuracy slipped between several layers of shields like a guided, angry wasp. The fencing blade had nearly reached him before being parried away.

A saber joined the skilled dance, swinging where Henry's sword failed to be and impacting his armor. The armor didn't chip, the sonic shell activating and sending the saber flying to the ground, the stunned weapon skittering across the arena floor.

But it had hit him.

A bevy of swords slipped past Henry's shield wall all at once immediately after, the proactive protections barely able to veer into a blocking position in time as their effects went off one after the other. Most of the sword hail was rebuked, but each wave returned every few seconds like an angry swarm. A few swords breached the gaps each wave, and when they did, they all gained that Capoeira mobility as they danced towards him, slashing and cutting at his sonic shell. Each impact sang like thunder being drummed from a cloud.

Nothing got through.

When Henry spotted Artorian through the rain of offending blades, the man was carefully keeping track of his defending shields, watching the reactions. Tallying the effects. The Administrator's eyes then landed on a tower shield that drew a particularly large load of Mana each time it activated, releasing a hurricane of rolling, dense flame that Pag the Pyroclasm would nod his head at in approval. Purely due to collateral damage.

Henry thought that must be Artorian's target, to aim for one of his best shields, and slip by moments before the cast triggered, leaving that shield weak, and slow.

Not on his watch!

When Artorian made his move, Henry was ready. Parrying more of the sword hail that was quickly becoming an annoyance rather than a threat, he let some slip through specifically so they struck his sonic protections instead. The blades hit, and clattered away. He was considering giving up on parrying altogether with how weak the strikes were, as foes in great numbers meant nothing when they accomplished nothing.

The tower shield was fed Mana preemptively, Henry grinning under his helmet as Artorian made a face of surprise when he was right in front of it, and the effect triggered before he could touch the shield and slip by. "Ha, ha! *Got you!*"

Henry pumped the flaming hurricane hard, straining the inscription on the item well past the point where the tower shield cracked and was at high threat of *boom*.

Runes, or inscriptions, breaking in the middle of use was not pretty.

A nova of force, fire, pressure, and ridiculous heat scorched the coliseum; wiping the entire western stands clear of illusions, and engraved serious scorch marks where the rest of the rogue Mana seared itself into place. Marie's Aura was nowhere close enough to eating it all up with any kind of celerity.

Henry hurriedly surveyed the scene as he soldiered through his own Rune-detonated bomb. His helmet flicked through modes of vision as the lingering heat outside of his armor felt wet, palatable, and thick. He'd been behind a shield wall and still felt rattled, so Artorian might be toast. Or reduced to seriously burnt crackers.

Instead, Henry's jaw hit the floor when a vision mode found success and gave him a clear view of the scene.

Artorian held a horse stance inches where the shield had obliterated itself, at the very center of the explosion. He was breathing deeply. Cultivating, from what Henry could tell. What Henry could also tell was that there wasn't a scratch on him or that ridiculous outfit of his. Only the glitter had perished, his beard spotlessly white. Artorian felt much, much stronger than before, his density considerably more compact and intense. Henry grit his teeth when that feeling registered. He should have put in more effort to cull the threat when it was still a

Hare. Now the presence in front of him felt like an absolute monster, freezing him to the spot.

Space around Artorian bent and expanded, wobbling back to normality when he released the tension. The old man exhaled slowly, rising out of his stance to roll his arms, and then his shoulders as the Mana in his vicinity swirled into him rather than Marie's overwhelmed field. Like some kind of inverse sun.

Artorian grunted with relief as his bones popped in sequence, the tapestry of good sounds serving as a precursor to his broad smile. "Theeeere we go. Topped off at A-rank seven! Now we've got something to work with."

He then beamed at Henry when the frozen, armored man dumbfoundedly raised his sword as **Valor** cuffed him across the back of the helmet and spurred a reaction. "Hello Henry! Ready for round two? I had to get the rust off."

CHAPTER THIRTY-SIX

Counter to Henry's expectations, Artorian aggressively shifted to the offensive. The beach-dressed party-goer took off straight at him, making Henry reflexively readjust his shields. Shields that were used as fancy footholds when Rail Palms from Artorian's feet sent the ornate protections flying, steering them off course before their automatic inscriptions were fed and triggered, spewing destruction across the arena.

Artorian leapt across Henry's shields like leaves in a pond, pushing off the last one with an extra powerful Rail Kick to gain enough height for his next trick, and to send that shield smack into Henry's helmet with a *k'thunk* as bonus, making the regent dodge his own defensive effects as a metal spike the size of a palm tree shot out to impale him! Sparks exploded from the side of his helmet as the spike sheared past, penetrating the sonic shell from sheer velocity and force. This cost Henry valuable moments of attentiveness, Artorian's nimble escape assured.

Making it just high enough with the Rail Kick—even with Marie's Aura pushing him back down and hunting for the

normal signs of Mana-based flight to steal resources from—
Artorian stepped foot onto the head of Henry's statue.

Marie didn't know where the old fox thought he was going
to go, or escape to. Her Aura still had the region boxed in, and
no further footholds were available above the southern statue.
She also knew about his platforms, and was ready to absorb
them if he tried it.

Artorian instead twisted on his heel, pressed his hand to his
mouth, and blew them a brilliant kiss. In response, the blade
hail swarmed away from the arena as they registered the change
in instructions. Connecting and merging behind Artorian with
the ease of clicking into a preset pattern that they merely
needed to slot, the swarm of blades formed and filled the
outline of owl wings.

Henry roared like an agitated lion, the side of his helmet
hot and white from the fresh brush of near death. "Get back
down here and fight me!"

"If fighting is sure to result in victory, then you must fight, even
though the ruler forbids it. If fighting will not result in victory, then
you must not fight. Even at the ruler's bidding." Artorian rattled off
the ancient proverb from the Art of Peace like he'd learned it yesterday, mocking the regent's order like an insubordinate soldier while
he was at it. He wasn't going to stick around. He had other plans!
Like not fighting in a venue that put him at a horrible disadvantage.

Artorian saluted with contempt. "Sayonara!"

Power sputtered in trembling flares from his adaptive legs,
tiny turbines and thruster vents deploying with sequential clicks.
This gimmick had proven disastrous before, but now? Now it
was showtime! "Go go gadget rocket legs!"

The display dazzled the regents long enough for both of
them to miss Polly's broken blade zipping in from left field at
Mach two. The hilt of which spun to exactly the right angle for
Artorian's grip to smoothly enclose it, the crack of an upset
sound barrier in hot pursuit right behind the blade.

Knowing that Polly's initial pull would only get him so far, as Excalibur was here to provide direction for his own force rather than be solely responsible for getting him out of this bind, Artorian spent his freshly stolen Mana as Bellini laughed over their connection like a proud rogue, adding some drums to the endeavor.

The Striker Mark IX legs fully burgeoned to life as they were fed glorious amounts of Mana, condensed white flame erupting with deafening sound. Unlike a normal flight effect, all his legs did was create and provide thrust. Lots, and lots of thrust. Like a bat out of the Abyss, Artorian took off to Bermuda with the speed of a firework suffering from social anxiety in a crowded setting.

He was *g-g-g-gone*!

Mach two was an easy speed to match as he and Polly switched roles. Blade igniting, Polly's rainbow surged from the broken business end, poised to pierce and strike.

Marie rose to chase him, but was dragged back down to her throne by her own Mana as she was still paying the invoking cost to keep memory-recreating the Phoenix Kingdom, and it wasn't done. **Glory** kept her tied down, as Marie's own **Law** took exception to its bound Mage leaving such a grand task incomplete.

"Does he think he's the only one who knows excerpts from the Art of Peace?" She grit her teeth, feeling the hands of her **Law** pressing on her shoulders. She wasn't going anywhere. "If you know the enemy and know yourself, then your victory will not stand in doubt. Henry! Go!"

Henry's instant flight was not impeded, his launch cratering the coliseum floor. The damage made him wonder why Artorian's launch hadn't damaged the statue, but a glance after flying high enough proved him very wrong. A conical hole melting straight through from the brass head down to the chest cavity was still filled with the equivalent of magma, based on the visual effect. No, it was lava. Magma was the underground stuff. So lava was what was currently turning his brand spanking new statue into a colander, by melting it from the inside out, the exterior boiling open and leaking thick ropes of the molten slag. "The distinction is probably unimportant."

Somewhere on the Silverwood, a volcano dungeon threw a hissy fit. Henry swore he could hear it, but couldn't afford to be distracted. He cursed and took up the chase. He would catch up in short order, not impeded by Marie's Aura body slamming him with pure weight.

Marie's Aura would slow Artorian down to a crawl. The effect became worse the closer he got to the edge, because that was how they'd set up their borders. In hindsight... a terrible idea, but those were the tools they had for now. In current circumstances, it meant Artorian would have to gamble being crushed in order to leave! The old man would surely not take that... Why was he not slowing down?

Marie raged from her seat. "That fleeing rat! He's rolling the dice!"

"*Wheeeeee!*" Artorian sped up in continued defiance, indulging in a case of the *nyooms*. Celestials, he loved the feeling of going fast! One of his eyes closed while the other narrowed, his flight path straightening more and more as he cranked up the Strikers' output. The blade wings clung tight to his back, positioned like those of a diving falcon. He aimed right for the densest Aura that he could detect, shooting towards it.

In retaliation to an interloper attempting to leave the region, the energy condensed like water on a glass window and globbed together to intercept him. That was his cue! "Polly! Ready?"

"Ready!" Polly scintillated with color, the rainbow blade kept directly ahead of Artorian like a spear-tip leading a charge, the multicolored edge flashing with a gleam of moonlight.

"Excalibur Style." Artorian engaged the newly minted martial maneuver, and informed Marie exactly how he felt about her border system.

Rather than gamble with unfair dice favoring a penchant for rolling natural ones, Artorian altered the method of expected interaction. Esoterics were his wheelhouse! Instead of moving through the border that was meant to keep him contained, he flipped the script. Forget passing through Marie's border Aura as was the expectation, Artorian *stabbed* it!

A line of moonlight flickered as Excalibur cut through the barrier. "Punctured **Pride**!"

From the central plains of Camelot, Artorian once again heard that fellow named Wilhelm scream. Honestly, people should stop letting their sensitive Auras just hang around! He could have grabbed and twisted Marie's Aura like an ear, or treated it with the same displeasure Odin tended to bring to bear. However, given the prior mention of her Aura having been insufficiently stabbed, this felt far more fitting.

Plus, it would buy him time! Precious, precious time.

Cutting right through the barrier like scissors gliding through paper, sound included, Artorian felt firm relief when he felt the repressive sovereign space effect leave him behind. No longer contained by the Camel-lot, he prodigiously pulled on Mana.

The excess energy in the air reacted like a platoon of lazy recruits that realized too late that their commander had entered the room, shooting upright to pretend they'd been ready for action the whole time. Staggering over their own feet before hurtling towards him, the Mana trumpeted the charge and shouldered itself into formation, answering Artorian's intense will.

Artorian exploded to the stratosphere as fresh fuel hit the mechanism. Mid-flight, Artorian drew in enough resources to top himself right back up, the clouds vanishing in his wake. Fighting as an A-rank two and a half was not... optimal. A-rank seven? Much better!

The odds were finally starting to show favor. Or rather, the odds were crawling out of the dark hole he'd lost them in, and there was more climbing to do.

Artorian took the moment to calculate. "Quick maths! Six ranks of Aura *Oomph* times Tier thirty one is... one hundred eighty six? That beats Henry's base value of ninety-eight, but I don't have the numbers for what actively spending Mana to boost yourself does to that formula. That's normally such an expensive drain that anything other than a quick burst goes unconsidered. I'm sensing similarities to… Eternia's Empowerment mechanic? The shape of how Henry's Mana flares out is telling. It definitely isn't his Aura getting that done. Techniques have beefier output, but I'm not worried about techniques. I'm going to pretend he's at A-rank one, with a full rank invested in his physique. Let's start the math at double and see if anything comes of it."

Holding up two fingers, he called out the numbers. "Two times ninety-eight is one hundred ninety six. So if I punch one of his shields coated in his Mana, and it doesn't scratch, then active expenditure provides a modifier of at least two."

Polly's rainbow blade fizzled out, the tired parrot expended from **Pride**-busting straight through Marie's Aura. Artorian did not have the luxury to turn around and play observer for the moment to survey the true extent of the damage. "Polly, how much extra time did that stunt buy us?"

"Not much!" The tired sword faltered, her voice huffy. "It'll give you an edge if you need to fight her later, but for now all it did was let us bowl over the border. The impact must have felt like a stone pillow to the seed Cores, but still. I'm tapped, Sunny. Stow me!"

"Good job, Polly. You're done for today." Artorian reached the blade out towards his sword wings. "Penkins! Get Polly home to Olympus Lake."

"You got it!" Conductor Penkins replied, the saber adopting the form of a bright yellow Oriole. Penkins gripped Polly in his talons, the broken blade condensing to the size of a pendant for easy transportation. "Good luck!"

"Thank you, Conductor." Artorian thanked Penkins as the Oriole shot away. "I'll need it."

Artorian stole a glance over his shoulder. Henry was catching up.

His Strikers were doing an impressive job of creating distance, but they were no match for a direct application of

Mana-based flight. Noticing the strain they were under, the thought occurred that he was going to lose them if he kept this up. He dove towards the Aquarium to set his final direction, and cut the feed. The lack of continued thrust, unfortunately, meant Henry got a hold of him long before he was there, resulting in a mid-air collision as the sky turned into a Mana-wrenched combat zone.

Henry surged with dark violet light, preparing for an attack. Artorian frowned when he inspected Henry mid-tumble. Henry's passive, if expensive, defenses had some finesse to them. Surely that offensive technique he was spinning up wasn't supposed to be so obviously full of flaws?

"Imperial Lion. Ultraviolet Ultraviolence!" Henry released a barrage of claws as if he were in Eternia, and fully capitalized on the extra show of calling out a big attack. A myriad of unseen Mana claws turned Artorian's position into a blender. The displacement of air cut lines of fire and plasma into the mauled spot, turning the general hue of the target area a bruised purple.

Henry thought he'd easily and quickly secured the win, until the side-effects dissipated and Artorian gave him a hands held high, 'what was that supposed to be' expression. The old man was contained in an easy orb of basic light, which none of the claws seemed to have scratched.

The regent was baffled, choking on his words. "Wait, what? How!"

Artorian felt offended. "Really, Henry? You thought I wasn't going to be able to see that?"

He then put two and two together, based on Henry's flabbergasted demeanor. "You're not used to people being able to see that attack, are you? I figured out ultraviolets as a C-ranker, you daft man. The whole point of attacking in that spectrum is to not let your opponents know what you are up to, or specifically for use against undead. Ultraviolet doesn't work on people who know the gimmick!"

Artorian scoffed, modulating his voice to stoke the fire. "You think luminance is your ally? You've merely adopted the light. I was brought into cultivation by resplendence. Molded by it! You clearly didn't touch true brightness until you needed flavor for your gimmick."

"It's not a gimmick!" Henry shook his fist as he veered back in on his flight path, readying a different attack as he yowled. "Try this one!"

Artorian effortlessly altered the color of his shield, the red claws faring no different than the equally violent violet ones. "Henry, that's infrared. That... You didn't change anything! That was even less effective! That's not what you use infrared for!"

"Yes it is!" The regent hurled a ball shaped as a lion's head in complaint.

"No it's not!" Artorian Capoeira spun to punt that soccer ball back with rocket-infused force as the strikers' white flames flared for a boost of thrust. Henry took his own bite-y ball to the face like an unlucky goalie, the lion-shaped energy orb trying to gnaw his own head off on impact.

"It's very effective!" Henry wrestled the lion's head away to flatten the emanation between his gauntlets, rebuking the claim as the ball slipped free. This resulted in the head biting onto his gauntlet, refusing to let go as Henry swung his arm about like trying to get a wet cat—that had been very upset about surprise bath-time—off of him.

Artorian wasn't having it. "It... Henry. You fool. Land and fight me properly. This is ridiculous. I don't know what kind of techniques you keep hidden in your sleeves, or what you carried over from the old Lion Kingdom, but that was terrible! Those soupy techniques were so sloppy that I could stuff the contents into a sandwich. That claw strike was coming apart at the seams like a teddy bear plushie that was all plush and no bear! I have seen spun sugar hold up better after being dunked in hot water than the cohesion that technique had just now."

The old teacher fumed. "Intent was the only thing holding that slap-dash dish of noodles together, and you overcooked them for an entire hour before serving the platter. Forget pasta. You gave me paste, Henry, paste! Claw manifestations in the light spectrum? At least make them fully *solid*. Those claws were goopy porridge! I had to do nearly nothing to block that. Any half-abyssed Mage could have backhanded that swill out of the air."

"It looks great!" Henry fumed, irritated at the impromptu review.

"That's all it did! *It looked good*." Artorian punched one of the kite shields when it swung into range. The shield, unharmed, veered off course before the inscription triggered and spewed yellow snow. This silently made Artorian grumble as it confirmed his 'at least two times' math. Meaning he was still not going to win here. Henry's *Oomph* out-oomphed him, and if he was going to do this without big flashy techniques, then he was going to need a higher baseline Tier. "Crackers, Henry. Yellow snow? Are you *five?*"

Henry hid that shield in the mess of the others, like an embarrassment to be hidden under the bed. "Hey, I didn't make them! I just collect!"

Artorian whistled and fanned out his arms, sending his blade wings out while coating them in **Celebration** Mana. He was at a loss for a specific effect to apply, but Brasilia slid back into her seat with a foreboding grin, ready with an assist. <Vovô! I've got a line to one of your happy tree friends. Bellini and I miss you already, but you gotta go!>

The blades flashed like fireworks lighting up a night sky, forcing Henry to use his vision filters, distracting him from the true action as he blocked the flashing sword swarm with his shields. He still had the sonic shell, and his armor would likely protect him all by itself from attacks like this, but special effects were Artorian's specialty. Better to defend than to risk it!

Following a drum riff, Artorian's outfit returned to being Brianna's well-designed Ao Dai. The sunglasses were a great loss. His **Celebration** effects and knowledge of Capoeira left with the elite outfit. Artorian had gotten limited use from the art, but he'd gotten a full Samba de Janeiro song out of it, before Marie had dropped her **Law** on the table like freshly packed bear sausage.

Artorian's Aura adopted a pure silver overtone as he was, with help, pulled up the Tower by two distinctly different nodes at his point of arrival. Floor forty-seven! The **Law** holding onto him, the one he wasn't using as a foothold, whispered a detail. One that Artorian quickly invoked as he directed the will towards the swarm of swords. The thought of one thousand cherry trees visualized before his eyes. "Senbonzakura!"

Adopting a pink, cherry blossom hue, the hail of swords all burst into tiny, glimmering pieces. Artorian's gut instinct was regret, but silvered hands on his shoulder fueled the certainty that the birds holding those blade forms were all entirely fine.

As small, razor sharp flecks, the blossoms whirled through the gaps of Henry's protections, wild as a localized tornado. His shields, while triggered, offered no added defense or use as he was surrounded in a maelstrom of cutting sounds impacting the sonic shell. The shell, thankfully for Henry's sudden burst of well-deserved panic, held. Henry's courage in overcoming the fear of being swarmed by razors also triggered a sufficient amount of checkboxes for his **Law**.

Henry did not waste the moment, taking the power up. "**Valor**!"

An omnidirectional shockwave that erupted like a war cry repulsed all the cherry blossoms. The razors reconstituted back together into swords before all those swords couldn't contain their weapon forms and shifted back into a flock of birds. The sword-storm was expended, the birds flocking away. Their role was played, and while they had extra durability as weapons, their real bodies were considerably more squishy. They would not be blamed for their decision.

Artorian was too busy to pay the distraction of fleeing feathers much heed, kicking at a shield that flew too close with his Aura. The act stopped his wild sky tumbling, but put him in the precarious situation of being above Henry. His opponent had aerial movement options, while his Strikers were on cooldown. Not good on the tactical positioning front.

Artorian distracted himself with some math. "A Tower Tier of forty-seven times six ranks of Aura. An *Oomph* of two hundred eighty-two. Surely that's enough to break a shield?"

Henry constantly doing his utmost to close the distance gave Artorian plenty of opportunity to interact with that spherical wall of shields. When another veered into a good enough position, he treated the heater shield like any other floor and kicked off from it. Evading the coldfire torrent that burst free from the rune via sheer height and distance, the heater spiraled out of control, bouncing into other shields and setting them off as well.

Artorian cursed under his breath at the result while he played a dangerous bunny-hopping game on explosive surfaces. The darn thing had been kicked away without suffering a dent! Much more *Oomph* than this, and he wasn't sure if he was going to be able to play his 'weak enough to not activate **Glory**' card. **Arbor's** Tier of forty-seven wasn't cutting the mustard if it still couldn't damage one of Henry's shields. "Eclairs! What is it going to *take*?"

The other **Law** gripped his shoulder. <I've got you.>

Argent's feminine voice was softer than Zelia's, but had that Arachnid knack to it. The accent wasn't forced, but it definitely sounded like **Argent** had picked the speaking manner up from Zelia, rather than the other way around. She repeated herself when the old man experienced a spike of anxiety, affirming her statement with additional strength. <*I've got you.*>

Argent moved her silvered support under his feet, steadying his cultivation base when **Arbor's** guidance faltered. That Heavenly was fully distracted by the flock of fleeing birds. Waves of concern for their well-being poured from **Arbor's** mental link, her attention torn.

Artorian would never fault someone for caring, but felt obvious relief when **Argent** took over and prevented another Tower Tier tumble. She took over the guidance, and provided a stable platform of glowing silver power that rolled over his skin, filling him with strength and confidence when his plans just weren't panning out as hoped.

As his anxiety spike abated, **Argent** smiled while she spoke. <A technique that isn't a transfiguration, but an actual attack, perhaps? **Arbor's** thousand cherry blossom technique to turn weapons into razor swarms was... cute.>

Argent then grinned like a vengeful god, her arms draping around his neck and shoulders as her whispering voice growled to his ear with predatory delight. <Try *mine.*>

CHAPTER THIRTY-SEVEN

"Imperial Lion! Wrathful Reaver!" Henry closed the distance in a blur of heat and roaring war cries, the Lion emanation over his helmet forceful and intense. His entire arm burst into bright orange flames, the Mana claw coating his gauntlet sinking into a deep violet hue as the business ends sharpened and solidified.

His offhand was poised to strike as a follow up, blade at the ready.

The existence of a sudden silver disco ball made him reconsider. The metallic object so casually tossed in his path rapidly built up with energy and a sharp pitched whine, giving the distinct sensation that it was going to be pouring out lines of deadly silver light. Or explode. Henry instantly remembered Dawn's fight with Artorian in the desert of the earliest iteration. How the old man had turned an entire section of the sky into a house of mirrors, before a massive device filled with lenses had—

The gears clicked in the Regent's head. The energy build up was the same!

Henry broke off his strike, expecting bright death beams while spotting brand new silver mirrors forming below. Those were angled to intersect their descent path, and a beam bounce would certainly redirect a line attack to slam into him from behind. Ah-ha! It was a trap! He knew it!

The disco ball shot Henry's expectations instead, because that cheeky bomb exploded into chunks of luminous shrapnel. The resulting concussive *boom* pushed all of Henry's shields out and away, blinding him with a light that his helmet failed to filter. While the disco-grenade accomplished little in terms of damage, it allowed Artorian a clean path out of the aerial entanglement. No more bunny hopping!

The opportunist blitzed straight down the newly opened path, rockets flaring to life and burning at full bore. Silvered streaks flickered in his wake as he shot straight for the stunned regent, his own hands becoming a luminous **Argent**.

"*Bomb* Dia, Henry!" Artorian could feel Brasilia and Bellini fist bump before twiddling their fingers up at **Argent** for a smooth team play. The old man was in the armored regent's face not a moment later, his own fist coursing with power as he stole Henry's playbook, copying the Empowerment trick and layering it into the Aura coating his fists.

The resulting impact of knuckles to helmet completely shattered Henry's lion head emanation, bent the sonic shell, and cratered the helmet underneath with enough raw force to crack it like an eggshell. Being a High Mageous was the only thing protecting Henry from both a serious concussion, and dastardly discombobulation.

The flashing silver impact slammed Henry away with the air-thundering force of a zero to Mach four acceleration. His shields rushed to follow as he spun and swirled downwards before impacting a mountain range like a burning meteor, adding a molten gorge.

"Safe!" Artorian shook the silver out of his hands, his feet smoothly touching down on grassy ground. He'd landed in the zone next to the Aquarium, and that was good enough! "Good guidance, **Argent**! Apologies for not using the mirrors as planned; he was open for a sockin'! So *boom* it was."

DENNIS VANDERKERKEN & DAKOTA KROUT

Recouping the **Argent** Mana still hanging in the sky, Artorian reformed the mirror constructs nearby instead. He then immediately let his legs vent heat by keeping those funny little flaps open. The steam pouring out was no joke, and the angry red heat his metal legs contained was equally serious. Hopefully, one rank of A-rank Mana kept any of the heat from being an immediate problem? The Cores in his knees swirled like happy marbles, which was a detail that made Artorian chuff. "Well, that's nice. Maybe it's not my singular body rank preventing me from being burned by Iridium at who knows what temperature."

Pressing his hands to his hips, he pursed his lips and blew out some air, addressing the **Law** supporting him. "Alright! What happened just now? That output was way off the survey. His helmet full-on shattered and Henry became a mountain ornament. I was expecting to slap him out of the way and keep tussling on the ground down here. Is my math that wrong? What variable am I having so much trouble with?"

Argent grumbled as her voice lost its amusement. <Pi.>

Her disco ball had been repurposed into a bomb. Not the use she'd suggested to really show off what her Mana type and thematic affiliation could do. Artorian could feel her arms pulling off his shoulders, the sensation of fingers kneading into temples replacing the prior sensation. <The math you do... it's...>

She tasted her words, mentally leaning on his shoulder again. <What you are doing is like watching a student show their work, seeing they got half of the formulas wrong, and then being very confused. Because somehow they ended up with a result that was the same answer you would have gotten if you'd done the math right. You're still off with your calculations, but you're close enough on the end result that... The math you're getting wrong? It's not important right now.>

"*Oof.*" Artorian felt concern for his numbers, murmuring as he was handed a less than stellar report card. "That bad? Surely my math is not *that* bad?"

<**Love**'s most dearest, darling little boy.> **Argent** pressed like an educator with forty years in the field, who had more than likely had this exact same conversation with the mother about the exact same problem, when the mother had pulled this stunt herself as a child. <You are eyeballing cosmic physics, calling out a number, and to my baffled bewilderment, are getting it right enough to be able to work with the results. Your luck is ridiculous. What is it with all you **Love**-aligned and having insane luck?>

Artorian silently kicked a rock, his head looking down as he moved his hands behind his back like a chided five year old, face pursed in the expression of hiding that he utterly and completely did whatever he was being accused of.

"*Three*-something, then?" Lacing his fingers together, Artorian mumbled apologetically. Really not having a better answer for the Heavenly as he latched onto her reference of Pi, trying to figure out where that was supposed to go in his ramshackle formula. Was **Argent** perhaps referencing his random guess at *Oomph* doubling from before? Was it a multiplier of three, rather than two, that he should be keeping in mind?

Argent could be felt rubbing her whole face with a hand, leaning back to sigh at the sky like a scorned noblewoman, before sharply dropping her palm towards him. Her voice was one of frustration, direly needing to correct him within the confines of what she was allowed to say. <Change your... You don't know what redneck engineering is yet, but it's what you're doing. Change your eyeballing-it math to three point fourteen, instead of two, and don't think about *why* too hard. Because it's going to hurt when you learn what logarithms are.>

His facial expression got a response before Artorian could complete the thought and form a sentence. <Don't ask. Do your... silly little napkin math, beat the high-horsed one with my mirrors, and consider giving Wo'ah of the **Empyreal** a visit when you want to suffer through the headache of rectifying your redneck engineering. Ask him about mass effects, the first

law of motion, and the deadliest son of the heavens in all of space. He will gladly tell you why you do not *eyeball* it.>

Argent cut him off before he'd fully inhaled to vocalize his next thought, reading his mind before it finished percolating like quality coffee. <Don't ask me about that either. **Arbor** already went up to see about a more fitting platform for what you need, and we're all too enthused about being here, and being involved, to deter you from getting to know as many of us as possible. I know how it goes with Ascended of **Love**, you'll get the word out. Now get your head back into the game, the lion is coming for your throat.>

Artorian blinked back to reality, then panic leapt behind one of the stationary mirrors as Rend of the World swung with full intent to relieve his head from his shoulders, carving a violet-orange line through the air as Henry roared on by. A set of precast energy blasts shaped as Lion heads smacked square into Artorian's **Argent** mirror as they followed up from behind Henry. On impact, their colors shifted to pure silver as they bounced skyward, the Heavenly gasping with glee at finally getting to show off one of her themes.

Switching their allegiance to Artorian, the silvered lion heads gathered into a pile high above the ground flashed in sequence, then aimed ominously towards Henry. Thumping with dull thuds as they rattled off in sequence, the rapid fire bolts launched towards their target.

Henry broke a piece of the landscape making his explosive U-turn, fought through his own traitorous Mana blasts, and then came face to face with the unexpected. Henry took a silver mirror to the face like a steel chair. Eating the damage, he punched the obstacle. His fist crashed through the mirror, and buried deep into Artorian's unsuspecting stomach, who had not been ready for that very quick counter attack.

The **Argent** mirror and all other mirrors like it in the vicinity were obliterated in tandem as **Valor** broke through **Argent**'s reflective properties. Artorian's Mana construct couldn't hold up against that kind of force.

Argent herself shoved both of her hands into her hair. <That's not how you're supposed to use those! You were doing so well, and now... *Aaaargh*. Get off my node! You ridiculous Ascendant. **Love**, the boy is one of yours alright. A completely lunatic! Zelia had sense!>

An accusing finger evicted him. <You? Out! *Out!*>

Henry tumbled across the plains, the momentum of his own strike carrying him all the way back to the mountains while Artorian turned into a flaming tumbleweed.

When Artorian's wild rolling momentum ran out, he stumbled to his feet only to immediately fall and hit the grass. Looks like High Magi could suffer from discombobulation after all! His equilibrium needed time to re-adjust, so Artorian remained on his rear as he exhaled hard, a hand pressed to his stomach as he poured in some healing. "*Oof.* Henry hits like a high speed palanquin."

Smashing **Argent**'s mirror into Henry's face may not have been the wisest choice, but it sure had been satisfying. Making **Argent** upset? Not so much. She'd been wanting finesse, and here he'd used her fancy mirror as a bashing implement.

Groaning and flopping flat on the ground, he tossed the justifications as his Mana state entered a very unpleasant feeling of flux. Like a coyote that had run off a cliff, and was slowly becoming aware that gravity, working for **Acme**, was merely toying with him before letting the drop happen. Artorian mentally held up a tiny wooden help sign as a metaphorical roadrunner *meep-meeped* at him in passing.

The sound of upset Dwarven feet stomping down a creaky mental staircase reached him before the beginning of that most unfortunate drop. Grasped by his proverbial britches, Artorian was dragged up the Tower as the node that had come to fetch him grumbled through an extreme mustache, a beard about which there were at minimum two legends, and a layer of coal that was so thick that his real clothes were going to have soot marks.

<Ya *dense* wee ninny.> The Dwarf shook him like an empty

mug. His drawl huffed out in full complaint, until he turned to face a most lovely lady going up the stairs with them, his tone changing on a dime when he addressed her. <Not you, polished gem. Ya be a most precious sapling and I am nothin' but fond ya came to knock on my mineshaft.>

Arbor pecked a flowery, cherry blossom kiss to the flushing Dwarven entity's cheek, the coal burning hot red on his face. The man held his hard hat with an embarrassed shuffle when they arrived on the miner's home floor, the other **Law** waving with a shy smile before giggling her way back down the steps.

Artorian's smile was all teeth, eyes sparkling and gleaming as there wasn't a chance in the abyss that he would ever let this fresh, new, prized piece of delicious gossip go. *Romance* in the Tower? The girls were going to have a field day. Entire book clubs would sprout out of the ground from this.

<Shut it!> The Dwarf cawed like an upset crow, his hard hat slapped back on his head as the soot fell off his form in thick clumps. <I don't need yer sass! Now git on up! There be blastin' tah do!>

Artorian was roughly placed on his feet, released from the Dwarven grip. Brushing himself off, the mental version of his clothing was certainly coated in Dwarven-handed soot stains. <Apologies, sir, but do I know you? You sound like you know me.>

An imaginary pickaxe that quickly gained non-imaginary weight was flung into his hands, Artorian catching it with an "Oof!"

The scene around him altered from a Tower floor and into that of a mineshaft leading to a wide open cavern filled with glittering materials that Artorian had never before laid eyes on. The weight of the pickaxe was quickly forgotten as his eyes took in whole walls made of gemstone.

<Aye. I know ya.> The Dwarven man ground his knuckles into Artorian's head, gaining more physicality as the seconds ticked by.

Artorian shifted uncomfortably, the ground turning from

rock into metal? Metal paneling under his feet moved as he stood still, shaping into some kind of square box with walls constructed from chainmail. One *ka-klunk* later, and they were descending, the contraption lowering them deeper into the depths as they passed lit up shaft after shaft. The caverns at the other end of each point they didn't stop at were all filled with diverse, different, wild… Wait.

Artorian needed to double take that particular opening. <Moss? Was that bright one we just passed stuffed with nothing but glowing moss?>

<Aye.> The Dwarf motioned at the forbidden fruit. <Dun eat it.>

Artorian felt his mind turn like rusted gears as he struggled with the accent. <Was that don't eat it, or do eat it? Sounded like you said both.>

<Try it an' find out, ya daft hunk o' pyrite.> The Dwarf's tone had a distinct layer of good amusement to it. <Ya can tell me when we're done scraping ya off the ceilin'.>

<Speaking of ceilings.> Artorian swiftly decided not to eat the glowing moss, moving away from that terrible mental image. <Where are we? I know the Tower is all very mental la-la land, but these new interactions are… different. Very fresh. More physical? No Heavenly has been able to move up and down so easily before and—>

<Will ye shut yer trap?> The miner cuffed Artorian.

Artorian's mouth stopped making noise and snapped shut. Of his own accord, as this was neither the hill, nor hole, he was going to fight and die on. Or in? They were in a hole, right? Abyss, if they went any deeper, they'd come across his odds of victory. Those should be around here somewhere.

The metal cage rattled, coming to a stop before the chain-mail acting as partition parted. One layer slid up, another moving to the side. Artorian chose not to ask why the metal box had multiple doors, it came fourth or fifth in the queue of questions as he followed the Heavenly and stepped into another cavern, this one coated in 'danger, explosive!' signs.

The coal- and soot-coated Dwarf pulled a glowing piece of highly-unstable-looking mineral from the wall like a piece of candy to bite a piece off from. He shoved it into Artorian's confused, open hand. The pickaxe was quickly taken away from him as he was made to cradle the hunk with both palms. <On secon' thought, best ya not be swingin' that.>

Artorian looked all around, then back at the chunk of glowing mineral in his hands that appeared like it was angry at all of existence for… really no reason. Aside from waking up today and choosing violence.

<Dun drop it.> The grumbling miner gave his massive beard a beating, rather than a pat down to get some of the blackness out of it. <Ye be holdin' plasmid nitroglycerin-concentrate in crystalline form. It's no fifth element like ye are, but it'll slap ya with a *big* bada-boom. It's what ya get when Essence tries to make the stuff, rather than lettin' good ol' physics have her due, and doin' it proper. All this cultivation hanky-panky blinds ya to the incredible natural order that happens when ya let fully corrupted, non-malleable materials cure, rest, and develop like a good Dwarven wine.>

Artorian paled. Even in non-reality, this was not something he wanted to be holding. <Please tell me why this is in my hands?>

The miner hacked into the nearby wall, unearthing a massive rock with the pickaxe. He dragged it across the ground before sitting down on it to show off a pearly white smile. <Cuz! If I'ma do you the courtesy of using my Mana type proper, ya gotta know about the dangers of what you're actually holdin'! Mine's not as kind or sweet as some of them' other baby Mana flows. Mine'll kill ya, proper and quick!>

Artorian looked at the Dwarf, his entire being still coated in soot. Like it was both a coat of protection, and a measure to hide his appearance. <Then thank you kindly for the courtesy, Mister…?>

<Torgue!> The dwarven miner laughed, putting the pickaxe down next to his rock. <Torgue Mayev Stoneking.

Grandfather to a lass that ye've been showin' proper respect to, if you added a dice-roll of 'grands' to the title. The lass ye fulfilled the last wishes of. Along with yer feisty friend currently doin' some very *solar* work.>

The pearly grin widened. <Welcome to the mines! Let's not dig around the aquifer, and see about your multi-pass. Tell me *everything* ya know about the life of muh sweet li'l flower, Ephira Mayev Stonequeen, and **Explosions**.>

CHAPTER THIRTY-EIGHT

Henry appeared back on the scene after clawing himself out of another rock face, when he saw Artorian press a hand to the ground, blow up part of it, and come to a perfect, exact upright stance. Little pops and crackles of dangerous Mana playing on Artorian's open palm.

The old man blinked, then stretched hard as he said words Henry didn't understand. Bending left and right as his bones popped. "Good heavens, that took *weeks*! I thought I was never getting out of that mine. I've licked enough danger-rocks to last a lifetime. I'm so done being a Petrologist. At least Torgue gave me my E.O.D. certification, even if he never told me what it was short for."

He then shook both his sleeves out, getting the flecks of white phosphorus off. "What was I doing again? Right! Hi Henry! We were fighting, I believe?"

"Yes?" The regent squinted in confusion, strolling towards Artorian as he picked the remaining broken pieces of helmet out from his bevor. He did not seem bothered about the loss of protection. With Marie's sonic shell still in place, and Artorian out of mirrors, he felt favored. "Did I gut-check you so hard that you forgot?"

Artorian observed the approaching giant of battle, packed into a small form. Against anyone else, Henry would be cleaning the Camel house right now. No wonder he'd been subjugating most Mages so handily. The new math said that A-rank one, times three point fourteen, times ninety-eight, resulted in a raw oomph of three hundred and eight. That was more than enough against opponents scared to spend Mana. In the old world, efficiency and retaining energy was a big deal, but Henry and Marie hadn't developed as Mages with those conditions in place. They didn't just have both a power advantage and a cheat Pylon, they had a psychological advantage.

"You may have." Artorian kneaded the back of his neck. "I'm pretty sure I was out cold on the grass for a bit there. But sweet celestials, Henry. Not a scratch on your face? That armor is exquisite! If my napkin math was anything to go by, that steel chair ought to have taken your head off."

"Chair?" Henry stopped in confusion, needing to give Artorian a once over. "I definitely hit you too hard, old man. You swung a weird silver mirror that tried to reflect my damage back at me? **Valor** overcame the effect, and I got you right in the food pocket."

Bouncing on his toes, Artorian watched Henry recoup all his shields into his spatial rings. The Lion emanations around his body were intense and bristling as they built up to a visual critical mass. Then, Artorian felt it. The *twinge*. The tingle on the nose. "You really are just doing all of this purely because you love Marie, huh? The regent stuff comes second. All you really want is to finally see her happy."

Henry pressed his hands to his hips as he looked down, his expression bashful before forcing an apologetic shrug in reply. "It's always 'when we finish this one last thing,' and 'when we meet this new next goal,' and 'when we have this we can spend time,' which becomes 'well, we really should…'"

The regent trailed off, his face turning foul. "You're not

wrong. I've put ruling, and being a good ruler, second, or maybe third, if not fourth. I admit, I've been blinded by my affection for Marie. Like… my actions have had a carpet to be brushed under. You have no idea how happy it would make me to live in some quiet cottage with her for a few decades. But…"

"Marie will be Marie, with her own wants, drives, and goals." Artorian scratched his chin as he finished Henry's sentence, nodding in understanding. "Which you wouldn't, for the life of you, want to get in front of. And if you support her through those ordeals and get them done, you'll have both been there for her, and with her, and you'll hope she sees that when all the chips are finally on the table."

Henry's colorations warbled to show his emotional discord. "You've poked a very raw bear, Sunny."

"**Love** can be blind." Artorian shrugged, responding with an equally apologetic tone, his face a painting of understanding and shared sorrow. "You do what you can. You strive to do your best. That your best can seem like it's not enough is no fault of yours. I can only offer the suggestion that you talk with her of this feeling and stance. Then talk, talk, and keep talking until the last vestiges of the worry have left you. I'm sure she'd be receptive, especially for you? She does share your feelings, I'm certain of it, even if they are buried under the self-imposed burdens that she… carries."

Artorian frowned at the end of his own sentence, the words from the Heavenlies of the fourteenth floor coming back to haunt him.

Henry chuckled, momentarily not feeling like fighting. He would continue, but not for the next few minutes. "I have an entire list about levels of friendship, you know. It's… the ideas? Those I can make and understand. The concept of friends is something with which I have no struggle. The actual upkeep? My head feels like it can be full of holes, and I forget people when I shouldn't."

The old man leaned into the momentary reprieve. If he could dissuade Henry from fighting on entirely, that would be a far greater win. "Don't suppose you have that list on hand? If I'm not the person you want to be hearing from about this, then I really must lean on the idea that you get help from other people that you trust, in a way that you want to be helped. The social sphere is a critical component to one's well-being, even for a hermit like me. Venting to close friends, or being close to friends and not talking, merely to feel the company. These things help. If you don't feel like reaching out, or for some reason feel like you do not deserve the help, please know that my door is open regardless. Meander in, don't meander in, that door is there for you, Henry."

The regent appeared conflicted, the critical Mana around him drowning the man in waves of coruscating energy as the energy itself clearly did not know what its user wanted of it. A good chunk of that turning-rogue Mana was instead starting to look to Artorian, but his silent message was that the energy should do its best to keep supporting Henry until he figured it out. The critical Mana mass did just that, smoothing out around Henry rather than reaching the kind of tipping point that would cause a Mana storm.

An uncertain Henry made jerky motions as he moved to take something out of his ring, paused, tried to continue, then paused again. Double-guessing his own actions. In the end, he pulled a scroll free and tossed it over in a loose arc, Artorian easily catching the writ.

The old scholar unfurled it for a quick glance, but only a quick one before furling it back in and absorbing the scroll into his spatial bracelet.

Desert Wisdom: A lion's 13 levels of friendship.

Note that most friends are level five or below.

One. A fellow of the same age, or other circumstantial connection.

Two. An acquaintance that you can nod with on a given topic.

Three. A colleague, or person you can sit and have a long conversation with.

Four. A person with whom you sit around, able to have a good conversation.

Five. A companion in conversations that occur at odd, or otherwise unreasonable times, yet you do not mind the intrusion. One to offer a drink even in the middle of night.

Six. A companion, with clear concern for your wellbeing.

Seven. A close companion or comrade, particularly in travel, whom you are certain that you can depend upon to hold your money.

Eight. The proper attribution of the word 'friend,' a person who comes to you without ulterior motive.

Nine. A close friend, worthy of intimate secrets, whose very presence makes you happy.

Ten. A friend whose presence can bring you calm, peace, and happiness. An inducted member of the family that one's mother considers part of the table.

Eleven. A person whose comfort and familiarity is second nature, whom you trust with not only your life, but your money and wife.

Twelve. A chosen best friend. Held in regard above all others. One whom you tell your most closely guarded secrets and sins, for their burden is safe to share.

Thirteen. As is the Kin of Ana to the Obi of Ken, this person is your spiritual double; inseparable from you, and so entwined with your sense of self that their loss would shatter you whole. Striking your name from all ledgers, as even if you lived, who you were would forever be dead.

"I don't know if what you want is truth seeking, or advice, Henry." Artorian softened his words, the tone dipping into grandfather land. "If you need to vent, then I'll listen, and keep quiet. However, I'm of the view that you need both validation and problem solving. That you need to be both heard and understood."

The old man, at the minimum, opened his arms for a hug. Even if the situation for it was poor, he was going to make his stance clear. "If I'm not who you need, tell who you do need this: Begin with listening to understand, not listening to respond. Have them reflect your experiences back in their own words. It will validate that it shows they are listening, giving you their full attention, which helps you both to understand what is actually going on."

Henry rubbed the back of his head, but didn't take the peace offering. His mind was so clearly on Marie that Artorian wasn't going to make the comment. Artorian dropped his arms, holding his own hands. "If what you hear back is not what you intended, then you can address it. However, if you let misunderstandings sit and fester…"

Henry growled, his uncertainty sharply falling into a pit of frustration. "I will feel exactly how I'm feeling?"

Artorian did not dismiss the rising anger. "Yes. If I went through what you were going through, and was facing those conditions, I would be so miffed that it was happening to me."

Henry deflated like a fish. The regent's entire Mana signature turned around, as if that validation and understanding was the first big step in something he'd direly needed. The idea that his emotions made sense, and he wasn't experiencing something that was unnatural. A bevy of psychosocial stressors still lived on his shoulders, but that particular chip packed its bags and checked out of the casino.

"Regardless of how we end this, old friend." Artorian smiled, trying to lighten the mood. "In Avalon, where my dear Lunella is dragging her town through the mud on the path of betterment, kicking and screaming, you may find what you seek. In order to make something truly good out of it, one of the goals is to help all the people who… don't feel like they fit. Who feel like they've missed out. People who need help because they don't know who they are, or who they want to be in this new world they've come back to. Go see her. Tell her I sent you to get help."

Henry shook his head, his emotions pushed under the rug as his thoughts kept going back to Marie. "Maybe, Sunny. Maybe."

The claws over his gauntlets flared back to life, dashing Artorian's hopes to resolve this easily. Henry's Mana signature resolved, determined to continue the brawl rather than change the initial plan. There was more fighting to do, so Henry upped the ante and pulled out his big ballistae. The shields had been a measure more useful for when Marie was present. Now that it was just them two in an open plain, Henry's sudden roar and transformation made Artorian click his tongue.

"I was complaining about transfigurations and humanizations not too long ago. I take it you acquired a Lion form in Eternia?" The Administrator grumbled, seeing that grandpa time would have to wait, as his station had clocked back in.

Henry's entire head became a bright orange, thick-furred Lion's head, flecked with violet Auric effects as his admittedly **Valorous** Aura tried its best to cohesively stick to him. A burst of power later, and Henry's armor overlapped a Lion's frame instead of a human one. The battle tyrant equipment was not limited to a mere human shape.

Artorian glared up at the armored beast that was staring him down, Henry's snarls unmistakable as a challenge for him to step up to the plate. Rend of the World pierced from Lion-Henry's forehead like a Basher's horn, the longsword curving into the shape that matched this intent.

"A Beast Dreamer, indeed." Artorian did some math in his head. The *Oomph* of **Arbor** and **Argent**'s forty-seven, with six ranks worth of investment, was a solid two-hundred eighty two. That output hadn't dinged Henry's pretty armor, nor his buffed threshold of three hundred and seven, or three hundred and eight, depending on the rounding. Empowering **Argent**'s tier forty-seven effect on the other hand, if the math held, multiplied his own two hundred eighty-two *Oomph* value by three point fourteen, reaching either a very clean eight hundred eighty-five, or a slightly more accurate eight hundred eighty-six, depending on how he rounded the numbers on that one as well. That was the move that had sent Henry flying.

Eight hundred eighty-five handily overcame three hundred and eight. So even if Marie's sonic shell had that same value, then he needed to add it to Henry's. Thus, making the formula eight hundred eighty-five versus a value of six hundred sixteen. With those numbers, his strike getting through the sonic shell, the armor, and Henry's Mage *Oomph* made plenty of sense as far as the math seemed concerned. So, now he needed to test whether the value he had to overcome to deal damage was three hundred and eight, or six hundred and sixteen.

Explosion sat cozily in the Tier fifty-five hole. That *Oomph*, times six ranks worth of Mana, came out to a very clean three hundred and thirty. Enough to both toe the line, and be just above Henry's individual output, Empowerment buff included. Not having to use the sudden Empowerment mechanic himself should keep the checkbox unticked on **Glory's** spreadsheet, if the value he had to overcome was three hundred and eight.

A hope to hold on to, and a valuable checkbox right now, as it was becoming ever more clear that Marie was going to be the big problem, rather than Henry. Henry would be satisfied with a loss, if he was beaten fair and square. Marie... Marie was going to be difficult.

That also meant he should try to wrap this round up.

Perhaps... he could be a little flashy? A little pizzazz wouldn't hurt.

Marie wasn't watching, and what **Glory** didn't know, **Glory** couldn't use.

"Alright, lion-lad." Artorian rolled his shoulders as he hopped on his metal toes, panels of hard light forming around him as the armored lion prowled in continued challenge. "You wanna go beast mode? Let's go *beast* mode."

CHAPTER THIRTY-NINE

The Lion regent roared! "Cape of the Beast King!"

Henry's sonic shell refreshed with a noisy and sharp synthesized screech, before a coat of orange flame fully overlapped the monstrous regent. The effect spread over him entirely, ending with particularly vicious looking burning claws where the extra fire burst free.

Artorian's Aura responded in kind, the old man disappearing into the Liger construct's chest cavity as it was forming, taking a dramatic stance, and roaring back in an explosive blaze.

Enacting a territory dispute between two great beasts.

Artorian shook himself out when the sensations and motions of the Liger form kicked in, empirical and tactile feedback electrifying to life. He felt the grass under his claws. The stiff breeze that clashed purely because they were both exerting power. The warmth of the light breaking through fleeing clouds. The smell of a brewing Mana storm. All of it came to him, detail after detail, as the construct encompassing him became more and more real to his senses, rather than a mere boxy-looking Liger shell that he was using as a wessel.

Vessel? He still liked wessel. It was funny.

Weekly lessons with Decorum had borne fruit!

No longer tumbling over one's own feet was also a feat, and he could sympathize with the story of Sleipnir. Multiple legs? A tragedy waiting to happen. Four was plenty to trip over.

The Liger construct, previously tinted in celestial colorations, now bloomed with metallic flecks of white phosphorus when the plating merge locked and completed. Places where his joints rubbed together sparked and flared with flashes of blinding white sparks, while a roll of the shoulders came with a clattering set of fireworks. Indicators for adjustment points that got some quick attention, slightly improving his range of motion.

Henry was undaunted by the pop rocks, stalking up.

As they prowled and closed the distance, Artorian noticed that Henry appeared to be gaining in strength as they closed the gap. The reason was difficult to discern, until it clicked. His perspective was higher? He was physically larger, and the size difference was giving Henry's **Valor Law** a tick box to check. That burning coat around Henry was doing its best to make him look bigger, and it distinctly felt like **Valor** at work.

Luckily, size had become something Artorian was more at liberty to alter, as he condensed his form down to match size. Liger too big? Shrink down to not give **Valor** an advantage! The resulting change was instant, as Artorian's smaller form made Henry's burning coat dissipate outright. **Valor** no longer had a foothold to provide additional strength, when the threat Artorian posed no longer required as much courage to tackle. A grand opponent poses great danger, but an equal opponent is one against which a soul tests their measure, and not their courage.

The *ding* of a bell flicked his eyes over to the zone next to them, the bordering Aquarium zone filled with people. Oh hey! Look at them! So many of them were sitting atop the cube without problems. That was so good! They'd been such an ant's nest before, all stuck and struggling.

"Get 'im, Pa!" Tychus shook his fist and boomed from up high, a big dumb grin on his face as he frantically waved and jumped to get attention. It appeared 'Pa' had been adopted as a nickname from Wu. Artorian liked it. It easily bridged some unseen gap between father and grandpa, and since he played both roles for a lot of them, it felt fitting. Pa it was!

The bell-ringer appeared to be Irene, who was giving him the most jealous eyes he'd seen on her to date. Right! Liger! She was pure Morovian, her mouth didn't need to verbalize the words for him to interpret her sharp hand motions as 'you are teaching me that and I am going to chase you down until you do.' She would, too.

A *cheeeeep* cut in from behind Irene, Blanket bursting from the gelatinous cube. The Beastie licked his own face as if he'd spent the last hour trying to eat the Aquarium. Cal *had* mentioned it was tasty.

Jiivra popped her head up from the back of Blanket's fur, looking around to check the commotion before following everyone's attention. The Celestial Mage landed her eyes on the title match, attentive to the Liger's lineage versus Lion's lineage tussle.

Experiencing a Nixie tube moment, she then produced flags and streamers with frightening speed, the crowd swiftly equipped with objects to wave and kazoos to blow, creating a cacophony of irritating noise that was enjoyable only to the fanclub crafting them. A particularly sharp whistle caused a jerking movement in the Liger when Jiivra showed off.

Artorian's distraction was Henry's opportunity!

Or so he thought.

"Imperial Lion." Henry's more beastly voice indulged in calling out his attacks, while a roiling burst of furious air rushed over his claws. "Mauling Storm!"

"Dream Weaver's Delirium." Artorian smoothly spoke his ruse into being. The rumble in his own voice was unavoidable since he was using the big construct to speak. The way he said it, on the other claw, was far too calm for a combat setting.

Artorian's Aura released a wave that diffused and mixed all colors around them, the environment stirred like a fancy drink. Stirred. but not shaken, as a cavity formed around the Liger. "Bubble in the Wine Glass."

The Lion's physical attack struck a glassy spherical shell. Upon touching the bubble, the edge hissed with angry yellows and reds. Followed by crackling pops of an impending... *boom*! Henry's own strike rebounded away as he was sent tumbling back. Mauling Storm's Mana effect then resolved, electric blades of solid air shattering the protective shell only to be obliterated in turn as the bubble cracked to pieces and shattered into wild, prismatic fireworks.

Turns out? Fueling a protective bubble with explosive Mana was a very double edged sword. As the protection collapsed, physics instantly slapped on the cap of the taxman, and demanded its share.

Weak points on Artorian's form cracked and shattered in several places, his entire Liger construct body coated in fractures as Torgue laughed in his head. **Explosion** Mana was indiscriminate, and he should know better! "Rather tha' construct than you! Regardless of it hurtin' just the same. Now Focus! An' try not to blow yerself' up again, ya daft vein o' Opalite. What are you thinking? *Defendin'* with explosions. Ha!"

Artorian smirked, exhaling the words under his breath as he watched the regent recover and get back on all fours. "Wasn't a *defense*."

Henry managed to escape the majority of the explosion's effects, but the lingering tremble in his paw was cause for concern. Mana intentions had been heavily intermixed, and he was being served the idea inherent in his own shields. The physical harm of the attack wasn't what stuck? There was something else creeping in.

A sudden slap of vertigo and all the colors in his vision being stirred was clue enough.

The blocky beast had attacked him mentally, adding a layer of reactive offense into that bubble which he had no chance of avoiding. One needed solid Auric protections against such mental attacks. The explosion felt like it was part of the Mana type, but the other effect felt more sinister, as a calm wave of fuzzy serenity rushed up Henry's forearm.

Like the limb was waking up from being asleep, except that he was quickly losing feeling in the entire limb, the effect spreading. Some flexing got rid of that peaceful yet prickly sensation, the orange fire flaring back to life over his claws thereafter. Surely the sneaky old man wasn't going to try to lay him low with sneaky mental trifles and—

"Decorum's Dance!" The fractured Liger took a stance with all four paws braced to create maximum steadiness. Like that glowing light gathering in his open mouth was going to blow him backwards. "Shining Ray!"

Henry dodged preemptively! He flung himself out of the way, which was the only motion that saved his life as his instincts screamed. First, a hefty ball of energy had gathered in Artorian's maw. From that condensed power, a teensy, narrow beam of twisting yellow and red light stabbed faster than Henry could see towards the horizon. The line of light pierced the space he had occupied mere instants ago as he rolled over the grass to duck, dodge, and roll.

The light line was barely a sliver thick! Not at all flashy.

Given the power density, Henry had expected a big, tree-sized laser! With the ray ongoing, he changed his mind and performed the limbo to slide underneath the deadly line as it swung towards him. Shining Ray worked as a sustained blast rather than instant effect? That cheeky waffle! Then Henry heaved and tensed after snapping to his feet, having pulled a hamstring, feeling a sudden, sharp pain in the back of his thigh. He'd foolishly exerted himself in a body that he wasn't very used to.

Artorian moved the beam with hardship. That condensed energy was difficult to control as he leveled the line parallel to the ground, the teensy thing dividing the mountainous land-scapes in its path even as he failed to connect the beam with his intended opponent. Henry's reaction speed was far too good, and if the Lion dodged it once, then he could dodge it twice, placing Artorian in a terrible position if Henry closed the distance before he was ready.

Ending the effect rather than continuing this tragedy, as Henry was glowering him down with wide eyes and a gaze of pure constipated focus, Artorian snapped his mouth shut. The Liger exhaled a hot white cloud of phosphorus from his construct's nose, not at all bothered by the wave of tiny explosions that crackled. The rest of his form steamed with accumulated heat, clearly strained.

Henry had been too fast, and too furious, for the turn speed of the ill-controlled beam to catch him. Artorian had gambled and hoped that the instant casting time—going from no threat to full murderhobo light beam—would have scored him the victory point. Had the initial shot connected, it would have been the win.

No dice. All snake eyes.

Hearing the construct creak like crystalline lattice snapping, he knew his joints were toast. Artorian needed to buy a lot more time in order to not get walloped right in the face like he'd offered a free hit to some new upstart in prideful hubris. The self-inflicted damage locked him in place as he recovered from Shining Ray's sustained effort, his body requiring precious seconds to mend at the joints that had been put under intense pressure.

Time that Henry might just give him with all that staggering the Lion was doing!

Torgue had no time for this leisurely well-digging, and slid Artorian a fat, double helping of erudition. A mental bolt of lightning, thicker than the muscled mass of Viscount Luke Von Murderhobo—a literal murderhobo from a different and specifically non-connected universe—jumped up from the depths of gifted memories and broke onto the scene like a head-cracking strike of a battering ram goat horn.

Artorian felt knowledge of ancient times, buried in old dusty scrolls, surface and come to light as Scholar Peterovia and Saint Karlussen's discourse on shapes came to mind. While the majority of the talks came down to segmented two hour conversations on their favorite tomes and flaws therein, they did hash out a nugget of wisdom that shot from the bottom of the ocean and breached the waves like a lecturer who had just heard one of his points being disputed.

With the stoic also wielding a battering ram goat horn.

All the better to educate a junior greenhorn with.

Artorian would have ordinarily rebuked such an involuntary thought, but then realized that this gift was an opportunity that fit his current predicament. Energetic discs were a favored subject of Scholar Peterovia's many scrolls, while orbs were considered superior by Saint Karlussen. Both measures required the caster to remain stationary, and he was plenty stuck!

Saint Karlussen loved his experimental rocketry and kabooms, while Scholar Peterovia was one of those famed combat-lore fanatics that would and could bring entire books of warrior styles to a conversation to gush over a fight done well.

First, the P.P.C.—Particle Projection Cannon—of Saint Karlussen!

Molding brand new construct cylinders onto the sides of his current form was a piece of cake! The transformer change came accompanied by a very distinct, mechanical, clicking *cho-chu-cha-chi* sound. Charging the new cannons up was only a hint more complicated; agitated particles electrified, orbified, and were condensed to a stormy intensity as he concentrated the round to critical mass. Firing K.P.R.—Karlussen Pulsation Rounds—from the P.P.C. made him lurch! Artorian was really happy that he was still in a four-point stability stance, because that alone wasn't enough as the tubes lit up with a *ska-doom*!

Torgue loudly cheered, applauding in approval. <Whooooo-hoo! That P.P.C. has more kick to it than yer Shining Ray! Karlussen knows his kabooms! Always loved his banger lectures.>

Swift launcher construction came with flaws, as anything

hastily assembled would be just as hastily be disassembled. Which was why Artorian grit his teeth when both of the tubes exploded in spectacular, firework fashion. On the positive side, the intended projectiles moved so fast towards the intended opponent that they left lines of lightning in their wake.

Henry paddled the pulsing electric balls away with the back of an ultraviolet claw, sending them spiraling into the sky before the particles destabilized, detonating in a big electromagnetic pulse that made normal fireworks feel like they should up their game, the fizzy particles popping and causing visual static. "Too slow, old man! Your line was faster."

Henry, seizing the moment of Artorian clearly being in a bind, employed a far more ingrained viciousness and closed the distance with ease. Seeing that the construct once again suffered its moment of emplacement vulnerability, he bit through the pain of his own injury and went for the kill.

Henry landed a solid blow! Cracking a burning orange claw across the Liger's face that displaced a mountain of air, pushed clouds apart, and destroyed vast chunks of Liger construct.

The impact sent Artorian tumbling and rolling over the plains as Henry followed in hot pursuit, successfully ripping entire glowing chunks out of the Liger's back and neck. Injured or not, Henry was employing smooth, highly skilled killing motions. The Lion focused on digging through to the tender, juicy, critical bits of Artorian's actual body.

The endeavor would have been very effective had the Liger not been an **Explosion**-fueled construct that saluted like a sooty, grinning Dwarf. The ripped away panels promptly detonated in the Lion's mouth as the **Explosion** Mana did what it and Saint Karlussen loved.

Cause the *kabooms*!

CHAPTER FORTY

Artorian and Henry both needed a breather after that moment of mutual destruction, separated from one another by pure concussive force. Pain was not a stranger to either of them as Artorian's construct repaired itself, while Henry hacked and coughed. That sonic shell neither protected the inside of his mouth, nor did armor help any when you bit into a bomb.

Henry's face hurt very badly, several Mana cracks lining up and over his appearance. There was likely more damage currently hidden under the Lion's armored plates, but rather than check, Artorian used his momentary advantage of recovering first to prepare his next attack instead of mending his form back to full health.

Henry hit as hard as Artorian feared, his construct jaw feeling like it had gotten whacked with a knockout punch. Being in claw-range was a grave danger! He wasn't going to be able to take a second hit like that, the *Oomph* math altered as both Shining Ray and Karlussen's trick had been costly.

He currently felt closer to an oomph of two-ninety or two-eighty, and that got its keister handed to it by Henry's *Oomph* of three-hundred and eight. He needed to shift tactics, and scrolls of knowledge unfurled before his eyes as he experienced the thought. The Saint had stood center stage, now it was time for the Scholar to speak.

"Peterovia Style." A sharp whistle from Artorian summoned Blanket down from the top of the Aquarium. A projection of a circle formed on Artorian's back, making it clear to the Sugar Glider what the game was. "Disc Wars."

Blanket's ears twitched before he deposited Jiivra and leapt from the cube like a tubby C'towl that was clearly not going to make the other side of the armrest. Dropping like a rock, Blanket twisted, called it mighty morphin time, and turned into a chakram to the sound of an electrical riff! Descending on a bolt of Celestial lightning, Blanket's chakram built up spin before slotting exactly in the place of Artorian's open ring.

Combining into the Liger construct, the open middle of the chakram flashed bright blue as the Liger's shell clicked into the weapon's interior. Blanket hummed with power as his existing effects were empowered with the sweet, sweet gift of **Explosion**. The infused power caused the chakram to illuminate, serrate, sharpen, and spin even faster.

The rising whistle of Blanket's spin reached a level that sounded notably threatening, the edge hazardously aglow with a bright, unstable blue.

Artorian quirked a brow at the color. Wasn't **Explosion** supposed to be a mixture of yellow and red? Blanket's affinities must be playing their part.

Blanket and Jiivra, who relied on one another for their cultivation, shared the Tier one **Celestial Law** in a way that Artorian didn't have time to unpack. What he did understand was that Blanket offered a plus to the *Oomph* of the formula, and more importantly, allotted him a mobile weapon to guide with telekinesis while he himself kept out of angry claw range.

Henry may have dodged his beam, but could he dodge a weapon with a mind of its own, that was dead set on tracking him down, plus guidance?

The old Liger grinned wide.

Coating the edge of Blanket's whistling disc with additional **Explosion** Mana appeared devastating! The destructive force was so visually captivating that the contained danger could be considered art. What should he call Blanket's upgraded chakram? Destruct-o-disc?

Artorian's momentary mirth was halted when the texts of Scholar Peterovia politely stepped to the side, graciously making way for another that had stepped onto the podium.

Flittering visions of Yuki interspersed his thoughts. Artorian felt a Heavenly hand, silent and cold, touch his back. To his ear alone, **Kenopsia** whispered a lonely fate fit for an empty king, trapped in a realm abandoned by both people and time. Artorian's mood dropped to solemn acquiescence. He inhaled deep, feeling **Kenopsia** sustain the expectation.

He nodded in silence, felt Karlussen's texts approve the modification requested by the Heavenly without retort, then spoke with an empty voice. "Hollow Knight Style."

Artorian launched the disc up from his back, then struck with the downwards swing of a sword guided by needle and thread. Blanket, ready for action, and not remotely affected by the change in battle plan, engaged the assault. He cut deep into the dirt, the earth muting the brass noise and hiding Blanket's intended trajectory past the initial bulge of ground that was kicked back up. Before becoming imperceptible, the single line of dirt pushing up from the ground split and became three.

Artorian did as **Kenopsia** requested, adding a nail to the coffin while Blanket was hidden from sight. "White Palace."

Henry had seen the landshark-themed attack launch, but was in a bad spot to keep track of it without his helmet. He wasn't quick enough with the change in vision modes to let him defend, or know where to dodge, against homing saw blades that would be erupting from below. He hopped around without knowing exactly where to go, and that proved to be a disaster as the metallic carving sounds drew ominously close.

Screeching out of the dirt, Henry had the acuity to dodge the copies. Both bubbled with explosive sheen, but didn't instantly release their payload. Henry felt victorious regardless! He had dodged two! That meant only one left to…

Angled platforms blinked to life around them. The swift set of light-walls from Artorian provided the copies ample space to bounce around, eager to bite into their target. Mostly, they ate up Henry's attention span. Which was exactly what Artorian needed Henry to spend.

Busy dodging the copies, Henry didn't notice the real threat until it was too late.

Blanket's destruct-o-disc slammed home straight into Henry's unsuspecting chest, an entire festival of sparks instantly erupting! The energetic sheen on his chakram's edge now a blinding, accursed white.

Blanket hit so hard that the impact pushed Henry's claws off the ground, allowing the re-vectored copies to impact with enough force to send Henry flying, colliding with a nice particle-heavy *bang*!

Artorian easily tracked the damage dealt as the discs glued to their target, cutting and grinding through several layers of protection, while he mentally fist-bumped Scholar Peterovia for the texts on disc wars. He then checked over his shoulder, feeling an approving hand touch the top of his bald head, before **Kenopsia** left the stage. Her will had been done.

What a cold and insidious infusion that had been. White Palace? Henry didn't have a clue about the kind of curse he was now stuck with, and Artorian wasn't sure how to feel about playing courier. One successful hit by Blanket was all White Palace needed, and success had been immediate.

Shaking himself out of this, his ears instead attuned to his surroundings.

Shearing, shrill cries of saw blades at work drowned out the cheering from above. Even as Henry eclipsed the Aquarium in height before gravity got a proper hold of him again. The destructive discs kept merciless contact, racing over the armored Lion to find sweet spots, then rip and tear their way through. When Henry landed with a dull thud, he began to violently roll in a first attempt to get the gnawing discs off of him.

The explosive copies detonated when Henry rolled on them, adding some craters to this section of the plains. Blanket managed to inflict significantly more direct damage before being made to twist and veer away by Artorian's telekinesis.

Henry lashed out with an orange-violet tinted bite, while Blanket was in a prime position for a critical strike. Artorian couldn't risk it. Henry would take significant damage, but Blanket had to remain unharmed. So, regardless of the potential gain, the destructive disc was yoinked away, and Blanket was done for the day.

"Blanket, good job!" Artorian gently tossed the chakram like a yo-yo back up towards the Aquarium. The easy arc allowed Blanket to smoothly and with ease shift back into his house-sized Sugar Glider form, landing on Jiivra with zero grace. The glider flopped on her like a room-sized pillow being dropped from the second story of a tower rather than some plushie being caught.

If there was an *oopf*, it was completely muffled by glider fluff.

He *cheeped* loud after being returned to safety, proud to have been involved, regardless of his part having been very short as the leftover Mana dissipated. Artorian, however, wasn't going to put his favorite Glider in any danger. Once the surprise of the move had been spent, Henry was far too likely to have counters devised. He wasn't going to put any chips down on the bet that Henry wasn't a combat aficionado.

Better to gamble that Henry was potent, and not to be underestimated. That sword of a forehead horn had still not come to bear, and it was very difficult to ignore. Preferably, Artorian could avoid dealing with it at all. He had plenty of bad Basher memories already!

More important for the current dilemma was the damage assessment! Artorian guesstimated that the main disc's output provided an *Oomph* of roughly three-thirty or three-fifty. Because the purely explosive copies hadn't accomplished bonk beyond distracting Henry, and were therefore below the three-oh-eight mark.

The destructive disc appeared to have cut through Marie's sonic shell, and into Henry's armor. Unfortunately, there was strong indication that Blanket's disc had not *reliably* cut through Henry's armor, and in the places where that damage was clear, there was no harm done to the Lion form underneath.

"Crackers and toast." Artorian devised new plans mid-complaint. "So I *am* dealing with the six hundred and sixteen value? Abyss, Marie! You were supposed to be the more difficult fight. If I need to beat six-hundred to handle Henry, and you only need half, that is definitely going to trigger the **Glory** checkbox. You clever little runt!"

The intense ping of a Mana signature changing caught his immediate attention.

Now Artorian had a problem.

Two problems.

One. He shouldn't have spoken of the demon in the Abyss, for if you call them, they will come. Marie was done with her task, and no longer tied down to the Camel-lot. Her Mana signature was suddenly heading this way at terrible speed. Two, if Marie saw him defeat Henry with a power output at least twice that of hers, he was never going to get her to concede a victory, and the spiral he wanted so badly to avoid would happen.

He wasn't here to beat his friends down into the mud.

He was here to solve the problem.

Bonus issue number three, he still needed to actually defeat Henry. He supposed... he did have one particularly dumb idea he could employ. It would be... unconventional. Perhaps not particularly satisfying. However, if it bought him that precious, precious time, then maybe? What if he was fighting Henry and Marie in the wrong order?

He was out of alternatives.

The glorious trumpets of greater *pwaaamp* had arrived.

Marie was here.

Henry charged at him with a killing blow, and Artorian didn't bother dodging.

The roaring claw came down with enough force to add another sizable crater to the landscape, but instead Henry found himself upside down, twisting through the air, and being flung into the distance.

"No Style." Artorian had shifted stances, his Liger standing upright as a man. Artorian's front paws had flowed through a windmill motion that allowed the back of Artorian's construct wrist to intersect the attack, redirect the force, and send Henry hurling away. "Deny the Blow."

With vast centrifugal force as all of Henry's might was turned into velocity, the armored Lion was, without ceremony or honor, spun right into the Aquarium. There was no impact noise when Henry passed through the external barrier, the regent sinking deep from the momentum. He sank right through the outermost layers of the gelatinous cube, coming to a complete standstill on the Aquarium's grassy yellow ground before fully and truly becoming aware that he was stuck.

Henry released the unsettled meow of an inconvenienced cat.

His form remained unmoving, as rather than being unwilling to move, he was solidly unable. No amount of Mana was going to help him here. An infinite supply of Mana was useless when this lack of Auric skill resulted in his untimely downfall, without the need for a bloody defeat. **Valor** kicked in at full force to fight back the panic, but slowly bled away when the **Law** sensed the minor push to help people escape that was in place.

Henry was slowly being moved back towards the Aquarium's edge by Cal's safeguards, but it would not be in time for him to rejoin the fray and become a notable addition to Marie's fight against Artorian. It was, however, enough to avert Henry from feeling he would be stuck in the Aquarium forever. A minor comfort.

He couldn't verbalize his complaint, but the result of the match ending in his effective loss wasn't lost on the regent. Rather than dwell on the feeling, Henry instead began to wonder what his friend had been up to this entire fight. For the old Fox had employed some truly strange madness, and Artorian had not in the slightest faced him with all the might that he knew Artorian could bring to bear.

That was... strange. *Why not* use your full power to win?

It was what he'd been doing, but Artorian had been going up and down in density, the Administrator's signature adapting wildly in an attempt to match his. The old man had been fighting to win, but not the same kind of win that Henry was aiming for.

"In Kings and Castles, we call this move Castling!" Suspicion struck Henry when Artorian spoke, the puzzled feeling intensifying as the Administrator provided him a polite send off. "You're tagged out, Henry! Take a break."

Artorian dismissed his Liger construct, falling onto the ground into a three point pose before rising back up and brushing himself off. The injured Aura construct was recouped, and pulled tightly in around his body all by itself, like it was glad to be home.

Artorian then flashed the other regent a bright smile as she burst onto the scene. A regal halo of mystical illusions followed in her wake to herald her arrival. "Hello Marie. Tagging in?"

CHAPTER FORTY-ONE

"**Glory!**" Marie arrived with zero chill, and an equivalent amount of amusement in her voice as she started her round of the fight right away. She was in no mood to mince words, or to employ words at all when they didn't come with a sizable helping of satisfaction or power. Her tag-in came accompanied by an army-sized array of bewitching, mystical halberds that angrily flashed into existence. They filled the sky and instantly bore down on Artorian like a school of synchronized swimmers. The rain of easily a thousand Mana halberds blotted out the sun as they descended upon him like starving locusts on a singular sprig of wheat. "Halberd's Conquest!"

Artorian intercepted the national armory's worth of armaments, their Mana unraveled as he reached out, clenched his fists, and then snapped back into a horse stance. A bubble around him absorbed all their invested might, shoring his rank right back up to A-seven. The expenditures of expensive techniques were smoothly recouped thanks to his opponents not knowing about this peculiar defense of his, and giving him the bonus courtesy of blanketing him in so much of the light-blotting large scale attack that his effort was masked.

If Marie had spotted him taking her armament manifestation apart while it bore down on him, she didn't show any signs of it. Her attention instead focused on coalescing a frankly ridiculous amount of Mana before feeding it straight into her **Law**, and engaging a repeat of something he'd experienced already while the halo of overtures behind her trumpeted calls of victory.

"**Glory!**" Artorian knew what was coming from the feel of the Mana in the air alone, Marie's imperious, heralding voice confirming his expectations. "Imperia!"

Bombastic drums beat to life, a raging orchestra of trumpets hot on their heels. A recreation of the events in the Camel-lot quickly came to pass, more Phoenix Kingdom buildings pulling themselves from the ground as additional trumpets and drums deafened the zone with imperial marching music.

Each new building that rose fully formed added to the growing musical flair.

With the scene setting itself, Marie made sure her own sonic shell was fresh and active, then sent her illusions to attack Artorian without any warning. A whole city of mystical knights and bannermen descending down upon him as they burst from the buildings in droves, erupting in force from the doors and windows of every structure Marie willed into existence. A feat that happened considerably faster than when Artorian had been in their home zone.

"Straight to it then?" Artorian rolled his shoulders and asked in full deadpan, his fists extending out to either side as he got up from the horse stance, the last of her halberds used as a toothpick before he turned it into a cookie and had it as a snack. "No pleasant little chat?"

"Charge!" Marie dropped her hand as an order and boomed, commanding her illusionary troops that were certainly not harmless. Enough Mana was coursing through each and every single one to make even a solitary mystical knight a danger to a low B-ranker. "I will have victory!"

"I'm sorry, Marie." Artorian frowned, deeply apologetic. "You will find only…"

The old man opened his hands.

"**Sorrow**."

Artorian spoke with clarity and certainty, his hand closing around a hilt that manifested directly in grip-closing range. His entire being mottled down to a dull ashen hue, both his skin tone and bright clothing completely sapped of color, leaving only gradients of gray.

For just a moment, the old man was cold, calculating, and monstrous. The look in his eyes was utterly devoid of kindness as the dark katana remained silent.

A blue and white winter-themed lei hung around the blade's hilt. Fresh carnations had replaced the old, while the Wisp-patterned inscription engraved down the other side of the black blade looked complete. This engraving was but a single word, and Artorian the Ashen spoke it out loud. "Kaumaha."

Sorrow answered Artorian's call by collecting its due and flaring to life, allowing a huge torrent of bright pink flames to cascade out from the hilt, traverse down the blade, and flare out from the tip with enough might and pressure to triple the pitch black katana's effective range.

Artorian considered the trade satisfactory.

"**Compassion**." Within his other hand, a musical zither tuned itself as shapely, balanced mixtures of pink and teal flowed into existence. The Albion Principe joined him, directly to the hand. When gripped, the grayscale eating Artorian alive was rebuked, fought back by the effects of the second sword as colors swam over his being.

The first of the mystical knights reached striking range before the discord within Artorian settled. The first of those mystical knights also became the first to die when a musical staff of five fine lines, covered in teal musical notes that played as the sword swung, intersected their path and bisected Artorian's attackers.

Compassion was ecstatic to sing and dance, while the

pink flames from Sorrow lashed out all on their own, like hungry snakes leaping and snapping, consuming the mystic effigies as dozens of rosefire hydras coiled up from the black blade, leaving Artorian's previously undefended back very well protected.

Artorian flipped **Sorrow**, holding the katana in a reverse grip. The Albion Principe was raised in a more formal, common one-handed striking stance. As he moved, **Compassion** changed its color to a bright cyan, hexagonal mosaics of pink overlaying the entirety of the blade. The tip dropped, pointed at Marie in clear, direct challenge. With the swarm of violet illusionary forces rising up around him, he then held **Compassion** in front of his face while adopting an official 'greeting your superior' Phoenix Kingdom military stance, obscuring half of his vision to salute all his opponents, before dropping his blade back down towards them.

"Your swords didn't do much against Henry, Administrator." Marie spat in insult. Mocking in response to the mockery he'd made of the stance, not saving her commentary. "They will not help you now."

Artorian wasn't putting up with her attitude. "Only because you believe that I will be conservative, Marie. That the numbers of your army, and the tactics of a thousand cuts, will fell the great beast that has caused you grievance."

The Administrator had bad news for her, as he shifted from his own denial-based style to one that had been taught and beaten into him over many a desert scuffle.

"Pantheon Style." His Aura flared iridescent crimson, and then Artorian vanished in a flash, leaving behind only blurred afterimages of where his deadly strikes had passed.

When he reappeared on a rooftop, half of Marie's army became as impressive as sliced bread, removed on the spot as Artorian swung **Compassion** down, and declared himself as the decimated part of her arm exploded into particles of annoyed white phosphorus. "Endless Waltz."

He then lightly tinked the tip of **Compassion**'s blade

against the very real, solid stone crenellations with a metallic tap-tap-tap. This opened the floor to action as the army crumbled behind him, the phosphorus particles detonating as Artorian's Mana flavor du jour hit the drums after the opening riff. "Let's dance."

The sky exploded with new sound before Marie had a chance to push more power into her area of effect army empowerment effects. Her trumpets were pushed off key, and her war drums were muted as a wave of mental attacks slammed in from above.

When she snapped her vision up to pick out the culprit, Astrea stood front and center. Her face was one massive grin, her hands splayed out to play conductor. Surrounded by hundreds of geometric Gnomes in their octahedron shapes, each showing the face of one of the Bards that lived in the Odeum. These grins too, were proudly emblazoned on their die-sides. A joint effort had been prepared behind Artorian's back, great minds thinking alike. Astrea was here to both deliver and render aid, pleasantly surprised that Pa had set the stage for her.

Grandfather's introductory riff had been but an hors d'oeuvre.

With both her hands held high, she appeared to be ready for the big moment when the phosphorus detonated to start the show, then called out exactly what she was about as she copied Artorian's tapped tempo, and dropped one nightmare of a musical storm.

Her voice filled the sky, the beat hot on her heels. "Three, two, one, *drop!*"

The ground under Marie's feet betrayed her, bouncing her into the air before the mental effects laden in the music hit her like a blindly swung bag of bricks. She, like Henry, had incredibly poor defenses against this exact kind of attack. Astrea, having picked up on that nugget from watching her grandfather tussle with another Supervisor, had chosen to take this initiative to launch a surprise round.

With Grandfather having opened the floor by letting Blanket participate, the lead up had been too juicy not to act on.

Irene and Jiivra had initially been content to watch, unlike Ty who couldn't help from up here, and Blanket who had already leapt down and scared many others away from trying at the forces actually involved. Seeing anyone fight her grandpa was akin to a heavy-handed declaration of war as far as Astrea was concerned. Blanket had gotten first crack at the fight, but it had left her bristling to join, against Jiivra's attempts to calm her down until she too had changed her mind from watching the fight progress, and roping Irene into the effort to commence the Choir Formation. A bard and Gnome or two didn't go misplaced either.

They all loved their grandpa far too much to not try.

Much like Gomei, the skilled Moon Elf general, Marie had been taken aback at the effects of this attack. She too, suffered its headache-inducing consequences. Unlike Gomei, Marie did not share his ability and skill in Aura to not feel like she was a ball being shaken about in a large drum, as each time the thick, heavy beat slammed down like a sheet of water from above, she was slammed to the ground with it. Her physical might was the only thing letting her muddle through this unharmed, while she did all she could to get to her feet.

The dirty bass and heavy wub crashed into her troops at the same time. The damage dissolved most back to particles, and allowed Artorian ample time to close the distance to Marie. Slicing through her remaining army of troops in endless cuts of blurry, iridescent red, the old man got right up in her face. A waltzing dance of crimson slashes cut through Marie's protective shell, leaving a tapestry of lacerations in her armor while she herself remained unharmed.

The fight against Barry in Eternia had certainly taught him something about striking with speed and rhythm! Had Ammy seen this burning flurry of blows, Artorian believed she might even be proud, and give him the most minimal of passing marks. He could already hear her training resound in his head. Faster. Faster! Faster still!

The iridescent red flared in brightness, for he knew, without doubt, that Amaterasu was entirely correct. He could go much faster, and had too many flaws, but his style of fighting leaned to being endlessly adaptive. So adaptive he would be!

Marie was not given the courtesy of fighting with several of those precious advantages she'd become accustomed to. She made it to her feet while blocking with her arms, summoning and interposing her halberd between herself and a strike from the Albion Principe that traded speed for power. Sadly, the math was not in her favor when she braced. Brutally smashed away, she was sent crashing through an entire basilica, a full row of shops, and two vacant blacksmiths.

Coated in stone dust, Marie came to a crumpling, hard, painful, dead stop against an indestructible, immovable fruit cart innocuously standing in the middle of the street.

Unlike Marie's scuffed armor, there wasn't a dent on that cart.

Its squeaky wheels peeped as the cart, with incredible delay, seemed to notice it had been hit, coming to the realization that it was supposed to be moving a liiiittle late. Shamefully rolling itself out of the way like an unwelcome observer tip-toeing their way out of a place they should not be, to the sound of squeaky springs as the wheels turned, Marie could have sworn through the spinning swirls in her head that the cart mumbled: "Sorry, sorry."

Grandpa pretended not to notice the cart, bounced on his toes, and shot off to one of Astrea's well-timed beat drops. The iridescent red flared over his being once more, and combat was rekindled.

Artorian's natural *Oomph* of three-hundred and thirty *should* overcome Marie's empowered *Oomph* value of three hundred and eight. On Artorian's follow up strike, she was once more rebuked, pushed back, and sent crashing through numerous other buildings of her own making as physics decided that the lesser force was the one that would take flying lessons.

The environment was cut to assassin-approved thin ribbons as the old man continued the blade-chained-chase. What Artorian learned only now was that Marie's sonic shell must be giving herself some kind of lesser flat bonus to her defensive *Oomph*. Physics resolving the way it did told him he was on top, but reality was making a big X with its arms.

Was she changing the effects of her sonic shell?

Unlike Henry, who was getting Marie's full value on top of his, there was more at play. Aside from getting the physics treatment and kicking up a massive dust cloud as building after building crumbled or was sent to another zone, Marie herself remained entirely unharmed. That shell of hers rang out with a very telltale synthesized sound each time a **Compassion** sword strike knocked on the door. Artorian was certain he'd been cutting through it earlier.

He took a stab in the dark, and counted her sonic shell as an individual value of ninety-eight, on top of her prior number, bringing her *Oomph* up to a snug four hundred and five-ish. That meant it was time for testing! Or laughing, as Marie was comically flattened to the ground by another wave from Astrea's Choir Formation.

Marie was miffed, sick of getting to her feet from an effect that made her believe she'd properly been hit and thrown to the dirt. She was especially irked that the believing it portion made her own Mana throw her to said dirt.

Her world felt like it had been turned sideways, and had convinced gravity to do the same. The ground was constantly moving to her senses, even if she knew that she was standing otherwise perfectly still and on steady ground when her feet flattened against the cobblestone.

Centering herself was an effort lost to the booming thud and drop of more sound that rippled out of the Choir formation connecting the floating octahedrons, destroying her army just as easily as it unsettled her footing. Impressive, for a B-ranking formation to affect even an A-ranker! She would claim that knowledge as her own when this dispute was all—

Deng!

Artorian punted Marie away with all the grace of a sledge-hammer hitting a service bell, clear in the direction of the Aquarium. Marie, having seen that Henry was still very much out of the fight, and no happier for it, clenched her fist mid-spin and brought a Mana-copied version straight down on Astrea. The fist punching down from the sky silenced the entire affair as a rusty trumpet warbled at the very end of Astrea the Night-mare's cut-short performance, the Choir Formation shattering to pieces.

"Party's over!" Marie landed on her feet, in complete control of herself when once more without that terrible noise interfering with her skills. She was inches from the edge of the Aquarium, but she'd made the save, her feet having carved divots in the ground in order to stop. "No outside interference!"

Her demand was reasonable, but that didn't stop Artorian from being upset that Astrea had been gut punched. He'd felt one of those earlier, and unlike him, Astrea was likely out for the count. He looked, but the floating horde of Gnomes were all flashing white circles with red crosses in them. Medical atten-tion was already on the scene. She'd put on a good show! Gotten rid of those pesky mystical army effects to boot. Very helpful! He'd talk with her later. First, more Marie.

Marie, who now had steady footing, and was holding her halberd tight. Stepping in concert to the motions in the third movement of the Mauling Phoenix. One focused on advancing towards the enemy. "I will handle that upstart later. First is beating it into you that I am doing things my way, and you will abide! I refuse to keep playing second fiddle to a person who only reached his position through sheer luck. I am a monarch! You are a *brat*."

Intimately aware of the steps inherent in the third move-ment of the Mauling Phoenix, Artorian dodged, parried, and clashed his musical blade against Marie's halberd. **Sorrow** was keeping his back protected rather than joining the attacks, as pesky groups of mystical knights raged out of nearby buildings once more, ambushing him now that their reinforcements were not staunched. Their numbers rapidly replenished out of thin air as Marie's **Glory** Mana sunk into the zone and claimed it as her own.

Free troops were a powerful tool for a monarch.

Free, self-replenishing, infinite troops? That was an Empire-builder.

Especially when those troops were zealous, unrelenting, incapable of retreat or surrender, unaware of the concept of fear, and unquestionably loyal. Artorian knew that last part for sure, as he had just tried and failed to convert one with a Mana pull.

Glory was not having his pish.

Time for a new plan.

CHAPTER FORTY-TWO

"Mauling Phoenix!" Marie engaged her opponent without pause, breaking away from the edge of the zone to put serious distance between herself and that instant loss area. Her troops struck in concert as her mystic knights charged at Artorian from all directions. It was downright impressive how, once they made a formation, they kept it. "Second Movement!"

Artorian pulled his weapons close, then handed both off to arms made of Auric telekinesis. He was going to need more than two hands to face both the horde and their regent. So he did exactly that, flaring with power to exert his **Explosion** Mana. A glaive made of old memories shimmered to life between his hands, the comforting grip of an old friend met once more steadying his fingertips. The blade scintillated with explosive energy, arcing upwards to counter the second movement of the Mauling Phoenix set. Movement two was a full-blown downwards strike meant to cleave through a shield.

He shifted to movement four, Phoenix Feather's Deflection, the traditional defense against movement two. Planting his stance as his reaction kicked in, the movements followed like second nature.

Artorian instantly knew his weapon wasn't going to hold up when he saw the sonic warble around Marie's halberd intensify, and neither was the rest of him if caught in the axehead's path. The easy way out was to dodge! His stance, unfortunately, had been compromised to one meant for stability. Marie had pulled one over on him! This was his loss.

A flash of madness and inspiration struck him. No! All was not lost. He allowed the feeling to pass over his face, a wide-mouthed stare forming. "Cowabunga it is, then!"

Remembering to vector the angle of force this time, he tapped all his red Mana, slapping down a big card. Artorian hoped it wasn't going to make **Glory** spreadsheet-happy.

"**El Kabum**!" Pops, cracks, and flecks of phosphorus chipped from his hard light glaive, the entire blade popping with blips of luminance before violently exploding on impact. The sound-breaking, cloud-shattering, sky-immolating environmental catastrophe of explosive impact was visually identical to his prior use. The conical concussive thrust bought him his time as hints of a miniature sun going off brutishly separated Marie from him. The regent was sent clattering away, her armored form breaking through the troposphere and stratosphere in the same moment, Marie flung clear into the mesosphere.

His old friend dissolved back into particles as Artorian recovered first, his condition no rougher than he'd been before the blast. He took the moment to breathe, and recoup his senses, then Artorian stepped forwards to pursue Marie. He made it a single step before stumbling. The cost of keeping steady footing while playing such a big card, and not damaging the area behind or below him, while setting the invocation off in the first place, hit him all at once. A wave of exhaustion beat him over the head from the exertion, the old man dropping to a knee.

That the explosion also relieved several buildings from their rooted spot in the surroundings was happenstance, but you simply could not throw A-rank Mana and associated effects around without country-destroying levels of collateral damage.

A **Law** being used directly? Add some zeroes to that formula. A chunk of Caltopia would be gone if he hadn't vectored the damage upwards. During the first Odin fight, he'd had some leeway by being in the sky, but this time the effort had been truly draining.

A quick glance over the shoulder quickly made the cost worth it. Artorian had spared the Aquarium zone behind him from receiving so much as a bruise from **El Kabum**, but everything in front where he'd angled the force was now in an abysmal state of devastation. All of Marie's Imperia efforts were laid to waste, regardless of the regrowth kicking in right away as fresh structures once more began to pull themselves up from a foundation of blasted, molten rock.

From their spot up on the top of the Aquarium cube, onlookers threw up shields and defensive formations to protect themselves from the waves of heat and debris. Their shields cracking, denting, and eventually shattering. Entire buildings being flung as broken chunks to the next zone over, if not several zones over, would test even the mightiest wall.

The ringing in Tychus's ears made him to squint, groaning as he held the side of his face from how abysmally loud that boom had been. The spots in his vision from the sudden burst of brightness when weapons had clashed would fade, but that infernal ringing was sticking around even as he tried to heal the damage. In Grandpa's bout against Lady Loudmouth, and Lord Growlsalot, the collateral damage had been heavy, but at least it hadn't reached them with the intensity of the scene outside of the Aquarium.

Watching Grandpa go *beast mode* and cut the mountain range a few zones over down to size had been a sight to see, but the explosions that had pushed the beast forms apart, and damaged the plains zone, had been kept contained to that zone. Blanket becoming a grinding wheel had been spectacular, but aside from the sound having been intense, and the glider increasing in social respect and making that everyone's problem by demanding belly rubs, they hadn't been accosted all the way up on the Aquarium.

He'd been rubbing the fluffy tum-tum when the Abyss dropped by to leave them a tinnitus gift basket. Tychus had never experienced an explosion that big, his body still trembling through the aftershocks until Irene gripped him to help. Shock could get the best of anyone. Even the big brothers of the group.

They caught each other's eyes, Irene nodding as she checked him over. He read her lips more than heard her words. "You're alright, Ty. Get the others and retreat. This is going to get worse before it gets better, and we are in the way."

Ty rebuked nothing, moved to action. He sprinted up from his position to immediately throw people into his arms and over his shoulders. It was time to go! Jiivra was getting Astrea and Irene to safety, while Blanket took it upon himself to serve as mass transport, hugging the grand majority of the group and stealing them away to safety. The Glider did not need to be explained what the plan was, instinct doing plenty good of a job to equate 'big angry boom hot' to 'get the abyss out of here and be gone by yesterday.'

Artorian exhaled hard, the excess heat wafting from his being and unharmed Ao Dai like a mountain's worth of steam.

Seeing that he'd avoided hurting people was more valuable than doing more damage to Marie, and saving his own hide. He was down to A-rank two-ish? That hurt as an *Oomph*-calculation, and needing to stop the chase and put his hands on his hips was... well, that was an inevitability. He couldn't get through Marie's shell right now, much less the armor or the rest.

A Nixie tube popped to life above his head. Couldn't he, though?

He knew a thing or two about sound, and the thought of Megheara with her quick words popped into his head. A second Nixie tube brightly followed the first. Now he needed to employ the idea, and that was going to take some trickery.

Telekinetic arms still employed the services of the swords

that caused his colors and emotions to swirl, never having gotten the chance to stabilize that mess. He took that opportunity now, then placed his hand over his eyes since he was squinting into sunlight with the angle Marie had been yote. Not feeling the swirl was a boon, but not seeing Marie was a bane.

Buildings were still sprouting, so she was clearly still in the zone. Where, though? Mana signatures were impossible to pick out from the ambient surroundings with that blast wave mucking it all up. Nothing was stable, and he didn't want to start pulling in Mana in the event that Marie had a clear line of sight to him. Without the regents knowing the events of what happened to Odin, his Mana Loved feature needed to stay hidden in the pocket. He didn't even want to guess how **Glory** was going to measure a power like that on the spreadsheet.

A symphony of trumpets pulled his vision up high, looking straight up to see Marie descending at an annoyingly sedate, peaceful pace. Aw, Abyss, she'd taken note of his rank while it had changed, hadn't she? A-rank two was nothing, and Empowering it was not going to bring favor to the formula. It would net him... what? Three hundred and forty-five? Enough for Marie with her Empowerment up, but not enough to account for the bonus of both her armor and sonic shell. That shell would—

A third Nixie tube joined the first two, all three of them flashing like a slot machine ready for payout. "Hold the cracker. That might be just the ticket!"

Where were his concept weapons in the Tier list? **Compassion** at fourteen, and **Sorrow** at fifteen? Was that enough for his devious plan?

He was going to need to ham up the performance first. That part, he could do. Moving both his blades behind his back and keeping them in a hovering formation, he pressed his hands to his hips and cocked his head like a disappointed sports fan who had just seen his team make a set of incredibly dumb and avoidable mistakes, and he was taking that personally.

"There." He stood up and declared his irritation, loud

enough to be heard over the ringing that was still dying down. "Are you happy now?"

Releasing a pouty huff, he made sure to visually make his chest big and push all the air out for effect, his arms doing more speaking than his mouth as they waved about. "You win. You *moody* woman. I don't understand what you're mad about, and you, the only person who can tell me why, *refuses* to tell me properly. I thus refuse to feel responsible. I don't even know what's going on, and since I angled that blast wrong, I pushed you away from the we-can-talk zone and out into... wherever you went. Do you know how expensive that was to accomplish?!"

Marie landed in front of him, smug as could be as she removed her helmet. She looked no worse for wear save for golden lines that carved across her features. The damage of **El Kabum** was either non-distinct, simply not present, or Marie had defended against it somehow. "I knew it. I've become accustomed to seeing Mages bottom out their Mana, or get low enough to where they could not fight back. I will admit, Artorian, I would have relished in your defeat. I will, however, indulge a *surrender* just as well."

CHAPTER FORTY-THREE

Artorian wobbled left and right, hamming up his complaint as his insides churned. Marie should have been seriously injured. He grumbled more than spoke for a moment. "What, no **Glory** left to be angry at me for something I don't even know not doing? Yes, you insufferable regent, I'm close to being tapped. I hope you're satisfied. Now will you wipe that smug smile off your mug and tell me what I have been doing that's made you so mad? I really, *really* do not know."

Before Marie replied, Artorian took note that **Glory** felt... incredibly absent. That big blast of his, using **El Kabum** with Torgue laughing at him for it, should... certainly *should* have ticked a box? Was he way off on another survey? Cal was going to call *him* Ricky at this rate.

At least the dungeon was no longer pretending to be a fruit cart.

"I have won." Marie grasped empty air into a fist, her helmet kept under the arm as she planted her halberd. "That is the important first step, because I have been so angry for so long that working it out brought me a small modicum of relief."

Artorian moved his arms to drop them against his sides, as that was neither helpful, nor adding to any answers.

Then, Marie finally cracked.

"I see Henry is… chafed, but well." She nodded, appeased. "It's been several things. Several small things, that all compounded. In anger, I didn't care so much, but in reason, I'm aware that you cannot be everywhere at once. I accomplish the feat myself only rarely, though I do accomplish it."

Artorian crossed his arms, saying nothing as Marie got on her soapbox to begin a speech. "Where do I even start?"

"The beginning would be nice." Artorian rolled his wrist and grumbled.

"Before Cal." Marie pressed a hand to her sternum and segued without a hint of pause, like she had actually been ready and merely wanted the prompting. "Mountaindale. No, perhaps even before Mountaindale? I've gotten fuzzy on the details on anything in the pre-Cal days, but I'll paint you a nice picture of the parts I remember, that have my goat."

She waved with a hand, arcing a mocking rainbow motion. "Picture this. You're an important royal family member, and you're sent off to some nowhere land because your family is convinced it will keep you safe. Politically, you give many other reasons for why you go, to the point that I don't remember if I got to Dale's fancy hill before a war, during a war, or after a war. Especially not to some little corner of the world where one unknown Baron got lucky with a dungeon. That happens all the time. That the dungeon was… well, Cal, was not in the calculations. Not too long after, you are in no uncertain terms informed that you are now the last surviving member of that royal family. Let's plant a flag in that detail as an important one."

Artorian raised a brow, but did not interrupt.

Marie got going. "Then, in a sick turn of events, you have to flee into a place that by all reasonable accounts shouldn't exist. Where you find out that some nobody you chose to run the local academy is now being installed in a position higher than yours. Because, you know, to the abyss with a lifetime of border-line unbearable scheduling, study, and regent lessons. Right?"

Her grip on the halberd squeezed. "Shortly after, some concessions happen and you get a Supervisor position, and attain some say about the local goings on. Only to be relegated to a broken floating island where half of reality hasn't been implemented, and you have to contend for territory with a madwoman of a cook, who holds kudzu plants in higher regard than anything you stand for."

The halberd hummed with power, Marie leaking Mana as the anger was coming back. "Then you discover that the very person who slaughtered your family, your lover's family, and the families of just about every friend you have ever had is, in fact, *also* working with you under a new name, and is turning a new leaf. That this person, having done their best for the dungeon's survival in the face of yet another world-ending threat, and everyone who made it into the Soul Space, is lauded for these actions and thus exonerated of past crimes. Because S-rankers, right? Wonderful how that madwoman of a cook and The Master 'share history' to say it politely, and she's now untouchable."

She began to growl. "It only makes sense he would be above you in the hierarchy, right? That you are relegated to tasks you'd supposedly be good at, with everyone else in your position shoved into much the same, before being completely abandoned by both Cal, and the supposed Administrator left in charge? You checked up on us... what? Once? Twice? Then after Brianna, we're all just supposed to forgive you and move on? While we get thrown into other realms, with other rules, and other needs? Doing the same life over, and over, and over, until it grinds you down and burns you out. In places where each realm or iteration is no better than the last, but with different issues?"

She stabbed an accusing finger at him. "That little hodge-podge get together in the sun was the least of my complaints, but can I vent properly? No. Can I release my frustrations and full opinions? No. Because there are not one, but *two* S-rankers hanging from your shoulders, and that woman *Loves* you with a capital L. When Dawn, or Ammy, or whatever name she has now, says something is not happening, then it is *not* happening. So I had to let you *be*."

Her finger pushed deeper. "When you gave up the Administrator position at the end of my little rant in the sun, I was so relieved. Then imagine how bristling and angry it must make me, to discover that Cal said *no* when finally being back, and you were reinstated like you were never gone. When you clearly couldn't hack it."

Marie could not hold back her frustrations. "Even before you vanished into Eternia to play with Algorithms, I told you in no uncertain terms that: 'My enthusiasm is at rock bottom, and all the constant changes drive me up the wall.' I was done *back then*, and the situation did not get better. So I do my best to be cordial, my best to play friend, and my best to keep going. Because from day one it was clear that if we don't do what Cal wants, regardless of the amount of leeway he shows, and 'we should just let things run,' our *nicest* death is one of Mana deprivation."

Artorian paled a bit.

"I am furious, Artorian." Marie vented physical heat, completely upset. "I am livid at the very concept that you were the Administrator, and not Henry and I. That you have Cal's ear, and not Henry and I. That you get leeway to go where you want, when you need, with a brand new private airship. While we get put to sleep when Cal decides we're done with whatever we are doing, and wakes us back up when there's another game to try, or problem to test, or realm to build. Bannermen playing cards and cursing to burn me under their breath when I fetch you from a brig is the least of my problems."

Artorian's paleness increased.

She grit her teeth, stabbing the butt of her weapon into the ground so she could use both her hands. "I am sick and tired of being moderated and treated like a gilded pawn. Of having all the people aside from Henry that I cared about stuck in a wall, in pretty little gems, until someone else decided it was decanting time."

The ground cracked loud. "Henry has eyes only for me, and I love the boy for that, but my anger will not let me slow down to the speed that he abyss-well deserves from me. Because say I *do* slow down, what family can I give him? Did you not remember how stricken we all looked at the news that no new souls entering the Soul Space also meant no new children?"

The ground shattered outright, the halberd digging several fingers deep. "What kind of a family would I be having, exactly? Who would those souls belong to, when recycled? Could I ever look at my future son, my child, fully knowing that not only is he not my child, but some other B-ranker just waiting to reconnect to the tower and get the rest of their memories back?"

Marie leaned in further, visibly furious.

"*I can't.*" She hissed loud. Releasing the breath through gritted teeth, her eyes burning a hole into the old man's skull. As judgment, pain, and years of this knowledge digging a hole in her heart leaked through. "I just *can't.*"

CHAPTER FORTY-FOUR

Artorian knew the sky was listening, and he didn't miss the uncomfortable swallow. Marie was laying it out, and everyone keeping their ears open was far from steady on their feet.

Marie took several long moments to recompose herself. "**Glory** has everything it needs to step on you and turn you into a puddle of past-tense pastels, Administrator. I'm just not calling on it. Because I know that you always have something up your sleeve, and the entire method with how you've been fighting me has been so suspicious that I can see the wrinkles on Henry's face from here with how much *he too* is thinking about it."

She frowned deep. "*Explosions?* That's not you. Construct forms? Strange, but that theme fits. Physical combat instead of leaning into techniques like you love to do? Uncanny. Your density wreaking havoc with itself, your signature having a conniption fit, and the Tier of your strength constantly feeling like it's changing? Changing suspiciously to exactly the point where you're *right about* on par with us before the sensation cuts out? I felt you slipping when you copied Henry's empowerment all the way from the Camel zone, and then you immediately repressed it. Did you think I would miss you expending huge swaths of energy, only for it to suddenly recover every time Henry hit you with a particularly big technique?"

She stepped close enough for their noses to nearly touch. "Did you think I threw out a wasteful technique like Halberd's Conquest, and not pay attention to what was going on underneath? I know that my infinite source of Mana isn't normal, but whatever you are doing is of an entirely different level. You would, and should, and could have been able to win any of these bouts in seconds."

Her words dripped venom. "*Seconds*, Artorian, if you went back to the Tier that you belong to. **Glory** was kind enough to tell me that you weren't there, and there was a lot of activity in a place where there shouldn't have been. **Revelry** apparently was all excited about one of his compatriots on a lower level, **Celebration**, having a great time with you. **Revelry** having forgiven you for something that happened with its own Ascended, and wanting you to come up and join the party."

Her eyes narrowed. "Now *why* would a Tier seven-twenty **Love** Mage be toying around all the way down on the thirty-first Tier? *Hmm?* **Glory** and I are both incredibly curious."

Artorian tactically remained silent. He was uncertain how to resolve the matter going forwards. This issue had definitely progressed from a concern based on 'a problem to be solved' into 'a person to be helped.'

Marie's army was replenished and waiting, the zone already back to a full scale copy of a sprawling kingdom, and all the damage that had been present seemingly erased in favor of nicely detailed structures and roads. Not one piece of cobble had a scorch mark, and Marie's Aura was already blobbing out and establishing sovereign space.

Artorian took a step back to have more than a nose worth of space between them, and squeezed the bridge of his nose. "What do you want me to say, Marie?"

She held up a finger, pointing it to the roof of a nearby two story home. "First, I have claimed the space here. So I can see *you* just fine, Brianna."

"*Tsk.*" The Dark Elven lady in a lovely Ao Dai dress clicked her tongue. "I was just thinking about that exact concern. I suppose that now I know."

"Why are you here, Brianna?" Marie bristled and straightened her back with more venom in her tone, her army moving the pointy bits of their many weapons.

Brianna smiled broadly.

"This is about the part where I would have expected our dear Administrator to begin speaking of stabbings." She grinned back cheekily. "I wished to be ready this time. I do *so enjoy* the topic."

"That'll be alright, Brianna." Artorian's shoulders bobbed with a half chuckle, not wanting a worse incident. "I am suddenly no longer of the conviction, nor thought, that defeating Marie in combat would yield results that would be satisfactory to all parties. She has also deduced that I have been mucking around with my available platform of power."

He then turned back to the armored regent, and gave it to her straight. "I am the Administrator, Marie, whether you like it or not. I'm sorry life in Cal has neither been what you'd hoped, or what you wanted, and I deeply wish you would have come forwards with all these worries. I don't like standing on the authority provided by my assigned office, and I don't like finding out this way that the severity of what is eating away at you is... what it is. I'm honestly at a near loss for words with what you've just said. Because good Heavens, Marie, what the Abyss."

He shook his head, deeply conflicted. "That unfortunately doesn't change that, Cal being heavy on the leeway or not, the way you've gone about things this time around was unacceptable. So we're plenty clear, I don't want a ruler like you to have anything to do with the way my family is taking care of Avalon right now. You're so heavy-handed on the entire matter that I'm just not going to stand for you getting to plow your way through the fields. You won't rule the world, Marie. If that's even what you want."

Her scowl dug deep. "Tell **Glory** and I what we want to know. Maybe I'll be merciful."

"Fine." Artorian shoved his hands into his pockets and grumbled, in no small part annoyed at being kept out of the loop from issues this significant. "I had a theory."

Marie's scowl didn't change one iota, her arms crossing expectantly as Artorian explained. "My theory was that **Glory**, your **Law**, thrives and strengthens you based on your ability to lay low enemies, threats, and obstacles that you can derive stories from. Public opinion of positive rapport, and the like. The presence of strong, warm reception in the collective consciousness. **Glory** doesn't just want to be lauded? I am of the biased opinion that it wants to be **Loved**, regardless of the fact that accomplishments, good or ill, both count for your progression."

He waffled slightly. "I think Henry explained it best. Achievements. Renown. The voices of the masses, shouting, lauding her actions, proud whispers of her name ready on every set of lips."

Marie flicked her eyes to Henry for a moment, but said nothing.

"What you want is reflected in your illusions. People shouting for you in recognition. Wearing your colors and symbolism. Lauding your actions of great, positive renown, for having made their lives better. Thus becoming your banner-men, and your knights." He nodded lightly, grasping how such a concept could draw people to it. "The greater the posited threat, the greater the benefit you derive. Much like Henry, but on a more... Well. I see the army."

Artorian straightened his back, continuing. "A grander scale. I was also of the mind that, if I approached you with power that you could not defeat, rise above, or otherwise come to terms with, that you would simply never in a million years accept a defeat. You've already made clear that you will abide by the will of S-rankers, but that you certainly aren't happy about it. The grudge is obvious, as, given the opportunity of their current absence, you revolted. So, you would rise back up and come for me, or wait until I was out of the picture to strike at my interests. Because I had done more than merely defeat you, I had stepped on your pride, and your honor, and that was more damaging than any physical wound."

Marie nodded, as that was entirely correct. "So you theorized that fighting me with a type of power that was weaker than mine, thus not giving **Glory** ground to stand on, as my opponent would be lesser, and thus not qualify for a worthwhile achievement. That I would concede and accept a loss had you managed to inflict it, purely because my pride would not be hurt at being defeated by measures of skill and ability, rather than an overt application of raw power. Which you easily have at your disposal, and thus would have led to growth in my renown."

She cocked her head, still annoyed, but considering. "That only works if you incur the win, Administrator. A feat you did not manage. I admit, a clever measure to accomplish your goal, even if incredibly convoluted. Unfortunately, **Glory** and I already have plenty of dirt on you to go all out. What you have seen so far is nothing more than an application of all this Mana I have to work with. You're perhaps not out of tricks, but you're certainly out of luck."

Marie then grinned, assured of herself. "In no uncertain terms, if I feel you increasing in density then I am striking you down. So make it easy for both of us, surrender, and accept that regardless of what you want, or what your supposed position is, that this isn't going to go your way. Cal isn't coming to save you. Not that he can't, but that he won't. Letting the world run is something that has to happen, and unless an issue comes up that interferes with that very concept, he will stay behind his curtain. I'm also very aware that there's no Incarnates present. So *nobody* is coming to save you. After all these years in their shadow, I can, in fact, just *tell*."

She pulled her halberd free, giving it a twirl. "This iteration will be *my* iteration. Cal gets his world to run as it naturally would have run. That it happens to be with Henry and I in charge for a change, is simply a fate long overdue. The state of the world will remain that way until Cal can release people, and only then will we check on how people's behavior has been. If that day never comes, then that's just how your cookie crumbles. I don't believe any of the news about 'new bodies' and the like, beyond it being more than a cute trick to make me give up my power, and be forced to continue more of the cycle that I am already sick of."

The pike on her weapon stabbed into the ground. "Cal would have to successfully let people out before I even begin to consider that idea as a possible truth. I will not be dissuaded, so do not even try. I will only get angry again, and I already have plenty to be angry about."

Artorian looked down at his feet, his thoughts a churning mess. "Well, this is a pickle."

CHAPTER FORTY-FIVE

"That distinctly didn't sound like 'I surrender,' Artorian." Marie glared him down and quipped back, interested only in another checkbox being added to her victory march.

He was quiet for a moment, then inhaled. "So I am certain of your position. Do you consider me a friend, Marie? I know Henry does. Difficulties considered."

"I am very done with *wanting* to play pretend, old man." She threatened, the irritation creeping back at lightning speed. "You try having a bunch of S-rankers around dictating what you can and can't do with your life. See how well *your* friendship with them and the people under their wing goes."

The air went still.

Silence became the loudest sound.

Artorian felt cold.

So cold that his heart felt gripped by ice, his stomach turning further. When **Sorrow** hovered close to press against his shoulder, not a hint of gray was stolen away. **Sorrow**, rather than take, empathized with Artorian's current pit of feelings, being exactly the kind of concept to apply here. The demon of the blade was gone entirely, Urcan the Garuda had relinquished its nature, the mind fully stepping into the role of a conceptual exemplar. Now there was Kaumaha, a manifestation of **Sorrow**.

Artorian closed his eyes and tried not to be struck by flashes of memories, back during the gathering in the sun of them all having a good time together.

Artorian reached back, his hand overlapping not the hilt of the dark katana, but the guard. There was no demon left to hate. No soul to return to a prior state. The soul had healed all by itself, having found place and purpose. Feelings of denial raged, followed by anger, traded out to bargaining, and laid silent by depression. Accepting that not only was the Marie he knew gone, but that she may never have existed as he'd seen her. The mask of the hollow regent coming apart.

He hurt inside. Encountering a pain he didn't know what to do with, aside from feeling it, breathing deep, and pulling his face up like it weighed a sack of stone. So his eyes leveled with Marie's.

His voice trembled, emotions worn on the sleeve. "Brianna? Could you deliver a message to Richard? I will not be able to keep an appointment."

A quiet nod was enough. "He's likely right outside the Camel zone, which doesn't actually have any camels. Your spitting distance joke went over my head."

"Yes it does." Both Brianna and Marie corrected him in unison, though after an unpleasant look between the two, only Brianna continued. "They were there. They just have Camel-flage."

"Camel—" Artorian closed his eyes. "A pun. Of course."

Brianna grinned, then shoved her chin up at him for the message. Artorian got it over with. "The Church affiliates and company are waiting for a talk on... friendship. Please inform them that the secret is threefold: We have no problem finding friends when we are young because we go to the same place for a long time. Say, school, or a playground. The first key in making friends is to show up somewhere regularly so that people there could remember you."

He swallowed and kept going, mouth unnaturally dry. "What is important in a friendship is to share some kind of interest or viewpoint. Think of things you want to do or try, and go for it. If you are a familiar face in a place where people share your interests, you'll make friends. So become a fixture at these places."

He fiddled with his sleeves. "I estimate that it typically takes more than two-hundred hours, ideally over six weeks, for a stranger to grow into a close friend. The luckiest will find people who want the same things as them, at the same time as them. Shared experiences, shared difficulties, and shared proximity, all contribute. Some people you won't click with, but you'll never click with anyone if you don't put in the effort to try. In truth, the best friends evolve from the most unlikely of people."

Artorian laid a meaningful look on the Dark Elf.

Brianna smiled, and was gone in a shadowy blur.

The old man nodded in thanks even if the recipient had left, coming to several conclusions that this tale could reach. Many were bloody. Some led to victory. Only two could remotely be considered to include **Love**. That made the narrowed verdict clear. He had two acceptable outcomes, and only those two. "Then it seems our scuffle will continue a slight moment longer, Marie. Regardless of how it ends, you want your tale, your story, your victory, to be known to the world. Yes? To help you in claiming the rest of it?"

Marie thought that was strange.

He was giving her both a concession, and accepting she would win, but he refused to surrender and make it easy? A thought dawned, providing some understanding. "*Ah.* You want to go down fighting. I see. You want me to, in my grand tales that will be told in future histories, have your name come up as the last great obstacle that stood in my way. So that when people can come to whatever little office I shove you in after you are revived in a new body, you may recount the details of my **Glory**."

"Something like that." Artorian felt distraught mid-mumble. "Mostly I'm worried about the people I will be disappointing by being gone for a while. Many wish to spend time with their old man, and the blip between this body and the next... well. I already feel like I am missing out on so much. Airship or not, we do what we can with the time we have."

Marie chucked, her halberd pulled free and presented above her head, the weapon poised to strike. "I never understood you, Artorian. Though I will admit, I did love the flag. I'll make sure to keep it."

Artorian gripped **Sorrow** as the blade slipped him exotic eldritch knowledge, the elder sliding into a low striking position meant for an instant attack. One performed at the exact moment of the draw. An Iai. His form turned grayscale in an instant, feeding the pressurized pink flare that burgeoned back to life. "I will make it swift."

Marie called his bluff, her weapon trilling with sonic power as she cut down to end this particular thorn in her side, sound warbling as she moved to split her intended target. "Your tooth-picks have proven to do nothing."

"Megheara Style." Artorian was calm as water and cold as ice as he vanished in a blur from in front of Marie, appearing directly behind her as the Iai strike culminated, the katana having finished its striking arc as a visible layer of sonic frequency vibrated across its edge. The landscape behind Arto-rian detonated, his feet having fired Rail Palms. "Dark Resonance."

The resulting sharp ring overpowered all other sounds as the tone lived in both their ears. The world deafened as a split-ting line formed across Marie's battle tyrant armor, most powerful of its kind. Marie stumbled in her strike. Mana then wildly gushed out at high pressure from the sudden wound on her chest that her divided sonic shell did nothing to contain.

A value of four hundred and five-ish was big cheese. Though ninety-eight of it came from that sonic shell. A sound based effect that, with the correct vibration and frequency, might as well be empty air. The armor's protective value was unknown, but even in Eternia, **Sorrow** had never cared for concepts involving protection. That trait was not lost in translation, and the armor proved to be little more than paper against the black blade.

This left a base value of three-hundred and eight to deal with, plus whatever defensive gimmick she might have up her sleeve. What a shame it was, that even with only two ranks of Tier fifty five as a basis to work with, the resulting one-hundred and ten it provided, multiplied by pi, reached an easy three hundred and forty-five. Overcoming Marie's *Oomph* by a full thirty-seven points worth of pain. Plus **Sorrow**'s bonus of fifteen, which had been enough to also overcome any secret gimmicks.

Glory gasped at the sight, too slow to have been of any use.

Marie dropped her halberd mid-stumble, clutching at the Mana-bursting wound that refused to stifle, the cut tearing open wider and wider as an infinite supply of Mana came with an infinite amount of drawbacks when it had an exit point other than directed will.

Artorian then trembled as he released **Sorrow**, drawing in a massive breath as that strike had taken far more out of him than the physical effort required. The blade clattered to the ground, the gray of his skin going with it. He fell to his metal knees, then gasped as he heard rather than felt the stress fractures crack through his legs. Artorian had been forced to steal the rank invested in his body away in order to add it to his Aura, so he'd had enough *Oomph*. This had resulted in some of that damage Deverash had been so worried about.

Partially turning to look at the destruction he'd caused while weak of breath, he dismissed both swords so that they wouldn't be caught up in what was likely going to be Marie blowing up in a **Glory**-based encore of **El Kabum**.

What Marie actually did felt like it tore one of his hearts out. She stopped stumbling, then turned to his kneeled form with a smile, a word ready on her lips. *"Kintsugi."*

CHAPTER FORTY-SIX

Artorian whined, receiving a front row view of Marie's damage turning into golden lines on marble skin. The entire wound fully healed in seconds while he was still mending his own. "Well, that's not fair at all."

"Says the man who healed through all his problems in Eternia." Marie reached out a hand and chided, the halberd flying back to her grip with ease, as her own dramatic act concluded. "What was the line? Tasting one's own medicine?"

She had him by the collar a moment later, hurling him into the Aquarium. "You enjoy being stuck. See if that won't change your mind and opinion on surrender after I've—"

Artorian moved through the Aquarium not at all like either of the regents expected. Henry was still stuck in the same physical position he'd been in when passing the barrier, give or take a few smidges from the safety field scooting him. A few other stragglers inside were moving slowly, as if through dense pudding, but it was still clearly a struggle as they relied on the safeguard to get them out from a measure of their own hubris. Some of the displaced buildings from the zone next door had given them convenient new handholds, but the improvement was minor.

Rather than be affected by either of these effects, the Aquarium appeared to hug the old man as he moved with full three-dimensional freedom. Requiring neither Mana, nor effort, to move as if with the most perfectly controlled flight. Artorian twisted on his hip axis like resistance was a concept eagerly handing him a hall pass, a constant pink sheen coating his being like a crayon-smudged outline.

"Did I hear that intent correctly, just now?" He exhaled with a demure huff, his hands pushed into his pockets. "Change my mind and opinion on surrender after you've what, Marie? After you *what*? What actions and leverage were you about to go stick your nose into, in order to convince *me* to lay down arms?"

His feet slid onto the ground like a pod of dolphins carried him down, not a hint of difficulty present in his motions as he strolled right around Henry and doubled back.

"For that matter." He increased in volume, grumbled irritation taking over his cold demeanor as he also allowed anger to fill the void of hollow betrayal. "Where's all this dirt? You're still not using **Glory**. Instead of striking me properly and claiming your so-called win, you toss me like some dwarf awarded three hairs of the fairest head?" *Tsk tsk*.

Artorian looked up from his feet, the glare in his eyes cutting. "So is it a *won't*, or are you lying to me some more, and it's a *can't*? You're just dangling bait from the hook to make me use all that might, which you know I have, so you can actually do what you say you can do."

He paused right on the Aquarium's edge, watching her from the other side of the wall. "Or shall we delve into the topic on how a very expensive **Law**-invocation appeared to not scratch you, and Kintsugi doesn't do what I was told it does?"

He repeated Henry's words. "'The art of putting broken pottery pieces back together with gold—a metaphor for embracing your flaws and imperfections. Marie took it more literally.'"

Artorian then cocked his head. "Or is that you took it purely literally, as a measure of accepting scars and making them part of you? As a modicum of pride and accomplishment, rather than self-reflection and character growth?"

Marie scowled at him.

"Nail in the coffin, then?" Artorian scowled back, his thoughts flickering with images of Yuki smirking, **Kenopsia** leaning on her shoulders.

She spat her words at him. "**Laws** have more meanings than the ones you accept, Artorian. Opinion and perspective does not encompass all there is when it comes to concepts made manifest. Just because you are of the viewpoint that Kintsugi is meant to mend the cracks of character does not mean that is all it could do, or is the only interpretation of the idea. Not only is it the case that it does work that limited way, but the case that it *must* work in this broad way. Interpretations are limited, and our **Laws** can do a lot more than we think they can. We limit ourselves to the views we agree with when engaging with them, thus limiting what we can accomplish. But I suppose you've never gotten to have that talk with Dawn yet, have you?"

Artorian felt rage and anger course up the back of his neck. She'd said that to tick him off. Unfortunately, all it ticked was a checkbox that he was right about her **Glory** limitations. Regardless of her words, trying hard to make him believe the contrary, she still wasn't using the biggest stick in her arsenal.

Instead of replying to her, he turned his back to Marie and walked to Henry. With a motion of the hand, a bubble opened up around them, allowing Henry to collapse to the ground as normal gravity took hold, the effects of the Aquarium pressed away. "Henry, I know Marie and I are in a tiff right now, but are you alright?"

Henry got to his feet, then checked himself over with serious confusion. "Why…?"

"I need to prove a point, Henry, and I need you to help me prove it." Artorian paced.

Henry looked to Marie on the other side of the Aquarium

wall, then back at Artorian. "Why would I want to do that? I'm still on Marie's side… difficulties considered."

"Because it involves you hitting me, Henry. It involves you hitting me as hard as you can." Artorian looked at the regent fully deadpan. Being entirely honest.

"O…kay?" Henry blinked back, at a complete loss on where this was going. "Elaborate?"

Artorian shook his head. "No elaborations this time. I'm going to stand here. You're going to power up. Then you're going to throw your fist into my cheek as hard as you can. Straight power, nothing fancy. So long as you do that, I won't budge."

Artorian reached out to the bubble in the wine glass he'd created, and touched some **Love** Mana. The pink energy fueled into his Aura, his crayon-colored sheen burning bright neon. "There was a complaint about me not fighting to my utmost capacity, so I want to show you something. I won't be attacking you. There will be no retributive effect, and aside from me feeding some intent into my Aura, I will be operating at the *Oomph* of an A-rank two on tier fifty-five. So you'll floor me on impact."

Henry looked at Marie, completely lost.

"Hit the man, Henry." She crossed her arms, half requesting, half commanding.

Henry looked at Artorian, who gave him a nod.

"I… Okay!" Henry felt conflicted as he got started. "You asked for it."

A full Lion-formed coating of orange-violet energy surrounded Henry with a roar. He then took a stance, Empowered to the utmost, gathered the business portion into his fist, and exploded his armored knuckles into Artorian's cheek.

The hum was what caught everyone's ears first.

"Well, Henry?" Artorian leaned his cheek closer, the fist barely not reaching him. "Gonna hit me?""

Henry frowned, roared louder, and put more power into the strike as his fist felt like it was fighting itself. His empowered punch didn't manage to gain a single millimeter of distance closer to Artorian's neon sheen as his gauntlet fractured, the fist underneath cracking with atrocious damage to his Mana body. The power around his fist clearly showed volition for more velocity, like a thruster raring to go and being stopped by unseen forces.

Henry had to pull away from pain, gasping as he half stumbled to a knee and winced. Holding his own injured hand and forearm. "*Ow...* How? I'm going to sound like an owl here, but who the what now? What was that? I swung at you with *every- thing* except the sink. How was *I* the one hurt? Was I supposed to use an offensive technique?"

"What did you attack me with, Henry?" Artorian calmed, cool as a carp. "What were you feeling when you meant to crack my jaw?"

Henry was too busy wincing, shuddering, and groaning in pain. Gasping as the mere act of opening and closing his hand brought agony to his being and sent tears down his face. Artorian leaned down, touching the damage with a finger. This made the cracks in both his jaw and hand seal up as if they had never been there. This act was so much easier to do for Artorian than getting his legs fixed up, which were... functional, right now. "Better?"

"Yes." Henry felt baffled and confused. So far out of the loop of what was going on that he defaulted entirely to taking- orders mode, his other hand on his jaw. "What?"

"What were you feeling, or thinking of, when you swung?" Artorian adopted his prior stance.

"Marie, mostly." Henry got to his feet while completely fascinated by his flawlessly mended arm and hand.

"*Mm.*" Artorian nodded, thinking that might be the case. "I'll help. Your **Love** for Marie is an inherent, required, and requisite part of your actions. Particularly when you work for her interests. So when you do something for Marie, which seems to be most everything these days, you do so out of **Love.**"

Artorian then gave him a very apologetic, old grandfatherly

smile. "A strike born from **Love**, cannot hurt that which *is* **Love**, Henry. You weren't hitting me because you were fighting my defenses. You weren't hitting me because you were fighting yourself, and all the Mana you are made of, both new and old, will follow that ruling. You can't fight your own source of power, or it will betray you, and fight back."

He then turned to Marie. "Which is a topic that appears to be the lesson of the day."

Henry still stared at his own hand. "You didn't fight me at full power, because I wouldn't have even been able to lift my hand against you?"

Artorian patted his shoulder. "Think of how well it would go for you if you tried to use **Valor** while choosing to take the most cowardly actions at the same time."

Henry blinked. "That wouldn't work very well…"

"That it would not." Artorian nodded to confirm. "I didn't fight you at my Tier because I have a problem with you, or intend to look down on you, Henry. I didn't fight you at my proper level of power, because I wanted you to feel that what you were fighting for had the merit you believed it did. Why would I ever want to dissuade you from doing things out of **Love**?"

A flash of insight filled Henry's eyes. "You just… you just wanted to help. But how do you help the blind when it is their choice to refuse to see?"

Artorian's eyebrows shot up, surprised. "Well, look at you! Was that wisdom I just heard? Where did that come from?"

"I'm still just really confused, my friend." Henry winced and shrugged to apologize. "I'm sorry. I want to help Marie, but it's hard to stay blind to that with the way things have gone. It's all about to take some very unpleasant turns, isn't it?"

"Indeed. Some *very* unpleasant turns." Artorian closed his eyes, nodding deeper. "Henry, could I ask you for a kindness?"

"You can certainly ask?" Henry raised an upturned hand and questioned more than confirmed.

"Get out of the public eye for a bit." Artorian sharply

moved his nose towards the horizon in request. "Pause the tasks, the kingdom stuff, pause it all. Spend some time with Marie, when this culminates. I'm about to serve her some very *expensive* perspective soup."

Henry looked back and forth between Marie, still on the other side of the Aquarium, and Artorian, who... was once again acting strange. "I'm getting the distinct sense that you won't be killing Marie?"

"What would that accomplish?" Artorian raised a brow, now also confused. "No, my boy. You are still my friend. Marie... Marie appears to be a person I need to meet all over from scratch. To that end, we have a scuffle to settle, and I want you to stay out of it. Know I don't blame you, even if I should. Following orders really is no excuse for enacting heinous events. Perhaps one day, we can come to that reckoning. For now, I believe the road of your intentions took you down a path that you perhaps would not have wanted to walk, in hindsight. Yet you will find yourself at the end of that very road when you stop to check your surroundings. I want you to make the delib- eration yourself, rather than being told what to do. For that, I need you to reach the end of that cobble, and look."

Henry looked to his opposite, words hesitant. "And... Marie?"

"Marie, after spilling all the beans and the rest of the cooking pot about what the actual problem is, still needs to be held accountable." Artorian smiled. "I'm here to collect. What happens after... Just, keep an open mind. Alright, my boy? Look for the path that leads to prosperity and happiness. Not the path of blind loyalty."

The neon glow around Artorian faded, his back turned to Henry as he walked away, returning to the wall of the Aquar- ium. He did collapse the bubble, leaving Henry once more stuck to be gently dragged to the edge. An act of kindness, as far as Henry was currently concerned.

Artorian's 'request' was one of those politically laden state- ments that was more of an 'if you choose to act out here, I will take you apart like a children's toy, and we will be having this conversation again with much more words, many of them heavily emphasized so you get the point.' Henry knew that he would like none of them.

He was sitting this one out.

Artorian stopped, only the Aquarium barrier now between himself and Marie. "Alright, Marie. We have some disagreements to work out. I'm going to stand on this A-rank two power platform, of which I will use *one*. Then I'm going to ask our Tower friends to pull me up to exactly Tier ninety-seven. One below yours."

He frowned at her hard, his eyes ablaze with power as they surged to include green Ulam Spirals that flared to life while he stepped through the wall. Already there.

"Riddle me *why*."

CHAPTER FORTY-SEVEN

Marie fumed, stepping away. "I'll riddle you with nothing except holes."

She reached back with her halberd, handing the weapon off to her mystical knights. She then held a gauntlet up to stop her army, and dropped both her Empowerment and her sonic shell, which had already proven to be circumventable. The irritation that she was just shy of no longer being too strong, chafed. A little more, and she would have been at par.

Glory remained unpleasantly quiet to her ears. The power was present, but awaiting those Abyss-cracked conditions. Hungry for her to do more than flood its most basic of functions with overabundant energy. Substantial proof was required, as circumstantial proof was considered insufficient.

An *Oomph* of ninety-eight faced an *Oomph* of ninety-seven.

Artorian then punched air, as if warming up for a fist fight before he adopted a butterfly-hopping stance and directly challenged her by brushing his thumb across his nose, a **vhump-vhump** of air being displaced by his shadow jabs.

Marie forced him to enter a protected stance instead as she sent a straight jab for his face on her immediate approach. Her lunge didn't break cobble, as the entire road appeared to clench and squeeze together to increase the stability of her foothold, pinning Artorian between the zone that he was clearly not going to use as a crutch, and thus making it a wall he was trapped against. A series of rapid jabs were blocked, dodged, or sidestepped as Artorian tried to duck out from under Marie's ham-fisted barrage. She was clearly not geared for this style of fighting, but had just as clearly accepted the challenge.

Anything that could serve as a stepping stone in order to get the **Glory** engine going was a piece of staircase that she would chance, no matter how rickety or unstable. She had not expected that this barrage gave Artorian the opportunity to then execute devastating offensive maneuvers in turn, an opening in her many jabs turned into a full reversal.

Artorian countered with one of his favorite measures as he flashed red.

Speed. "Pantheon Style. Gatling."

Marie instinctively flared her sonic shell to life without thought, but a resonating vibration hummed to life across Artorian's knuckles at the same time. His single punch struck battle tyrant armor dead on target. Then a second, third, and fourth strike landed before he'd visually pulled his fist back as a growing number of impacts developed, raining hundreds of pounding impacts into her metal shell. The sonic shell protections were turned moot as he sped up considerably, and threw a thousand punches as one. Hammering directly into her armor that rang like an accosted bell that sang the tongue-trilling song of *B-R-R-R-R-R-R*.

The final punch from his glowing, red hot fists sizzled with a teapot's whine. The air against Artorian's knuckles resonated with green-red plasma when Marie was finally knocked out of her footing and was bowled down her own main street like a cannonball. Physics was very unhappy about that much energy moving that quickly, the static crackling and oppressive heat dissipating in a hurry as Artorian rubbed his thumb across his nose again. "Marie, if you knew who I hung around, that sonic shell is not the surprise tool I'd be relying on to help me later."

Grunting as her feet carved divots into her own street before it repaired, Marie growled while getting back into stance. Her ribs ached. The impacts had still carried through even if the armor had eaten the brunt of the damage, the tyrant plate now a tapestry of fist marks. Marie hopped away with her arms up, the sonic shell dropped since it was balancing the math further out of her favor, and she was dependent on that scale to win. That Artorian had a method to ignore that defense outright bit into her pride. She would find this 'Megheara' when this was all over and 'gently ask' about this vibration and resonant frequencies business.

Marie needed Artorian to one-up her so she could respond in kind. That she might have to make the first move appeared to become more of a requirement. The annoying old man had sussed out too many of her checkboxes and conditions, and was being incredibly cautious about checking them off. Merely knowing what he could do was insufficient for **Glory**. Her opponent had to actually be doing those things, or it didn't count. Stoking the fire under his butt to make him think that her knowing equated to him already having ticked the box had borne no fruit. She had failed to make him rush to that expected level of power, stealing from her an easy power creep victory.

Glory could provide far more than mere additive bonuses, but the multiplicative ones required those abyss-blasted checkmarks!

"Dream Weaver's Delirium." Artorian took the initiative when Marie faltered, too focused on the conditions to scale her power up that she hadn't paid attention to a scheming old man being left to his private, intricate devices. Devising devious and dubious attacks that would indubitably lead to her downfall. "Daymare."

She took a clean hit to the jaw, sent tumbling to the ground as flecks of marble crackled off from her statuesque face. Little smears of gold dribbled from the wound before the sticky material sealed her injury. When she got up, she instantly collapsed again as her vision swam, gravity once more feeling like it turned sideways at a whim. Marie groaned, but could tell that Artorian was using more of those sly mental-effects since she didn't have an Aura worth any salt, and thus couldn't protect herself from the mental pushes.

She got her hands back up, then saw visions of terrible things.

There was a fire in a library. The words 'it's not the suppression squad that will kill you, it's the librarians,' swam through her head like a smoky paste. Followed by splotchy flashes. Librarians melting out from full shelves and dark alcoves, personally appearing to murder her for starting a fire.

"I didn't start the fire!" Marie yelled at her swimming vision, rather than reality.

'No matter. You are collateral damage.' She heard the snide words in her head. The librarians hissed through hate stained lips. 'Everyone dies, to show all arsonists that there is no escape from justice.'

Then her vision twisted, a gorilla erupting from the aether and traveling at non-Euclidean speeds to clothesline her into another dimension.

Her eyes shot wide, hands pressing to her knees as Marie suddenly suffered cold sweats and heaving breaths, the visions fading as she squeezed her eyes shut and shook herself. She wiped her mouth of spittle, then glared daggers at Artorian. "You are cruel."

"Am I?" Artorian scratched his head and questioned, the bouncy butterfly stance readopted. "I have no idea what you saw. I just induce the condition. What you see is whatever your mind needs to process. Like a bad dream during sleep. Except while you're awake! So, Daymare! Since you punched out my favorite Nightmare. Or did you think I wasn't going to get you back for that?"

Marie lunged and flung herself forward several city blocks

as mystic warbling surrounded her fist. A group of French horns accompanied the power surge, as the gallop of cavalry traversed her wake. Artorian countered, having baited the wild swing. Marie's fist passed by Artorian's ear, the clashing sound of swords and war tearing down a few buildings behind him. A swing and a miss, as the old man got an uppercut right into her center mass. The impact, Marie expected, was going to be minor. So she could twist on her foot and bring her elbow d—

Zwiiiiiiii!

"*Ooph!*" Marie's perspective spun in a twisting circle as she took off into the sky. A glowing green drill had formed around Artorian's fist as chunks of her armor rained back down to the ground. The uppercut had done nothing to her Mana form, but her armor now had a gaping hole in the center, and her chest definitely ached as residual damage drilled through.

She landed on her feet, watching Artorian manifest a pillow from seemingly nowhere as the spiral themes in his Aura, currently coating his whole body, simmered back down. He flurried and struck it about like some kind of poofy nunchuck, then shook his head like some idea he had wasn't going to work. "No, I tried this. Pillows and drills do not grok."

"What was that supposed to be?" Marie coughed and chided, trying to rile him up to use more power. "Your latest flavor of toy? Casting away an attack before you even try isn't going to get you the win."

The old man put the pillow back, had an epiphany from her question, looked at his fist, then at Marie, then back at his fist. Culminating in a giant smile. He slid into a striking stance, the fist kept behind his side as a swirl of green spun up with a whine. Those grand spirals put pressure on the landscape behind him like a sideways hurricane passed through, her troops fleeing and attempting to dodge before being swallowed up along with whole buildings. The entire lot flung into the distance to sprinkle more zones with falling ruins.

"I cast Fist!" Artorian punched and howled back, suddenly in her face as the ground behind him detonated. His knuckles crashed into her chin, mouth, and nose as the green glow coating his hand unraveled and drilled through, once again sending her spiraling off into the distance as mere flecks of marble were ground from her face. Her human skin tone bled away as more and more of the alabaster look filled Marie's features, revealing just how many of those golden Kintsugi cracks she already had.

A sizable amount from the look of it, accounting for a life-time of scars. Her trumpets turned to drums, Marie upping the ante as this couldn't keep going the way it was when she twisted and landed flat on her feet. Artorian paused his own charge, his own feet skidding to a halt as the vibe in the air changed, and it was impossible not to notice.

"Warlord's Call, Hel-taker!" She snapped into a straight position, her stance wide and stable as she reached out and formulated her own soul item. She fractured her own armor and burst free from within, a very different set summoned and equipped from her own storage ring.

In her extended hand, to the sound of war drums joined by a thousand tribes, and backed up by imperial trumpets, a battle standard doubling as a spear formed in her grip. The weapon was gargantuan in comparison to her own form, as a luminous flag of pure light unfurled from the top, the war banner showing an image of a Lionix. The head of a Lion surrounded by Phoenix wings. The images integrated to form a single, cohesive whole.

"I *will* have my nation, Artorian! No matter the price. If I have to do that from nothing but ashes, then I will give you a front row seat to how a Phoenix claims its prize. My *Ardania* shall rise!" Three stanzas of text then burned into the flag, each searing into being below the other as Marie called the words into being. "Battle Tyrant's Flag! Pride of the Nation! Heart of Conquest!"

Power tormented the sky around Marie, mystical light and fog filling her surroundings until a rage-fueled godray descended upon her, allotting her the sole position of illumination in the darkened zone as rain began to pour down as if grumbly clouds had been gathering for months on end. Her new armor set was clearly of Eternia make, but the design—unlike Cal's seamless smoothness with the battle tyrant set—was all horns, spikes, and dark metal. A central core fueled and streaked her completed set in bright, oppressive lines, like magma boiled beneath the plates as a flaming set of Phoenix wings unfurled from her back.

"Oh. We gettin' serious?" Artorian measured his opponent, determining Marie's godray to be an envious step up from the one he'd caused with help. She was definitely upping the ante, not going to stand being the lesser story. A cautious backwards step was proactively taken as all the troops in the vicinity flared with deep violet blacklight. Their armor turned new colors as their mystical flair dipped into the darker spectrum to follow suit with their regent. "*Oooooh*, showing off some of **Glory's** dark side, are we? The bits of scraping an empire together that you don't want people to see?"

He nodded, rolling his shoulders as they crackled with green spiral energy as Marie pulled together her preparations. Rather than interfering, he chalked this up as a necessary step to the ending he wanted to accomplish. Artorian mentally checked in on his current **Law**. <Gurren, any requests?>

The coat-wearing **Law** on the ninety-seventh floor that he was currently using as a platform smiled wide, leaning forwards while pushing sharp sunglasses back into place. The **Law** then swirled its finger in a circle, grinning. <*Samba*. And call me Ulam. Gurren is for strangers.>

Artorian did as requested, slid two fingers to his mouth, and whistled loud. Mentally, he felt Brasilia and Bellini saunter onto the ninety-seventh floor with their hands already up, pumping for more while they swaggered in with a serious bounce to their hips. He then felt a tremble, as **Revelry** poked his head in from above with a serious frown, a wounded expression on his face. Like a ceiling cat that could not contain its curiosity. <Ulam! Right beneath my feet, and *no* invitation? You wouldn't.>

The smirking **Law** of spirals and lover of prime numbers looked over his sunglasses at his math-abundant friend. Artorian had been putting serious effort into accounting, and Ulam very much liked that. The silent question made Artorian smile both on the battlefield, and in the mental space that was getting very crowded. <You know what I'm about, Ulam. Is my answer not self-evident?>

Ulam chuckled, then moved his hand up to grip **Revelry's** begging, wild grabby hands. The **Law** acted like a whiny child that did not want to be left out when it came to a good party. A pink spark flickered from Artorian's Aura, as both **Arbor** and **Explosion** popped into being on dance-floor ninety-seven, where **Celebration** and his friend had set up some kind of spinning-disc station, strange muffling contraptions covering their ears.

Sakura and Torgue both looked about, not too sure why they were here, until Artorian's unseen pink hands nudged them together. Like the sole occupants on a ship. Ulam cheered, **Revelry** hollered for them to kiss, and Torgue just about swung on an axle to sock the other **Law** one before Sakura caught that turn and swirled Torgue into a deft spin, catching her lips right on target where they needed to be as she held the Dwarf like a bent ballerina.

The Tier exploded in cheers, cries of disbelief, and utter outrageous yelling. **Celebration** got a massive power boost and **Revelry** threw out flower blossoms like that smooch had been seven whole universes in the making, and it was about time!

Artorian shrieked with laughter. Unfortunately, he was doing that both in mental time and real time, and in real time, a very real Marie was taking that reaction very poorly.

Her response was to create a tiny paper dragon, and attach it to the top of her standard, making Artorian snap out of his pleasant moment and devolve into a deep groan. His hand moved up to point at the paper addition palm up. "Really?!"

CHAPTER FORTY-EIGHT

Dark clouds rumbled above. Rain fell in unforgiving torrents. The architecture illuminated only when lightning broke through and lit part of the scene. A dark day in the Phoenix Kingdom was on direct display as Artorian felt the mood sink in, understanding what the reflection of the scene meant to Marie. An empty kingdom, of vacant buildings, with only ghosts and illusions to accompany the memory of what was left.

The party that had been building in the shared mental space lost its footing, breaking to pieces as the good times stopped before they began. All the **Laws** were rubber-banded back to their respective floors when Artorian couldn't keep the conditions in place for the festivities to continue. Leaving floor ninety-seven rather quiet and hollow once more.

<That displeased me.> Ulam was scowling in Artorian's head, the **Law**'s tone equally dark. <Are you sure you want to apply that plan of yours, **Love's** Ascendant? It is *very* costly.>

<I'm sure, Ulam. Cost will have to come second, because I want a very specific outcome to make as many people win as possible. I am on the path of **Love**, after all. Marie made some unpleasant choices. Like with any child that has thrown a

tantrum, Grandpa's job is to clean up.> Artorian mentally bumped fists with the **Law**, a thin shield of Aura keeping the rain from directly touching him and ruining the Ao Dai clothing.

<I'm not any happier about the sudden hole in the heart, Ulam. Or seeing this part of… Empire building. I spoke to a friend of my discomfort about this exact subject, and seeing it on display does nothing to dissuade how much I dislike the requirement of 'displacing' the existing, to 'emplace' one's desires. It would kill me to paint on such a canvas.> Artorian felt a pull, his attention shifting.

"Zone attack: Diffusion." Marie cut his line of thought and pulled all his attention back to the forefront. Diffusion attacks were big cheese, with frighteningly complex effects, his ears tuning out the rain and focusing on Marie's voice. Artorian silenced himself, his eyes flicking around to try to find what it might be, as he wasn't seeing a lot of her empire or troops through all this abyssal rain.

"City of Tears." Marie raised her battle standard and declared her attack, her form vanishing as wisps of steamy fog rolled between the waves of falling water. A torrent that became so loud that Artorian could not hear his copper coin drop against the cobblestone ground.

A melody by a famous Phoenix Kingdom artist, Marissa the Songstress, chimed between the impacts of droplets. She was its foremost prodigy, before the fall, gathering crowds that flooded in to fill even the widest hall. She sang like people cried, the pull of her words moving the heart, and wrenching it all night.

She sang for those crowds, until she sang alone.

When all that was left was Marissa, and the rain coating an empty throne.

Unlike Marie's, Artorian's Aura was a fortress. So when the normal rain turned into something vastly more dangerous than mere wetness coming down in heavy sheets, Artorian was not caught flat-footed. He felt the attack try to creep through the cracks incurred during the Liger fight, but rather than let the song stab cold through the fragile heart, he gripped the hands of the singer, and became the dancer.

Compassion flicked into existence, but the blade twisted and reshaped, forming a shield the size of a pendant that pressed to Artorian's sternum and hung from a self-forming chain. He gripped gaps in the rain that formed hands, and danced with the phantom in the water that rebuked the falling night. Marissa's tears found no handhold of a heart to squeeze and pour her sadness into, but they did find the warmth of the stage that greeted her as an old compatriot. Her own **Love** of the craft mirrored back at her, as from the perspective of the hollow in the rain, Marissa was holding hands with a warm, nondescript pink cloud of energy.

This cloud did not judge. This cloud did not take. This cloud had not one, but two hearts to hold her pain. Yet the cloud, instead of holding her pain, held her sorrow like it was used to balancing out that opposite.

Tugging her through the water as music began to bustle and flow from the cloud as a section of viola, Marissa danced. The cloud led with growing fervor; the viola grew louder, louder, and louder still until they drowned out the pitter patter of heavy rain entirely. Until Marissa stood upon a bright stage, surrounded by a brand new crowd sitting on the edges of their Tiered floors. Organized in some tall Tower, where the grand majority of guests clapped in standing applause when her song reached its inevitable end.

Roses rained down on her stage. Applause filled her antechamber. Marissa reached out, and found a whole host of hands willing to receive her memory. The Tower was powerfully fond of artists, in all their shapes and colors.

Marie reappeared in the central square of her **Glory**-bound Phoenix Kingdom recreation. She gripped at her armored chest, gasping incredulously as a key component of her own attack had been ripped away. Except that the component had left willingly, and her diffusion attack crumbled to pieces as result as all the rain returned to being little more than water. Her own effort at a mental attack proved far less viable than those used by her opposite.

Her opposite stood in the square with her, gently taking a pendant off as it flashed with pinks and blues, reforming into a steady Albion Principe. His colors swirled with extra bright variants until he released the blade, and it vanished out of being, the colors of emotional discord vanishing with it.

"I'd say it's about time, Marie." Artorian wistfully moved his hands against his lumbar, unbothered by the rain.

"Time for you to fall!" She advanced spear-first until Artorian appeared in front of her with a hand already pressed to her dark, magma-red pulsing chestplate. Her sweeping strike with the battle standard was now in the wrong range, and very ineffective.

"Bass Cannon." Artorian's eyes were soft. He calmly unleashed the attack, as a booming *wub* moved both Marie and miles of rain sideways in a single, concussive blast. Marie tumbled through space, but got a hold of herself quickly enough as a host of troops caught and redirected her like a giant bungee cord, bringing her face to face with an already-advancing Artorian who had a follow up in the works. His palm in her face. "Kaleidoscope."

Marie dodged to the left, veering past him with incredible momentum and thinking she'd dodged the next attack. Until a five by five width beam of solid light bounced away right outside of her peripheral vision before slamming into her from above, and letting her keep a suddenly scheduled close appointment with the ground. Or the new well she had dug from being slammed through the ground, and going straight for long enough to hit a cavern filled with accumulated water.

Water that she stood on to catch her footing, the beam of light slapped away with her standard, shattering the effect to her satisfaction. Marie then exploded out of the well and reappeared back in the sky over the zone's kingdom recreation.

Artorian was waiting for her up there, solid light weapons

coated in Megheara's Dark Resonance effect already in hand. "Welcome back! Back to it, then?"

"How are you faster than me?" Marie pointed in accusation. She angrily snapped in complaint, the flag on her standard shining with a thick blacklight that filtered through the rain. "We should be going the same speed!"

"I know a thing or two about **Acceleration**, one could say." The old man grinned back with an apologetic shrug of the shoulders. He then looked up, and snapped his fingers. Exploding a big hole through the cloudscape above, and making a massive clearing of bright, fresh light that tore away the dreary setting Marie was keeping them trapped in.

"Cal?" Artorian addressed the clear sky. "Could you make sure to tell everyone about Marie's big victory? I do mean *everyone.*"

The sky looked to ask him what he was on about, when Marie's spear-tipped battle standard pierced Artorian's back, erupting through the chest. Flickering sparks of blacklight tore through to the other side as the weapon dug deep. The sharp pointy bit stabbed true as Marie capitalized on even the slightest distraction, not wanting to be one-upped again in another contest of speed. At first, elation broke over her features. Then concern, as Artorian's words registered, the Mana cracks breaking open and tearing through his body.

Then she saw the smiling, apologetic expression on his face.

"What did you do?" She shuddered in sudden fear. Marie instantly released her standard and backed away a dozen paces.

Artorian moved his weapons out to either side, then let them vanish into thin air. "Nothing much. Fulfilled the conditions I was seeking, and you played your part so terribly well. Congratulations, Marie! You win. This body of mine is dying. I won't be around for a while."

"What? No!" Marie panicked. "Fix it! I know you can fix it! This is not how I need to win!"

"No." Artorian sagely bobbed his head, pulling her standard

free with a little grunt. His body descended as his ability to fly was compromised to the point of his legs pulsing to life. The thrusters picked up the slack when the Mana circuit Artorian had been using to fly failed. The internal pattern was now incomplete. "We have, however, gotten you the win that fits my criteria. No **Glory**! In fact, I planned around your plans. So thanks for planning so many. It was a good time, I'll admit. I had micro-suns in my back pocket, but once I realized what it was that would actually help you, so that when we meet again in the future I can see about making a new friend... well. You'll find out shortly."

Marie howled, her fists balled up. "Why would you *do* this?"

Artorian, voice cracking, slid into a parable. "The novice says to the master, 'What does one do before enlightenment?' 'Chop wood. Carry water,' replies the master. The novice asks, 'What, then, does one do after enlightenment?'"

The tired grandfather smiled. "'Chop wood. Carry water.'"

Marie flailed incomprehensibly.

Artorian then slid off his spatial bracelet, tapped it against both his legs to store the Strikers, and commenced a freefall. He spent a significant portion of Mana to teleport Ammy's object to safety on his way down. It wasn't like he needed to be conservative at this point, his body already breaking apart into particles as he gave Marie a final send off. "Toodeloo!"

Scholar D. Kota appeared on the scene to grab the last vestiges of Artorian's breaking Mana, the glittery pieces dissolving in his open hand when he looked as he double, then triple, and quadruple checked that Artorian was properly saved and stored in his Silverwood Seed Core. That Silverwood spatial bracelet of his laid on the sphere like a fashion-statement circlet.

Marie suddenly didn't feel so good. She had, in fact, riddled Artorian with holes. One big one to be specific. From a strike that had slid in like a knife through butter, as Artorian had definitely not been standing on tier ninety-seven when she'd stabbed him.

"I... I can explain." Marie defensively put her hands up.

She stammered loud, her army, soul item, and armor all vanishing so it was just her in normal clothes. Nice, royal clothes, but normal ones. Cal showing up had not been an expected play of the cards. He was supposed to be neutral and stay out of it all! The environmental effects faded to obscurity, and her attempts to call on **Glory** were coming up so empty that she wondered if the **Law** had abandoned her.

"I don't need you to explain, Supervisor." Cal's words were cold and heartless. Like a dungeon should be to its occupants. "I was watching. I likely shouldn't have, but I couldn't help it."

Marie's stomach turned, her words dying in her mouth.

This was not supposed to happen.

"Tell *everyone*, he said?" Cal frowned and looked at the Silverwood. He requested confirmation from the air around them, confirming the statement to nobody but himself. "Yes. Very well."

Marie moved backwards, then forwards with an outstretched hand, then backwards again as she pulled away.

"Good morning, my neighbors!" Cal shoved his arms to the sky, shouting with a clear voice through the entire Soul Space. Like a prince from a foreign, yet-to-exist land with some adorable little name like Nigeria. Not a single occupant would be able to miss this.

"Hey, Abyss you!" An upset Mage who had just woken up from a dead sleep yelled back.

"Yes!" Cal shook his arms with mirth. He happily mewled back, his accent pure chipperness. "Abyss you too!"

Some sonic feedback caused an unpleasant sound to shudder through the Soul Space like feedback, Cal continuing. "Grand news! My Administrator, Artorian, has been slain! Killed on the spot! Sent all the way back to his Seed Core. A place I needed him very badly not to be, as Tim and I don't have a new body ready for him, due to the peculiar nature of his soul imprint being a wee bit different from the normal. Two hearts and all. Y'know?"

Cal then clapped his hands together, smiling for the

message, but turning in the sky and making it plenty clear for Marie that this smile on his face was anything but kind, happy, or pleasant. The kind of villainous expression reserved only for people that were caught in the web, and didn't yet know how bad of a fate they were in for. "I can already feel a lot of you becoming rather upset at this news. So worry not! I know who did it."

Cal let the sentence hang, and Marie could feel something... unpleasant, happening to her **Law**. Like she was rapidly gaining power. But... not the right *kind* of power.

"Queen Marie!" Cal clapped hands together during his explanation as images of Marie fighting Artorian appeared all through the Soul Space, showcasing the good snippets of their bout, and ending with her spear through the Administrator's chest.

Cal then cut the feed, and his Soul-Space-wide voice, now speaking only to the Supervisor. "Oh, wow, look at all that power from renown flooding in. Not bad, not bad at all. Big achievement, huh? I tell ya, Marie, I had this option pinned to the board, but I was really wishing, hoping, that this was not the card Artorian would play."

His hands rubbed together. "Imagine my intense surprise and displeasure when it became ever more evident that he was either going to play that one, or another card that was even worse! For him, I mean. Worse for him. Card three was unplayable because he already made a Mana-oath with Ammy that he wouldn't blow himself up. To his credit, he did not. You, my dear Supervisor, who is very correct that I want to keep my nose out of the way my world runs, have entirely new problems!"

Cal smirked. "I think you can already tell."

Marie looked horrified, her hands clutching her own chest as her face paled, eyes wandering down to Caltopia below. "Ab... Abyss. The... The—"

"Infamy." Cal helpfully informed her with a little bounce. "That's called infamy. Sprinkled with notoriety, a bit of turpitude, and a lot—*a lot*—of contempt. Congratulations! You've got your renown, alright! Unfortunately, not the good, positive, words shouting your praises renown that would really put pep in your step for getting any kind of monarchy going in *my* Soul Space. Because I'm pretty sure that you just ticked off... everyone."

Marie became the definition of distraught.

"Everyone?" Cal tasted the words like fine wine, squinting at his own sky before nodding. "*Everyone.*"

CHAPTER FORTY-NINE

"Now don't worry!" Cal played at being chipper. "I don't think I'll be doing anything to you. I'm upset, but I'd be lying if I said that I didn't see the possibility coming. I just didn't want it to happen. I need that old man to be my Administrator. In part because he cares for everyone, and everyone in turn loves him for it. He has this uncanny knack that, even where he is biased, he is willing to wear that bias on his sleeve and factor it in for who he speaks to. A difficult feat, that. You've put me in a serious pickle, but retribution is not what you'll find from *me*."

He turned, but stuck a finger in the air. "So it's not a secret! Administrator is not a position you will ever have. You rule with authority. What I need from an Administrator is understanding."

"Fine." Marie deflated, the news not that surprising. "So... I can just nab Henry, and get back to it?"

"Oh, yes!" Cal giggled, that villainous smile back as he steepled his fingers and faced her once more. "Please, do feel free. Good luck with getting anyone on Caltopia to not oppose you and your... goals. I won't fuss about the Supervisor thing. Again, it's one of those things that I saw coming. I just wasn't the right soul for the job. I'll admit, the outcomes I see available here… Well played, old Fox, well played. That's some sneaky Kings and Castles towards that checkmate at the end."

Marie looked down, then back at Cal, as it slowly dawned on her what this particular victory type actually meant for her. It was a win, yes, but she had really needed a win by surrender, or a win by **Glory** getting good fuel. **Glory** now had fuel, but it was not… the *correct* fuel. She had won the wrong way, and if she wasn't careful, the old man's note about fighting her own source of power was about to bite her in the butt.

Glory was with her, but with a hand covering its face. Embarrassed for its Ascendant who had conquested herself into a dead corner.

Marie could feel the surge of might, the Exemplar path definitely tread with bold steps. She could also, however, feel the source bubble and boil with a double helping of trouble. As there wasn't a single soul on Caltopia—save perhaps Henry, who would always try his best for her—that wasn't currently out and about looking for her, fuming up a storm, and planning serious regicide.

To continue her empire building from this point, she would have to defeat, contain, and conquer every single person in the Soul Space. Every single one.

"Well…" Cal chirped, his tone elongated. "There is *one* thing that I'm going to do. Though, it isn't a punishment, as much as… a concluded experiment."

Marie felt horrible as her source of infinite Mana was cut off, leaving her at A-rank one, pushing towards two from her recent achievements. She bumped to A-rank two, then felt both the ceiling preventing her ascent into rank three and a distinct wall blocking her ability to move up. The sensation of finite energy also hit her in that same moment, as all her active feeds to **Glory** cut off as she couldn't pay for even the weakest upkeep effect.

Her buildings were real, so those remained.

Everything else… the environment ate right up.

Marie saw all her plans falling apart before her eyes, her voice faltering. "What happens now?"

"Now!" Cal leaned back, smacking his lips. "Now I watch the show! You see, when I mentioned that I told everyone in the Soul Space, I did mean it. Tatum just got word a few seconds ago through the tangle that is the grapevine. Which means that Amaterasu is about to find out in... three... two..."

The sky above the Silverwood Tree broke.

A black hole bloomed into existence, eating up all there was as a pair of supernova eyes burned to life, newborn suns opening in its depths. From the gap in existence, an arm of galactic flame tore free as Amaterasu's voice caused earthquakes to shudder the entire planet. "Mariiiiie!"

Cal whistled. "Ooooh, she's angry!"

"Get over here!" Amaterasu's anger rolled over the planet, causing more ground-shattering damage. The clouds skipped to hug one another as the very sky shrank away in pure fear from the burning hand that turned its attention towards Cal and Marie. From Amaterasu's palm, an opening split apart as Jorm —the world-sized serpent—surged free, bursting forwards in a serpentine hunt. The sky-blotting snake opened his maw wide in a cobra-strike, collapsing Marie's world to utter blackness as Jorm's jaws snapped closed a mere fraction of time afterwards, drawing the regent deep into Eternia as both the world serpent and supernova arm receded back into the black hole that collapsed into itself.

The sky was peaceful and serene a few seconds later.

Tatum stepped from the void and appeared right next to Cal, Tim joining the duo with haste. Tatum was holding his face as Tim surveyed Caltopia's damage, his lip pursed and not wanting to say anything. Cal merely exhaled and pressed a hand to the back of his head. "Well, we started this way. Might as well end it this way. Shame we've got no pleasant Armillary Tourbillon to share the moment over this time."

Tim clicked his tongue. "We were just about ready for him too."

"The way through the ice is carved, yes." Tatum kneaded the bridge of his nose. He let his arms drop afterwards. "Cal, what just happened?"

"Artorian died, like you heard." Cal crossbow finger-snapped to deliver his joke.

Both the other dungeon and Occultatum turned their heads towards the Silverwood Tree, spotting a very concerned group of Wisps all bundled around Artorian's Seed Core. They, in unison, then turned back towards Cal, with Tatum speaking. "He seems fine. A little grumpy from likely getting the body-rejection prompt as we didn't have one for him, but alive and well. Even if it's in a proxy. That's what Seed Cores are for. The nap will even help fix damage we weren't aware of."

Tim glanced over his shoulder, then winced. His hand pressed to his rotund stomach, rubbing it like he was having the same indigestion. "*Oof*, Ammy's got one of those big-mad moments. She's not gonna be done anytime soon, is she?"

Cal and Tatum both shook their heads, because no, no, she was not going to be done anytime soon.

Tim then winced again with a hiss. "*Auwch...* I heard that stony face fracturing from here. Cal, I'm going to stay in your Soul Space for a hot minute? Ammy's got your Supervisor by the hair, and buried her knee into Marie's face with enough power to make an Ackerman nod in approval. There are *Titans* in Eternia very politely giving them a lot of space right now. Several worldbreaker variants are shaking their heads going: 'I don't care that they're moving through my territory, I'm not breaking that up.' Titans gaining in wisdom score is not something I needed today, bud."

Tatum then looked down, spotting Henry being safely deposited from the Aquarium, and looking all sorts of lost. "Do either of you need me? I think... I think I finally need to have my talk with Henry."

Tim slapped him on the back and nudged him along with a nose-motion. Cal shook his head no and instead hand-motioned that he was going to need to talk to Tim first, and that Tatum's portion would come after. The topic of Artorian's new body was no longer one they could avoid, and was now quickly moved to the top of the list.

Not having him around was going to cause more problems than many other issues could accomplish if bundled. Cal relented on the topic. "Artorian technically did as he promised. The problem is solved! That he did it using the 'helping people' category... Well, that's for us to deal with now. Good luck with Henry."

CHAPTER FIFTY

"Hello Henry." Occultatum landed soft and silent, doing his best to be a friendly face. "Tough day?"

"Tough day." Henry ran his fingers through his hair with a weak set of nods, the regent sitting without his armor on the cobble outside of the Aquarium's wall.

"Do you mind if I sit and chat with you for a minute?" Tatum fidgeted, his hands already fiddling with an object behind his back.

"Someone to chatter with right now would be very nice, I think?" Henry winced, his mood understandably subdued.

"That's good." Tatum nodded as he replied, sitting down next to Henry in his plague doctor attire, the mask missing. He then procured the object he'd been fiddling with, bringing it out to meet the light. It was a simple memory stone. A pre-Cal design, but of astounding purity and quality. "Because I've got a few things to apologize for, and unfortunately, now might be the best moment. I've been putting this off for a very, very long time. Guilt is a hard pill to swallow."

Henry shrugged, his head barely pulled up for him to see the memory stone. "We all have a lot to be sorry for lately."

"Yes." Tatum agreed with a strong nod, trying to keep the flow of conversation steady. "This hiccup in particular... This one has been eating at me. I don't make promises lightly, and I have been remiss to keep this one. But here we are. Could I ask you something?"

"Fire the bow." Henry chuckled, feeling like nothing could be worse than losing Marie, the entire plan, all the ambitions, yet another region and zone... "I think I'm fairly tapped on spoons."

"Do you hate me, Henry?" The Incarnate frowned. Tatum queried his concern with a raised brow, not intending to drag this out. "I am the very reason you are here. That Marie is here. That the old world went to the abyss. That you no longer have your family. I killed them. Did you know?"

Henry closed his eyes, sinking down onto the cobblestone like a sorry pile of gelatin until he faced the sky. His hands resting on his chest as his face twisted into a bleak expression. "I knew."

Tatum regretfully swallowed. "Do you also know what I promised your father, King Garron?"

Henry shook his head, not having a clue.

Tatum observed the memory Core closely, like it held the weight of a thousand burdens. "I said, and I quote: 'This is for you. A way for your legacy to continue on. I'll pass it on to your son if we ever meet.' So, hello, Henry. It is nice to meet you, and I am sorry that it took me this long."

With a small motion, the Core was offered to Henry. "Your Lion's Lineage. Your legacy. All of it. Everything your father ever knew, learned, and went through. Every skill he developed, every craft he tended, every choice he ever made. Every building he erected. Every mistake he overcame."

Henry blinked at it, turning to look at Tatum's remorse-filled face, the man doing a poor job of copying Artorian's more genuine versions. "Wait... Really?"

"Really." Tatum pushed the memory Core closer, confirming what was true. "I think it would serve you well for when you chase Marie into Eternia. You're obviously going. Ammy is going to drive her point home, but she's not going to kill her. It wouldn't accomplish much. Plus, Eternia's beta run is going to have a lot of issues that..."

He paused. "Once we can get Ammy and Artorian to kick-start things, a major problem is outright going to require conquest. A skill that, while ending regrettably here, is going to serve you well *there*. A long war awaits, and while some punishment might still be coming down the pipeline with significant delay, the better you do there, the more you'll mitigate what's coming. You and Marie are already good at what you do. The correct conditions to do them in have been far too long in the making. They aren't ready yet, but they will be soon. The moment they are, your celerity with Ardania's progress will mean the world, and make all the difference."

Henry took the offered memory Core, at a loss for words as he hung on Tatum's. Artorian had asked Henry to keep an open mind, and while he could easily indulge in being both judgmental donkey, and igniting a whole barn's worth of blame right now... he merely listened.

The Incarnate exhaled, pained. "I'm sorry, Henry. I don't know how to make any of it better. They're all gone, and I did it. The bits I did not do, either Barry or Xenocide cleaned up. That I was influenced by a Whisper of **Madness** changes nothing. I did it."

The man wrenched his own hands together, frowning. "What am I supposed to do about that? Because I certainly do not know. I have held the delusion that almost every Incarnate being wiped from the face of the old world was in some way a good thing. I no longer hold that delusion. I couldn't bring... your father back. I could not bring any member of your family back, Henry."

He grit his teeth, chuckling through built up emotion. "Trust me, I tried. *Oh, I tried*. I tried a lot of things. With the success of Dev's **Remembrance Law** getting an entire Gnomish race back on track. The Wood Elven trick that Birch and Mahogany pulled where they pooled their memories together. The developments of inviolable information and how to pluck it from the ether. Every little trick to get a single fresh soul back into Cal. Never tell the Wisps that the resurgence of their entire race was one built on an unmitigated disaster."

Tatum took a deep breath. "Yet, for your father. Nothing. Just... nothing."

He then sharply pointed at the memory Core, like it was the object of his greatest bane. "And *that* thing, that thing right there might be why."

Henry looked at the memory Core, but didn't understand.

Tatum swallowed, his fingers trembling before he laced his hands together. "So I've a question, and a choice."

Henry bobbed the Core to ask the Incarnate to continue.

Tatum bit the arrowhead. "Do you want your father back? Or do you want your Lion's Lineage, and all the memories? Because you can have one, but you cannot have both. Destroying that Core is the lynchpin of what has been preventing me, all this time, from accomplishing that. And I got both of Rose's fathers back, so I know I can do it."

Henry's conflict lived on his face with all the obscurity of an open book that played three dimensional pictures of every scene, in Dolby surround sound. *"Oh."*

"Oh? It's about on par for a response." Tatum tried and failed to lighten the mood.

A beat of silence reigned.

"I think..." Henry was slow. His mind and voice both apprehensive and wary. "I think that regardless of how much I would like my father back, we have all gotten a bit too used to immortality. Bodies to come back to. Death being meaningless. Life being lived too much, too repetitively. There's a limit to what can be handled, and if it is my choice, then I would rather not make my father handle the brunt of the task we contend with in Cal. People die. That's part of life. Bob would judge me if I didn't respect that, more than I already disrespect it by still existing."

Henry tilted his head. "Tim keeps a log, you know. You probably do. I've died a hundred times, and I will die a hundred more. Like I would walk five hundred miles, and then would walk five hundred more, so long as I fall down at Marie's door."

Henry replied with a difficult smile. "I barely remember my father, Master. I know it's 'The Master,' but that 'The' is too hard to say. I have... vague, flickering thoughts of those times. Brief imprints. Moments of cold clarity in cold rooms. Even if I had him back, I couldn't, and wouldn't, look at him the same. I am an ageless monster of countless iterations, and he is a man who contended with the real. Where there was only ever one chance. He built up a whole kingdom from scrap and scratch, and he did it right, the first time around. That doing it *right?* That means more to me than all the fathers you could give me, Master."

His smile turned genuine. "Because at the end of the day, when I get back on my feet, Artorian was right. Why would anyone ever want to fight against what they love? I'm going to shuffle and stumble my way to Marie, and like always, I'm going to make the best of it. Regardless of how much I fail, or how many problems might arise in Ardania when we build it in Eternia. No matter how much I will inevitably miss, or whatever snake of an organization fills my boots? Marie will be there, and that is the only thing in all versions of life that makes me truly, proudly, deeply happy."

He swallowed, holding the memory Core close to his head. "I have failed a lot of my friends, and I have failed a lot in general. However, my soul item isn't a *shield* for nothing. I am **Valor**, and courage will always be with me to keep striving, and striving on, until I stand on the hill that I can finally die on."

Henry pressed the stone against his head. "And on that day, Master, on *that* day, you can repay me for all the loss you have caused by standing with me, with your arm around my shoulder, as one of the best friends that I have ever had the pleasure of having. And there will be no bad blood between us. And there will be no secrets. There will only be two ancient friends, seeing off one last sunset."

He swallowed again, preparing himself. "I don't know who I'm going to become once all these new memories live with me, in me. But I, Henry, as you know him, loved it when you snuck me those stupid resurrection titles and saved me from my own stupidity. So I'll see you at the next dawn, my friend. I, unlike her, will likely be keeping my name the same."

Henry smiled with silent tears as a flash of light pulsed from the Core. The Core that was empty a moment later, as Henry fell completely unconscious as all that new knowledge and experience swirled in. Far too much for his already spent mind.

Tatum didn't need to catch Henry, as he was intelligently already lying flat and down on the ground. So he picked his unconscious friend up, bit away his own tears, sniffled hard, and brought his friend home. Home, to Marie. "Towards that last sunset then, my friend. Towards that last sunset, together we go."

EPILOGUE

Artorian woke like it was just any other day.

A to-do list sprang to mind, but the comforter he was wrapped in was warmed just right. Embraced in that morning toastiness that would be lost with even the slightest hint of a nudge of most precariously pulled covers. The indulgence was too tantalizing to let slip, until the squeeze of an arm around his relatively small-feeling neck rang the bell that he was not wrapped up alone.

Speaking of a small neck. All of him felt small. Almost... child-sized.

"*Oh no.*" His voice was barely in its teens, peeping like a mouse that had noticed the shadow of a cat. "Not a *third* time."

He tried to pull on his Mana, but there was none.

He tried to knock on any kind of mental door, but there were none.

The very effort brought him a distinct sense of not even being able to try, like every single possible requisite condition was missing entirely. He tried to shape his Aura gently to expand so he could get a better sense of his environment, but there was no Aura to shape. The field was definitely there. He could feel the *barest* hints, from an awareness built over decades not simply lost to inability.

Artorian tried to draw on Essence at all, and found only one very big gap in his center. Like a gaping maw with not a particle in it. Worse than that, he felt precariously *mortal*. Mortal, powerless, and with not an F-rank to his name as not only was there no Essence in his system, but he did not have a cultivation technique present to speak of.

He was, well and truly, starting over from bunk-bonk-bust-nothing.

"The new body project." He hushed himself. His childlike fingers held the comforter tight, and felt every handsewn fluffy detail of it. A sensation of reality so raw that the tingles shooting up his arms stole all of his attention. No Mana body ever beat or had come close to the purity of sensation that came from mortal senses. Once Essence got involved, 'enhancement' threw one's average out of whack. Once Mana got involved, you had to rebuild sensation and everything that allowed it.

Getting it right was a rare occurrence, because what things were supposed to feel like were lost as a measurement.

The darker-skinned arm around his neck squeezed tighter, nearly choking him as he wriggled for space and turned, coming face to face with the teenage eyes of Ember. Those Iridium irises were impossible to mistake, even if the norm of swirling supernovas had become such a commonplace sight.

"Morning, sunshine." She cooed at him, a big grin on her face. "I was hoping you were gonna wake up soon."

"Ammy?" He frowned, uncertain about everything in life right now.

"In the flesh." She grinned wider, clearly pleased to see him up and running. "Literally, by the way. Non-cultivator fresh start. When Cal and Tim got a body together that could work, I had them include me in the pile. There isn't a cold chance in the Abyss that I was going to live this round out without you."

She spoke through gritted teeth. "You have no idea how *jealous* Henry made me when he got back to Marie, after Tatum got him the memories of the old Lion Kingdom. *So* jealous. I don't know where that boy suddenly discovered an entire life-time's worth of charm, but oh man, can he suddenly lay it on *thick*. Marie was *wooed*. Okay, well, I do know, but that's not the point."

Artorian's mouth popped open and closed like a goldfish.

"Ember, by the way." She placed a very mortal, very real, very non-Incarnate finger on his mouth to correct him. "This is like going through the ranks all over again for me as well. I started as Ember then, I will start as Ember now. Es-illian-Yaran is a mouthful, and I think I'll skip it. Dawn is a step that I will make when I Incarnate again. So, for *now*, Ember."

She smirked with a look of pure mischief. "Of course, 'Yes dear', on the other hand, is also acceptable."

Artorian broke into a smile, gasping out a laugh that was all air. "Yes dear."

He sighed with heavy amusement. "So, we're okay? No world-shattering problems? Our lives aren't in deep, direct, horrible danger?"

She curled a brow. "No, we're still in Cal, so nothing different there. We are, on the other hand, on track to get these real bodies going and *exit* Cal once the opportunity arises. They found a way. It's going to take... a lot, admittedly, but they found a way. New souls as influx too, before you ask. We already told Marie, and you should have seen how fast her ass found something to sit on."

That was extremely surprising news, Artorian barely believing it. "Are you serious? A way out?"

Ember nodded with rapid movements, glad about the news herself. "Confirmed and everything by Zelia. You've also been plenty safe. Yuki, Halcyon, and Decorum have had a running visitation schedule on your sleeping form running for years. I had a... pink-sparkly feeling that today was the day, so I of course *took* today. Plus I needed snuggle time."

She then cleared her throat rather powerfully. "*Snuggle time.*"

"Oh, right, yes!" Artorian hurried, entangling himself with

Ember until she was content, could kiss his forehead, and make a very delighted happy-cat-purr rumble from her throat. "Better?"

"Much." She hummed, adjusting a bit more to slam her face into his relatively small chest. Artorian felt the breath get knocked out of him with a wheeze. Holding back was still not Ember's forte. She mumbled from her cozy spot. "Stay."

Artorian squeaked. "I missed you too."

"Everyone missed you." She huffed, loudly jealous. "I, of course, missed you most of all."

Young-torian held Ember without another word, applying a serving of head-rubs that, much like a C'towl, Ember was content with. "So... aside from, you know, not having even an F-rank to the name, what are we looking at for coming challenges?"

Ember mumbled, half-muffled as she kept pressed to his shirt. "All of Eternia's beta run. We've got a sun to restart, several objects to remove that Tim can't get rid of himself—think the liminal objects from Cal that he couldn't see—and our cultivation to rebuild. A chunk of which we will be able to do in Eternia as it is rebuilt from the flotsam and jetsam that we can dredge together. Then prepare for life in the real world, which we might get temporary trips to before permanent decanting. We're gonna make mythology and make sure humanity has a foothold."

Artorian squeezed Ember with discomfort. That was a big bowl of soup, and he was going to need to take tiny sips. "Build up in Eternia? As F-rankers? That is... That's going to take very long if we can't use the abilities that were locked to the prior bodies."

The miniature Ancient Elf put her hand on his face like a cat laying down its paw. "Tim is starting us off with a feature that's only supposed to become available when you finish all the Eternia realms, plus the moon. He calls it 'New Game Plus.' We get to cherry pick old abilities for the new run-through, and we keep the highest cultivator title that we have obtained. So you get those attributes in the seven-twenties from the get go, but I'm pretty sure the base stats will need to be rolled again."

Ember made a surprise noise, as she'd recalled something important. His face was used as a platform as she pushed herself up, burying him into the pillows before she realized what she'd done, and sheepishly pulled the flailing boy free. "Sorry, sugar. Still gettin' used to it all myself. The spark of insight was that we can go home at any time. That was a sensitive point from the alpha run I was sure to really lean my sharp stick into. A complete bypass on needing a gazebo to enter and leave. Silverwood Bracelet perks."

"You're fine, Emby." Artorian rubbed his nose, then coughed out before finding a new cozy spot and mentally making a new checklist. The scroll began with 'never lose the bracelet' planted right at the top. "Tell me more."

She counted on her fingers for a moment after flopping onto her side. "We've got carte blanche access to everything. Even Cores that aren't past the concept phase, or maybe only have so much as a single chair together. So if we wanted to exit Eternium because we were tired of Midgard and the related 'Nordic' realms, as we're calling them? Nothing is in the way for us to pop into Incursus and try a Grecian realm. Think the Elysian Fields we had going in the sun? Different dungeons are going to group together based on their thematic interests."

The finger tally was put away in favor of some hand holding, Ember stealing his grip. "The current consensus is that if about fifty dungeon Cores are in agreement on a theme, then they get their pass."

Artorian hummed, forming a question. "Grecian?"

Ember giggled and shook her head. "We've got funny names for it all. Like Dregs with Mayan themes, or Mu with Egyptian themes. Dregs—with her **Eruption Law**—really loves her volcanoes, and sacrifices to Pele. Xan, her green wisp, is not in agreement with any of it and keeps preventing sacrifices. Mu, having a big affinity for bags, loves big intricate temples that are internal mazes. Mu's environments sadly keep being deserts, but give that dungeon a pyramid and you're in business. Mu's current obsession is a Pharaoh's Pyramid of Panacea."

Ember waved it off, the allotments of realms still speculative. "There's going to be hundreds of them. Just... avoid Murderworld. Invictus's dungeon has it out for everyone with those goats of his."

Artorian squished her hand. "Sounds convoluted."

Ember grumbled and pressed close, as that had been her exact response. "The basic idea is that until they all get a copy of Eternia's base world, with Pylons that let them actually do more than dabble, all of these dungeon Cores will be playing support roles for Tim. Making instant dungeons, guiding zones, practicing for their own worlds, toying with area bosses, making prompts for players with their own particularity for kindness or snark. The works. It's going to be a big hodge-podge of ideas until Tim has enough Pylons working for a clean handoff."

She then poked his nose adoringly. "Eventually you will be asked to play Administrator."

He nodded, pulling the blanket half over his head. He didn't feel ready. "That can wait until after breakfast. To quash the growing anxiety, I'm human, right?"

Her silence chilled him. "Ember?"

"Sugar, I don't know how to answer that." She held his hands tight to start. "Your body is... let's start off with the concept of 'new species.' Let's slap on the name 'Nascent Being.' Let's also immediately tell you that you technically also have a dormant Beast Core waiting to develop, that there is definitely bone-scripting in place, and that you definitely still have two hearts. With the soul-imprint you left behind mixing Dragon, Liger, human, Ascended, and some connection muddling from the two dungeons considered... Just nod and smile when someone asks you, say human because that's what you look like, and try not to think about it."

She then smiled while fluttering her eyelashes.

Artorian once again popped his mouth like a goldfish.

Ember once again, stopped it with a finger, then hugged him hard. "You're okay. You're functional. You're here, and most importantly it's *you*-you that's here. So take time getting used to life and new things. We'll be busy in no time."

She then smiled wide, hitting her own shirt-covered chest, and enacted some dramatics. "It will be Sunny and Ammy, infiltrators of the Red Inkquisition. Agents Y and Y, we ask ze questionz! We will investigate rituals, regicides, and strange dinosaur-handed people. We will raze nations, and apprehend the ruthless. To give them a good shake by the lapels and say: do not inflame the Inkquisition! Or else we must invent a solution and send... ElCazorro!"

Artorian sputtered and pulled the blanket over his face to laugh, his shoulders bouncing while his outburst was muffled. He drew a big breath when moving the blanket away, feeling okay enough to sweetly touch foreheads with her and lay back down. "So, Ammy, after all?"

"What?" Ember appeared puzzled. "No. I... Oh, Celestial feces, I did it myself. That's what I get for name flipping like a noble obsessed with their seventeen titles."

Artorian stifled his next laugh, his face utterly betraying him as it turned red with bloated cheeks and a held breath.

"You better hope you're not ticklish." She smirked at him with warmth.

"I'm glad you're here, Emby." Her hands were squeezed back in his. "I... I would not have been doing too well if I had to do this a third time, all... different from everyone else. Missing out even more."

Ember sighed and closed her eyes, coping with a thought.

"The only bits you missed? Wu and Ty would both give their left arm in order to forget. You're more okay than you think, and Grimaldus has it all tucked away in his Grimoire for when you want to know anyway." Ember chuckled, patting him as her voice lowered. "Sugar, I know a thing or two about being different. Did I ever tell you about my last talk with Bob? The last words he said to me?"

"Tell." He requested the information with a tug of her hand.

"Bob and I had many talks." Ember got snug before recounting her experiences. "He looked at me like plants must look at the sun. Then with a wistfulness, like he knew it would soon be time, he said where he was a gate, I was an engine. All before me is laid to waste. All his eyes saw were the ashes in my wake. True death. The gentle death, for people who forgot to live. He then laughed, just... laughed. Like something was funny? Top six regrets of the dying, he then said."

She freed a hand, counting. "I wish I'd had the courage to live a life true to myself, not the life others expected of me. I wish I hadn't worked so hard. I wish I hadn't missed my child's youth and partner's companionship. I wish I'd had the courage to express my feelings. I wish I had stayed in touch with my friends. I wish that I'd let myself be happier, and realized happiness was a choice."

She let her hand drop, and rubbed at his cheek. "I love you, you clever doofus. I have loved you for thousands of years, through iterations on end, ever since a wily old man in the forest dropped everything to see me for me. I don't care what you look like. I don't care if you're bald and have a beard three miles long. I don't care if you're not even twenty in this form. You have my love, and my proper 'I love you.' So I would like, very much, to heed Bob's last advice to me, and live a life where all of those wishes can be crossed right off."

She squeezed his hand. "Regardless of if we're ten, twenty, fifty, or five-thousand years old. Because we're probably going to make five-thousand without any problems, and dates at that point might have to be in the stars. I adore you to pieces. When I first heard that Marie had offed you? My entire world fell apart, and I knew. I have no interest in a world that doesn't have you in it, honey bunches of bees."

Artorian squeezed and held her, nodding. He opened his mouth, then felt her entire hand slap onto his face. Ember was flushing hot pink, her words hurried. "Don't say it back yet. *I know.* I am also currently a mortally embarrassed wreck. *I know.* I want to hear it, but don't say it back yet."

Artorian chortled, a big smile on his face as he nodded again, and squeezed her hand for comfort. "Alright, dear. Where would you like to start?"

"Right here!" She gleefully pulled him upright and off the bed, helping him get on his very real and complete legs! All in order to look out of the window to showcase a very familiar bonfire living in the center of a gorgeous town. Complete with blooming flowers and delightful fresh winds, refined architecture, smiling faces as far as Artorian could see, and a big sign obviously written by Lunella that read: 'If the brat wakes up, I wanted to be told yesterday!'

Ember broadly motioned at their town, where all their people lived.

"Home, in Avalon!"

ABOUT DENNIS VANDERKERKEN

Hello all! I'm Dennis, but feel free to call me Floof. Credit of the name now being accumulated by the vast and powerfully cultivated viking beard, that grows ever more in potency. I'm now counting my writing experience in years, so let me say it is my great pleasure that you are reading this, and welcome back to the goodness!

I have been the designer, plotter, and writer of Artorian's Archives since its inception, and look forward to gracing your eyes with ever more volumes of the story. Indulging my dear readers in secrets otherwise forever obscure.

If you have any questions, or would like to chat, I live on the Eternium discord server. Feel free to come say hi anytime! I will keep you entertained for years to come!

Connect with Dennis:
Discord.gg/mdp
Patreon.com/FloofWorks

ABOUT DAKOTA KROUT

Associated Press best-selling author, Dakota has been a top 5 bestseller on Amazon, a top 6 bestseller on Audible, and his first book, Dungeon Born, was chosen as one of Audible's top 5 fantasy picks in 2017.

He draws on his experience in the military to create vast terrains and intricate systems, and his history in programming and information technology helps him bring a logical aspect to both his writing and his company while giving him a unique perspective for future challenges.

"Publishing my stories has been an incredible blessing thus far, and I hope to keep you entertained for years to come!" -Dakota

Connect with Dakota:
MountaindalePress.com
Patreon.com/DakotaKrout
Facebook.com/DakotaKrout
Twitter.com/DakotaKrout
Discord.gg/mdp

ABOUT MOUNTAINDALE PRESS

Dakota and Danielle Krout, a husband and wife team, strive to create as well as publish excellent fantasy and science fiction novels. Self-publishing *The Divine Dungeon: Dungeon Born* in 2016 transformed their careers from Dakota's military and programming background and Danielle's Ph.D. in pharmacology to President and CEO, respectively, of a small press. Their goal is to share their success with other authors and provide captivating fiction to readers with the purpose of solidifying Mountaindale Press as the place 'Where Fantasy Transforms Reality.'

Connect with Mountaindale Press:
MountaindalePress.com
Facebook.com/MountaindalePress
Twitter.com/_Mountaindale
Instagram.com/MountaindalePress

MOUNTAINDALE PRESS TITLES

GameLit and LitRPG

The Completionist Chronicles,
The Divine Dungeon,
Full Murderhobo, and
Year of the Sword by Dakota Krout

Arcana Unlocked by Gregory Blackburn

A Touch of Power by Jay Boyce

Red Mage and
Farming Livia by Xander Boyce

Space Seasons by Dawn Chapman

Ether Collapse and
Ether Flows by Ryan DeBruyn

Dr. Druid by Maxwell Farmer

Bloodgames by Christian J. Gilliland

Unbound by Nicoli Gonnella

Threads of Fate by Michael Head

Lion's Lineage by Rohan Hublikar and Dakota Krout

Wolfman Warlock by James Hunter and Dakota Krout

Axe Druid,
Mephisto's Magic Online, and
High Table Hijinks by Christopher Johns

Skeleton in Space by Andries Louws

Dragon Core Chronicles by Lars Machmüller

Chronicles of Ethan by John L. Monk

Pixel Dust and
Necrotic Apocalypse by David Petrie

Viceroy's Pride by Cale Plamann

Henchman by Carl Stubblefield

Artorian's Archives by Dennis Vanderkerken and Dakota Krout

Vaudevillain by Alex Wolf

Made in the USA
Coppell, TX
28 October 2023

23532813R00246